The Counterfeit Wife

Nathan Case

ISBN 978-1-969342-15-8

TwainWorks Publishing LLC

For the ghosts we carry,
and the fire we become when we learn to let them go.

Disclaimer

This is a work of fiction. Names, characters, businesses, places, events, and incidents are either the products of the author's imagination or used in a fictitious manner. Any resemblance to actual persons, living or dead, or actual events is purely coincidental.

While the story and its characters are fictional, the novel explores a number of real-world locations, organizations, and technologies. The private banking protocols of Zurich, the secretive world of "ghost work" intelligence operatives, and the traditions of the Klausjagen festival in Küssnacht, Switzerland, are based on extensive research to provide a realistic backdrop.

Furthermore, the concepts of quantum computing, behavioral economics, biometric authentication, and mass data surveillance, while dramatized for the purposes of the narrative, are grounded in established scientific principles and the ongoing, urgent global conversation about the nature of privacy in the twenty-first century. Project Panopticon is a fictional construct, but the questions it raises are very real.

Man is least himself when he talks in his own person. Give him a mask, and he will tell you the truth.
— Oscar Wilde

Three may keep a secret, if two of them are dead.
— Benjamin Franklin

We are all now living in a world that Bentham merely dreamed of. We are all living in the Panopticon.
— Edward Snowden (paraphrased)

Chapter 1: The Long Fall

There are two kinds of deaths in Hollywood.

The first is the kind where they find your body. The second is the kind where you disappear so completely, it's like you never existed at all.

Sloane Devereaux was about to learn the difference.

***

The September heat in North Hollywood was a special kind of hell. It wasn't the clean, dry heat of the desert. It was thick. Smoggy. It had teeth. It pressed through the rattling window unit and settled over the apartment like a shroud.

The Oscar lived on top of the fridge now. A golden tombstone gathering dust next to a half-empty box of baking soda. Sloane had moved it there during a 3 AM spiral six months ago, some half-formed idea about keeping it out of sight. It turned out the Academy Award for Best Actress wasn't small enough to forget. It was just small enough to make the top of a rental fridge feel like a grave.

She opened the refrigerator door. Hoping for a miracle.

The small light flickered, revealing the grim reality. One yogurt, expiration date a mocking suggestion from last week. Half a bottle of white wine from a forgotten time. A takeout container of pad thai she was pretty sure was from last Tuesday.

Or the Tuesday before that.

Her phone buzzed on the counter. She didn't need to look. Capital One, Chase, or American Express. They called in rotation now, a three-headed hydra that had already devoured two hundred thousand dollars of her future. The interest alone was eating her alive.

She'd stopped answering a month ago. She stacked the red envelopes on top of the fridge, next to the Oscar. Face down, so she didn't have to see the words.

FINAL NOTICE. DEMAND FOR PAYMENT. LEGAL ACTION PENDING.

If she couldn't see them, they weren't real.

A harder-to-ignore, more immediate notice sat on the kitchen counter. It wasn't a threat from the landlord. That battle had been lost weeks ago. The court had already ruled. This was not a warning. This was the verdict, printed on official Los Angeles County Sheriff's Department letterhead.

FINAL NOTICE OF EVICTION ENFORCEMENT

Sheriff-Enforced Lockout: Friday, September 19th, 12:00 Noon

She'd found it taped to her door this morning. The clock was already running.

Three days.

Three days to find eight thousand, two hundred dollars. Back rent, late fees, court fees. The total sum had to be paid. Or a man with a badge and a gun would physically remove her from the apartment and change the locks. The court had ruled against her two weeks ago when she hadn't shown up for the hearing. She'd had no defense. She genuinely couldn't pay.

And even if she could, the credit card debt would still be there, a two-hundred-thousand-dollar tumor growing in the dark.

This was the end of the road.

She glanced at a stack of dog-eared scripts on her coffee table—the half-finished screenplays she'd poured her soul into during the long, silent years. Brilliant ideas, sharp dialogue, stories that went nowhere. In this town, you were either a commodity or you were invisible. She had tried to become a creator, but no one was reading.

Three days. Then she'd be on the street with an Oscar, a pile of useless scripts, and two hundred thousand dollars of debt she could never repay.

She closed the fridge. Walked to the window. Stared out at the hazy sprawl of North Hollywood, the palm trees wilting in the heat, the endless grid of failure stretching to the horizon.

Her phone buzzed again.

This time she looked.

Unknown number. 310 area code. Probably another collector who'd bought her debt for pennies on the dollar.

She almost didn't answer.

Almost.

But something made her thumb hit the green button. Desperation, maybe. Or just the faint, stupid hope that maybe, this one time, the universe would throw her something other than knives.

"Hello?"

The voice on the other end was male. Professional. Warm in that specific way that meant expensive and practiced.

"Ms. Devereaux? This is Blake Feld from Briarwood Casting. I have an audition for you. This afternoon. One PM. It's a prestigious national commercial. Union scale plus residuals. We had some cancellations this morning—honestly, we're scrambling. Plus, you came highly recommended by a client. Can you make it?"

Her heart did something complicated in her chest. Hope and humiliation fighting for space.

A commercial. Not a film. Not even a decent television role. A commercial.

But the union scale was seven hundred for the day. Residuals could be another few thousand if it ran. It wasn't eight thousand two hundred dollars. But it was something. It was more than the nothing she had now. And maybe it would open other doors. She desperately needed to believe that it would.

"What's the product?" she asked, trying to keep her voice steady.

There was a pause on the other end. The kind of pause that meant bad news.

"It's a... pharmaceutical," Blake said carefully. "For hemorrhoids. The client loved your work in *The Turning Point*. They're looking for someone with gravitas. Someone who can make the product feel... aspirational."

Aspirational hemorrhoid cream.

"This afternoon?" Sloane heard the edge in her own voice.

"I know it's incredibly last minute. But we were told that you might be... available." The pause felt deliberate. He knew. "But if you're busy—"

"No!" The word came out too fast. Sloane caught herself. Forced her voice into something smoother. Casual. The performance of a woman with options. "No, I just—let me check my calendar real quick."

She stared at the red envelopes on top of the fridge. Counted to three.

"Okay. Yes. I can move some things around. One o'clock works."

"Briarwood Casting. Burbank. Do you know where it is?"

"I do," she lied.

Blake gave her the address anyway. She didn't have anything to write with. She'd remember it. She had to.

"And Ms. Devereaux? The client wants someone who can really sell the relief. The... comfort. If you could bring that vulnerability you had in *The Turning Point*..."

He wanted her to cry about hemorrhoid cream.

"I understand," Sloane said.

She hung up. Looked at the eviction notice on the counter. Friday, September 19th, 12:00 Noon.

Three days to pull off a miracle. Or at least, to sell hemorrhoid cream with gravitas.

She closed her eyes.

Her career had become a punchline. An Academy Award got you nothing when the industry decided you were done. Not just rejected. Not just forgotten. But offered the kind of roles that were designed to humiliate. To remind you exactly how far you'd fallen.

She should say no. She should hang up and preserve whatever microscopic shred of dignity she had left.

But dignity didn't pay rent.

"I'll be there," she said.

She ended the call and stood there in the heat, in the silence, in the apartment that would stop being hers in three days. The humiliation was a hot flush that made her want to claw at her own skin. She dug her nails into her palms, the sharp, grounding pain a welcome distraction from the shame that was burning her from the inside out.

Her gaze drifted past the eviction notice to the Oscar, the golden tombstone on top of the fridge. This is what winning looks like, she thought. This is what happens when you stop being useful.

She'd won the Oscar at twenty-two. A supernova, burning brighter than anyone in a generation. By twenty-five, she was a global icon. An empress of her own making, her name on every casting list in town.

She remembered the speech. The impossible weight of the Oscar in her hand, the heat of a thousand lights, her own voice, small and shaking, echoing through the theater as she thanked her mother, Caroline, "who believed a trailer park girl could be a queen."

She'd meant every word.

Her mother had died six months later. Never saw Sloane become a queen. Only saw her become a target. Maybe that was a mercy.

At the absolute peak of her power, she had said *no* to the wrong man.

That was five years ago. Five years of a slow, grinding crucifixion, orchestrated to make an example of her. A brutal descent from the A-list to the blacklist to... this. This suffocating room. This suffocating heat. This audition for rectal itch cream on the cusp of her thirtieth birthday.

She walked into her bedroom and opened the closet. The scent of lavender hit her first—the cheap drawer liners her mother had taught her to use, back when "making things nice" was an act of defiance against the Oklahoma dust. The ghost of her former life lived in there. Tucked in the back was a single garment bag. Inside, a Celine blazer. Black. Perfect. A relic from a time when her name opened doors instead of closing them. The last piece of the woman who had won the Oscar. The woman who mattered.

This is what erasure feels like, she thought, her hand resting on the cool, perfect fabric. Not a bang. A whisper.

She walked to the bathroom, turned on the shower, and cried under the water where no one could hear.

This was the last time she would cry as Sloane Devereaux.

Chapter 2: The Taste of Ash

The Honda smelled like old coffee and failure. It had been her first real purchase after her first real movie, a practical, reliable car Manny had helped her negotiate when she was nineteen—a temporary step, she'd told herself, on the way to a Porsche. Even during the years when she could've afforded that upgrade, she kept it. Part superstition, part rebellion, part refusal to let Hollywood turn her into someone she didn't recognize. Fourteen years in this town, and the Porsche was still an impossible dream. But the Honda was still here, a loyal, sputtering reminder of the girl she used to be.

The drive from North Hollywood to the casting office in Burbank was a tour of her own personal graveyard. She took Laurel Canyon, the engine whining as it climbed the winding road. She passed the turnoff for Lookout Mountain, where she'd attended her first real Hollywood party, a dizzying, dazzling affair where she'd nursed a single glass of champagne for three hours, terrified of saying the wrong thing.

Then down into the Valley, past the studio lots. Universal. Warner Brothers. Huge, monolithic gates that she used to walk through with a nod and a smile. Now, she was just another anonymous driver in a sea of them, a ghost haunting the edges of a kingdom that had exiled her.

There had been men, once. A writer. An agent. People who loved the light that reflected off her. But when the spotlight turned off, they vanished. In this town, intimacy was just another networking opportunity, and Sloane Devereaux was no longer a value-add.

Billboards rose on either side of the 101, advertising the faces of the new gods. A superhero movie. A gritty new streaming series. A smiling, nineteen-year-old actress who had just been declared "the new face of her generation." Sloane had been the new face of her generation once. It had lasted about six months.

She parked three blocks away from the casting office to save six dollars on parking. Six dollars was two boxes of pasta.

This was her life now, a series of small, grim calculations.

***

The waiting room at Briarwood Casting was a study in quiet desperation. The air was thick with the scent of stale coffee and cheap perfume. Actors sat in uncomfortable plastic chairs, their faces a mixture of forced calm and raw, buzzing nerves. They were all beautiful, in that specific, reproducible way that Hollywood demanded. And they were all holding the same script pages, the "sides," their lips moving silently as they rehearsed their lines.

I used to avoid summer picnics. The itch. The discomfort. But with Velvasitz, I can finally say yes to life again!

Sloane took a seat in the corner, pulling out her own copy of the sides. She didn't look at the other actresses. She didn't want to see her own desperation reflected back at her. Instead, she did what she had been trained to do. She began to build the character.

Who is this woman? she asked herself. *Let's call her Linda. Linda is thirty-eight. A ghost of a life she had run a thousand miles to escape. She loves her husband, but the spark is gone. The hemorrhoids are not just a physical affliction; they are a metaphor for the small, secret pains that have made her close herself off from the world. When she says yes to the picnic, she is not just saying yes to a social event. She is saying yes to intimacy. To joy. To herself.*

It was bullshit, of course. It was a hemorrhoid cream commercial. But this was her process. This was the work. The discipline that had taken a scared girl from a trailer park in Oklahoma and put an Oscar in her hands. She had to find the truth, even here. Especially here. Because if she couldn't find the truth in this, then she had nothing left.

She closed her eyes, shutting out the waiting room, and found Linda. She felt her quiet shame, her longing for a life without discomfort. She was ready.

"Sloane Devereaux?"

A young man with a man-bun and a clipboard stood in the doorway. Tyler. He looked bored already.

Sloane stood up, her professional smile clicking into place. It was showtime.

***

"Whenever you're ready," Tyler said, not looking up from his phone.

The audition room was small, gray, and windowless. A blue backdrop. A single camera on a tripod. The glamour of Hollywood.

Sloane took a breath. Centered herself. Let Linda's quiet sadness settle into her bones. She looked at the camera, her expression a perfect blend of vulnerability and hope.

"I used to avoid summer picnics," she began, her voice soft, relatable. "The itch. The..."

"Sorry, stop."

Tyler held up one finger, his thumb still flying across the screen of his phone. He was texting. A small gold stud winked in his left nostril—the kind of carefully curated "edge" that cost three hundred dollars at a boutique piercing studio in Silver Lake.

Sloane held her smile. "Problem?"

"Can you make it more... I don't know. Real?"

Real.

She'd spent six weeks living with actual cowboys in Montana to prepare for *Copper Moon*. She'd learned to speak conversational Mandarin for a role in a film that never got made. She had once made Meryl Streep cry in a table read.

"Of course," she said, her voice impossibly pleasant. "From the top?"

"Actually—" He finally looked at her. Really looked. His eyes, devoid of any real interest, did a quick, brutal calculation: the lines around her eyes, the fading relevance, the scent of desperation she had tried so hard to mask. "I think we're looking for someone more... relatable."

The word landed like a slap. He had delivered it with the casual cruelty of a man who had never been told no in his life.

"More relatable," Sloane repeated, her smile frozen in place.

"Yeah. You know." He gestured vaguely. "Someone people see themselves in." He was already looking past her, to the door, to the next warm body in the waiting room. He had already forgotten her name. "Thanks so much for coming in, though. Really. Huge fan of your work."

He'd never seen a single frame of *Copper Moon*. She could tell. He was probably in middle school when it came out.

"Thank you for your time," she said. The professionalism was so deeply ingrained it was a reflex. She walked out of the room, her spine straight, her head held high. She was an actress. The performance wasn't over until she was in her car.

***

The girl in the waiting room looked up when Sloane walked out.

Twenty. Maybe nineteen. She was luminous, in that effortless, artless way that only youth could be. She was holding a cold-pressed juice and scrolling through her phone, and when she saw Sloane, her face lit up with genuine, unadulterated awe.

"Oh my God. Are you Sloane Devereaux?"

Sloane stopped. The performance was cracking. "Yeah."

"I loved you in *Copper Moon*. I've seen it, like, six times." The girl stood up, her energy a bright, painful spotlight. "You made me want to act. Seriously. That scene, in the canyon, where you have to choose between your brother and the law? The way you just... held that moment. You are the reason I moved to L.A."

Run, Sloane wanted to tell her. *Run while your face still opens doors. Run before they start calling you "difficult" for having an opinion. Run before you wake up at thirty and realize you were never a person, just a product with an expiration date.*

Instead, she smiled. The muscles in her face ached.

"Break a leg in there," Sloane said.

"Thank you!" The girl beamed, her face a perfect picture of hope. "Oh my God, I can't believe I just met you."

Sloane walked out into the blinding, indifferent sunshine of the parking lot. She didn't cry. Crying was a luxury she couldn't afford. It made your eyes puffy.

She unlocked her car, the old Honda groaning in the heat. She climbed inside, the hot vinyl of the seat burning through her jeans. She closed the door, sealing herself in the small, stifling space.

She let out a single, silent scream, her throat raw, her mouth wide, a perfect mask of tragedy that no one would ever see.

Then she pounded the steering wheel. Once. Twice. The sharp, ugly pain in her knuckles was a welcome distraction. It was real.

The pain, and the man who had caused all of it. Mitchell Carver. A Hollywood titan who made careers. And unmade them.

The memory hit her, sharp and unwanted as a shard of glass under a fingernail. It wasn't the slow fade of a star. It was a crucifixion, and it had happened on the best night of her life.

The Golden Globes after-party, five years ago. She was twenty-five, the Oscar still shiny on her mantelpiece, the world at her feet. Carver, his face flushed with champagne and a possessive, predatory entitlement, had cornered her by the terrace, away from the crowd.

"My beautiful little investment," he'd murmured, his hand sliding too low on her back, fingers pressing with an intimacy she'd never invited. "Time to talk about the next project. Just you and me. Upstairs."

The meaning was clear. The transaction explicit.

She'd stepped back, carefully, her smile still in place. Trying to defuse it with grace. "Mitch, I'm so grateful for everything you've done for my career. But I think we should keep things professional."

Professional. Polite. The kind of boundary any reasonable person would respect.

The warmth drained from his face. "*Professional?*" He spat the word like something rotten. "You think you got that Oscar on *professional*? You think I championed you for two years because of your *talent*?"

The circle of agents and publicists nearby had gone quiet, pretending not to listen while hanging on every word.

"I think," Sloane had said, her voice steady despite the ice spreading through her chest, "that I earned that Oscar. And I'm grateful for the opportunities you've given me. But I'd like to keep our relationship exactly what it's been—a working partnership."

She'd meant it as an exit line. A polite shutdown. A way to let him save face.

But he'd heard refusal. Rejection. A *no* from someone who owed him everything.

The humiliation on his face had been a flash of lightning, illuminating the monster he truly was. He'd leaned in close, his breath hot with champagne, his voice a low, vicious whisper meant only for her. "Watch me," he'd hissed. "I'll unmake you with a single call."

His revenge had been a masterpiece of corporate strangulation. Quiet. Thorough. Invisible.

No one would work with her. No one would return her calls. Her agent had dropped her with a regretful email citing "creative differences." Projects she'd been attached to suddenly went in "a different direction." Auditions dried up. Then stopped entirely.

She'd been erased. Not loudly. Not publicly. Just... gone.

This suffocating Honda, this audition for hemorrhoid cream, this eviction notice—this was the dividend. This was what happened when you told a king you wouldn't sleep with him.

The worst part? She'd done everything right. She'd been polite. Professional. Respectful. She'd tried to let him save face.

And it hadn't mattered.

Because the only answer Mitchell Carver would have accepted was *yes*.

***

The five years since had been a masterclass in erasure. A slow, grinding descent designed not just to punish her, but to unmake her. The A-list projects that suddenly had 'creative differences.' The party invitations that stopped arriving. The friends who went incommunicado, their assistants suddenly unable to find a single opening for lunch in a calendar year. Carver's invisible hand was everywhere, turning her from an icon into a pariah, one whispered rumor at a time. It was a war of attrition, and she had hit rock bottom after rock bottom. Would this ever end?

Her phone buzzed on the passenger seat.

A text. From Manny.

Gable's. One hour. Don't be late.

Chapter 3: The Last Honest Man

Gable & Crane Grill smelled like 1927 and felt like salvation. It was the only place left in Hollywood that hadn't been gutted and replaced with gray minimalism and Edison bulbs. The leather booths were the color of old blood, worn smooth by the ghosts of screenwriters and movie stars. The air was thick with the scent of char-grilled steak, gin, and a century of whispered deals.

The hostess, Gina, a woman whose face was a beautiful roadmap of a life lived, smiled when she saw Sloane walk in. It wasn't the pitying smile Sloane got from casting directors. It wasn't the "oh honey, what happened to you?" smile she got from old acquaintances at the grocery store. It was just a smile. "He's waiting for you at his table," Gina said.

His table. Manny Goldman had been holding court in the same red leather booth since Carter was president. Sloane wove through the crowded room, past agents closing deals on their phones and tourists hoping to spot a celebrity. For the thirty seconds it took to cross the floor, she felt like a person again. Like she belonged.

Manny looked up as she approached. He grinned, a big, broad, unapologetic grin that lit up his corner of the room. He was a glorious dinosaur. Seventy-two years old, clad in a silk shirt patterned with what looked like turquoise peacocks, enough gold on his wrists to fund a small independent film.

"There's my girl," he boomed, his voice a gravelly mix of Brooklyn and fifty years of cigars. He stood up, a minor miracle of physics, and enveloped her in a hug that smelled of Old Spice and defiant optimism.

***

"You look like shit," Manny said, which in Manny-speak meant *I love you and I'm worried about you*. He settled back into the booth as Sloane slid in across from him.

"Commercial audition," Sloane said, picking up the heavy water glass. The weight of it felt good in her hand. Solid. Real.

"Let me guess. A cruise line for the recently bereaved? A new medication for restless leg syndrome?"

"Hemorrhoid cream."

"Jesus Christ." Manny winced as if he'd been physically shot. "What'd you tell them?"

"I didn't have to say anything. They told me I wasn't 'relatable.'"

"Not relatable?" He threw his hands up, his gold bracelets clattering. "You're the most relatable goddamn person in this town! You're broke, you're pissed off, and you're surrounded by schmucks. That's the entire population of Los Angeles!" He signaled the waiter—Eddie, a man who had probably been working here since the silent film era—without looking. "Two martinis, Eddie. As dirty as this business. And bring the lady a steak. The big one. Medium rare."

"Manny, I can't let you—"

"Did I ask if you could?" He leaned back, studying her with those sharp, dark eyes that missed nothing, that had spotted the fire in her when she was a terrified sixteen-year-old fresh off the bus from Oklahoma. "You're not eating. I can tell. You get that look. All cheekbones and bad decisions."

The martinis arrived, impossibly cold, the olives plump and glistening. Sloane took a sip. It tasted like twenty-dollar olives and Manny's unwavering loyalty. For a moment, the knot in her stomach loosened.

"I got a call," Manny said, his voice a little quieter. "From Barry at CAM. He saw you at the Gelson's on Franklin."

Sloane tensed. Barry Feldman was her old agent, the one who had dropped her like a hot rock the second the blacklist whispers started. The big-time Hollywood player she'd left Manny for after the Oscar, chasing bigger roles and studio deals. Manny had taken her back without a word when Barry bailed. Just: "Welcome home, kid."

"He said you looked... thin," Manny finished, his gaze steady.

"I'm fine, Manny."

"Bullshit, you're fine. You're a ghost. You're haunting this town, and it's killing me to watch." He rubbed his face, suddenly looking every one of his seventy-two years. "Five years. Five years I've been working every connection I've got, and I can't even get you a callback. Not even a hemorrhoid cream commercial." He reached into the inside pocket of his ridiculous jacket and pulled out a thick, white envelope. He slid it across the table. It landed with a soft, heavy thud. "For the rent," he growled. "And for God's sake, buy some groceries. Don't say no."

Sloane stared at the envelope. It was thick. Probably ten thousand dollars. Maybe more. Enough to buy her another sixty days of dignity. Enough to fix the Honda. Enough to breathe. But woefully inadequate to make a dent in the mountain of her debt.

The shame was a hot flush on her cheeks. "I can't take this."

"You can. You will."

"Manny—"

"Listen to me." He leaned forward. His voice dropped, stripped of the showbiz patter, becoming the serious, frightened voice of the man who was the closest thing she had to a father. "The game is rigged, sweetheart. It was always rigged. You just had the bad manners to spit in the Hollywood god Mitchell Carver's eye and expect a fair shake after."

His left hand, resting on the table, trembled slightly. A faint, almost imperceptible tremor. He saw her notice and pulled it back, defensive. "It's nothing. Just the coffee."

But she knew. The way his hand had shaken when he'd hugged her. The way he'd gripped his martini glass a little too tightly. This wasn't caffeine. This was time, running out.

"Manny—"

"Don't," he cut her off, his voice fierce. "We're not talking about that today. Today we talk about you surviving."

The thought of a world without Manny's steadfast, boisterous presence was a black hole she couldn't bear to look at.

"I'm not taking your money," she said, her voice quiet but firm. "I'll figure it out."

"How?" he demanded, his voice rising again. "By being the face of ass cream? By selling that goddamn blazer you love so much? That's not a plan, Sloane. That's a slow-motion suicide."

"It's my pride, Manny. It's the only thing I have left."

"Pride won't feed you, sweetheart!" He sighed, the fight going out of him. He looked old. Tired. The tremor in his hand seemed more pronounced. "You think this is charity? This is an investment. You're gonna come back. With a bang. I've seen a thousand actresses in this town. Most of them were pretty. Some of them could act. You? You're a goddamn supernova. And supernovas don't just fizzle out."

Her throat was tight. The unshed tears burned behind her eyes. "What if you're wrong?"

"I'm not wrong." He smiled, a sad, tired smile. "I'm never wrong about talent. I'm only wrong about people. And you're the best person I know."

She stood up, the legs of the chair scraping against the old floor. She left the envelope on the table. It sat there, fat and impossible.

"I love you, Manny," she said.

"I know," Manny said to his martini glass. "That's why I'm not letting you starve, you stubborn idiot."

She walked out of the restaurant, past the ghosts of Hollywood past and the predators of Hollywood present.

The envelope sat on the table between Manny and the life she was about to lose. It was the only power move she had left, and it felt exactly like defeat.

Chapter 4: The Serpent's Crest

The apartment was exactly as she had left it: hot, silent, and smelling faintly of despair. The late afternoon sun cut sharp lines through the cheap vertical blinds, illuminating dust motes dancing in the dead air. Sloane tossed her keys onto the small counter that separated the living room from the kitchenette. They landed with a clatter that felt obscenely loud.

For an hour, she did nothing. She sat on her worn-out sofa and stared at the eviction notice, which she had propped against a salt shaker on the counter. The red ink of the date she had circled seemed to pulse in the heat. Less than seventy-two hours now. The math was getting brutal by the minute.

She thought about Manny. About the tremor in his hand. About the fierce, terrified love in his eyes. He was the last honest man in a city built on lies, and she couldn't take his money. It would have felt like a surrender. Like admitting that the bastards had finally, truly won.

Her stomach growled, a low, embarrassing rumble. She walked to the kitchen, her bare feet sticking slightly to the linoleum floor. She opened a cupboard. One box of pasta, half a jar of marinara sauce, and three cans of off-brand soup. She pulled out the pasta. It would have to do.

She was filling a pot with water at the sink when the knock came.

It was too polite for a process server, too firm for a neighbor.

Sloane set the pot down. Wiped her hands on her jeans. Her heart gave a stupid, nervous little kick. She wasn't expecting anyone. No one ever just dropped by.

She opened the door. A man in a charcoal-gray suit stood in the dingy, beige hallway of her apartment building. He was holding a single, cream-colored envelope like it might either bite him or grant him three wishes. He looked impossibly clean, impossibly out of place. His shoes cost more than her Honda.

"Sloane Devereaux?" His voice was as starched as his collar.

"That's me."

"Delivery for you, ma'am. Signature required. Time sensitive. You are requested to read it immediately, please." He produced a sleek, slate-gray tablet and a stylus.

She signed her name on the glowing screen. The elegant, looping signature she'd practiced for a thousand headshots felt like a forgery. The man nodded once, handed her the envelope, and turned and walked away without another word. His footsteps made no sound on the worn carpet.

Sloane closed the door, the lock clicking shut with a sound of finality. The envelope sat in her hands, heavy as a grenade. The paper was thick, textured, expensive. The kind of expensive that whispered old money, the kind that didn't need to shout. In the top left corner, embossed in a shimmering silver foil, was a single, elegant crest: a stylized letter 'L' entwined with a serpent.

No return address. Just the crest.

Her hands were shaking. This felt... different. Dangerous. And her only way out.

***

She sat on the sofa, the envelope on the coffee table in front of her. For a long time, she just looked at it. The serpent seemed to glitter in the dim light, watching her.

This was how it happened in movies. The mysterious invitation. The offer that changes everything. But Sloane knew better. She had lived in the real world for five hard years. In the real world, mysterious envelopes from men with limitless money did not contain fairy tales. They contained traps.

Her mind flashed back to a night fourteen years ago. During her early days in Hollywood. A producer's sprawling guesthouse in Malibu. The scent of salt and gardenias. The "private audition" that was never about the lines on the page. She'd been sixteen. Saved, that night, by a miracle—a ringing phone at the perfect, terrible moment. But she had never forgotten the cold, transactional look in his eyes. The look that said, *I own you.*

This envelope felt like that.

Her eyes drifted to the eviction notice on the counter. Sixty-five hours to homeless. Eight thousand, two hundred dollars.

She picked up the envelope. Her fingers were steady now. She slid a nail under the wax seal and broke it.

The note inside was not a letter. It was an invitation that read like an order, typed on a matching piece of heavy cardstock, the font a clean, merciless sans-serif.

Ms. Devereaux,

You are invited to discuss a matter of mutual and significant benefit. In exchange for two hours of your time, you will receive an honorarium of fifty thousand dollars, regardless of your ultimate decision.

If you are interested, call the number below within the next two hours to arrange a meeting.

Below the text was a phone number. An international line. A country code she didn't recognize at first, then did, with a jolt.

+41.

Switzerland.

Sloane read the note three times. The words didn't change. Fifty. Thousand. Dollars. For a meeting. It wasn't a salary. It wasn't a loan. It was an appearance fee. More money than she had seen in two years, just for showing up.

Every instinct she had—the ones she'd honed in fourteen years of navigating the treacherous currents of Hollywood, the ones that had kept her alive—screamed *trap*. It was a honey pot. A test. A game she didn't understand. No one gave away that kind of money for nothing. Men with money wanted things. Men with Swiss bank account money wanted things she probably didn't even have a name for.

But fifty thousand dollars wasn't just rent money. It wasn't just grocery money. It was breathing room. It was six months of life. It was the power to tell the world to go to hell for a little while longer. It was a shield.

Her gaze fell on the Oscar, glinting dully from its perch on top of the fridge. She remembered the weight of it in her hands that night. The impossible, breathtaking feeling of being seen. Of mattering. She had been on top of the world. Now, she was here, in a hot, dusty room, contemplating a deal with a devil she hadn't even met.

She picked up her phone. Her fingers hovered over the numbers. It was insane. It was a trap. It was the stupidest, most reckless thing she could possibly do.

The eviction notice stared back at her. *Tick, tock.*

She dialed the number.

It rang once, a strange, European tone. A crisp, female voice answered, speaking perfect, unaccented English with the practiced neutrality of a professional answering service.

"Good evening, Ms. Devereaux. Did you receive the courier on time?"Sloane's mouth was dry. They were waiting for her call. Expecting it even.

"I did," she said, her voice a stranger's.

"And your answer is..."

Her heart hammered against her ribs. For a second, she almost hung up. Then she thought of the eviction notice, of the pity in the casting director's eyes, of the tremor in Manny's hand.

She took a breath.

"Yes, I accept the meeting."

The line went silent. Not hold music. Just dead air. Ten seconds. Twenty. She could hear her own breathing.

Then the voice returned, brisk and efficient.

"Thank you for responding promptly. Your interest has been noted. A local representative in LA will contact you within the hour to arrange a meeting for tomorrow morning. Please ensure your phone remains available."

A click.

The line went dead.

Sloane stared at the phone in her hand. That was it. No questions. No negotiations. No explanation. Just confirmation that she'd taken the bait.

The local contact called within seventeen minutes. A different voice, this one American and just as cold. She was to meet Mr. Fairweather at 9 AM sharp the next morning.

Show up. Get the money. Get out.

Chapter 5: The Glass Tower

The law offices of Fairweather & Associates occupied the entire forty-third floor of a glass and steel spire in Century City that scraped at the hazy Los Angeles sky. The lobby was a study in threatening minimalism: vast expanses of white Italian marble, a single, brutalist steel desk, and a silence so complete it felt like a held breath. The air was chilled to the point of discomfort, smelling faintly of expensive leather and money so old it had forgotten how to shout.

The receptionist looked like she had been sculpted from ice and disapproval. She greeted her without a flicker of a smile. "Ms. Devereaux. Mr. Fairweather is expecting you." Her voice was a soft, precise weapon.

Sloane followed her down a long hallway lined with abstract art that probably cost more than her childhood home. Through floor-to-ceiling glass walls, she could see cavernous conference rooms where silent, impeccably suited figures conducted the business of empires. No one was laughing. No one was shouting. They were just moving pieces on a global chessboard, their faces impassive. This wasn't a law firm. This was the temple where money prayed to itself.

She was shown into an office that was less a room and more a panorama. One entire wall was a single pane of glass overlooking the city, from the distant shimmer of the Pacific to the haze-shrouded Hollywood Hills.

Mr. Fairweather was not a man. He was a function. The firm's founding partner, a man with a small and ruthlessly exclusive clientele. Mid-fifties, perhaps, with silver-templed hair and a bespoke suit that looked like it had been woven from shadows. He sat behind a desk of polished black granite that was completely empty except for a single, sleek monitor. He didn't stand when she entered. He didn't smile. He simply gestured to the single leather chair opposite him.

"Ms. Devereaux. Please sit."

She sat. The leather was cool and smooth against the back of her legs. She felt like a specimen under a microscope.

"Thank you for coming on such short notice." His voice was measured, emotionless, exact. His left hand rested on the desk, and Sloane noticed the wedding ring—a simple platinum band that looked like it had never been removed. As he spoke, his thumb moved in a slow, unconscious circle around it, polishing metal that was already flawless. "As per our letter you received yesterday evening, fifty thousand dollars has been wired to your account. You should have received the confirmation."

She had. The alert had popped up on her phone on the way over, a number with so many zeroes it looked like a typo. It was real. This was real.

"Before we proceed," Fairweather continued, "I must ask you to sign a non-disclosure agreement." He slid a slim, slate-gray tablet across the vast expanse of the desk. The document on the screen was dense with legalese. "It is standard confidentiality. It covers the contents of this conversation in perpetuity. The penalty for breach is five million dollars, to be paid in full within thirty days of judgment."

Sloane looked at the document, then at him. "I haven't agreed to anything yet."

"The NDA covers this conversation. Not any subsequent arrangement."

She picked up the stylus. What did she have to lose? You couldn't squeeze blood from a stone, and she was the stoniest person she knew. She signed her name. The elegant signature felt like a lie.

Fairweather nodded once, a barely perceptible motion. He retrieved the tablet. "My client represents a consortium with significant global interests. He has a unique and highly sensitive problem. A problem for which you, Ms. Devereaux, represent a unique and highly sensitive solution."

Client.

The word snagged in her mind.

The same "client" who loved my work in The Turning Point? The one who recommended me to the hemorrhoid cream people?

No. Absurd. She let it go. She gave Fairweather the smallest nod.

Fairweather pressed a button on his desk. The glass wall behind him, which had been showing a panoramic view of the city, went opaque, then flickered to life as a massive, high-definition screen.

And Sloane saw her own face staring back at her.

***

The woman on the screen was her.

Not exactly her. But close enough to make Sloane's skin crawl, to make the fine hairs on her arms stand up. Fairweather's voice cut through her shock, clinical and precise. "The resemblance is not coincidental, Ms. Devereaux. But you'll get to know about that later. For now, simply observe."

The same angular bone structure, the same high cheekbones. The same wide-set hazel eyes that shifted from green to gold in the light. The same widow's peak where her dark blonde hair met her forehead. Even the way she moved—a slight, almost imperceptible tilt of the head when she laughed—was a gesture Sloane recognized from her own films, a gesture she thought was hers alone.

The woman—*not me, not me, NOT ME*—was standing on the deck of a magnificent yacht, *The Ariadne,* the sails taut against a sky the color of a sapphire. She was wearing a simple white linen dress that probably cost more than Sloane's entire wardrobe. She turned, laughing at someone off-camera, and the low winter sun of the Tyrrhenian Sea caught the spray in her hair, creating a momentary halo.

She looked happy. Confident. Effortlessly wealthy. Loved.

She looked like everything Sloane used to be, and everything she had lost.

Another scene flickered onto the screen. The same woman, this time in a glittering emerald gown at a Parisian gala, a diamond necklace sparkling at her neck. Then on a ski slope in Gstaad, her face flushed with cold and exhilaration. Then walking through a field of wildflowers, her hand held by a man who remained just out of frame.

"This was Livia Crestwell," Fairweather said, his voice cutting through Sloane's daze. The video froze on a close-up. Livia's face filled the screen, smiling, her eyes bright with a light that Sloane's no longer possessed.

Sloane couldn't breathe. It was like looking at a ghost. Her ghost.

"She's the wife of my client's partner, Mr. Damian Crestwell," Fairweather continued, his tone as flat as a morgue slab. "You will not have heard of them. They are obsessively private individuals. Mr. Crestwell grew up in the US, launched two public companies by age twenty-five, and moved to Switzerland to work on his third venture, which is a privately held research firm with a limited web presence."

He let that sink in, a deliberate pause to ensure she understood the scope of the world she was looking into. Then he delivered the first blow.

"She died nine months ago."

The words hung between them, heavy and cold.

"A tragic yachting accident," he continued, his voice a clinical report. "They were on a private cruise out of Naples, late last December, along the Amalfi Coast. Her body was not recovered for three weeks."

He let the silence hang in the room, letting the full, shocking weight of the resemblance settle.

"My client," Fairweather said, his eyes locking onto hers, cold and reptilian, "would like to offer you one hundred million dollars to become her."

Chapter 6: The Role

The number was so vast, so absurd, it had no meaning.

Sloane's mind screamed a single, deafening word: TRAP.

They would take her to Switzerland and she would just... disappear. A breathing doll in a golden cage.

"I see the skepticism," Fairweather said, his voice cutting through her panic like a cold blade. "You are thinking we could hire a lookalike for a fraction of that. But we are not paying for a lookalike, Ms. Devereaux."

He tapped the screen where Livia's face shone. "We ran the biometrics. You are a statistical impossibility—a perfect match with world-class acting ability. You are a market of one."

He leaned forward, the reptile closing in. "Furthermore, we are calculating the cost of failure. The interests at stake are... substantial. Institutional. In that context, one hundred million is an acceptable insurance premium to ensure absolute perfection. We are paying for your face, your talent, and most importantly—your permanent silence."

Her first instinct was to stand up, to run, to get out of this cold, sterile room and back to the hot, ugly reality of her own life.

But then the other part of her, the actress, took over. The professional who had learned to mask her terror with a perfect, cool veneer. She took a slow, deliberate breath, pushing down the tidal wave of panic.

This was an audition. She would not be the desperate girl from the hemorrhoid cream commercial. She would not let this man see cracks.

She found her voice. "I don't understand."

Fairweather's lips curled. "Think of it as a role. The role of a lifetime."

He leaned back. "I saw *Copper Moon*. Oscar at twenty-two. You didn't just play a part—you resurrected someone. Brought a dead character to life." His gaze sharpened. "The question is: can you do it again? For a much bigger stage?"

Her heart kicked. For one insane second, all the other implications fell away. She was just an actress again, hearing the words she'd longed to hear for five years.

"You already passed the audition," he continued. "Five years in the wilderness. Your refusal to break. My client values resilience. Livia herself was a great admirer of your work. She would have approved."

One more word and you'll blow it. Shut up and listen.

"There is nothing to say yet," Fairweather said, clocking her silence. "Only questions to ask. Now. The why."

His thumb traced a slow circle on his wedding band. "My client's partner, Mr. Crestwell, is devastated by the loss. His grief has rendered him... unable to engage with the world as he once did. He needs the comfort of Livia's presence—or the appearance of it—to function. To continue. It's an unusual request, I grant you. But grief makes us all seek unusual remedies."

Sloane stared at him. "What?"

"The official story for the past nine months is that Livia Crestwell survived the boating accident, but with profound physical trauma and near-total amnesia. She has been in a private Swiss clinic, recovering in absolute seclusion. The world has been holding its breath, waiting for her to re-emerge."

"And now she will," Sloane whispered, the chilling logic of the performance falling into place.

"Precisely," Fairweather said. "Your job is not to play the happy, healthy wife. That would be unbelievable. It is to play the recovering survivor. A woman slowly, tentatively, re-emerging into the world. Your fragility is your cover. Any inconsistencies in your memory, any emotional distance... it will all be attributed to the trauma. It is the perfect cover story. You are to provide the illusion of his recovery by embodying the illusion of your own."

Sloane's mind was racing, the actress in her assessing the role, the survivor assessing the risk. "What you're describing," she said, her voice carefully neutral, "is impersonation. Fraud. This is... illegal, isn't it?"

Fairweather laughed. It was not a warm sound. It was a dry, rustling noise, like old paper being crumpled. "Ms. Devereaux, they say anything that's truly fun in life is either illegal, immoral, or fattening. I can assure you this role is none of those. It is a private arrangement to ensure the stability of a significant global enterprise. Quite simply, you are to be Mr. Crestwell's muse. It is a performance, not a crime."

He leaned forward, his smile thin and sharp as a razor. "And I can guarantee you... it will be fun. Never a dull moment."

Sloane didn't return the smile. She let the silence stretch.

She leaned forward, her posture shifting from that of a victim to that of a professional negotiating terms. "A hundred million dollars is a compelling number, Mr. Fairweather," she said, her voice now steady and clear. "But before we discuss the terms, there is a more fundamental question that needs to be answered."

Fairweather's eyebrows lifted a millimeter. "Proceed."

Sloane held his cold, reptilian gaze. "This 'tragic accident.' Was it really an accident?"

The question landed in the silent, sterile room like a block of ice. It was a direct accusation, a test of the entire premise.

Fairweather did not flinch. His expression remained a mask of polite, professional calm. But his thumb, which had been tracing a slow circle on his wedding band, stopped. Dead still.

"The official investigation by the Italian authorities was exhaustive," he said, his voice a flat, legalistic instrument. "They ruled the death an accidental drowning, caused by a freak weather event. The case is closed."

"That's not what I asked," Sloane pressed, refusing to let him off the hook. "I'm being asked to live in a house with a grieving man. I need to know if I'm living with a man who is grieving his wife, or grieving what he did to her."

For the first time, a flicker of something that might have been genuine amusement touched the corner of Fairweather's mouth. "Ms. Devereaux, your talent for melodrama exceeds the facts. Let me be unequivocally clear: Mr. Crestwell was below deck at the time of the incident. He is a victim in this tragedy, not a perpetrator. His grief is profound, genuine, and the very reason for this entire, unorthodox arrangement. Is that clear enough for you?"

Sloane held his gaze. He had answered the question without answering the doubt.

"Clear enough," she said, her voice now steady and clear. "My next question, then. Mr. Crestwell. Does he know about... this arrangement? Does he know I'm an actress? Or am I expected to fool him as well?"

"Mr. Crestwell is... aware of the arrangement," Fairweather said, the words chosen with a lawyer's surgical precision. "His grief is profound. He has chosen to embrace a solution that provides him with the necessary stability to continue his work. Your role is to be that solution. Lift his spirits. Be his muse. You will not break character. Not for anyone. Not ever."

The ambiguity was a chilling answer in itself. Damian knew, but he had chosen not to know. A willed delusion.

Sloane continued, "The terms of this... performance. What are the expectations regarding... intimacy?" The word was a piece of ice in her mouth, but she said it without flinching. She had learned long ago in Hollywood to ask the ugliest questions before they became assumptions.

"None," Fairweather stated, his voice flat, absolute. "You are not required to have any physical relationship with Mr. Crestwell. It would be inconsistent with the narrative. You are a woman recovering from severe trauma. The lack of intimacy is a feature of the performance, not a bug. You will be his partner in public, his emotional anchor in private. Is that clear?"

"Crystal," Sloane said, the relief a cool wave she did not allow to show on her face. "Next. My liberties. Am I a guest or a prisoner? Can I leave the estate?"

"Argentis is a secure, controlled environment," he countered, a masterpiece of corporate doublespeak. "Your safety and discretion are paramount. All of your needs will be met on-site. For the six-month term of the contract, you will not leave the grounds without explicit authorization and a security detail. It is not a prison, Ms. Devereaux. It is a sanctuary."

A sanctuary with invisible bars. "And success?" she pressed. "What is the metric for a successful performance?"

"The successful completion of the six-month term without incident," he said. "You will make a handful of public appearances with Mr. Crestwell. Your presence will reassure the investors and satisfy the board. After six months, 'Livia' will return to a life of quiet seclusion, and you will be free to become... whoever you wish to be."

Sloane nodded, trying to absorb the nature of this unusual 'role' that she was being offered.

"But above all," Fairweather added, his voice dropping to a low, confidential murmur, "the most important element of your role—the reason my client is willing to pay one hundred million dollars—is your appearance at the Crestwell

Foundation Gala in approximately eleven weeks. On the surface, it is a simple charity event, a way to reassure the board and the stakeholders of Mr. Crestwell's stability. That is *the* performance you will give to the world."

He held her gaze, letting the silence stretch. "But charity is not the true purpose of this event."

"The gala," he continued, his voice now barely a whisper, "is a front. The real event is the covert final summit for my client's most proprietary technology project—created by Mr. Crestwell. It is the one night when all twelve members of The Consortium will be in one room. They will be watching you and Mr. Crestwell.

"But they are not looking for romance, Ms. Devereaux. They are verifying the stability of the Chief Architect.

"This is not a party. It is the culmination of a deal that will redefine the strategic landscape for the next century. And your performance is the final linchpin."

He paused, letting the weight of that sink in.

"Mr. Crestwell has been... emotionally compromised since his wife's death," he continued, the pieces now clicking into place for Sloane. "The members of The Consortium have expressed... concerns. They are about to make an unprecedented financial commitment, and they will not do so if they believe the system's chief architect is unstable. Your performance at this gala must convince them that Mr. Crestwell has recovered. That the project will continue on schedule. That the woman they knew as Livia Crestwell is alive, well, and fully supportive of her husband's work."

The words were sterile, corporate, but Sloane heard the subtext loud and clear. The Consortium. Ready to walk away. Untold riches on the line. *Proprietary*. A lawyer's word for secret. A word used for things that were valuable, dangerous, and heavily guarded.

"I must emphasize something critical," Fairweather continued, his voice even quieter now. "These stakeholders—and indeed, virtually no one outside of an extremely tight circle of trust—know that Livia Crestwell died. Her death was kept *very* private. Contained. As far as the world knows, she has been recovering from an accident in seclusion. And that fiction must be maintained absolutely.

"At the gala, and in every interaction thereafter, the members of The Consortium must believe, without doubt—that you are Livia Crestwell. Not an actress playing her. Not a stand-in. Her. That is the success metric, Ms. Devereaux. Total, flawless, undetectable impersonation. If even one of them suspects the truth, the deal collapses. And if the deal collapses..."

He didn't finish the sentence. He didn't need to.

Chapter 7: The Fine Print

"It is not just for Damian's comfort that you are here," Fairweather continued. "It is because Livia Crestwell—or the woman everyone believes is Livia Crestwell—lending her face and reputation to that gala gives the project legitimacy. When Mrs. Crestwell stands beside her husband and endorses this technology, when she smiles for the stakeholders and raises her glass to the future, it signals safety. Stability. Continuity. And that, Ms. Devereaux, is worth far more than a hundred million dollars to my client."

Sloane understood then. She wasn't just a replacement wife. She was the linchpin of an astronomical business deal. The beautiful lie that would prevent the whole house of cards from collapsing.

"And the money?" she asked.

"One million dollars upon signing the final agreement," he stated. "The remaining ninety-nine million will be placed in an escrow account, to be released to you upon successful completion. Should you breach the terms of the contract at any point—by revealing your identity, by failing to maintain the performance, by any action deemed detrimental to my client's interests—the contract will be terminated, and the penalty will be... significant."

Sloane held his cold, reptilian gaze. She knew what "significant" meant. It meant erasure. A different kind than Mitchell Carver's, and far more permanent.

"Before I decide," Sloane said, a new question forming in her mind, "how did you find me? There are thousands of actresses in Los Angeles who need money. Why me?"

Fairweather's thin lips curved into the ghost of a smile. "My client has extensive resources, Ms. Devereaux. Resources that allow us to... identify opportunities before they become obvious. We've been aware of your situation for some time. Your talent. Your... desperation. Your relationship with Mr. Emanuel Goldman." He said Manny's name with a deliberate, almost clinical precision, as if it were a data point in a file. "A loyal man. A fierce advocate. The kind of person who would do anything to protect you."

The implication hung in the air like a threat.

"I want to see the contract," she said. "All of it. Before I decide."

"Of course." Fairweather's expression didn't change, but something in his eyes suggested satisfaction.

Sloane bit her tongue, stopping herself from asking the one question she desperately wanted to. *Manny.* Fairweather had mentioned him. Knew about him. Could she talk to him?

As if reading her mind, Fairweather cut her off. "No doubt you feel compelled to discuss this with your agent, Mr. Goldman, as you would with any other offer," he said, his tone smooth and reasonable. "We would generously interpret the NDA you've signed to accommodate such a consultation. We can trust his discretion if you can, I'm sure."

He paused, letting the ostensibly magnanimous gesture settle before delivering the poison.

"However," he continued, leaning forward slightly, "I would advise against it, for purely pragmatic reasons. First, Mr. Goldman, for all his talents, has never negotiated an offer of this magnitude. Not even close. He operates in a far minor league. Second, and more importantly, his primary concern will be your safety, as it should be. However, he might blow this concern out of proportion. If there is even a small chance that he might dissuade you from accepting this once-in-a-lifetime opportunity... is that a risk you are truly willing to take?"

The question hung in the air, a perfect, poisoned dart. Fairweather didn't need to wait for an answer.

***

He handed her a slate-gray tablet. It was cool and heavy in her trembling hands.

"These files contain hundreds of hours of Mrs. Crestwell's home videos, her correspondence, her social media archives. Everything you would need to study her."

He leaned forward and tapped the screen, highlighting the file header.

"And the full seventy-four-page performance and confidentiality agreement, filed under its operational code name: Project Chimera."

Chimera. A monster stitched together from pieces that didn't belong.

Sloane turned the device over in her hands. On the back, etched in silver, was the serpent crest.

She flipped it back to the screen, staring at the wall of text.

"Seventy-four pages," she said. "Legalese designed to protect you, not me. I will require my own counsel to review it before I sign anything."

Fairweather's thin smile didn't waver. He simply tapped a finger on his desk. "Of course," he said, the words dripping with condescension. "You have forty-eight hours. The same time your eviction is due. I'm sure your 'counsel' is a competent international contract lawyer who is available at a moment's notice, can be trusted with a hundred-million-dollar contract, and happens to be an expert in Swiss corporate law. If you do have such a unicorn, by all means, send me their details."

The dismissal was absolute. It wasn't a "no." It was a demonstration. He was showing her that, in his world, access to the kind of resources she would need was a weapon she did not possess. He had given her a right she had no practical way of exercising.

"You have until Friday noon to decide, Ms. Devereaux," Fairweather said. "During that time, you will speak of this to no one. If you accept, a car will pick you up. If you decline, or if you breach the confidentiality of this meeting, the consequences will be... significant."

He saw the question in her eyes, the flicker of a modern reflex. *Google it?*

"By all means, do your research," he said, a thin, dismissive smile touching his lips. "You will find the public narrative to be perfectly... curated. A tragic accident. Livia recovering in the comfort of her home. Nothing more. My client is a master of information control."

He gestured to the slate-gray tablet she held. "The real story, the one that matters to you, is in that device. Everything you need to know will be provided. We value efficiency."

"After forty-eight hours," he concluded, his voice turning back to ice, "this offer will disappear. As will any record of this meeting."

Sloane stood. Her legs felt like water, but she walked out.

She didn't remember the elevator. Didn't remember the lobby. One moment she was in the glass tower, the next the violent sunlight of Los Angeles hit her like a fist.

She pressed her back against the building's concrete facade. Clutched the tablet to her chest.

Livia's perfect face. The eviction notice. A hemorrhoid cream commercial audition that she had failed. Or...

One. Hundred. Million. Dollars.

Chapter 8: The Ghost in the Glass

The drive back to North Hollywood felt like a journey between dimensions. One moment she was in a glass tower with a hundred million dollars within her reach; the next, she was back in the gritty, sun-bleached reality of her own life.

She didn't turn on the air conditioning. The suffocating heat felt appropriate. A penance.

The eviction notice still sat on the counter, red letters screaming. She pulled out her phone. The alert glowed: *Wire Transfer Received: $50,000.00.*

Her fingers moved fast. Banking app. Landlord payment. Eight thousand, two hundred dollars. Transfer Submitted.

For one dizzying second, she was saved.

She picked up the eviction notice and tore it into pieces. The sound was satisfying. Violent.

Then her gaze fell on the credit card bills. FINAL NOTICE. FINAL NOTICE. FINAL NOTICE.

Two hundred thousand dollars in debt. Growing every day. What was left would barely touch it.

A single sandbag against a tsunami.

The fifty thousand wasn't a gift. It was bait.

She opened her laptop first. The instinct was automatic—verify the source. She typed "Damian Crestwell" into the search bar.

The results were... curated. Sterile. A Wikipedia page that read like a corporate press release. A few articles from *Wired* and *The Economist* from a dozen years ago, praising his early genius. No paparazzi shots. No gossip. No recent news.

Then she typed "Livia Crestwell accident."

A handful of identical articles popped up. "Near-fatal boating incident." "Recovering in private." No photos of the wreckage. No hospital leaks. Just a polite, corporate wall of silence that echoed Fairweather's story.

Fairweather hadn't been lying. The public narrative was a blank wall.

She looked at the tablet on her sofa, the serpent crest glittering in the dim light.

The role of a lifetime.

That's what Fairweather had called it. An Oscar-winner reduced to hemorrhoid commercials, now offered a hundred million to become someone else entirely.

Trap or resurrection. Survivor or artist.

She sat in the gathering dusk, staring at the tablet.

Then she turned it on.

***

The screen glowed to life, the serpent crest dissolving into a simple, elegant user interface. There was only one folder, labeled *LIVIA*. Inside were hundreds of files. Videos. Audio recordings. Scanned journal entries. Photo albums. An entire life, digitized and cataloged.

She tapped on the first video file. *Naples, December 2024.* The last of Livia's videos.

The screen filled with the impossible blue of the Bay of Naples. And there she was. Livia. Her face. Laughing as the wind whipped her hair. She was speaking, her voice a low, melodic murmur with a faint, unplaceable European lilt. It was Sloane's voice, but polished, softened, moneyed.

Sloane's finger hovered over the screen. She felt a sick, voyeuristic thrill, a toxic cocktail of envy and professional fascination. This was the ultimate challenge for an actress. Not just to mimic a person, but to become them from the inside out. To absorb their memories, their mannerisms, their very soul, until the line between the performance and the self blurred into nothing.

Exhilarating. Demanding. Frightening.

All it demanded was the complete annihilation of Sloane Devereaux.

***

The thought was the last coherent thing she had before exhaustion, a tide she had been fighting since the courier delivered the mysterious letter, finally pulled her under. Curled on the worn-out sofa, the tablet still glowing in her lap, she slipped into a strange, twilight state—a fever dream bathed in the cool blue light of the screen.

The apartment dissolved. The oppressive heat vanished. The world became Livia.

She wasn't just watching anymore. She was *there*.

She watched her in Paris, ordering coffee and croissants in flawless French, her gestures fluid and confident. Sloane had played a scene in a Parisian café once; she had spent a week with a dialect coach just to get three lines right. Livia simply lived it.

She watched her in Gstaad, skiing down a mountain with a casual grace, her laughter echoing in the crisp alpine air. Sloane had learned to ski for a role, a clumsy, terrified week on the bunny slopes of Mammoth Mountain.

She watched her at a charity dinner in New York, navigating a room full of powerful people with a disarming warmth. She remembered their names, their children's names, asked about their last vacation. She was a master of the soft power that Sloane, with her confrontational honesty, had never learned to wield.

She watched the intimate moments. Livia and Damian, curled up on a sofa in a vast, minimalist room, a fire crackling in the hearth. He was reading a slim volume of moral philosophy—one of those books that asked more questions than it answered. She was sketching in a notebook. He would read a passage aloud, and she would look up and smile—a private, knowing smile more intimate than any kiss. They were a team. Intellectual equals. Sloane had never had that. Her relationships had always been a battle, a negotiation, a performance.

The envy was a sharp, physical pain in Sloane's chest. Livia had everything. Everything Sloane had clawed for and lost. The money. The career—Livia had been a brilliant cryptographer before she married Damian. The respect. The love.

And now Livia was dead.

And Sloane could have it all. She just had to become a dead woman.

***

She woke up with a start, her mind rattled by the strange fever dream, and straggled into her small, dingy bathroom. She flicked on the harsh fluorescent light and stared at her reflection in the cheap, builder-grade mirror.

Her face was pale, her eyes hollowed out with exhaustion. She saw the fine lines of stress around her mouth, the faint shadow of desperation in her gaze. This was the face of a woman who was losing.

She thought of Livia's face on the screen. The same bone structure. The same eyes. But Livia's face was relaxed, confident. Alive.

Sloane took a breath. She raised her chin, just a fraction. She softened the set of her jaw. She let a small, enigmatic smile play on her lips, the kind she had just seen Livia give Damian in a dozen videos. She tilted her head, a gesture she had already memorized.

The transformation was instantaneous and terrifying.

The desperate woman in the mirror vanished. In her place was a stranger. A woman of wealth and confidence. A woman who belonged in Paris, in Gstaad, on the deck of a yacht in the Tyrrhenian Sea.

It was Livia.

Sloane stared, her heart pounding. The line had blurred. For a disorienting, terrifying moment, she felt a wave of vertigo. Who was the real person? The woman in the mirror, or the woman looking at her?

She whispered a phrase she had heard Livia say a dozen times, a soft, French endearment she used for her husband. "Mon cœur."

The voice was not quite hers. It was lower, smoother. The accent was perfect.

A thrill, sharp and electric, shot through her. She was good at this. She had always been good at this. Becoming someone else was the only thing she had ever truly mastered.

Then her gaze dropped to her left hand, resting on the edge of the sink. She saw the scar.

A thin, white, diagonal line across her palm, a permanent reminder of a hot August afternoon in Oklahoma, a smashed butterfly jar, and a father's casual cruelty.

Livia Crestwell didn’t have a scar.

The ghost in the mirror vanished. Sloane was herself again, a thirty-year-old woman in a shitty apartment, a single, ugly scar branding her as a survivor of a life Livia could never have imagined.

The thought was both a relief and a profound, aching disappointment.

Chapter 9: The Warning

The next couple of hours dissolved into a haze of heat, anxiety, and fine print. Sloane didn't leave the apartment. The forty-eight-hour clock Fairweather had given her was a silent, relentless drumbeat in the back of her mind.

She attacked the seventy-four-page contract first, her eyes burning as she scrolled, the dense legalese a foreign language designed to conceal, not clarify. When the words started to blur and a migraine began to pulse behind her eyes, she took a break and ordered cheap Chinese food, the delivery guy giving a little start of recognition when she opened the door. "Hey, you're that actress, right? From... yeah, that movie." He couldn't remember the name. She smiled, a brittle, practiced thing, and closed the door on his pity.

Mindlessly chewing her favorite food without any joy, she found herself vacillating between two extremes. One moment, she was convinced it was a trap. A sophisticated scam. A human trafficking ring for the 0.01 percent. They would take her to Switzerland and she would disappear, another tragic story for a true-crime podcast a decade from now. Her Hollywood-honed paranoia, the survival instinct that had kept her safe from predators for fourteen years, screamed at her to throw the tablet in a dumpster and change her name.

Then she would think about the eviction notice she had barely escaped. She would think of the casting director's bored, dismissive face. She would feel the phantom weight of the hundred-million-dollar offer, a number so vast it felt like a key to a different dimension.

In that dimension, she wasn't invisible. She was relatable. She was powerful. She could resurrect her career. She could start her own production company. She could pull those dog-eared scripts off her coffee table and finally make one of them real. She could fund the strange, beautiful, difficult films that no one else would make. She could finally have the one thing she'd always craved more than fame: control.

The back-and-forth was making her physically ill. Her hands shook. A low-grade hum of anxiety vibrated behind her ribs. And then she checked the time.

Forty-three hours remaining.

She needed an anchor. She needed the one person in the world whose bullshit detector was even more finely tuned than her own.

She picked up the phone and called Manny.

***

"A hundred million dollars?"

Manny's voice on the other end of the line wasn't just loud; it was a physical force, a sonic boom of pure, unadulterated shock that made Sloane pull the phone away from her ear.

"You're kidding me," he bellowed. "This is a joke, right? You're doing a bit. A very, very unfunny bit."

"It's not a bit, Manny," Sloane said, pacing the length of her small living room. She had told him everything. The courier. The law firm. The doppelgänger. The yacht accident. The grieving husband.

There was a moment of rare, terrifying silence on Manny's end. She could hear the faint clink of ice in a glass, the low murmur of the early dinner crowd at Gable & Crane.

"Are you out of your goddamn mind?" he finally exploded, his voice a raw, terrified roar. "This isn't a role, Sloane! This is a disappearing act! You don't take a hundred million dollars from people like this and just walk away six months later with a tan and a thank-you note!"

"Manny, calm down—"

"Calm down? Sweetheart, you just told me you're thinking about willingly climbing into a cage with a monster you've never met for a pile of money that could buy a goddamn country! There is no calm! There is only the screaming panic of a man who is watching his favorite person in the world walk off a cliff!"

"It's not like that. There's a contract. Lawyers."

"Lawyers?" He laughed, a harsh, ugly sound. "Honey, for a hundred million dollars, they're not hiring lawyers. They *own* lawyers. They own judges. They own the goddamn police. A contract means nothing when the other side can afford to buy the entire legal system. It's toilet paper. You'll be a loose end, Sloane. A loose end with a hundred million dollars' worth of secrets in her head. What do you think they do with loose ends like that?"

The brutal logic of his words hit her. This was the part she hadn't let herself think about. The "after."

"I don't know," she whispered.

"You end up at the bottom of a lake wearing cement shoes, that's what happens! You have a 'boating accident' off the Amalfi Coast, just like the first one! Jesus Christ, Sloane, do you hear yourself? You'd be replacing a woman who already died under mysterious circumstances!"

"It was a tragic accident," she recited, the words feeling thin and stupid even as she said them.

"Says who? The guy with the hundred million dollars to buy a replacement? That's not a grieving husband, sweetheart. That's a man cleaning up a crime scene!"

"But Fairweather said it wasn't Damian who's paying for the contract," Sloane protested weakly. "He said the client was Damian's partner..."

"The client?" Manny's laugh was a harsh, incredulous bark. "The 'client' who wants to spend a hundred million dollars to help his grieving partner? Sweetheart, listen to yourself! Who is this phantom? He hides his own name, but he's happy to give you Damian's? Why? And why does this ghost have this much power over a man like Damian, the billionaire? It's a shell game, Sloane, and you're the pea!"

Sloane sank onto her sofa, the phone pressed hard against her ear. His terror was a contagion, seeping through the line and chilling her to the bone. This was what she had called him for. The dose of sanity. The voice of reason.

"Just... just say no, kid," Manny pleaded, his voice cracking now, the bravado gone, replaced by raw, paternal fear. "Walk away. We'll figure something out. I'll sell my condo. We'll move to Montana. You can do community theater. I don't give a shit. Just don't do this. Please."

Sloane could hear the tremor in his voice, the raw, terrified love. And in that moment, another voice, colder and smoother, echoed in her memory. Fairweather, in his glass tower.

"His primary concern will be your safety, as it should be... If there is even a small chance that he might dissuade you from accepting this once-in-a-lifetime opportunity... is that a risk you are truly willing to take right now?"

Manny was offering her a life raft. A small, safe, honorable life in Montana. Fairweather was offering her a rocket ship to another dimension. Manny was trying to save her soul. Fairweather had warned her that Manny's love would try to keep her chained to a life of failure. The poisoned dart had found its mark.

She looked at the tablet on the coffee table, its screen dark, the serpent crest a faint, silver gleam. She thought of his hand shaking at the restaurant. Of him getting old, of the world becoming a place that would one day not have Manny Goldman in it. The thought was a physical pain, sharper than any rejection from a casting director.

"Okay, Manny," she said softly. "Okay. I hear you."

"Promise me you'll say no."

"I..." She looked at the tablet on the coffee table, its screen dark, the serpent crest a faint, silver gleam. "I promise I'll think about it. I have to go."

"Sloane, don't—"

She hung up.

***

She stood in the center of her silent apartment, Manny's terror echoing in her ears. He was right. It was insane. It was a one way trip. She should throw the tablet in the trash, block the number, and go back to her life of quiet desperation.

But his fear had done something else, too. It had ignited a tiny, defiant spark in the cold, dead center of her soul.

Who the hell was he to tell her what she could and couldn't do?

Who was anyone?

Her entire life had been a series of men telling her what she was, what she could be, what she was worth. Her father, telling her that pretty things get crushed. The producer in Malibu, telling her what her body was worth in exchange for a role.

The studio titan, Mitchell Carver, telling her that he would unmake her with a single call.

And now Manny, the man she loved most in the world, was telling her she was a victim. A lamb walking to the slaughter. He saw her as a fragile thing that needed to be protected, spirited away to Montana to do community theater.

The spark flared into a hot, angry flame.

She was not fragile. She was a survivor. She had survived a violent father. She had survived the shark tank of Hollywood. She had survived poverty and humiliation and erasure. She was still standing.

Fourteen brutal years. She had arrived in this city a terrified sixteen-year-old fresh off a Greyhound bus, won an Oscar at twenty-two, and was blacklisted by twenty-five. Fourteen years of fighting, clawing, compromising, and refusing to disappear, only to end up here, thirty years old and auditioning to be the face of rectal itch cream.

The opportunity that had knocked wasn't just a role. It wasn't just money. It was a chance of a lifetime. A chance to take control. To be the one pulling the strings for once.

She was a damn good actress. Maybe the best there ever was. She could play this part. She could walk into that gilded cage, take their money, and walk out again, leaving them all in her dust. She could beat them at their own game.

The fear was still there, a cold knot in her stomach. But now, it was mingled with something else. A wild, reckless, exhilarating surge of her old ambition. The ambition that had told a sixteen-year-old girl she could conquer a city of monsters.

She looked at the tablet. The serpent seemed to be mocking her, daring her.

A clock was ticking on Fairweather's offer. But for Sloane, the choice was no longer about time. It was about defiance. She had already decided the moment she hung up the phone.

She would not be the victim. Not this time.

***

The silence in the apartment felt hotter, smaller, thick with the echo of Manny's terror. He was right. It was insane. A suicide mission. She sank onto the sofa, the tablet on the coffee table looking like a sleek, gray tombstone. She was a fool to even consider it. She should call them back, tell them no, and go back to her life of fading auditions and fluorescent-lit rejection rooms.

An hour after her call with Manny, as the late afternoon sun began to bleed into a hazy, orange dusk, a hard, impatient knock on her apartment door made her jump, her heart seizing in her chest.

It was too firm for a neighbor, too insistent for a courier. Her mind flashed to the men in the glass tower, to the serpent on the crest. Had they been watching her? Listening to her call? Had they come to collect their answer in person?

She crept to the door, her bare feet silent on the cheap linoleum, and peered through the peephole. Her breath caught in her throat.

It was Manny.

She swung the door open. He stood in the dingy hallway, looking utterly out of place, a glorious, hibiscus-blazoned dinosaur in a cage of beige stucco. His face, usually a mask of defiant optimism, was a wreck of raw, paternal fear. He didn't say hello. He pushed past her into the apartment, his eyes taking in the torn eviction notice in the trash, the oppressive heat, the scent of failure. The frantic drive across town had clearly done nothing to calm him down; it had only solidified his resolve.

"I couldn't do it," he said, his voice a low, gravelly growl. "I couldn't just sit there after that call, waiting for the world to eat you alive."

He turned to face her. He wasn't holding the envelope of cash. This wasn't about money anymore. This was about survival. He pressed a small, cheap, blister-packed object into her hand. A pre-paid burner phone.

"What's this?" she asked, her voice a near whisper.

"It's my paranoia package," he said, his voice dropping, his gaze intense. "You're not thinking straight. I get it, I see this place, I get it. But if you're really going to consider this Swiss thing... if you're going to talk to these people... you do not use your real phone. Ever."

He tapped the back of the package, where a small, neat stack of SIM cards was taped in a tiny plastic baggie. "This isn't your corner store special. It's a clean phone, no GPS, no frills. And these..." he tapped the baggie again, "these are the important part. Ghost SIMs. Global roaming. They'll work from the top of the Matterhorn if they have to."

"And listen to me carefully." His voice dropped even lower, urgent. "If—and I'm saying IF—you end up somewhere isolated, somewhere they're watching you,

you DO NOT power this thing on indoors. These people, whoever they are, if they're worth billions, they'll have surveillance. RF sweeps, signal detection, military-grade stuff. This phone only gets turned on when you're OUTSIDE their walls. Away from their cameras. You find a reason to leave—shopping, a walk, whatever—then you call me from somewhere public. You understand?"

Sloane nodded, her throat tight.

He scribbled a sequence of digits on a yellow Post-it note and pressed it into her hand.

"And you memorize this number. Right now. Not my regular cell—assume that's compromised. This is a ghost line, just for us."

He tapped the paper in her hand.

"Don't store it in contacts. In your head only. Once you have it, burn this or flush it. Because if they find this thing and search it, you don't want to leave a trail." His eyes were fierce. "After every call or text—and I mean every single one—you clear all logs and power down. And after three, maybe four uses—or if anything feels wrong, if you think you've been made—you pull the SIM, snap it in half, flush it, and swap in a new one. The phone stays clean. It's the SIM that's the snitch."

He met her eyes, his own fierce and unwavering. "This little package... it's your new religion. It goes where you go. In your purse. In your pocket. You never, ever let it out of your sight. You hear me? I'm not letting you walk into the dark alone, kid. Not without a flashlight. Even a cheap one."

She looked from the cheap plastic in her hand to his worried, fiercely loyal eyes. The tremor in his own hand was more pronounced up close. He was terrified for her, and his response was not to try and cage her, but to arm her. She couldn't refuse this. This wasn't a handout. This was his heart, made manifest in a piece of plastic and a stack of global SIM cards.

"Okay, Manny," she whispered, her throat tight. "Okay."

He gave a single, curt nod, the mission accomplished. "You call me," he said. "That's an order."

He turned and left without another word, a whirlwind of vermilion silk and terrified love, leaving her alone in the quiet, suffocating apartment. Sloane closed the door, the lock clicking shut with a sound of finality. She looked down at the burner package in her hand, a small, secret piece of armor.

Chapter 10: The Dream

That night, sleep was not a refuge. It was an ambush.

Sloane fell into a heavy, dreamless state at first, the exhaustion of the last few days finally claiming her. But then, the dream began. It wasn't a story. It was a series of images, sharp and cold as shards of glass.

She was standing in a closet. Not her own cramped, cluttered closet, but the one from the videos. Livia's closet. It was a cathedral of wealth, vast and silent, the recessed lighting making the rows of shoes glitter like jewels in a treasure chest. Gowns hung in temperature-controlled glass cases like priceless works of art. The air smelled of cedar, leather, and the faint, cloying scent of ghost orchid and bergamot.

She was wearing a simple, white slip, her bare feet cold on the polished marble floor. She felt like an intruder, a ghost haunting a life that was not hers.

A single dress was laid out on a velvet chaise lounge in the center of the room. It was the emerald gown Livia had worn to the Parisian gala. In the dream, it seemed to glow with its own internal light. A voice, cool and precise, echoed in the vast space. It was the voice from the videos—Livia's—a polished, melodic ghost of her own.

Put it on.

Sloane's hands moved, but they weren't her own. She lifted the gown. The fabric was impossibly heavy, a cascade of silk and hand-sewn crystals. It felt cold against her skin as she slipped it on. It fit perfectly. Of course it did.

Turn around.

She turned to face the three-way mirror that dominated one wall. And her breath caught in her throat.

The woman in the mirror was Livia. Not Sloane playing Livia. It was her. The eyes were brighter, the smile more confident, the posture more regal. It was the woman from the videos, radiant and alive.

Sloane lifted her hand. The reflection lifted hers. But as Sloane's real hand came up, she saw the faint, white scar on her palm. In the mirror, Livia's palm was flawless.

***

The woman in the mirror—Livia—smiled, but it was a cold, pitying smile. She spoke, but her voice was in Sloane's head, a venomous whisper.

You think you can wear my clothes? You think you can live my life?

"I can," Sloane whispered back, her own voice a dry rasp in the silent room. "I'm a good actress."

Livia laughed, a sound like shattering glass. *Actress? You are a beggar, dressed in a queen's robes. You are a ghost, trying to haunt a house that is not yours.*

Sloane took a step back from the mirror. The reflection did not. Livia remained where she was, her hands now pressed flat against the glass from the inside, her smile gone, replaced by a mask of desperate, silent fury.

They will kill you, Livia's voice echoed in her mind. *Just like they killed me. This dress is not a costume. It's a shroud.*

"Who?" Sloane asked, her heart hammering against her ribs. "Who killed you?"

Livia's mouth opened in a silent scream. She pounded on the glass, her face contorted in a mask of terror. The mirror began to crack around her, fine, spiderwebbing fractures spreading out from her fists.

RUN, the voice screamed in Sloane's head, no longer a whisper, but a raw, animal shriek of pure terror.

Sloane stumbled backward, away from the cracking mirror, away from the screaming ghost who wore her face. She turned to flee the closet, but the door was gone. The walls were closing in, the rows of shoes and gowns becoming a suffocating, silent crowd, pressing in on her. The scent of ghost orchid was overpowering, thick and sweet as poison.

She was trapped.

She looked back at the mirror. Livia had stopped screaming. She was just standing there, on the other side of the shattered glass, her expression now one of calm, heartbreaking pity. A single, perfect tear rolled down her flawless cheek.

The glass of the mirror dissolved like smoke.

Livia stepped out.

She reached out and touched the scar on Sloane's palm, her fingers impossibly cold.

You poor, stupid girl, Livia whispered, her voice no longer a scream, but a sigh of profound sadness. *You really think they're paying you to act?*

***

Sloane woke up with a gasp, tangled in her cheap cotton sheets, her body drenched in a cold sweat. Her apartment was dark, the only light the faint, orange glow of a streetlight filtering through the blinds. Her heart was a wild, frantic bird beating against the cage of her ribs.

The dream was already fading, the sharp edges dissolving into the muddy confusion of waking. But the feeling remained. A deep, primal terror. And the echo of Livia's final, haunting question.

She sat up, swinging her legs over the side of the bed. Her hand went to her own palm, her fingers tracing the familiar, raised line of the scar. It was real. A part of her. Proof that she was Sloane Devereaux.

For now.

She stood up and walked to the window, pushing aside a slat of the blind. Outside, the city was asleep, a vast, sprawling creature of concrete and faded dreams. In a few hours, the sun would rise, and the deadline would be closer.

The dream was a warning. Her subconscious, her survivor's instinct, screaming at her to run.

But Livia's final question was not just a warning. It was a challenge.

You really think they're paying you to act?

If not for that, then for what?

The fear was still there, a cold, hard knot in her stomach. But now, it was mixed with something else. A flicker of her old, defiant curiosity. The part of her that didn't just want to survive the game, but wanted to understand it. To win it.

The dream had been meant to scare her away.

Instead, it had sealed her fate.

She was no longer just thinking about the money. She was thinking about the mystery.

She had to know.

Chapter 11: The Promise

Thursday disappeared in a fog of paralysis.

Every time she reached for her phone, her hand stopped. Every time she tried to imagine saying "yes," her throat closed. And every time she tried to imagine saying "no," she thought of the eviction notice she'd narrowly escaped. The three-headed hydra. The unending hell of being blacklisted. The life of irrelevance that continued slipping away.

The clock wasn't just ticking anymore—it was thundering, each hour a hammer blow against her skull.

Sloane didn't watch any more of Livia's videos. She didn't need to. The ghost of Livia Crestwell was already living in her apartment, a silent, judgmental roommate. Livia's voice was in her head, her perfect, confident smile burned onto the back of her eyelids.

The eviction notice was gone—paid, dealt with, a problem from another life. Then another forty thousand to the credit card companies. Not enough to kill the debt, but enough to let her breathe.

For now.

She had finished reading the contract once the night before, a frantic first pass. Now she attacked it again, a second reading, then a third, her eyes burning as she searched for the serpent's fang, the single clause that would reveal the trap.

There wasn't one.

The more she read, the more the words blurred into a single, inescapable truth: she was signing away Sloane Devereaux. Completely. Irrevocably. For six months, she would cease to exist. And if Manny's paranoid fantasy were to be right, forever thereafter.

And the most terrifying part? For a hundred million dollars, the terms almost felt reasonable.

Then she tried to clean. She scrubbed the small, stained bathtub until her knuckles were raw. She organized the mismatched books on her particle-board shelf. She threw out the expired yogurt. It was the frantic, useless activity of a condemned woman trying to put her cell in order.

With twenty hours left on the clock, the final blow came.

Her phone buzzed. A 310 number, but not one of her saved contacts. She almost didn't answer. But something—instinct, paranoia, the same curiosity that was about to ruin her life—made her pick up.

"Ms. Devereaux?" The voice was female, professional, apologetic in that California way that wasn't really an apology at all. "This is Jessica from Dr. Patel's office."

Sloane recognized the receptionist's voice, but not the number. “Hi Jessica. Did the office number change?”

“No. Sorry, our phones are down. I’m calling from my cell phone. About your account."

Sloane's stomach dropped. Dr. Patel. Her therapist. The one she'd been seeing twice a month for the last three years, the only thing standing between her and a complete psychological collapse after the blacklist.

"Your card was declined after your last month’s appointment," Jessica continued, her tone shifting from apologetic to firm. "And you currently have an outstanding balance of forty-eight hundred dollars. Dr. Patel has asked me to inform you that we can't continue sessions until the account is current."

Forty-eight hundred dollars.

The number hit her like a fist.

She'd forgotten. In the chaos of paying the landlord and the credit card companies, she'd completely forgotten about Dr. Patel. The bill had been sitting in a stack of unopened mail for days, buried under the red-envelope avalanche of more urgent threats.

"I—" Sloane started, then stopped. What could she say? That she'd had the money two days ago but had already spent it keeping other wolves from the door? That she'd prioritized credit cards over her own sanity?

"I understand," Sloane heard herself say, her voice hollow. "Thank you for letting me know. I'll look into it."

She ended the call before Jessica could launch into the scripted speech about payment plans and financial hardship programs.

She stood in the middle of her apartment, the phone still in her hand, staring at the remaining balance in her banking app. The last pathetic remnant of her war chest.

It wasn't enough. It would never be enough.

Five years. Five years of hemorrhaging money with no real income. A few commercial residuals here, a voiceover gig there, a humiliating industrial training video that paid three hundred dollars. And all the while, the rent kept coming. The utilities kept coming. The groceries, the gas, the car insurance, the phone bill—the thousand small, relentless cuts of just existing in Los Angeles.

She'd burned through her Oscar-era savings in the first two years. The rest had been a slow, grinding spiral into debt. Credit cards to pay rent. Cash advances to pay credit cards. Payday loans to pay cash advances. A Ponzi scheme with herself as both the con artist and the mark.

And now, the one person who'd been keeping her functional, keeping her from disappearing completely into the darkness—gone. Cut off. Because she'd forgotten a forty-eight-hundred-dollar bill.

She looked at the number on her screen again. The meagre account balance stared back at her. She could ask Dr. Patel for a payment plan, and pay a portion to keep her lifeline intact.

But then she'd have nothing. Soon the forty-eight-hour deadline would expire, and Fairweather's offer would disappear, and she'd be back to zero with no way out.

The choice was grotesque in its simplicity: mental health or survival. Sanity or salvation.

She already knew which one she'd choose. She'd known since the moment Fairweather had said "one hundred million dollars." But knowing and accepting were two different kinds of hell.

She set the phone down on the counter, her hand shaking. She needed air. She needed to get out of this suffocating little box.

***

She didn't sleep that night. Not really. She lay in the dark, the ceiling fan rattling above her, turning over the impossible choice.

By 5:30 AM, she gave up on sleep. The answer had been there all along, written in the stark mathematics of her bank account. She just wasn't ready to say it out loud yet.

She needed to see the sunrise first. Her last one in Los Angeles. For six months at least. Maybe forever.

She climbed the stairs to the roof as the sky began to lighten, the city below still wrapped in darkness, the Hollywood sign barely visible against the hills.

***

The roof of her apartment building was flat, tarred, and littered with old satellite dishes and cigarette butts. But it had a view. If you stood at the southern edge, you could see them: the distant, iconic letters of the Hollywood sign, stark white against the brown summer hills.

Sloane walked to the edge. The wind was hot and carried the scent of asphalt and exhaust. She leaned against the low parapet, the rough concrete digging into her forearms.

She had first seen that sign when she was sixteen, fresh off the Greyhound with two hundred dollars and a universe of desperate hope. It had looked like a promise then. Proof that you could build a heaven in the middle of a desert.

She closed her eyes.

She thought of the girl she had been. A girl running from the ghost of a violent father, armed with nothing but a pretty face and a will of iron forged in the fires of a miserable childhood. She remembered the promise she had made that first night in L.A.: *I will never be invisible again.*

For a while, she had kept it. She had burned with the fire of a supernova.

Now, she was just ash.

The memory of the butterfly jar rose unbidden—the sharpest fragment of her past. Nine years old. A dying monarch with a torn wing she had trapped in glass, feeding it sugar water, trying to make its last moments beautiful enough that her mother would finally look at her.

Her mother had found her crying over the jar that evening, bone-tired from a double shift: "Oh, baby, you can't save everything."

I tried to make it beautiful enough that people would look.

That was it, wasn't it? The core of it all. Acting had been the jar. The Oscar had been the sugar water. And in the end, her career had died just like the butterfly—trapped in a glass cage, watched by people who didn't care if she breathed or suffocated.

The sky was changing now. Black bleeding to navy, navy to gray. The city below was beginning to wake.

Sloane opened her eyes and looked at the Hollywood sign again. In the dawn light, it didn't look like a promise anymore. It just looked like letters on a hill. A prop. A piece of a set for a movie she was no longer in.

The choice was clear. She could stay here, in this city of ghosts, and become one herself. Or she could take the deal.

It was a way to disappear, yes. To erase Sloane Devereaux completely.

But it was also a path back to power.

One hundred million dollars wasn't just money. It was rocket fuel. It was a resurrection.

She was not Livia Crestwell. But she could play her. She was one of the best actresses of her generation—Mitchell Carver and his bastard friends hadn't been able to take that away from her. It would be the greatest performance of her life. And at the end of it, she would be free. A queen again, but this time, of her own kingdom, built on her own terms.

The sun broke over the horizon. Gold spilling across the sky.

A beginning. An ending.

Both.

She turned her back on the Hollywood sign. The fear was still there, a cold, hard knot in her stomach. But beneath it, something else was stirring. A flicker of the old fire.

She took out her phone to call the mysterious number in Switzerland.

The girl with the butterfly jar was gone. The Oscar-winner was gone. The blacklist victim was about to be gone.

Someone new was about to be born.

Chapter 12: The Signature

The air in Fairweather's office was the same: chilled, sterile, and smelling of power. Sloane sat in the same leather chair as before, but this time, she did not feel small. She felt a strange, cold calm. The desperation was gone, replaced by a crystalline resolve. She had walked through the fire of her own fear and come out the other side, forged into something new. Something harder.

She had called the Swiss number watching the sunrise from her rooftop. The same crisp, female voice had answered. Sloane had said only two words: "I accept."

An hour later, a black car, silent as a shark, had been waiting outside her apartment. Now, she was back in the glass tower, the city sprawling beneath her like a map of her own ambition and failure.

Mr. Fairweather entered the room, his movements precise and without wasted energy. He did not smile. He did not offer a pleasantry. He simply sat down behind his black granite desk and looked at her, his eyes like polished stones.

He gave a single, almost imperceptible nod of approval toward the slate-gray tablet she had placed on the desk between them. He gestured for her to wake the screen.

The display glowed to life, revealing the title page she had spent the last forty-eight hours dissecting. The bold letters seemed to stare back at her:

PROJECT CHIMERA: PERFORMANCE & CONFIDENTIALITY AGREEMENT.

"You have read the terms," he stated.

She had. Seventy-four pages of dense legalese. Forty-eight hours in her hot apartment, agonizing over every clause. Passport surrender. Cosmetic procedures.

Termination rights. A penalty clause that would make her current debts look like pocket change.

A slave contract, wrapped in elegant legal language.

"I have a question," Sloane said.

Fairweather frowned slightly. "Yes?"

"The initial payment. The contract states one million dollars upon signing. I need to pay off my—"

"That is correct. Immediately upon signing," Fairweather interrupted smoothly. "Furthermore, as a special consideration, I've been authorized to settle all your debts—every last one—and restore your credit. We want your transition unburdened. You are embarking on a great journey, and you shouldn't have to concern yourself with mundane details. Leave those to us."

"Thank you," Sloane said, and meant it. The gesture was unexpectedly generous. Almost... kind.

She felt something shift inside her chest—a dangerous, treacherous loosening.

Maybe Manny had been wrong. She wanted to believe that. God, she wanted to believe it.

"And the remaining ninety-nine million?" she asked.

"It will be held in an escrow account in Zurich and released to you in full upon the successful completion of the six-month term, as determined by my client."

"And if your client determines that my performance is... unsuccessful?"

For the first time, a flicker of something that might have been a smile touched the corner of Fairweather's mouth. "Then you will have had a six-month, all-expenses-paid vacation in the Swiss Alps. In a home where the wine is older than you are and the art is priceless. And you will leave with one million dollars for your trouble. Provided, of course, that you maintain absolute and total confidentiality for the remainder of your life."

He was lying. She knew it. He knew she knew it. It was part of the game.

There would be no consolation prize. No safe exit. You succeeded, or you vanished.

She could feel the room closing around her, sealing her choice in stone.

Sloane took a breath. "I'm ready to sign."

***

The signing was a ritual of erasure. She signed the performance contract. She signed the power of attorney. She signed the declaration of her intent to "disappear." With each stroke of the stylus, another piece of Sloane Devereaux flaked away.

When it was done, Fairweather produced a small, heavy, platinum card from a drawer. "Your initial payment has been transferred to this account. It is a private Swiss bank. We could not wire a sum of this magnitude to your domestic account without triggering federal flags that would compromise your anonymity. This account is untraceable. The PIN is the year of your birth."

He slid the card across the desk. Sloane picked it up. It was cold and heavy. The year of her birth. The day she came into the world, now the code to leave it.

"Your affairs in Los Angeles will be handled," Fairweather continued. "Lease terminated. Debts paid. Your possessions will be placed in secure storage. A car is waiting downstairs to take you to the airport. And as per the contract, you'll have to surrender your cell phone."

It was happening. Now. The machine was already in motion.

"Wait," Sloane said, her mind reeling. "My apartment. My things. I need to pack."

Fairweather gave the ghost of a smile. "That will not be necessary, Ms. Crestwell." He let the name hang in the air. "You are no longer Sloane Devereaux, remember? You have no home to go back to."

He gestured to a sleek, brushed aluminum suitcase in the corner. "We have provided for your immediate needs. Everything else you require will be waiting for you. Consider your old life... in storage."

The cold, clinical efficiency of it was breathtaking. The suitcase wasn't a convenience; it was a tool.

She thought of the Oscar. The Celine blazer. She pushed the feeling down. The woman who treasured those things was a ghost. She gave a single, curt nod.

"My agent," she said, her voice distant. "Manny Goldman. I need to call him."

"Not possible," Fairweather said, his tone final. "All communications from your old life have now ceased. Mr. Goldman will be informed you've accepted a film role abroad. He will be... compensated for his troubles."

The brutality of it took her breath away. They were cutting her off.

Her fingers, hidden inside her purse, closed around the cheap plastic of the burner phone. *Manny's paranoia package.* A drowning woman's piece of driftwood. The last real piece of her life.

She looked at Fairweather. A wall.

She stood, her legs unsteady. The platinum card felt like a block of ice in her hand.

"It's time to go, Ms. Devereaux," Fairweather said. He stood—the first time he'd moved since she entered. "For the last time."

Her name. He was burying it. With her consent.

***

The car was a Bentley Flying Spur. Black. Heavy. It looked less like a vehicle and more like a mobile vault. The door closed with a soft thud, sealing out the city.

She looked out the window, but saw only her reflection, a pale ghost against the dark glass.

She was leaving. Just like that. No tearful goodbyes. No last look. Just a clean, surgical extraction.

But she had one loose thread to tie.

She glanced at the rearview mirror. The driver's eyes were fixed on the 405, indifferent behind dark sunglasses. Keeping her movements small, she reached into her purse and found the cheap plastic blister pack Manny had forced on her.

Shielding the action with her jacket, she cracked the seal. Popped the SIM card. Slid it into the burner phone. It powered up with a cheap, cheerful chime she muffled with her thumb.

She typed the number from memory. Her fingers shook as she tapped out the lie that was supposed to protect him.

Took the job. Car service taking me to private jet. Total blackout for now. Don't worry. Love you.

Send.

She watched the signal bars flicker, then vanish as the message went through. She immediately powered the phone down, pulled the battery, and buried the pieces deep in the lining of her bag. A lifeline. Or a breadcrumb.

She thought of the girl on the rooftop, promising herself she would never be invisible again. Now, she was being paid to do just that.

The panic was still there, a coiling serpent in her gut. But beneath it, the actress was taking over. The performance had begun. Her old life was the backstory. This car, this silence, this journey—this was the first scene.

She took a breath. Sat up straighter. Composed her face. She was no longer Sloane Devereaux, failed actress.

She was a woman on her way to a new life. A woman with a secret.

She was ready for her close-up.

Chapter 13: The Ascent

The private terminal at Van Nuys Airport was another world, a hushed sanctuary of wealth and power tucked away from the chaotic sprawl of LAX. There was no security line, no crying babies, no stale smell of recycled air. The Bentley glided directly onto the tarmac, stopping beside a Gulfstream jet so sleek and white it looked like it had been carved from a single piece of ivory.

A pilot stood by the stairs. Sloane handed him her passport. He verified it against his tablet, slid the document into his jacket pocket for Swiss entry, and gestured for her to proceed.

The mid-afternoon sun glared off the polished fuselage, blinding and absolute—a stark, overexposed backdrop for the end of her life.

A woman in a crisp, tailored uniform stepped forward. She had the posture of a ballet dancer and a single, thin white scar bisecting her left eyebrow—the kind of scar that told a story she would never share. She smiled, a polite, professional smile that didn't reach her eyes. "Welcome, Ms. Devereaux. My name is Anna. I'll be your flight attendant for our journey to Buochs."

Sloane nodded, her own professional smile clicking into place. The actress was now fully in control, a necessary shield against the overwhelming vertigo of the situation. She walked up the stairs, her worn-out sneakers silent on the plush carpet.

The interior of the jet was a masterpiece of understated luxury. Cream-colored leather seats, polished dark wood, and brushed platinum accents. It was larger than her entire apartment. There were no other passengers.

"May I offer you some champagne before we depart?" Anna asked, her voice a soft, pleasant murmur.

"What have we chilled?" Sloane asked, her voice carrying Livia's cool, casual authority.

The line felt right. Not a request—an inquiry into the state of her own assets.

Anna returned a moment later with a single, delicate flute of pale gold liquid, tiny bubbles rising in perfect columns. "Salon, 2002. Le Mesnil," she said, as if Sloane would know the difference.

Sloane took the glass, her hand surprisingly steady. She had once done a scene in a film where she'd had to drink premium champagne. The prop master had given her sparkling apple cider.

This was not apple cider.

She took a sip. The bubbles were tiny, sharp, and tasted of green apples and something else. Money. It tasted like money.

She settled into one of the large leather seats as the jet began to taxi. She looked out the small, oval window. The lights of the San Fernando Valley were beginning to flicker on, a vast, glittering carpet of failed dreams and desperate hopes. Her home.

The jet turned onto the runway. The engines spooled up, a low growl that vibrated through the floor, through the seat, into her bones. Then, a powerful, relentless push, and the world outside became a blur.

The jet lifted off the ground, a smooth, effortless ascent. Sloane watched as the sprawling, glittering grid of Los Angeles fell away beneath her. She could see the dark, winding ribbon of the 101, the distant cluster of skyscrapers downtown, the vast, black emptiness of the Pacific Ocean. The city that had made her and broken her, the city she had loved and hated in equal measure, was shrinking, becoming a map, an abstraction.

She felt a sudden, sharp pang of grief, so intense it was like a physical blow. She was leaving everything she had ever known. Manny. The ghost of her mother. The dream she had chased for half her life. It was all down there, getting smaller and smaller.

But as the jet climbed higher, banking east into the darkening sky, another feeling began to surface, pushing through the grief. It was a terrifying, exhilarating surge of pure, unadulterated power. She was leaving it all behind. The failure. The humiliation. The eviction notice. The ghost of Mitchell Carver and all the other men who had tried to own her.

She was rising above it all.

She took another sip of champagne. This time, it tasted like freedom.

***

An hour into the flight, Anna approached her again, her movements silent and graceful.

"Forgive the intrusion, Ms. Devereaux," she said, her professional smile never wavering. "I was instructed to provide you with this, so you might begin your research during the flight. To get ready."

She handed Sloane a sleek, slate-gray tablet identical to the one Fairweather had given her in his office. A fresh one, still sealed in plastic. Sloane unwrapped it. It powered on to the same simple interface, the same single folder: LIVIA.

"There is a secure satellite internet connection, should you need it," Anna said. "Dinner will be served in two hours. Chef has prepared a Chilean sea bass with a saffron risotto. Will that be acceptable?"

"That's... fine. Thank you, Anna."

"Of course." The flight attendant gave another small, perfect smile and retreated to the front of the cabin, leaving Sloane alone in the quiet, humming luxury.

Sloane stared at the folder on the screen. Livia. Her life for the next six months.

She had spent the previous two days in a frantic, obsessive deep dive, but it had been the work of preparing for the role. This was different. This was the moment the cameras rolled—no retakes. She had to do more than just mimic Livia. She had to know her. She had to understand her. She had to find the soul of the woman whose skin she was about to inhabit.

The tablet's blue light carved shadows across her face. Outside the private jet's oval windows, nothing but darkness at forty thousand feet. The hum of engines, the recycled air, the leather seat that probably cost more than her last car. Everything felt unreal. Like she'd already disappeared.

She opened the folder. The hundreds of files were still there, but now they were organized into sub-folders. Childhood. University. Intelligence Career. Marriage. Social Engagements.

And the final one: December 2024.

That last folder sat at the bottom like a tombstone. The end of the timeline. The point where the documentation stopped and the silence began.

It was an intelligence dossier. A complete psychological profile. The kind of file that shouldn't exist. The kind that took serious resources—and serious violations of privacy—to compile.

Someone had been watching Livia Crestwell for years. Maybe her entire life.

The thought should have terrified Sloane. Instead, she felt a strange, cold gratitude. She needed this. Every frame. Every secret. Every moment of a life she was about to steal.

She clicked on the folder marked *Marriage*.

The thumbnails that populated the screen were nothing like the dazzling, curated highlights Fairweather had projected on his office wall—the yacht, the gala, the ski slope. Those had been Livia performing for the world, moments of public perfection captured by press, friends, or Damian himself.

These were different. Raw. Unsettlingly intimate.

But it was the perspective that jarred her. The angles were high, wide, and steady—fixed points from the ceiling or the walls. No cameraman. No handheld shake.

Sloane paused. She knew cameras. She clocked it instantly.

It was surveillance footage.

She felt a chill. These weren't memories captured for love; they were moments captured by a system. Six years of marriage. Six years of a woman's private life, catalogued and indexed like evidence at a trial.

The first one was labeled *Argentis, Kitchen. January 2019.*

Soon after they got married.

The scene was the kitchen of the Swiss estate—a vast, sterile space of brushed steel and white marble that looked like an operating theater. Everything gleaming, cold, expensive. The kind of kitchen where food was prepared by staff, not the owners.

Damian was trying to make an omelet.

Sloane leaned closer to the screen.

He was clumsy, inept, focused with the intensity of a man trying to solve an impossibly complex problem. The spatula held like a scalpel, the pan approached with the caution of a bomb technician. He was treating breakfast like a simulation.

A quantum behavioral economist trying to predict the chaotic system of an omelet.

Livia stood behind him, her arms wrapped around his waist, her chin on his shoulder. She was laughing—a soft, genuine, unguarded sound that felt like an intrusion to hear.

"You're going to burn it, my love," she whispered in his ear, her voice warm with affection and amusement.

"I'm trying to model the emergent behavior," he muttered, prodding the eggs. His accent was faint—American, but with the flattened vowels of someone who'd spent too much time around Europeans. "The state change from liquid to solid isn't a linear progression. It's a cascade failure. If I can just find the tipping point before the browning reaction becomes irreversible—"

"It's eggs, Damian. Not a predictive model for market collapse." She kissed the back of his neck. "Let me."

She gently took the spatula from his hand. He relaxed into her embrace, his body—which always seemed so tense and coiled—suddenly finding its center with her. The transformation was immediate. His shoulders dropped. His breathing slowed. He leaned back into her like a child seeking comfort.

He was a different man. A man who was loved.

And who loved back.

His hand came up to cover hers on the spatula, not taking it back, just... touching her. A small gesture of trust. Intimacy. The kind of moment that exists only between two people who know each other's rhythms perfectly.

Sloane felt something twist in her chest. Not envy. Something worse. Recognition.

This was what it looked like when someone wasn't performing. When two people existed together without audience, without pretense, without the constant, exhausting work of being seen.

She'd never had that. Not once in her thirty years.

Every relationship she'd ever had was a negotiation. A transaction. Even the good ones—especially the good ones—had been about managing appearances, protecting careers, maintaining the illusion of normalcy in an industry that destroyed normalcy as a matter of course.

Watching Damian melt into Livia's arms, she felt the full weight of what she'd never had. What she'd maybe never even known to want.

She tapped the next file.

Gstaad, Chalet. December 2019.

Eleven months into the marriage.

Livia and Damian sat by a stone fireplace, playing chess. The room was all dark wood and leather, a massive window showing snow falling in the Swiss night. The fire crackled—Sloane could almost hear it through the silent footage. The scene looked like something from a luxury catalog. Two beautiful people in a beautiful room, playing a beautiful game.

But Damian's face told a different story.

He was winning, but she was making him work for it. He was muttering to himself, a low, rapid-fire stream of variables that the camera microphone picked up clearly.

"Queen to h5," he said, sliding his piece forward with a rare, boyish grin. "Locking down your escape. Forces you to defend. Then it's mate in three."

Livia studied the board. Her expression was serene. Unworried. Almost amused.

She picked up her own Queen. "You always leave your king so exposed, Damian," she murmured.

She didn't defend as he'd expected. She didn't retreat.

She moved her Queen across in a single diagonal slash, placing it directly next to his King.

It looked like a suicide move. But his hand, reaching for her Queen, suddenly stopped. He saw the trap.

Her Bishop, quiet in the far corner, had been aiming at that exact square all along. It wasn't attacking him. It was anchoring her.

She was protected. He couldn't take her Queen without walking directly into her Bishop's line of fire. And blocked in by his own pawns, he had nowhere else to run.

"Checkmate," she said softly.

Damian stared at the pieces. His grin vanished, replaced by a look of stunned, delighted disbelief—the expression of a man who'd just watched his wife do something he'd thought mathematically impossible. He looked up at her, and his eyes were full of an adoration so pure it was almost painful to watch.

"How?"

Livia smiled—that secret, enigmatic curve of lips Sloane had practiced in the mirror a hundred times. "You always underestimate the queen," she said.

Sloane's finger froze over the screen.

You always underestimate the queen.

The words hit differently now. Not a taunt. A warning. A signal from a woman who had calculated the endgame long before the first pawn was moved.

Had Livia known then? Had she been planning even that early?

Or was Sloane projecting meaning onto a private moment between two people who loved each other and played games and made omelets—two people who had no idea their world was already burning?

She opened the next clip.

Argentis, Study. March 2020.

The pandemic year.

The footage was grainier. Damian was at his desk, surrounded by screens showing data visualizations—probability cascades, behavioral models, the kind of abstract visual language that looked like art but was really mathematics. He was hunched over a keyboard, typing with the manic intensity of someone who'd been awake for thirty-six hours.

Livia entered the frame carrying a tray. Tea. Sandwiches cut into triangles. The kind of small, tender gesture of care that felt enormous in the context of a man who clearly didn't notice his own body's needs.

She set the tray down. Put a hand on his shoulder.

He didn't look up.

"Damian."

Nothing.

"Damian."

His fingers stopped. He looked up, and his eyes were wild—not seeing her, seeing through her, still running models in his head.

"I need you to eat something," she said, her voice gentle but firm. "And then I need you to sleep."

"I'm close," he said. His voice was hoarse, cracked. "The prediction accuracy is approaching ninety-three percent for individual actors in controlled scenarios. If I can push it to ninety-five, the applications for market stabilization—"

"Can wait six hours," Livia said. She knelt beside his chair, taking his face in her hands, forcing him to see her, to be present, to remember he had a body that needed rest and a wife who loved him. "Damian. You're going to burn out. And then all of this"—she gestured at the screens—"means nothing."

He stared at her. For a long moment, Sloane thought he'd argue. But then something shifted in his expression. The wildness faded. He nodded.

"Six hours," he said.

"Six hours," she agreed.

She helped him stand. He was unsteady—Sloane could see it even through the grainy footage. Livia supported him, one arm around his waist, guiding him out of frame.

The camera kept recording the empty study. The screens cycling through their endless data.

Sloane sat back, her heart pounding.

This wasn't a performance. This was a woman managing a brilliant, fragile, obsessive man who would work himself to death if someone didn't intervene. This was the hidden labor of loving someone extraordinary—not the glamorous galas and art patronage, but the daily, unglamorous work of keeping another human being alive.

And Livia had done it. For six years. Until she couldn't anymore.

She tapped another file.

Diplomatic Reception, Geneva. October 2023.

Fourteen months before her death.

The footage was professional this time—event videography. Livia in an ice-blue column gown that shimmered like liquid mercury, her dark hair swept into a sleek chignon, a triple strand of diamonds at her throat—simple, geometric, the kind of jewelry that whispered wealth rather than shouted it.

She moved through the crowd like water, effortless, graceful, stopping to speak with men in tuxedos and women in couture.

But Sloane wasn't watching her technique. She was watching her eyes.

They were working. Scanning. Cataloguing.

Livia laughed at a joke from a gray-haired man Sloane didn't recognize. Touched his arm. Leaned in to whisper something that made him smile. Then moved on, seamlessly, to the next conversation.

She wasn't just being charming. She was extracting information. Reading people. Building a map of who had power, who had leverage, who could be used.

This was intelligence work disguised as socializing.

And Sloane recognized it because she'd done the same thing at a hundred Hollywood parties—reading rooms, identifying allies, spotting threats, playing the game of soft power that was the real currency of any industry.

But Livia was better at it. Much better.

There was a moment—maybe three seconds—where Livia glanced toward the camera. Her expression didn't change. But something in her eyes went cold. Calculating. As if she'd just spotted a weakness. A vulnerability. A lever.

Then it was gone, replaced by the warm smile of the perfect hostess.

Sloane rewound. Watched it again.

There. That flicker. That's who Livia really was.

Not the loving wife making omelets. Not the chess player with secret smiles.

A cryptographer. An analyst. A woman who'd worked in intelligence and understood that information was power and people were systems to be decoded.

A woman who saw everything. And paid for it with her life.

She had to stop. Her hands were shaking. The tablet felt too hot, the cabin too cold. She was breathing too fast.

It was too much. Too intimate. She was not just stealing a woman's face. She was stealing her memories, her private jokes, her husband's love, her secret wars.

The moral weight of what she was doing settled on her chest like a stone.

She put the tablet down. Stared out the window into the black, featureless void of the night sky. Forty thousand feet above the Atlantic. Halfway between who she'd been and who she was about to become.

One hundred million dollars.

That's what a life was worth. That's what it cost to erase one woman and replace her with another.

Sloane closed her eyes.

Somewhere over the dark ocean, Sloane Devereaux was drowning.

And Livia Crestwell was learning to breathe.

***

She picked the tablet back up. She had to know more. She had to know everything. The actress in her was gone. The survivor had taken over. And survival depended on knowing every detail of the terrain she was about to enter.

She went back to the main folder. She didn't click on the videos. She clicked on a different sub-folder. One she hadn't noticed before. It was labeled: *Project Chimera: Subject Analysis.*

Chimera. That was the project name from the contract. And she, Sloane Devereaux, was the subject.

Chapter 14: The Doppelgänger

There was no title page, no author. Just pages of dense, single-spaced text. It wasn't a biography. It was a clinical, detached analysis, the kind of report a scientist might write about a lab rat.

It detailed her entire life, from her birth in Tulsa, Oklahoma, to her humiliating audition for the hemorrhoid cream commercial only three days ago.

They knew everything.

They knew her father's name, his DUI arrests from when she was twelve, the official cause of her mother's death. They knew about the Greyhound bus ticket, the exact timestamp of her arrival at the Union Station terminal, and the address of the youth hostel in Hollywood where she'd spent her first three nights. They'd even found an old radio interview from her first year in LA where she'd joked about arriving with "two hundred and forty-seven dollars—everything I'd saved from six months waiting tables."

They knew the name of the producer she had met for a "private audition" in Malibu. They knew about the blacklist, the whispers, the slow, methodical strangulation of her career.

They even knew about her dusty, forgotten Oscar, sitting on top of her refrigerator like a tombstone.

Sloane felt a wave of nausea, a profound sense of violation. She had spent her entire life building walls, hiding the shame and the trauma behind a fortress of performance and glamour. And these people, these strangers, had walked through those walls as if they weren't even there. They had dissected her, analyzed her, and laid her bare on a digital slab.

She scrolled down, her finger trembling slightly. The report continued, analyzing her psychological profile: *"Subject exhibits high-level resilience, a capacity for sustained deception (professional training), and a deep-seated need for validation, making her psychologically susceptible to the proposed financial incentive. History of trauma suggests a high tolerance for high-stress, morally ambiguous situations."*

It was a cold, brutal, and horrifyingly accurate assessment. They hadn't just chosen her because she looked like Livia. They had chosen her because she was the perfect psychological candidate: a survivor who was desperate enough to say yes.

***

Then she saw the final section of the report. It was titled: *Biometric Analysis.*

Her breath caught. The text was dense with scientific jargon she didn't understand, but one sentence, highlighted in the middle of a paragraph, leaped out at her, stark and clear as a headline.

"...Analysis of publicly available video and audio confirms an unprecedented 87% base correlation across key static biometric markers—facial topography and vocal print. The statistical probability of a non-familial match of this fidelity is estimated at one in five hundred million."

The text continued, and this was the part that made her blood run cold.

"The remaining 13% variance exists in dynamic facial biometrics: micro-muscular tics, emotional mapping, and subconscious reaction speeds. Standard lookalikes fail here.

"However, the subject, Sloane Devereaux, is a generational talent, an Academy Award-winning actress noted by critics for her total physical and emotional transformations. Her neurological control over involuntary micro-expressions is anomalous, unmatched.

It is our assessment that with prosthetic contouring and corrective cosmetics to address the structural deficit, combined with her world-class ability to overwrite her behavioral patterns, she can achieve a 99%+ composite match.

She is not a lookalike; she is a perfect baseline. For our purposes, she is a biological key that can be precision-cut by her own talent."

Sloane dropped the tablet onto the seat beside her as if it had burned her.

A one-in-half-a-billion anomaly.

This wasn't a coincidence. This wasn't a lucky break. This was a biological impossibility. She wasn't just a lookalike. She was a mirror. A statistical echo.

Or as Fairweather had put it: *"You are a market of one."*

The offer suddenly felt less random, and far more sinister. They hadn't just found an actress who could play the part. They had found the only person on earth whose very existence—her face, her voice, her movements—made her the perfect key. It felt like predestination. Like she had been a pawn in this game long before she even knew it was being played.

Her mind reeled, trying to process the impossible. The cabin of the jet, which had felt so vast and luxurious a moment ago, now felt small and suffocating, a high-tech coffin hurtling through the dark.

She closed her eyes, and a memory, sharp and unwanted, rose from the depths of her past.

***

She was seventeen. A year in Hollywood had been a brutal education. The scared, hopeful girl who had stepped off the Greyhound from Oklahoma was mostly gone, replaced by a survivor with harder eyes and a gnawing hunger that made her do stupid, dangerous things. The dream of red carpets and artistic integrity had been ground down by a relentless reality of crowded cattle-call auditions, predatory casting directors, and the gnawing loneliness of a city that didn't care if she lived or died.

She'd been sleeping on Manny's couch for three months. Her savings—the meager cash she'd arrived with—had evaporated in her first week. She'd survived the year on a patchwork of humiliations: convenience store graveyard shifts, extra work on sitcoms where she stood in the background holding fake grocery bags, a nightmare month waitressing at a Denny's in Burbank where the manager's hands kept finding her lower back. She had thirty-seven dollars left. Again. Always. Rent on even the worst studio in Van Nuys was twelve hundred a month. The fire in her belly hadn't gone out, but it was burning on fumes. This "private audition" was her last, desperate roll of the dice. And she knew it. She knew exactly what Elliott Shaw was offering, and exactly what he wanted in return.

She went anyway.

The producer's Malibu "guesthouse" was a palace of glass and white marble, perched on a cliff overlooking the endless, churning Pacific. It was a property his production company kept on a long-term lease—a place for visiting writers to find inspiration, he'd told Manny. A quiet space to work. Sloane knew, with the cold certainty of a survivor, that no writing ever got done here.

His name was Elliott Shaw, and he was one of the gods of the city. He had the power to make careers, and to end them. And he was interested in Sloane.

The official invitation had come via a phone call, Shaw's voice smooth and proprietary. He had called it a private audition. Manny, who was new to her life but an old, cynical veteran of the Hollywood game, knew exactly what that meant. He had been suspicious, his warnings laced with a weary anger, but he was ultimately powerless to stop a hungry, seventeen-year-old girl from walking into a god's living room. "Just be smart, kid," he had pleaded with her, his voice full of a paternal fear she was too young and too desperate to truly hear. "Don't do anything you can't live with."

She'd seen the look in Shaw's eyes when they'd met at that industry mixer two weeks ago—the same look she'd seen in a dozen other powerful men's eyes. The same look that made her skin crawl and her rent calculation spike with desperate hope at the same time.

She'd said yes before Manny finished his warning.

The house smelled of salt and gardenias. Shaw was in his fifties, with a predatory tan and eyes that looked at her like she was a piece of art he was considering buying. He didn't ask her to read from a script. He poured her a glass of wine she was too young to drink and asked her about her dreams.

She had played the part. The ambitious but naive young actress, grateful for the attention of a great man. She had laughed at his jokes. She had listened, wide-eyed, to his stories of the stars he had made. She knew what this was. She had known from the moment she got in the cab. It was a transaction. He was testing her, seeing how far she was willing to go. Her career, her entire future, was balanced on the edge of a single, unspoken question.

He had stood up, his smile knowing and patient. He walked over to the vast glass wall overlooking the ocean. "It's a beautiful view," he said. "You can see all the way to Catalina on a clear day. But you know what the best part is? The privacy. No one can see in."

He turned to look at her. The question was in his eyes.

Sloane's heart was a cold, hard stone in her chest. She thought of the trailer park. She thought of her mother's exhausted face. She thought of the promise she had made to herself. *I will never be invisible again.*

She stood up. She took a breath. She was about to pay the price.

And then his phone rang.

The sound shattered the tense silence. Shaw had looked at the phone, his expression souring. "What is it?" he snapped. He listened for a moment. His face changed. "Now? Are you sure?" A pause. "Fine. I'm on my way."

He hung up. He looked at Sloane, his predatory focus completely gone, replaced by a distracted annoyance. "My wife," he said, as if it were a curse. "She's gone into labor. A month early."

He had walked her to the door, his mind already a million miles away, at a hospital in Santa Monica. "We'll do this again," he'd said, a casual, dismissive promise he had no intention of keeping.

She had gotten in a cab, her body trembling with an adrenaline crash so violent her teeth were chattering. She had been saved by the bell. By the miracle of a premature birth.

Two weeks later, she got the role. She never knew why. Maybe he felt guilty. Maybe he admired her nerve. Or maybe, and this was the thought that haunted her, he just forgot who she was and his casting director had made the final choice.

She had been willing to pay the price. And that knowledge, the shame of that willingness, was a secret she had carried like a stone for thirteen years.

And here she was again. Making the same calculation. Only this time the price tag wasn't a walk-on role. It was a nine-figure payout.

***

Her hands shaking, she scrolled down past her own psychological autopsy to the second section of the file. It was titled: *Principal Profile: Damian Crestwell.*

This was him. The man. His photograph was severe and intellectual, with dark, intense eyes that seemed to look right through the screen. He was handsome, but it was the beauty of a storm cloud—full of contained electric power.

The biography that followed was the portrait of a modern myth.

A prodigy. He entered MIT at sixteen.

Launched his first company, Helios Data, from his dorm room at seventeen. By nineteen, he'd dropped out, bored with academia. He took Helios public at twenty, becoming a billionaire before he could legally drink. Disinterested in management, he handed off the reins the next year, retaining the equity to hunt for a harder problem.

By twenty-three, he had repeated the pattern with QuantumScape: IPO, fortune, exit.

By twenty-five, he'd built and abandoned two empires, disillusioned with the corporate world he'd conquered twice. Already one of the world's richest men, he now needed a bigger mission.

The file contained a clipped addendum from a rare academic journal. It described him as a "self-taught authority" in a field he had largely pioneered: Quantum Behavioral Economics.

"For decades, behavioral economists have understood *that* humans are largely irrational," the article read. "Crestwell is the first to prove *how* that irrationality can be mathematically modeled and predicted."

The article continued, its tone a mixture of awe and academic terror. "He was the first to write the mathematical code for human chaos—a feat most of the field considered a theoretical impossibility in itself. But formulating the equations was only the first miracle. Even the fastest supercomputer on Earth would need a century to run the simulation."

The article paused, as if for effect. "Crestwell's true genius was not just in writing the code. It was in building the machine capable of running it. He didn't just pose an impossible question; he built the quantum computer that could answer it."

"He has, in effect, built a machine that can calculate the incalculable: the human irrationality."

Damian's core mission, the file noted, was applying his revolutionary work for benevolent purposes. Helios Data used his models to predict stock market crashes, paving the path to an unprecedented financial stability. QuantumScape used them to build uncrackable encryption by modeling the irrational behavior of potential hackers. Both were hailed as world-changing, humanitarian achievements, cementing his public image as a visionary dedicated to creating a safer, more predictable world.

The file noted that this was when he met the man who would change the course of his life. The relationship was not framed as a simple investment. The file called this figure his "friend, patron and mentor." A section from a rare interview with a former associate was quoted:

"For his next venture, Damian didn't need any more money. He needed an even grander philosophy. He had the 'how,' but he didn't have a 'why' big enough for his genius. He wanted to be an artist in a lab, not a CEO in a boardroom. His mentor's pitch was a work of genius in itself: 'I will handle the entire world—the finances, the law, the people—and you will be left completely free to create a system that shapes chaos into order.' He didn't offer Damian a partnership. He offered him a crusade, wrapped in a cocoon of absolute freedom."

The file stated that at twenty-five, Damian moved to Switzerland, founding his third and current company, Crystal Vision SARL, in total seclusion, with this unnamed patron providing the operational infrastructure and ideological vision.

"As Chief Architect," the file read, "Mr. Crestwell works almost entirely alone from the Argentis estate. His core team—a hyper-elite unit of fewer than one hundred of the world's top behavioral scientists and programmers—operates from a secure, undisclosed remote facility in Europe. Mr. Crestwell is in constant contact via encrypted video calls and travels to meet them in person only a few times a year."

Sloane's blood went cold. She wasn't just walking into a house. She was walking into the isolated command center of a ghost-like, global operation. The fact that Damian worked alone at Argentis was not a sign of a small company; it was a sign of his immense, solitary power.

***

The chime of the seatbelt sign jolted her back to the present. The cabin of the Gulfstream. The dark sky outside.

Anna's voice came over the intercom, smooth and calm. "Ms. Devereaux, we are beginning our initial descent into Buochs. We should be on the ground in approximately thirty minutes."

Sloane looked at the tablet, at the clinical analysis of her life, at the impossible, chilling mathematics of her own face.

They knew about Elliott Shaw. They knew about all of it. They had chosen her not just for her face, but for her scars. They had chosen her because they knew she was a survivor. They knew she was a woman who understood, intimately, that sometimes the only way to get what you want is to be willing to pay an impossible price.

The jet banked, and through the window, she saw them for the first time. The Alps. Jagged, snow-dusted peaks rising into the brilliant light, their silhouettes sharp against the blinding clarity of the early morning sky. They were beautiful, terrifying, and utterly indifferent.

She was flying into the heart of a mystery she didn't understand, to meet a man she had never seen, to become a woman who was her biometric echo. And for the first time, she was truly, completely, and utterly alone.

Chapter 15: Argentis

The Gulfstream descended through cloud cover, and suddenly Switzerland was below—impossibly green valleys, villages like toys, mountains that made LA seem small and forgettable.

The private airstrip in Buochs appeared like a surgical incision in the landscape, a ribbon of impossibly black tarmac carved into the mountainside fifteen kilometers south of Lucerne, where the money stopped pretending to be democratic.

The landing was a whisper, so smooth it felt less like a descent and more like a surrender.

The moment the door opened, the air hit her.

It was so clean and cold it felt like a physical substance, a shocking, scouring force that made her lungs burn. Not the smoggy, forgiving warmth of Los Angeles, but air that had traveled across three hundred kilometers of glacial ice before reaching her. This was the air of altitude, of money, of absolute, untouchable privacy. It was the kind of clean, perfect air you only got to breathe after you had purchased your way out of the ordinary world, after you had built walls so high that the dirty air could no longer reach you.

At the bottom of the stairs, a border officer waited on the tarmac. He accepted her passport from the pilot, stamped it efficiently against a clipboard, handed it back to the pilot, and vanished. No questions. No line.

The only structure in sight was a single minimalist hangar that looked more like a modern art installation than a building—all titanium and glass, reflecting nothing.

A black Maybach sat silently on the tarmac, its engine a low, predatory hum that was felt more than heard. Not the S-Class that tech billionaires drove in Silicon Valley. Not even the stretched version that sheikhs used for airport runs. This was the S680 Guard—armored, bulletproof, with run-flat tires and a reinforced chassis that could survive an RPG strike. A car designed not to be seen, but to be inevitable.

A man stood beside the open rear door.

He was not what Sloane had expected. Not a hulking, neck-less bodyguard in an ill-fitting suit. He was lean and compact, mid-thirties, dressed in a perfectly tailored dark wool suit that couldn't quite conceal the coiled, efficient power in his frame. Short dark hair, strong jaw, eyes that never stopped moving—scanning the treeline, the sky, the jet, the access road. He moved with an absolute economy of motion that was more intimidating than any overt display of strength. The stillness of a man who knew exactly how much force it took to break a human neck.

He did not smile. He did not introduce himself. He simply held the door, his gaze meeting hers for a fraction of a second.

It was not a look of welcome. It was an assessment. A calculation. The look of a man cataloging valuable, unpredictable cargo.

Sloane slid into the back of the car. The leather was the color of cream and smelled of absolutely nothing—not new car, not cologne, not cleaning solution. *Nothing*. As if the air inside the vehicle had been sterilized. The door closed with a soft, hydraulic thud, sealing her in a world of profound, unnerving silence.

The man got into the driver's seat.

She knew from the dossier that this was Nico Sorrento. Head of Security. Former Italian Special Forces, 9th Parachute Assault Regiment. Expert in what the file had euphemistically called "ghost work"—the kind of operations that never appeared in any official record. Ex-filtration. Close protection. Targeted surveillance. Things that had other, darker names.

Her jailer.

***

The drive from the airstrip was a silent, hypnotic journey into the heart of the fortress.

The Maybach glided south along Route 2, skirting the lake, then turned east onto a private access road so narrow it didn't appear on any public map. The road clung to the side of a cliff, carved directly into the limestone face of the mountain. On one side: sheer rock, still cold from the night, streaked with mineral deposits that looked like veins of silver. On the other side: a continuous ribbon of reinforced steel and tensioned cable, waist-high and elegant, engineered to catch a tank yet disappear against the view. Beyond it: five hundred meters of empty air and then the lake.

Lake Lucerne.

Vierwaldstättersee, the locals called it. The Lake of the Four Forested Cantons. One hundred and fourteen square kilometers of glacial meltwater, fed by the Reuss River and a dozen mountain streams. Maximum depth: two hundred and fourteen meters—deep enough that entire buildings could sink without a trace, deep enough that the Swiss Navy conducted submarine tests here during the Cold War.

At this hour—just after dawn—the lake was still half in shadow, the western shore catching the early light while the eastern mountains kept the water dark. The color was extraordinary. Not the tropical blue-green of postcards, but something deeper, more complex. Turquoise near the shallows where the sun hit. Cobalt in the deep channels. And in the shadows, a blue so dark it was almost black, the kind of blue that looked *cold* even from a distance.

Sloane had seen beautiful things in her life. The Pacific at sunset from Malibu. The lights of Manhattan from a penthouse in Tribevale. But this was different. This wasn't the beauty of aspiration or achievement. This was the beauty of indifference. The lake didn't care if you admired it or drowned in it. The mountains didn't care if you built your fortress on their cliffs or fell from them. This was a landscape that had been killing people for thousands of years and would continue long after the last human was gone.

Intimidating beauty. The kind that made you feel small.

The road climbed. Switchback after switchback, each turn tighter than the last. The tensioned cables vanished against the sky. No warning signs. Just a meter of asphalt and then gravity.

They passed a single other estate—a modernist chalet perched on an outcropping, all glass and weathered wood, with what looked like a helipad and an infinity pool cantilevered over the void. The kind of place that would cost thirty million and still be considered "modest" by local standards. A sign near the gate read: PRIVAT – VIDEOÜBERWACHUNG.

Sloane recognized the architecture. This was the Bürgenstock, the mountain plateau that had been home to Swiss banking dynasties since the 19th century. Audrey Hepburn had honeymooned here. Sophia Loren kept a villa. The kind of place where prime ministers vacationed and no one ever saw a photograph.

But even the Bürgenstock estates were lower, more accessible. Her destination was higher. More isolated. More absolute.

After twenty minutes of climbing—twenty minutes without seeing another car, another person, another sign of civilization—they rounded a final sharp curve, and she saw it.

Argentis.

It was not a house. It was a declaration.

A series of interlocking boxes of glass, steel, and pale granite—the local *Alpenkalkstein*, quarried from the mountain itself—cantilevered dramatically over the cliff edge. The main structure seemed to float five hundred meters above the lake, its glass walls reflecting the water and sky so perfectly that the building looked like it was made of light. The architecture was aggressive, angular, a razor blade of human ingenuity pressed against the throat of the ancient mountain.

She recognized the style. Minimalist. Brutalist, almost. The kind of architecture that didn't try to blend with nature—that *dominated* it. Every angle was deliberate. Every line was a challenge. This was not a home that whispered. It *shouted*.

And it was a fortress.

As the Maybach approached the outer perimeter, Sloane saw the security. It was subtle, integrated, and terrifying.

A camera lens embedded in the rock face, its housing designed to look like a natural crevice. The faint shimmer of a laser grid crossing the road at ankle height—impossible to see unless you knew to look for the micro-reflections on the asphalt. Motion sensors built into the trees. An automated vehicle barrier disguised as a decorative boulder.

This wasn't residential security. This was military-grade defense. The kind of systems that protected embassies in hostile territory.

Through the tinted windows, movement caught her eye.

A figure stood at one of the upper windows of the main house—a tall silhouette backlit by warm interior light. The distance was too great to see details. But she felt the weight of his gaze.

Damian.

Watching her arrive. Watching the counterfeit wife come home.

Then, as quickly as she'd noticed him, he stepped back into the shadows and was gone.

The Maybach glided to a halt before the outer gate—not the main entrance, but the security checkpoint. A massive slab of brushed steel set into a concrete bunker that looked like it had been designed to stop a tank. The kind of gate that didn't open unless you were supposed to be there.

The Maybach glided to a halt before the massive, featureless slab of granite. The low hum of the engine was the only sound in the crisp, thin air. Nico killed the engine, and the sudden, profound silence was broken only by the faint, electronic hum of a sensor array set into the rock wall. Its single, recessed camera lens stared out, a black, unblinking eye in the harsh, clear light of the alpine sun.

Chapter 16: Welcome Home

Nico turned to look at her, his dark eyes unreadable in the rearview mirror. "Look at the sensor," he said. His voice was a low, gravelly baritone, stripped of all warmth. "State your name for biometric verification. Clearly."

Sloane's stomach dropped.

This was not a recording. This was a test. Her first real test.

She thought of the dossier. The cold assessment she'd read on the plane. The face was biology—a genetic accident. But the rest? The way Livia moved, spoke, held silence? That was performance. And performance could fail.

This sensor would measure everything. And if she failed—

Her mind raced back to the videos, the audio files, the hours she'd spent on the jet mimicking the soft, European lilt of Livia's voice, the subtle, confident tilt of her head. The way Livia held silence like a weapon. The way she breathed.

Was it enough?

She looked at the sensor. A small, black camera lens stared back at her, a dead, unblinking eye. Below it was a fine mesh grille for the microphone. The hardware didn't care about her fear. It would measure her in a second or two—the micro-tensing of facial muscles, the frequency spectrum of her voice, the rhythm of her breath. Cold data. Binary judgment. Pass or fail.

This was it. The performance had already begun. She could not be Sloane Devereaux, the terrified actress. She had to be Livia Crestwell, the lady of the manor, returning home.

Not imitating her. Not mimicking her. Being her.

Slightly annoyed, perhaps, at the tedious necessity of it all. A woman who had done this a thousand times. A woman for whom biometric gates and security protocols were simply the architecture of her life.

She took a breath—not a shaky, nervous one, but a slow, centering breath, just as she would before walking onto a stage. In through the nose. Hold. Release. The technique she'd learned in a stuffy, windowless method acting workshop in the Valley, a decade ago. The one thing from her old life that still worked.

She composed her face into a mask of neutral, aristocratic calm. Let the tension drain from her jaw. Softened the muscles around her eyes. Found Livia's resting expression—the slight downward curve of the mouth that wasn't quite disapproval, just... aristocratic neutrality. The face of someone who expected the world to accommodate her, not the other way around.

She let her voice drop, finding the precise musicality, the faint, unplaceable accent she had practiced until her throat was raw. European finishing schools and American universities. Old money diction with new world confidence. Every syllable weighted, nothing rushed. Livia never hurried.

She wasn't just saying a name. She was performing an identity. Proving she was more than a matching face.

"Livia Crestwell," she said. Her voice came out steady. Bored, even. As if this were an inconvenience, not a life-or-death audition.

The silence that followed was absolute.

Then: a soft mechanical hum.

A soft, red laser grid swept over her face, mapping every contour—the distance between her pupils, the angle of her cheekbones, the precise geometry of her nose and chin. She felt it like fingers on her skin, invasive and clinical. Measuring her. Judging her.

The 87% was easy. That was biology. A gift she'd done nothing to earn.

But the remaining 13% was far harder to bridge—the way she held her head, the micro-expression in her eyes, the emotional undertone in those two words—that was all her. That was craft. That was the reason they'd chosen her over every other woman on Earth with a similar face.

A single, agonizing second stretched into an eternity. Sloane held her breath, her hands clenched into fists in her lap. Her nails dug into her palms. She didn't move. Didn't blink. Stayed in character even though every instinct screamed to look away from the sensor, to break, to run.

In the rearview mirror, she caught Nico watching. Not the road. Her.

He was tense. Ready to intervene if this went wrong. This was her first test, and he was her failsafe. But she didn't want saving. She wanted to pass.

A soft, female voice, synthesized and perfectly calm, emanated from a hidden speaker.

"Identity verified. Welcome home, Mrs. Crestwell."

The system had accepted her. Not just her face—but her performance. The way she'd held Livia's silence, her breath, her aristocratic indifference. All of it.

She'd bridged the 13% gap. On her first try.

But the victory brought a cold realization. In Hollywood, a bad take cost time. Here, a bad take meant her life. There was no script to reference, no director to yell "Cut," and no stunt double to take the fall when the ground rushed up to meet her. She was improvising on the edge of a cliff.

Sloane let out a breath she didn't realize she had been holding. Her hands were shaking now—adrenaline crash, the body's delayed response to terror. But she kept them still in her lap. Livia wouldn't shake.

In the rearview mirror, she saw Nico's expression shift. Just for a moment—a flicker of something that might have been surprise, or respect, or both. He gave a single, almost imperceptible nod.

He had been testing her, too. And she had passed.

***

She was met at the entrance to the main house not by her enigmatic, grieving employer, but by the true ruler of this kingdom.

Her name was Katarina Zimina. She was tall, impossibly thin, and dressed in a severe, charcoal-gray sheath dress that looked more like a uniform than a piece of clothing. Her silver-blonde hair was pulled back in a chignon so tight it seemed to pull at the skin around her pale, intelligent, ice-blue eyes. She was a vision of severe, Eastern European efficiency, a woman who looked like she had never had a frivolous thought in her life. She was, as the file had noted, the estate's Chief of Staff. And, as the file had also noted, she was former GRU. Russian military intelligence.

"Welcome to Argentis," Katarina said. Her accent was faint but sharp as a shard of ice. She did not say Sloane's name. She did not offer to shake her hand. Her smile was a precise, surgical incision that did not touch her eyes. "I trust your journey was satisfactory."

"It was," Sloane replied, keeping her voice in the Livia register. The soft, European lilt. The slight upward inflection at the end. The tone of someone who expected satisfaction, not someone grateful for it.

Katarina moved closer. As she adjusted the collar of Sloane's coat, her hand brushed Sloane's neck. It wasn't a caress; it was a check. Two fingers pressed against the carotid artery for a split second, testing the pulse, while her eyes scanned the room's perimeter with the reflex of someone expecting a sniper. The movement was so fast, so practiced, that if Sloane hadn't studied stage combat for *The Assassin's Waltz*, she would have missed it entirely. Beneath the silk of Katarina's cuff, Sloane caught the glint of a ceramic knife sheath strapped to her forearm.

For just a fraction of a second—maybe half a heartbeat—something flickered across Katarina's face. Not quite surprise. Not quite pain. Something deeper. Recognition. As if she'd heard a ghost speak.

Her pale eyes narrowed, just slightly. The kind of micro-expression that a trained intelligence operative would normally suppress, but that grief had made vulnerable.

Then it was gone. The ice closed over again.

Katarina's head tilted, a predator reassessing prey. "Good," she said, her voice cooler now, more controlled. Katarina's gaze swept over Sloane from head to toe, a quick, dismissive appraisal that took in her worn-out jeans, her scuffed sneakers, her general air of dishevelment. "Though you sound somewhat... strained. The altitude, perhaps? Or merely fatigue from your journey?"

The words were solicitous. The tone was not.

Sloane understood immediately. This was not concern. This was a warning shot. A reminder that Katarina was listening. Evaluating. That nothing would escape her notice.

And that she would accept nothing short of perfection.

***

Sloane felt like a stray dog that had wandered into a palace. But she held Katarina's gaze and kept her voice steady, kept it Livia's voice. "I'm perfectly fine, thank you. Just eager to settle in."

Katarina's lips compressed into a thin line. Not quite approval. Not quite dismissal. Just... acknowledgment.

"Your luggage has been taken to your suite. The staff has been briefed. You will find them... discreet."

Katarina turned and began to walk, expecting Sloane to follow. "Allow me to show you the main living areas. Mr. Crestwell is in his laboratory. He will not be disturbed until I deem you to be ready for him."

The words, delivered in Katarina's flat, icy monotone, were not a courtesy. They were a judgment. A clear, unequivocal statement of the new hierarchy. Sloane was not a guest. She was an asset under evaluation. The tour that followed was not a welcome, but an exercise in psychological intimidation—an orientation for a new, high-stakes, and deeply dangerous job.

The interior was as breathtaking and inhuman as the exterior. Vast, open spaces with twenty-foot ceilings and floor-to-ceiling glass walls that looked out onto the lake and the mountains. The furniture was minimal, expensive, and looked like it had never been sat on. The art was massive, abstract, and cold. The only sounds were the faint hum of the climate control and Katarina's low, monotone voice.

"This is the winter garden," Katarina said, gesturing to a three-story glass atrium filled with exotic, pale-colored flowers. "Livia found it... calming." The subtext was clear: *You, the imposter, will likely find it overwhelming.*

"This is the main salon. Livia used it for entertaining." The unspoken addendum: *Something you will not be doing.*

"Livia's posture was impeccable. We will need to work on yours."

With every sentence, Katarina reminded Sloane of her place. She was the guardian of Livia's memory. Sloane was a cheap, necessary imitation.

Finally, they arrived at the master suite. The door slid open silently. The room was vast, dominated by a bed that looked large enough to sleep six, and another wall of glass that made it feel as though you were floating in the sky.

"Your quarters," Katarina said. "Livia's wardrobe has been maintained. It's yours... for now. You will find everything you need, and then some." She gestured to a door on the far wall. "The staff will be available to attend to your needs.

They are also instructed to report any... irregularities in your routine. Is that understood?"

"Perfectly," Sloane said, her voice a perfect echo of Livia's cool confidence.

Katarina's eyes narrowed almost imperceptibly... For the first time, a flicker of something that was not pure ice entered her expression. Respect, perhaps. Or simply a recalculation of the asset's potential.

She walked toward the door, then paused, turning back to face Sloane. She was no longer the tour guide. She was the spymaster delivering the mission brief.

"You are an actress, Ms. Devereaux," Katarina said... "You believe your job is to imitate a woman. Your job is to become a fortress... I require that you do not dishonor the memory of the woman I loved like a daughter with a weak performance."

"I won't," Sloane said, and the words were a promise.

"See that you don't," Katarina said, the ice snapping back into place. "The role of a queen is not to be liked. It is to be unquestioned."

She gestured to a sleek, gray tablet on the writing desk. "That contains the preliminary dossier," she said, her voice a cold, clinical instrument. "It covers Livia's immediate social circle and upcoming engagements for the next month. I expect you to have it memorized by morning. This is your first test."

She paused, her pale eyes locking with Sloane's. "Livia had a near-photographic memory. I expect nothing less from her replacement."

The door slid shut, leaving Sloane alone in the vast, silent mausoleum of Livia's life.

She stood in the center of the room, her breath hitching in the sudden, heavy silence. The air was chilled to the point of discomfort, but overlaid with a floral scent so thick and familiar it made her heart lurch. On a low, marble table near the window sat a massive crystal vase of white Casablanca lilies.

They had been her mother's favorite. On the rare occasions when a waitressing shift had ended with a surplus of tips back in Oklahoma, her mother would buy a single, bruised stem from the grocery store and arrange it in a chipped jelly jar. *To make things nice*, she'd say.

Sloane stared at the waxy, pristine petals. A momentary prickle of unease crawled up her spine. Was it a greeting? A test? She looked at the severe, minimalist lines of the suite and forced herself to breathe. Casablanca lilies were the shorthand of high-end floral design; they were in every luxury hotel lobby from Paris to New York. It was a coincidence. A cliché of wealth, nothing more.

***

For a long moment, she didn't move. She just stood there, Katarina's words echoing in the silence. *The role of a queen is not to be liked. It is to be believed.* It was a mission statement. A threat. A promise.

Her gaze was drawn to the door Katarina had indicated. Livia's wardrobe.

Taking a breath, she slid it open. It was not a closet. It was another dimension, a multi-room boutique dedicated to the art of being Livia Crestwell... a silent, beautiful accusation.

Sloane reached out a trembling hand and touched the sleeve of a cashmere sweater, impossibly soft. She could smell the faint, lingering scent of Livia's perfume—ghost orchid and bergamot. It felt like a violation. Like breaking into a stranger's home.

This is the job, a cold, professional part of her mind insisted. *You were hired for this. There is no need for guilt.*

But another, deeper part of her recoiled. Livia was dead. She had no say in this hostile takeover of her life. Was she watching from somewhere, feeling this invasion? Did Sloane have her permission?

She thought of Fairweather's words, the silken lie he'd spun in the glass tower. *"Livia herself was a great admirer of your work. She would have approved."*

It was a lie. It had to be. But in the silent, oppressive grandeur of the mausoleum, surrounded by the remnants of a life she was about to steal, it was the only lie she could cling to. She had to believe she had the ghost's permission. It was the only way she could survive the guilt of becoming her.

The panic was still there, but it had changed. This wasn't just about mimicry. It was an invitation.

And the ghost whose clothes she was about to wear had to be her first ally.

Chapter 17: The Search

Left alone in the vast, silent mausoleum of Livia's life, the panic that had been coiled tight in Sloane's chest began to change. It sharpened into something colder. Purpose.

She walked out of the closet, sliding the door shut. The suite was a perfect, sterile cage. Impersonal. But Livia had lived here for years. There had to be a trace of the real woman somewhere beneath the curated perfection. A loose thread. A hidden note. A secret.

Sloane began to hunt.

It was a quiet, methodical search, the work of an actress building a character from the inside out. Not by reading a script, but by touching their things. She started in the master bathroom. She opened the drawers. Expensive creams, perfumes, all arranged with geometric precision. Nothing out of place. She ran her hand along the back of the medicine cabinet. No taped-on keys, no hidden compartments.

She moved to the bedroom. The nightstand. A single, leather-bound volume of Rilke's poetry. A silver bookmark. Nothing more. She checked under the mattress. Behind the headboard. She was looking for something that felt real, something that hadn't been sanitized by Katarina's efficient, all-seeing eyes.

She found it in the bottom drawer of a massive, antique writing desk, tucked beneath a stack of old architectural blueprints. It was a thick Moleskine notebook. It was not hidden, but it was not displayed.

Sloane sat on the floor, her back against the desk, and opened it. The handwriting was a revelation—a perfect, elegant, looping script. The handwriting of a woman with time, with confidence, with a deep, unshakable sense of her own importance.

The first entry was from years earlier.

Damian showed me the plans for the Argentis renovation today. He has taken this beautiful, old fortress from the Müller estate and is turning it into a mad, beautiful, impossible dream. A house of glass that floats in the sky. He wants to build a sanctuary for us... His mind is the most beautiful thing I have ever known. He sees the world not as it is, but as a series of elegant equations waiting to be solved. And I, somehow, am the solution to his favorite one.

Sloane read the words, a knot tightening in her stomach. The love was palpable. She flipped forward, past entries about the renovation, the wedding, their honeymoon. She was looking for the first crack in the perfect facade.

She found it in an entry from three years earlier.

Another quarterly review with Damian's patron. Damian sees him as a visionary. I... am not so sure. He has the kindest, calmest gray eyes, the kind you'd trust with your life. But there is a dissonance. A professional coldness. The way he looks at Damian's work... it is not with a scientist's awe, but with a primary investor's calculation. As if he is weighing not its potential to save, but its capacity to leverage. I worry Damian, in his beautiful, abstract world, doesn't see the man, only the mission. He is so trusting.

Why would a billionaire genius defer to anyone? What does the patron have that Damian's wealth and brilliance can't provide?

Purpose. A mission grander than Damian himself. That's the only currency that could buy this kind of loyalty.

The words sent a chill through Sloane. The perfect love story suddenly had a villain.

Damian's patron? The primary investor? Was he the same as Fairweather's mysterious client?

And as Sloane read on, she noticed something strange. The entries were all perfect. Little literary vignettes. No mess, no self-doubt, no true fear. It felt... curated. It felt like a performance. A script.

Her bullshit detector, honed by years of reading bad scripts and watching insincere performances, was screaming. This wasn't a private confession. This was a document Livia had written to satisfy prying minds. A decoy.

Which meant there had to be a real one.

The thought galvanized her. She flipped through the remaining pages, no longer searching for truth, but for a pattern. For a message hidden inside the performance.

Most entries were mundane. Dinners. Travel. Notes about Damian's research. One mentioned rereading Bulgakov. "Still holds up."

Then she came across an entry that stopped her cold.

Damian upgraded the house systems again. Everything is encrypted. Biometric locks. I suppose he's right. Though sometimes I miss the old systems. The simple ones that just worked.

When all the modern doors are locked, remember: the old ways still work.

—Margarita

Sloane read it twice.

Margarita.

Her gaze drifted to the stack of old architectural blueprints she'd moved to reach the journal. Livia had hidden the lie *under* the truth. The blueprints weren't the decoy. They were the map.

***

That night, dinner was served in her suite. She was picking at a plate of seared arctic char, her mind still spinning from Livia's journal entries—the kind eyes, the calculation, the shadowy patron who smiled like a grandfather while pulling strings like a puppetmaster.

She pushed the fish around her plate, her appetite gone. The investor. The man Damian trusted. The man Livia had feared. Nameless. Faceless.

She tried to picture him. What would he look like when he finally appeared? What would he say to her, the replacement wife, the counterfeit?

Her imagination, trained by years of building characters from thin air, began to construct the scene. She could see it so clearly it was almost real—the door chiming, her looking up, expecting a housekeeper. Instead, a man in the doorway. Gray hair. Kind eyes. That warm, grandfatherly smile Livia had described.

"Forgive the intrusion," he would say, his voice warm as he entered, uninvited. "I was just arriving at the estate and couldn't resist saying hello."

In her mind's eye, he sat in the armchair across from her small dining table, a glass of red wine appearing as if conjured by invisible hands.

"You're the final piece, you know. Do you know why I paid one hundred million dollars for you specifically, Sloane? Not for any talented actress, but for you?"

She could almost hear her own voice responding, steadier than she felt: *"My Oscar-winning performance?"*

"Partly." His imagined smile was like watching a snake taste the air. *"But mostly because of who you used to be. The girl who said 'no' to powerful men and survived. You understand what it's like to be cornered."*

He would lean forward. Deliver the threat with the casualness of discussing weather. He would tell her exactly what he expected. Exactly what would happen if she failed. He would slide a photograph across the table—Manny, standing outside his apartment, a timestamp from yesterday.

Her blood went cold just imagining it.

"I don't make threats lightly. Investments that don't perform... can be liquidated. Along with everyone connected to them."

He would stand, button his jacket with practiced elegance. Remind her that he had eyes everywhere. Even here. Especially here.

"The gala is in a few weeks. Make them count."

Sloane blinked, the vivid daydream dissolving like smoke. She was alone in her suite, the arctic char congealing on her plate, her hands trembling. The door had never chimed. No one had entered. It had all been in her head—an actress's mind building the scene before it happened, rehearsing the confrontation before she even knew his face.

But somehow, she knew she'd gotten it right.

The words from Livia's journal echoed in her mind: *Kind eyes. Calculation. The dissonance of a predator in philanthropist's clothing.*

The shadow from the journal didn't have a face yet.

But when it finally appeared, she would be ready.

She pushed the plate away, her appetite completely gone, and walked to the window. Outside, the Alps rose like jagged teeth against the darkening sky.

Somewhere in this fortress—or in some villa across the world—the shadowy patron was waiting. Watching. Planning.

Or maybe she'd already met him.

Maybe he'd been the driver who picked her up at the airport. The housekeeper who'd unpacked her bags. The man at the gate who'd checked her passport without meeting her eyes.

Maybe he'd been watching her face the entire time, savoring her ignorance.

She turned away from the window. The fortress was beautiful. The cage was perfect.

And she had no idea who held the key.

Chapter 18: The First Domino

Sleep was impossible. The jet lag, the anxiety, the adrenaline from her discovery—her mind was a hive of racing thoughts. She lay in the unfamiliar bed, staring at the ceiling, replaying that journal entry over and over. *Kind eyes. Calculation. Dissonance.*

She needed air. She needed to hear a voice that wasn't a ghost's, wasn't Katarina's ice, wasn't the phantom investor in her imagination.

She needed Manny.

Sloane remembered the burner phone hidden in the false bottom of her cosmetics case—Manny's paranoia package, the last thread connecting her to her real life. She retrieved it, checked that it was charged, and slipped it into the pocket of her cashmere robe.

The villa was a labyrinth, but she'd memorized the basic layout from the briefing materials. She made her way down a service corridor, past the kitchens where she could hear the staff cleaning up from dinner, and found a side door that led to the gardens.

The night air hit her like a slap—cold, clean, alpine air that tasted of pine and snow. The grounds were vast, terraced into the mountainside, lit by discreet pathway lights that created pools of gold in the darkness. She could see the distant shimmer of Lake Lucerne far below, a sheet of black glass reflecting the stars.

She walked away from the house, down a gravel path toward what looked like a conservatory, its glass walls dark and empty. Far enough that her voice wouldn't carry. Far enough that the house's probable surveillance couldn't pick up her conversation.

She hoped.

She pulled out the burner phone and dialed Manny's number from memory. It rang three times. Four. She was about to hang up when his voice came through, rough and breathless.

"Sloane? Jesus Christ, kid, is that you?" She could hear him panting. "Sorry—phone was in the other room. I was making dinner."

"It's me," she whispered. "I'm okay. I'm—I'm in Switzerland. At the estate. Argentis. Overlooking Lake Lucerne."

"Thank God." She could hear him moving, lighting a cigarette. "I've been climbing the fucking walls. You just disappeared. The car service, the jet—I couldn't track any of it. Are they treating you okay? Are you safe?"

"I don't know," she said honestly. "Manny, I need to tell you what I've found. I don't know how much time I have. I'm being watched all the time."

"Talk fast, kid. I'm listening."

She took a breath, organizing her thoughts like she would for a character breakdown. "The house is a fortress. I've met Katarina—she's the chief of staff, former GRU. Ice-cold, terrifying. Then there's the head of security, Nico Sorrento. Former Italian special forces. He looks it. I haven't met Damian yet, just saw him briefly when I arrived. He looked..." She paused, searching for the word. "Haunted. But that's not what worries me."

"What worries you?"

"Livia left a journal. Moleskine notebook, perfect handwriting. All about her love story with Damian, their life together... mostly normal stuff." She paused. "But there's an entry from three years ago. She mentions Damian's patron without naming him. The primary investor in Damian's current company, Crystal Vision SARL. A man with kind eyes. Gray eyes. But she noticed something—a calculation beneath the kindness. A dissonance. She was worried about him. I suspect that this shadowy patron might be the same as Fairweather's unnamed client."

"The patron. Do you have a name?"

"No. That's the problem. It's vague. Like she was afraid to write it down, even in her own journal. Either that or she wanted to leave just enough breadcrumbs in there." Sloane looked back at the lit windows of the villa, watching for shadows, for movement. "And here's the thing, Manny. The whole journal feels... wrong.

Too perfect. Too curated. Every entry is a little literary vignette. No mess, no second-guessing, no fear. It reads like a script, not a confession."

She could hear Manny's wheels turning, the click of his lighter, the exhale of smoke.

"You think it's a plant. Something they left for you to find."

"I think if Livia was smart enough to suspect that Damian's patron was dangerous, she was smart enough not to write the real story in a journal they could find. This feels like a decoy. The public version." Sloane's breath misted in the cold air. "Which means there's a private version somewhere. The real journal. The one with the actual truth."

"Can you find it?"

"I don't know. But I'm going to try." She glanced at the darkened conservatory, the manicured hedges, the perfect, beautiful prison. "Manny, I need you to do something for me. Research Damian's funding. His investors. There's someone behind this company, someone with serious money, and Livia was afraid of him. Find out who."

"I'm already on it." Manny's voice carried the edge of a man on a hunt. "After you disappeared yesterday, Fairweather's people contacted me with that cryptic bullshit about a 'remote film location with no cell service.' I didn't buy it for a second. I started digging immediately. Open internet first, standard stuff."

"And?"

"And your husband is perfect. Too perfect." She could hear him flipping through notes, the rustle of paper. "Damian Crestwell. Genius entrepreneur. Considered the brightest kid at MIT. Launched a predictive analytics company at seventeen. Dropped out two years later to take it public. Made a fortune, got bored. Rinse and repeat with a second company. He was worth over a hundred billion by twenty-five. Moved to Switzerland to work in seclusion. His current company is expected to be bigger than the stock market's Magnificent goddamned Seven put together."

“It’s the same story they gave me,” Sloane said, her voice flat but trembling underneath. “The official myth — the prodigy who rose from nowhere. Too clean. Too safe.”

“It’s a goddamn ghost story,” Manny said. “The company website? A masterpiece of nothing. Just enough filler to pass the smell test without telling you a damn thing. Pure corporate bullshit. One photo of Damian looking like a tortured poet, and a 'philosophy' page that says less than his Wikipedia entry. No board. No team. And sure as hell no investors."

"I even went down the rabbit hole," he continued, a note of frustration in his voice. "Reddit threads, old Quora posts, tech-bro forums. It's all the same recycled legends and a bunch of juicy, unverifiable rumors. The guy went dark a dozen years ago, and the internet, for the most part, just... forgot about him. For a private company, that's their right. It's also convenient as hell."

He took a breath, his voice dropping, getting to the real meat of it. "And then there's the wife. The official story, scrubbed clean across the entire internet, is that Livia Crestwell had a 'near-fatal accident' at sea and is 'recovering' in his loving care."

Manny's tone put heavy, skeptical quotes around the official line. He didn't need to say she was dead. They both already knew.

"To rewrite a narrative that cleanly," he continued, his voice now a low growl, "to make a death disappear from the public record? That takes more than money. That takes power on a level I haven't seen in a long time."

"Can you find out who's really behind this?"

"You got it, kid," Manny said, his voice dropping, taking on a grim, determined edge she hadn't heard in years. "I'm calling in the old guard. I've got an accountant for the money, a journalist for the bodies, and if they can't find him on paper, I've got a whiz kid who can find anyone in the dark. The best hacker I've ever seen. We'll find your shadow investor."

"How long?"

"Hard to say. This kind of digging takes time. But I'll find him." His voice softened. "Sloane, baby, you don't have to do this. You can walk away. Just say the word and I'll get you out of there."

She thought about the eviction notice. The Oscar on the fridge. The hemorrhoid cream audition. The suffocating apartment and the ghost of Mitchell Carver and the slow, grinding crucifixion of her career.

She thought about one hundred million dollars.

And she thought about Livia Crestwell, a woman she'd never met, who'd left breadcrumbs in a fake journal for someone to follow.

"No," Sloane said quietly. "I'm seeing this through. But I need you watching my back."

"Always, kid. Always." He paused. "Be careful. If you're right, if there's a shadowy patron with kind eyes who scared a cryptographer enough that she hid her real thoughts... that's not a man you want to underestimate."

"I won't," she promised. "I have to go."

"Find that real journal, Sloane," Manny's voice was a final, urgent command. "If she left it, it's there. You just have to look."

The line went dead.

Sloane stood in the cold Swiss night for another moment, looking up at the impossible spread of stars. She pocketed the burner phone, her hand closing around its hard, plastic reality.

She slipped back into the house, a ghost returning to her haunting. The adrenaline from the call and her earlier discoveries was beginning to fade, leaving a deep, bone-weary exhaustion in its wake. She had been awake for twenty-four hours, jet-lagged, running on pure, terrified will.

She wanted to collapse. To sleep. To let the darkness take her for a few hours.

But then her gaze fell on the sleek, gray tablet Katarina had left on her writing desk. The "preliminary dossier."

This is your first test, Katarina's cold voice echoed in her mind. *Livia had a near-photographic memory. I expect nothing less.*

Sloane's jaw tightened. She was jet-lagged, terrified, and running on fumes. But she was also a professional.

And Sloane Devereaux, the director's actor, never, ever showed up on set unprepared.

Chapter 19: The Queen's Gambit

The first morning at Argentis broke with a violence of light that Sloane wasn't prepared for. At this altitude, the September sun didn't just shine; it struck the glass walls like a hammer.

Katarina Zimina arrived at her suite at precisely 0800 hours, a specter in charcoal gray. She held a tablet. "Your regimen," she announced, her voice as flat and devoid of warmth as the marble floor. "We begin immediately."

The "regimen" was a grueling, eight-hour assault designed to strip away every last vestige of Sloane Devereaux and build Livia Crestwell from the bones up. The morning was spent in a private screening room, a dark, cold space with a screen that took up an entire wall. For four hours, Katarina made her watch Livia. Not the curated highlight reel from the jet, but raw, unedited footage. Livia arguing with a contractor in fluent German. Livia tasting wine with a sommelier in Bordeaux, her commentary sharp and intelligent. Livia reading a bedtime story to a nephew over a video call, her voice soft and full of a gentle, easy love.

Sloane, the actress, was taking notes, filing away gestures, vocal tics, the way Livia held her head when she was concentrating. But Sloane, the woman, felt like a voyeur, a thief stealing the most intimate moments of a dead woman's life.

"Observe her posture," Katarina commanded, pausing the video on a shot of Livia walking through a museum. "Shoulders back, but relaxed. A straight spine, not a rigid one. You hold yourself like a soldier expecting an attack. Livia held herself like a queen who owned the castle."

Lunch was a solitary affair in the vast, silent dining room. A single place setting at a table that could seat twenty. A Michelin-star-worthy plate of seared scallops and asparagus foam appeared, served by a silent housekeeper who materialized and vanished without a word. The food was exquisite, but Sloane could barely taste it. Every bite felt like a betrayal. The silence was the loudest thing in the room, broken only by the soft, synthesized voice of the home's AI.

"The current outdoor temperature is twelve degrees Celsius," Aura announced from a hidden speaker. "Would you like me to adjust the interior climate, Mrs. Crestwell?"

The name made Sloane flinch. "No, Aura. Thank you."

"You are welcome."

The AI sounded more human than anyone else in this house.

***

The afternoon was deportment. Katarina took her to the main salon, the vast space with the glass wall overlooking the lake.

"Walk for me," Katarina ordered. "From here to the window."

Sloane walked, every muscle tensed, hyper-aware of Katarina's critical gaze.

"No," Katarina snapped. "Stop." She walked a slow, critical circle around Sloane, her eyes cataloging every flaw. "Your posture is a ruin. Your core strength is non-existent. You have her face, but you have forgotten how to carry it."

Katarina's voice was cold steel. "Livia Crestwell was a disciplined woman. Yoga at dawn. Ten kilometers on the treadmill before lunch. Krav Maga twice a week with Mr. Sorrento. Her body was as sharp an instrument as her mind. You," she said, her gaze a withering assessment, "are a pale imitation. For the gala, for any public appearance, you must not just look like her. You must move like her. You must have her stamina, her grace, her power. Your physical conditioning is as critical as your German accent."

She tapped a command into her tablet. "Mr. Sorrento will begin your physical regimen tomorrow morning. He has Livia's exact training logs. You will meet every one of her benchmarks before the gala. Do you understand?"

"Yes," Sloane said, her jaw tight.

"Good," Katarina said. "Now, again. Walk for me. And try to remember what it feels like to own a room, not just rent one."

For an hour, Katarina drilled her like a cruel ballet master. Walk. Stop. Turn. Again. Shoulders back. Chin up. Slower. Let your arms swing naturally. It was brutal, humiliating. With every correction, Katarina was sanding away another piece of Sloane's identity, another piece of the Oklahoma girl who had learned to walk fast to escape trouble.

After the walking came the sitting, the standing, the way to hold a wine glass, the way to descend a staircase. It was a complete physical deconstruction and rebuilding.

As the sun began to dip behind the mountains, casting long, dramatic shadows across the room, Sloane felt a flicker of defiance. She was an Oscar-winning actress, not a show pony. She stopped in the middle of a turn.

"Is there a problem?" Katarina asked, her voice dangerously quiet.

"I think I have it," Sloane said, letting a hint of Livia's cool, unbothered tone into her own voice. She turned and walked back across the room, her movements now fluid, graceful, a perfect imitation of the woman on the screen. She had absorbed the lesson. She was a quick study.

Katarina watched her, her face an unreadable mask. "Adequate," she said, the word a small, cold stone. "We will continue perfecting your posture and your walk tomorrow."

***

But she did not dismiss her. Instead, Katarina gestured to the two severe, minimalist armchairs by the cold, unlit fireplace. "Sit."

Sloane sat, her spine straight, her hands resting calmly in her lap, a perfect imitation of Livia at a board meeting. Katarina sat opposite her, holding a tablet. The physical exam was over. The oral exam was about to begin.

"The Rothschild dinner in Geneva next month," Katarina said, her voice a flat, clinical instrument. "The French finance minister, Jean-Luc Martel, will be in attendance. Livia despised him. Why?"

It was a pop quiz. A test of the preliminary dossier she had been given less than twenty-four hours ago. Katarina was stress-testing her from the get-go, looking for a reason to declare her a failure.

But Sloane was an actress. Her entire career had been built on cramming impossible amounts of dialogue and backstory into her head on a moment's notice. This was no different from learning a new script overnight.

Sloane didn't hesitate. She was an actress who always knew her lines. "Because he was indiscreet," she replied, her voice a cool, confident Livia. "At a luncheon in Davos two years ago, he hinted to a reporter from *Le Monde* that Damian's work on quantum computing had applications in signals intelligence. Livia considered it an unforgivable breach of trust. She called him a 'peacock with the security clearance of a Parisian street mime.'"

A flicker of something—surprise? grudging respect?—registered in Katarina's icy eyes before it was extinguished. She swiped to the next page on her tablet.

"The Italian ambassador, Sofia Ricci," Katarina continued, pressing. "Livia admired her. Why?"

"Because she was a survivor," Sloane said, the words feeling sharp and personal in her own mouth. "She came from a poor family in Naples, put herself through school, and outmaneuvered every man in the Italian foreign service to get where she is. Livia saw her as a fellow warrior. A woman who understood that a smile could be both a welcome and a weapon."

For a long, silent moment, the two women just looked at each other, two very different kinds of warriors in a quiet, sunlit room. Katarina had expected a doll, a physical copy she could program. She was discovering a mind, a quick, analytical intelligence that could not only memorize the data but understand its meaning.

Katarina switched off the tablet. "We are done for today," she said, her voice clipped, a fraction colder than before. "Dinner is at eight. Do not be late."

She stood and swept from the room. That first session was a declaration of war.

And Sloane knew, with cold certainty, that it wouldn't end until she walked into that gala as Livia Crestwell—flawless, unbreakable, and utterly convincing.

***

But the day's battles weren't over.

As Sloane walked back toward her suite, her muscles already aching from the unfamiliar postures, a dark figure fell into step beside her in the cavernous hallway. Nico.

"Katarina is right," he said, his voice a low, gravelly rumble. He didn't look at her, his gaze fixed straight ahead. "Your posture is... terrible. Livia's physical conditioning was part of her fortress. We start at 0600 tomorrow. The gym."

The next morning, it was humiliation.

Sloane stood in the center of Argentis's private gym—all polished wood floors and floor-to-ceiling mirrors reflecting the dark, pre-dawn Alps. Nico was already there. Waiting.

"Push-ups," he said. No greeting. "As many as you can."

She remembered a time when she could do thirty without breaking a sweat. Back when her body was a disciplined weapon, sculpted for the role that won her the Oscar. Now, after five years of surviving on ramen and rage, she was a stranger in her own skin.

She dropped to the mat. Her arms shook.

One.

Two.

Three.

She collapsed on the fourth, her cheek pressed against the cold, unforgiving mat. The shame was a hot flush on her face.

Nico crouched beside her, his expression unreadable, his voice a flat, clinical assessment. "Your biological age is thirty," he said, making a note on his tablet. "Your fitness age is forty-four. Fourteen years of deterioration in five years. That's what a crucifixion in Hollywood does to a body. At age thirty-six, Livia body operated as if it were twenty-one."

He stood, a dark, unimpressed silhouette. "Get some rest. We have work to do. Same time. Six days a week. For the next ten weeks."

Humiliated, fighting fatigue and jet lag, and about to collapse, Sloane reached deep within. Nobody–not Katarina, not Nico, not the mysterious shadowy patron–was going to keep her down.

"No mercy," she said with a defiant smile. "Make it seven days a week."

Chapter 20: The Sentinel

By the second week, the air had begun to turn. The crisp, polite breeze of her arrival had gained a sharp, biting edge that hinted at the winter waiting in the wings.

Every day at ten o'clock, there was the walk. The only reprieve from the morning's brutal workout—even if her legs still burned and her arms hung like lead. Sloane had come to believe it was a special kind of torture. One she'd begun to crave.

"Livia valued her morning constitutionals," Katarina had announced, her tone suggesting it was a moral failing that Sloane did not. "It is important to maintain appearances. For the staff. For the security cameras."

The implication was clear: she was always being watched.

So at ten o'clock, Sloane found herself walking along a winding gravel path that snaked through a meticulously manicured alpine garden. The air was crisp and thin, smelling of pine and damp earth. The sun was bright, but it had no warmth. Below her, the black, still water of the lake was a vast, unblinking eye.

And fifty feet behind her, a silent, watchful shadow, was Nico Sorrento.

He didn't walk so much as glide, his footsteps making no sound on the gravel. He was a constant, unnerving presence at the edge of her peripheral vision. He wasn't looking at the scenery. He was looking at her. Or rather, he was looking past her, his gaze constantly sweeping the perimeter—the dense line of pine trees, the rocky outcrops, the sky above.

It was like being tailed by a panther. The silence between them was a heavy, physical thing, a wall of professional distance.

After ten minutes of the suffocating quiet, Sloane couldn't take it anymore. Her new mission—the library, the hidden journal—was a frantic, secret drumbeat in her mind. But how could she get anywhere alone, how could she find a single moment of privacy, with this ghost tailing her every move? She had to test his boundaries. She had to know the shape of her cage.

She stopped and turned to face him. He stopped instantly, his body perfectly still, his expression neutral.

"Is the shadowing really necessary, Mr. Sorrento?" she asked, her voice pure Livia—cool, amused, a little annoyed.

"It's Nico," he said, his voice a low, gravelly thing that seemed to absorb the light. "And yes. It is."

"Are you expecting an attack? A sniper in the trees? I thought this place was a fortress."

He didn't smile. The concept of humor seemed foreign to his hard-cut features. "I expect everything," he said, his eyes meeting hers. "That's my job."

"Fine," she said, turning back to the path with a dismissive flick of her wrist. "Just try not to breathe down my neck."

She started walking again, the gravel crunching under her feet. The performance was her shield. She was Livia, the lady of the manor, slightly irritated by her overzealous security detail. But underneath, she was Sloane, the actress, analyzing her scene partner, looking for a weakness, an opening.

The path forked. The main gravel trail, wide and impeccably maintained, continued to the left, winding back toward the main house. To the right, a smaller, overgrown dirt path led down a steep embankment toward a small, old stone boathouse she had seen from her window. A rusted iron weather vane squeaked atop its peaked roof, spinning lazily in the wind. It was the only part of the estate that didn't look like it had been designed by a minimalist architect with an unlimited budget. It looked old. Real.

A small, elegant sign, carved from local wood, stood at the fork. In four languages, it read: *PRIVATE - NO ADMITTANCE.*

Sloane turned right.

***

She took three steps down the steep, needle-strewn path before he was there. He hadn't run. He had simply materialized in front of her, a solid, immovable object blocking her way. He was closer now than he had ever been, and she could feel a palpable heat radiating from him, the coiled energy of a predator. He smelled faintly of clean laundry and gun oil.

"This area is off-limits," he said. His voice was the same low rumble, but there was a new, hard edge to it. A warning.

"Why?" she challenged, tilting her head in a perfect imitation of Livia's confident curiosity. She let her gaze drift past him, down to the small stone structure by the water's edge. "What's in the scary old boathouse? The family crypt?"

"Security infrastructure," he said, his eyes not leaving hers. "And it's not on the approved route."

"And who approves the routes? You? Katarina?" She was pushing, testing the chain of command, searching for a crack in the hierarchy.

"I do," he said, his voice flat, absolute. "And I don't approve of this one."

They stood there for a long, silent moment, a standoff on the edge of a cliff. He was a wall. A handsome, well-dressed, and utterly impassable wall.

Sloane remembered how to get her way. It was a muscle she hadn't flexed in five years, but the instinct was still there. She was used to men, even powerful men, bending to her will, seduced by a smile or a sharp word.

But Nico Sorrento did not look like a man who bent.

As she held his unblinking gaze, her eye caught a flicker of movement. He thought he was being subtle, but she saw it. His left hand, hidden from the direct line of sight of the house's cameras, held a small phone. On the screen, for a fraction of a second before he thumbed it off, she saw a photograph. A young girl, maybe twelve, with dark curly hair and his eyes, laughing as she held up an ice cream cone. A daughter.

And on his wrist, just visible beneath the cuff of his tactical jacket—a faded friendship bracelet. Cheap craft store beads in blue and yellow, the kind a child makes. Worn and fraying, but still there. Still worn.

The detail was so jarringly, incongruously human against his cold, professional exterior that it was like finding a wildflower growing in a concrete bunker. This man. This killer, this ghost who moved without a past, had a child. A child who'd made him a bracelet he refused to take off, even on a mission. A vulnerability.

His reaction was instantaneous, though almost imperceptible. He pocketed the phone, his body tensing, the professional wall becoming a fortress of ice. He knew she had seen it.

"This area is off-limits," he said, his voice clipped, final. The subject was closed.

She had hit a nerve. A deep one. She filed the information away. The impassable wall had a crack in it. A tiny, human-shaped crack. She wouldn't tell Manny about this. This was her secret. A piece of leverage, or perhaps something more, in a game she was just beginning to understand.

"So I am a prisoner, then," she said, changing tactics, her voice losing its lightness, taking on a brittle, challenging edge. "Confined to the pretty paths, not allowed to stray."

"This is a secure environment, Mrs. Crestwell," he countered, his voice a masterpiece of corporate-speak, deflecting the emotional core of her question. "My job is to maintain that security. For your protection."

"My protection," she repeated, letting a note of bitter, ironic amusement enter her voice. "Of course."

She knew she had lost this battle. He would not move. He would not break. And he would certainly not let her explore the one corner of this estate that felt real.

She forced a light, dismissive laugh that sounded exactly like Livia's. She gave a small, theatrical sigh of defeat. "Fine," she said, turning and walking back up to the main path. "You're no fun at all, Nico."

She heard him go still behind her. When she glanced back, his face had gone pale. His eyes tracked her movement with an expression she couldn't quite read—shock? Recognition? "You're no fun at all, Nico," he whispered, his voice barely audible. "Damn. That's what Livia used to say."

***

She didn't look back, but she could feel his eyes on her all the way back to the house. The silence that followed was different. It was no longer the empty silence of professional distance. It was a charged silence, full of the things they had not said. Full of the bracelet on his wrist and the journal in her mind.

Sloane had lost the skirmish, but she had won a valuable piece of intelligence.

First, she had learned that the physical boundaries of her prison were absolute. Nico was not a man who could be charmed, intimidated, or negotiated with. He was a wall, and a direct approach would always fail.

Second, she had learned that the wall had a crack. The sentinel who moved through the world like a ghost was tethered to it by a cheap, faded bracelet. He wasn't just a man of violence; he was a father. That knowledge was a key.

Finally, and most importantly, she faced the sheer, crushing magnitude of the hunt. Livia's real journal could be anywhere. Argentis was forty thousand square feet of locked rooms, hidden panels, and blind corners.

Searching it wouldn't be a casual act. It would require tearing the house apart, inch by inch. It was an act of espionage that required the one thing she did not have.

Privacy.

She couldn't do it in the dead of night; the house's motion sensors would flag the activity as an anomaly. She couldn't do it during the day; the staff was ever-present, and Nico was a constant shadow.

She needed a window. A moment of calculated distraction. A perfect performance that would carve a blind spot out of the light—and give her the freedom to hunt.

Chapter 21: Ghosts of Hollywood Past

While Sloane was learning to walk in a dead woman's shoes, Manny Goldman was waging a street-level war in the smoggy trenches of Los Angeles.

His dusty, two-room office above a tailor shop in Burbank, a relic from an era of landlines and handshake deals, had become a command center. The walls, once covered in the optimistic, smiling headshots of aspiring stars, were now a chaotic collage. Printouts of corporate filings. Satellite maps of a mountain in Switzerland. Handwritten notes connected by a spiderweb of red yarn. It was the paranoid, obsessive shrine of a man on a holy mission.

He hadn't slept. Not really. Not since Sloane's whispered, frantic call from a country he couldn't spell, a call that had been cut short, leaving a silence more terrifying than any scream. He was living on black coffee from the deli downstairs, cheap whiskey from the bottle in his desk drawer, and a pure, unadulterated rage that felt like the only clean thing left in the world.

The fear he had felt for Sloane, the raw, paternal terror, had not subsided. It had metastasized, transforming into a grim, cold determination. He looked at the framed photo on the corner of his desk. His daughter. Sophie. Gone twenty years now, taken by the slow, merciless attack of a disease he couldn't fight.

He would not fail another daughter. He would not be too late again.

He picked up a clean burner phone from a stack of five on his desk. His old network, the ghosts of Hollywood past, had been activated. Back in the nineties, he'd been a fixer—the guy you called when a starlet had a drug problem or a leading man had a gambling debt. He knew where the bodies were buried because he had supplied some of the shovels.

It was time to start digging.

***

He met Jerry Bostrom in a dark corner of a forgotten bar near the Burbank airport, a place that smelled of spilled beer and a century of bad decisions. Jerry was a washed-up forensic accountant, a genius with numbers who'd been stripped of his license for getting a little too creative with a studio's tax returns.

"Crystal Vision SARL," Jerry grumbled, squinting at a printout under the dim, greasy light of a fake Tiffany lamp. "Manny, this isn't a company. It's a goddamn nesting doll of offshore holding companies. You peel back one layer in the Caymans, you find another in Lichtenstein. It's a ghost."

"Every ghost leaves a footprint," Manny pressed, pushing a glass of whiskey toward him.

"Yeah, well this one wears slippers," Jerry shot back. He took a long swallow of the whiskey. "But I still have a few contacts. A guy in Geneva who owes me a very big favor."

He smirked.

"Just like you still owe me for that thing with the IRS back in '05."

"It's on my tab," Manny said, impatient. "What did your guy find?"

“He confirmed what the public records show: the early funding for Damian’s first two public companies appeared clean. Stanford endowments, Silicon Valley regulars. The usual suspects.”

Jerry let out a short breath.

“What the records don’t show—unless you know exactly where to dig—is who engineered those early rounds. The capital was layered on purpose. Endowments fronted the money. Tier-one VCs legitimized it. But the scaffolding—the shell funds, the legal architecture that made every dollar arrive compliant and untraceable—none of that belonged to them.”

Jerry tapped a line on the printout with a grubby finger.

“But the real money—the multi-billion-dollar injection that funded his move to Switzerland and the creation of this private entity, Crystal Vision—that’s where the smoke and mirrors start.”

“From who?”

"That's the thing," Jerry said, leaning in, his voice dropping to a conspiratorial whisper. "It doesn't come from one place. It's a dozen different investment vehicles. Shells. Pass-throughs. But I ran the transaction logs."

His finger tapped again. Harder.

"The funding is a maze. But every single wire—dozens of them, from all over the world—was authenticated by the exact same invisible hand. The final authorization signal, for every transaction, was routed through a single, hyper-secure data center."

"Zurich?" Manny guessed.

Jerry shook his head, a look of grudging admiration crossing his face. "No. Too obvious. Too expensive. A decommissioned iron mine in northern Finland. Perfect ambient temperature for cooling. Cheap geothermal power. Buried under a thousand feet of granite."

He looked up.

"The place is a digital fortress. Untouchable."

"And the company that leases it?"

"It's called the Lazarus Group," Jerry whispered.

Manny's jaw tightened. "Lazarus. As in, raised from the dead."

"As in, this guy's money is so clean it's like it was never dirty in the first place," Jerry confirmed, sliding over a second printout. "And he's not new to the game. I went back and pulled the original SEC filings for Damian's first two companies—Helios and QuantumScape."

Jerry met Manny's eyes.

"The Lazarus Group wasn't just in there. They were early. Quiet. And significant. Not a majority stakeholder—nothing that would trip alarms—but deeply embedded. The same group that later handled the entire operational infrastructure for Damian's private move to Switzerland."

"And Damian?" Manny asked.

"Still the largest single shareholder in both public companies," Jerry confirmed. "A completely silent one. His lawyers file the necessary paperwork, but he's a ghost. It's the only reason we even have a guess at what he's worth. Not counting the valuation of Crystal Vision SARL since it's private."

"So our ghost has a ghost of his own," Manny murmured. "The name on the Lazarus incorporation papers?"

"That's where it gets scary," Jerry said, his voice dropping. "My guy in Geneva says the whole 'secret numbered account' thing is a myth now. They have 'Know Your Customer' laws that would make the IRS blush. They *have* to know who the real owner is."

"So what's the problem?" Manny pressed.

"The problem," Jerry whispered, "is that for this guy, the rules don't apply. The beneficial owner of the Lazarus Group is a black hole. It means whoever this is, he isn't just rich. He's powerful enough to make the Swiss government itself look the other way. He's not using the system; he *is* the system."

"Keep digging," Manny said, sliding a thick envelope of cash across the sticky table. "I want to know who's pulling the strings."

***

The Lazarus Group. It was a name, but it wasn't enough. The money trail was a dead end, a series of elegant, professional illusions. Manny knew that when the money was invisible, you had to follow the blood.

He picked up another burner phone. He needed a different kind of ghost. Not an accountant. A storyteller. Someone who remembered the bodies.

He dialed.

"You have a lot of nerve calling me, Manny," the voice on the other end rasped, a sound like gravel and nicotine.

"Hello to you too, Sarah," Manny said. "I need a drink. Greasy spoon diner. Van Nuys. Thirty minutes."

"I'm not your source anymore. My career is ash, remember? You were at that party. You saw what they did to me."

"I know," Manny said, his voice softening. "That's why I'm calling. The MO. The scale of it. It matches. I think they're the same ones holding the match to my girl. Help me identify the hand, and I promise you: we both get to watch them burn."

There was a long silence on the other end. The sound of a cigarette being lit. An exhale of smoke.

"The usual place?" she asked.

"The usual place," Manny confirmed.

He hung up the phone. He had a name. Now he needed a pattern. He needed a story. He needed a ghost who remembered the other fires.

Chapter 22: The Piano in the Dark

The silence of Argentis wasn't peaceful. It was engineered.

Three weeks of Katarina and Nico's boot camps had stripped Sloane raw. The constant correction, the endless repetition of Livia's history, the grueling physical conditioning—it was eroding the edges of her own identity. Lying in the dark of her suite, staring at the ceiling, she felt a terrifying vertigo. She was forgetting what it felt like to just be Sloane.

She needed an anchor. Something tactile. Something real.

She left her suite, moving through the sleeping house like the ghost she was paid to be. The cameras watched her—unblinking glass eyes in the ceiling—but tonight, she didn't care about their judgment. She just needed to breathe air that didn't taste of filtered oxygen and secrets.

She found herself drawn to the main salon. Not for the view of the lake, but for the shape in the center of the room.

The Fazioli grand piano.

She didn't sit. She just stood beside it in the darkness, tracing the smooth, cool wood of the lid with her fingers. In a house of steel and glass, the wood felt alive. A tangible link to a world of art and beauty that felt a million miles away. She thought of her mother, of a life before all this, a life with music in it.

***

Damian Crestwell stood in the doorway of the salon, unseen, watching the woman at his piano.

He'd heard the footsteps—the house's acoustic design was flawless, every sound carrying through the open architecture like water through glass—and he'd come to investigate. Or perhaps he'd been drawn. He didn't know anymore. Didn't trust his own motivations.

She stood in profile, silhouetted against the vast windows overlooking the lake. The moonlight painted her in silver and shadow. Her hand rested on the closed lid of the piano, her fingers tracing the wood grain with an unconscious tenderness that made something in his chest constrict.

It was the posture that broke him. The slight curve of her shoulders. The tilt of her head. The way she seemed to be listening to music only she could hear.

Livia had never stood like that. Livia had approached the piano the way a mathematician approached an equation—with cool appreciation for its construction, its symmetry, its potential. She had understood its physics but never its soul.

This woman—this actress, this stranger wearing his wife's face—stood like someone who had loved music and lost it. Like someone who remembered what it felt like to have beauty in her life before the world took it away.

The rational part of his mind—the part that dealt in logic, probabilities and observable phenomena—knew exactly what she was. An actress. A performer. A woman named Sloane Devereaux who'd been paid an obscene amount of money to wear a dead woman's skin and say the right words at the right times.

But the other part of him, the part that had been hollow for nine months, the part that woke screaming from nightmares where the dark water closed over her head again and again and again—that part didn't care about rationality.

That part saw a woman standing alone in the dark, touching his piano like it was a relic of something sacred and lost, and felt something he thought had died with Livia.

Need.

He took a sip of his scotch, the burn grounding him, and spoke before he could stop himself.

"She hated that piano."

The woman spun around, her hand flying to her chest, a sharp gasp escaping her lips. For one crystalline moment before she caught herself, before the performance clicked back into place, he saw naked fear in her eyes. Real. Unguarded. Human.

Then the mask returned—Livia's poise, Livia's grace—but it was a fraction of a second too slow. He'd seen beneath it. And God help him, he wanted to see more.

"I'm sorry," she said, pulling her hand back as if the piano had burned her. The voice was perfect—Livia's British precision, the slight melodic lilt she'd affected after years at Cambridge. "I didn't hear you. I couldn't sleep."

"Neither can I." He walked into the room, moving carefully. For two weeks, she had been a theoretical concept living in the West Wing—a project report on Katarina's tablet. Now, standing ten feet away, she was uncomfortably real.

He stopped, suddenly aware of how this must look. A midnight encounter. The two of them alone. He cleared his throat.

"Katarina tells me you're... settling in. Splendidly."

The word hung in the air, absurdly formal, almost Victorian. He winced internally. *Splendidly.* Christ, he sounded like his grandfather at a state dinner.

He cleared his throat again, trying to recover.

"She was quite insistent that I not disturb you until you were 'ready,'" he said, swirling his glass and offering a small, conspiratorial smile. "But I suppose we've both broken the rules tonight."

"Yes," she said, and he could hear her searching for the script, the right line. "Everyone has been very... accommodating."

Accommodating. They were like two diplomats at a failed peace summit, lobbing pleasantries across a minefield.

The silence that followed was excruciating. He took another sip of scotch, she shifted her weight, and the floorboard beneath her foot creaked with a sound like a gunshot in the quiet.

"Livia played with a kind of terrifying perfection," he heard himself say, desperate to fill the void, gesturing at the instrument with his glass. "Chopin, Bach... every note precise. Every tempo exact. But she said it was just mathematics to her. Notes on a page. She had no interest in its soul."

Better. This was safer ground. Talking about Livia. The ghost between them was easier to navigate than the reality of two strangers standing in the dark, pretending.

He sat in one of the armchairs, the leather cool beneath him, and let his gaze rest on the instrument rather than on her. Safer that way. Less dangerous. "Do you play?"

It was a test. He knew it was a test. Livia had played with clinical precision—every note correct, every tempo exact. But there had been no joy in it. No warmth. He wondered if this woman would reveal herself by playing differently. Or by not playing at all.

The woman—Sloane, he reminded himself, her name is Sloane—hesitated. She looked at the polished black surface reflecting her face, then slowly sat on the edge of the bench. She didn't adopt Livia's rigid, professional posture; she leaned over the ivory keys like a curious child.

Then, with two index fingers, she pecked out the opening bars of "Chopsticks."

The simple, repetitive tune was a ridiculous, defiant act in a room built for Rachmaninoff. She played it with a clumsy, honest gravity that made the multi-million-dollar Fazioli sound like a toy. Sloane's fingers froze on the keys, creating a final, discordant clang. She looked at him, her face flushing in the dim light. "That's the extent of my repertoire. A bit of a letdown after Liszt, I imagine."

Damian didn't laugh. He leaned forward, the genius in him suddenly awake. "You know," he said, his voice full of a quiet, intellectual passion, "that simple piece is a fascinating study in diatonic harmony. It's a perfect illustration of parallel motion—something most classical composers actively avoided because it was too... honest. Too transparent."

He took a sip of his scotch, his eyes never leaving hers. "Livia understood the math. She could see the equations that governed the music. But you seem to understand the poetry."

His heart did a slow, painful roll in his chest. For nine months, he had lived in a room of static. To see this woman treat a master's tool with such unrefined levity—it felt like a window opening in a tomb.

And then something shifted. The accent slipped, just slightly, becoming softer, rounder, more American. More real.

"My mother did," she said, her voice quiet, almost a whisper. "Beautifully. I... never had the discipline."

The past tense. The catch in her voice. The way her fingers curled into her palm, as if physically restraining herself from reaching for the keys.

Damian's chest tightened. This wasn't performance. This was grief. He knew grief. He'd been drowning in it for nine months.

He took a step closer, swirling the amber liquid in his glass. He needed to break the spell. He needed to prove to himself that this was just a transaction, that she was just a woman reading lines from a dossier.

He decided to push. To find the edge of the script.

"Livia used to play Liszt's Liebestraum when it stormed," he said, his voice casual, though his eyes were locked on hers. "She said the thunder messed with the acoustics, so she had to play louder to compensate. Do you remember that?"

Sloane froze. Her mind raced through the thousands of files, the videos, the journals. There was nothing about Liszt. Nothing about thunderstorms. But she knew the character. Livia was a perfectionist. Livia controlled her environment.

"I remember," Sloane lied softly, turning back to the keys to hide her eyes. "But I think I played it to drown out the noise. I always hated the thunder."

Damian stared at her profile. The silence stretched, taut as a piano wire.

Livia had loved thunderstorms. She used to stand on the balcony in her bare feet and conduct them like a symphony.

It was the wrong answer. A crack in the performance. The proof he had been looking for.

He should have felt triumphant. He should have felt the cold satisfaction of a scientist identifying an error.

But then he looked at her trembling hands, at the genuine, unscripted grief in her posture. And he realized with a jolt of horror that he didn't care about the error. The lie was softer than the truth.

He should have stopped this. Should have sent her away before the counterfeit became more real than the memory.

Instead, he took a sip of his scotch.

"Discipline is a cage, sometimes," he heard himself say, the words coming from somewhere deep and unguarded. "What did she play?"

"Debussy," she whispered, and when she looked at the piano keys, he saw tears gathering at the corners of her eyes that she was too proud or too professional to let fall. "Sentimental things."

Debussy. Damian's chest tightened. The polar opposite of Livia's cold precision. The Impressionists. All emotion and atmosphere and the spaces between notes. Everything Livia had dismissed as "mathematically inelegant."

"Livia would have called that... imprecise," Damian said, and he could hear his own voice going soft, almost tender. "Emotion without structure."

He paused, looking at this woman who was and wasn't his wife, this stranger who'd somehow slipped past his defenses with nothing but a moment of genuine sadness over a dead mother and a piano in the dark.

"I think I would have liked your mother."

The words hung in the air between them, simple and sincere and more intimate than he'd meant them to be. Because what he was really saying, what he couldn't say, was: I think I'm starting to like you. Not the performance. Not the ghost. You.

And that was terrifying.

She looked at him then, really looked at him, and in her eyes he saw the same recognition. The same terrifying understanding that something had just shifted between them. That in this moment, in this darkness, they weren't captor and prisoner, employer and employee, widower and paid actress.

They were just two lonely people, talking about their ghosts, standing on opposite sides of an abyss and wondering if it was possible to build a bridge.

For a few suspended heartbeats, neither of them moved. Neither spoke. The silence wasn't empty—it was full of all the things they couldn't say, weighted with possibility and danger and the fragile, impossible beginning of something that felt dangerously like hope.

Then reality crashed back in. The house. The cameras. The contract. The hundred million dollars. The fact that they were always being watched, and this woman was a performance, and he was a broken man grasping at shadows because he couldn't bear to be alone anymore.

Damian stood abruptly, finishing his scotch in one burning swallow.

"You should sleep," he said, his voice professionally distant again, the walls rebuilding themselves. "Tomorrow Katarina will continue your... integration. It will be demanding."

He walked toward the door, needing to escape before he said something he couldn't take back, before he reached across the space between them and touched her hand and confirmed that she was real, that this moment had been real, that he wasn't losing his mind in his grief.

At the threshold, he paused. He shouldn't say it. He knew he shouldn't say it.

He said it anyway.

"Your mother would be proud of you," he said quietly, not turning around, not trusting himself to look at her. "For surviving. For being brave enough to stand in a stranger's house and admit you lost her."

He gripped the doorframe, his knuckles white against the dark wood. "I've spent nine months living as a ghost in this house, Sloane. But seeing you peck out nursery rhymes on that Fazioli… it's the first time I've felt human again since the water took her."

He left before she could respond, before he could see if the tears in her eyes finally fell, before he could do something catastrophically stupid like tell her the truth:

That he didn't just feel human. He felt alive.

And that was the most dangerous thing of all.

Chapter 23: The Equation of Grief

She found him in his laboratory one night, a month into her stay. Not the pristine study, but his real workshop in the sub-levels—a chaotic space of whiteboards covered in frantic equations, humming server racks, and the cold, clean smell of ozone.

He was standing in front of a whiteboard, staring at a complex equation, but his eyes were vacant. He hadn't slept in two days. Katarina had told her he was in a "downward spiral," lost in the labyrinth of his grief, a state that made him unproductive and, for his partner, useless.

"It's not balancing," he said, not turning around. His voice was a dry rasp. "The variables... they keep collapsing. The chaos factor is too high."

He wasn't talking about the equation. He was talking about his wife's death.

The old Sloane would have frozen—out of her depth, exposed. But the new Sloane, the one who had spent a hundred hours memorizing Livia's voice, her syntax, the rhythm of her certainty, knew exactly what to do.

She walked to the board, picked up a marker, and stood beside him. She looked at the sprawling, beautiful, and broken equation. It meant nothing to her. Not a single symbol. But she knew how intelligence sounded. She knew how conviction moved.

"You're trying to solve for a constant," she said softly, her voice perfect in its calm, its precision—a flawless performance of Livia's analytical certainty. "But grief isn't a single, fixed number. It's a non-linear dynamic system. You can't force convergence on a waveform in superposition. You have to account for the stochastic variance."

The words tasted like ash and metal—sounds she had memorized phonetically from Damian's old lecture videos without understanding a single syllable of their meaning. To her, "stochastic variance" wasn't math; it was just a line of dialogue. A cue. She delivered it with the same casual authority she would use to order coffee.

She uncapped the marker and, with a steady hand, circled one variable in his equation. A small, almost insignificant symbol —σ^2(t)—that she recognized only because she had seen it scribbled in the margins of Livia's journal next to a grocery list.

She didn't choose it because of the math. She chose it because it was isolated. Because visually, the scene demanded a focal point, a prop.

"You're treating her as an outlier to be discarded," Sloane said, her voice full of an understanding she was carefully, expertly counterfeiting. "She's not. She's a recursive function. The ghost in the machine. You can't remove her from the equation. You have to integrate her into it."

Damian stared at the board. At her hand. At the circle she had drawn. His own hand, holding a marker, was trembling. He looked at her—and for the first time, the vacant, haunted look in his eyes was pierced by a flicker of his old, brilliant light.

He took the marker from her. His hand was now steady. He drew a new line, connecting σ^2(t) to a different cluster of variables. He muttered something—"re-weighting the decay parameter"—that sounded like gibberish to her.

The equation shifted. It re-aligned. It began to make sense to him.

Sloane watched him work, keeping her face a mask of serene approval. She had no idea if the math was correct. She only knew she had delivered the scene.

He didn't thank her. He didn't speak. He just started to work, his movements now fluid and certain, the genius back in control of his universe.

Sloane backed away slowly and left the room. Only then did the tension drain from her shoulders. She had done it. She had spoken his language without understanding a single word of it. Like performing Shakespeare in a language she didn't speak—she had sold the emotion, not the definition. She had used the cold logic of computational modeling as an accent, a costume, a lie to describe the chaos of the human heart. She had proven her worth.

Fairweather's words echoed in her mind. *'Quite simply, you are to be Mr. Crestwell's muse.'*

She had thought it was a romantic, metaphorical term. A piece of corporate flattery. She realized now, with a chilling clarity, that it was a literal job description. She was a tool, a specialized key, designed to unlock the broken parts of his genius.

And she had just lied to him more deeply and more intimately than ever before. The guilt was a cold, hard stone in her stomach.

Chapter 24: The Human Variable

Some nights later, she woke to a sound that didn't belong in the engineered silence of Argentis.

It wasn't loud. Not an alarm or a shout. It was a raw, broken noise from down the hall. The sound of someone being torn apart from the inside.

Damian.

Sloane was out of bed before she'd fully processed it, her body moving on a primal, protective instinct. The silk of her pajamas was cool against her skin. The marble floor was a shock of cold beneath her bare feet.

His bedroom door was ajar, a sliver of darkness in the dimly lit corridor. She hesitated, her hand hovering over the wood. This was a line. A space she had no right to enter. A private grief she was paid to soothe, not witness.

The sound came again, a guttural, desperate cry choked off before it could become a full scream.

She pushed the door open.

The room was vast and dark, the moonlight through the great glass wall painting everything in shades of silver and gray. Damian was a storm in the center of the massive bed, thrashing against sheets that had twisted around him like chains. His face was a mask of anguish, his mouth open, the sound coming from him not quite human.

"Damian." She crossed the room, her voice a low, steady thing in the chaos. She touched his shoulder. "Damian, wake up."

He came awake violently. His hand shot out, clamping around her wrist with a strength that made her gasp. His eyes were wild, unfocused, staring right through her. He was seeing another ghost.

"It's okay," she said, keeping her voice calm, her body still. She didn't fight his grip. "You're safe. You're home. It was just a dream."

He blinked. Once. Twice. The madness in his eyes receded, replaced by the slow, dawning horror of recognition. And then, something worse.

Shame.

"Livia." His voice was a hoarse rasp. He released her wrist as if her skin had burned him, pulling back, putting distance between them. "I'm sorry. I didn't mean to wake you."

She should have left then. Murmured something soothing and distant. Retreated to her own room and her own role. That's what the actress would do.

But the raw vulnerability on his face—the grief that lived so close to his surface he couldn't hide it even in sleep—made her stay.

"You were dreaming about her," Sloane said. It was not a question.

His jaw tightened. He looked away, toward the window where the mountains were black, jagged teeth against a starless sky. "Every night," he said finally, his voice hollow. "The same dream. We were on the yacht. The *Ariadne*. I'm trying to reach her, but I can't. She's calling my name and I just... I stand there. Paralyzed. Watching her drown all over again."

Sloane's throat tightened. This wasn't in Katarina's dossier. This wasn't in the videos. This was a man being destroyed by guilt.

"It wasn't your fault," she whispered.

"Wasn't it?" He looked at her, and his eyes were full of a pain so raw it was almost unbearable to witness. "I was so focused on my work. On Panopticon. On changing the world. And I lost the only person who mattered."

He was quiet for a long time, lost in the memory. Then he started talking, the words pouring out of him in a low, confessional rush. He told her about meeting Livia at a quantum computing symposium at Cambridge, about how she was the only one who understood even a fraction of his work. He told her about their wedding, the wildflowers, the vows she'd cried through. He told her about the fights, the slow drift apart as the machine he was building consumed him.

"I built the cage we both lived in," he whispered, his voice breaking. "I just didn't realize the door only opened from the outside until she was gone."

She was supposed to comfort him as Livia. To say the right words. But the training had covered social grace and public personas, not how to reach a man drowning in a darkness this deep.

So she did something else.

She sat on the edge of his bed and, after a moment's hesitation, took his hand. It was cold. Trembling.

"You're not in the cage anymore," she said quietly. "Neither of us are."

It was the wrong thing to say. A mistake. A crack in the performance. Livia would never have acknowledged the cage at all.

But Damian's hand tightened on hers. His fingers laced through hers, a desperate, anchoring grip. And for just a moment, in the quiet dark, he looked at her not as a ghost, but as a person. "Thank you," he whispered.

He didn't let go of her hand. The plea in his eyes was unspoken. *Don't leave me alone in the dark.* Sloane didn't know what to say. So she did the only thing she could think of.

She lay down beside him, on top of the covers, and wrapped her arms around him, letting him hold her like she was the answer to a question he'd been asking for nine months.

"I'm here," she whispered into the darkness. "Right now. I'm here."

He held her tighter, his face buried in her hair, his body shaking with silent tears. They lay like that until dawn, until his breathing evened out and sleep finally claimed him.

Sloane stayed awake, staring at the ceiling, feeling the weight of him in her arms, feeling the terrible, crushing guilt of knowing that every moment of comfort she gave him was built on a lie.

She was falling in love with him.

The thought was a quiet, catastrophic detonation in her mind. Not with the idea of him. Not with the performance. But with the actual man. The brilliant, broken, desperately hopeful man who still believed people were fundamentally good.

And that made everything so much worse.

Chapter 25: The Tell

Late October brought the mist. It rose from the lake in thick, suffocating coils, swallowing the lower valley and turning the view from Sloane's window into a wall of shifting gray.

It was a fitting backdrop for the silent war being waged inside Argentis.

Sloane was fighting on three fronts. There was Nico, the silent sentinel whose lethal competence she had grown to respect, even as his watchful eyes kept her a prisoner. There was Damian, whose grief was becoming a dangerous gravity, pulling her into a shared intimacy she hadn't bargained for. And there was Katarina, the relentless architect of the simulation.

After another long day, exhausted and emotionally raw, Sloane couldn't sleep. The daily victories over Katarina felt hollow. She was perfecting the role, but she still didn't know who had cast her. The "Patron" from Livia's journal remained a ghost.

She opened her tablet, deciding to hunt in the video archives not for homework, but for a weakness—a crack in the perfect facade of Livia Crestwell. A tell. Something real.

She had watched hundreds of hours of footage. Galas. Dinners. Quiet mornings. Nothing.

And then she found it. A small video, innocuously labeled Argentis, Library. December 22, 2024. Six days before Livia's death.

It was a quiet, domestic scene. Damian in his leather armchair, reading. Livia at the mahogany desk, sketching. The camera was a fixed security angle from high in the corner of the room.

Livia was sketching furiously, her focus absolute. Then she froze, head cocked like a deer scenting a predator. She glanced at Damian; he remained lost in his own reading. Moving with urgent, fluid grace, Livia took the Moleskine she was writing in, crossed the room, and climbed the rolling ladder to the upper gallery. She reached into a high row of dark, leather-bound spines, her movements obscured by her own body.

Sloane slowed the footage to a frame-by-frame crawl, zooming in until the pixels blurred. The titles were mostly illegible, lost in shadow and age, but as Livia's hand lingered near a cluster of thick volumes, the light caught fragments of gold-leaf lettering.

Sloane squinted, parsing the partial words on the spines. On the left: "...WAR AND..." On the right: "...AND MARGARITA."

Margarita.

The word from the decoy journal entry she'd found in the desk. *"The old ways still work. Margarita."* Sloane had assumed it was a name. A person.

Now she realized it was a title.

She grabbed the tablet. Pulled up a browser. Typed: "Margarita book Bulgakov" — recalling the author Livia had mentioned in passing in the decoy diary.

The results loaded instantly. *The Master and Margarita* by Mikhail Bulgakov. A twentieth-century Russian masterpiece.

She scanned the summary, looking for the connection. Why this book? Why there?

Then her eyes landed on the novel's most famous quote, highlighted in bold:

"Manuscripts don't burn."

She stared at the screen.

Manuscripts don't burn.

Livia hadn't just signed her name; she had given coordinates. She had hidden her real journal—her manuscript, her testimony, her truth—inside a copy of a novel about art that survives destruction.

The signature in the decoy diary. The Bulgakov reference. This footage. All breadcrumbs leading to the same shelf in the Russian Literature section.

It was perfect.

Sloane returned to the video and continued the frame-by-frame advance.

A few frames later, Livia's hands were empty. She snatched a different notebook from a lower shelf—the sanitized decoy Sloane had found—and returned to her desk before Damian ever looked up.

"Everything all right, my love?" he asked.

"Perfect," Livia said, smiling her brilliant smile. "Just working out a new design for the guesthouse."

Sloane's heart hammered in her chest. She rewound the footage. Watched it again. The furtive glance. The quick, practiced movement. The switch.

It was a dead drop. A secret hiding place. Right inside the house.

The library. She had to get into the library, alone.

But how to do that in a house where privacy was the rarest commodity?

She checked the timestamp on the video: 20:15. The time of the evening shift change.

She remembered the rhythm of the house. The way the staff moved between the wings after dinner service. The vacuum cleaners in the main hall creating a wall of sound. The twenty-minute window where the eyes of Argentis blinked.

The only blind spot in the schedule.

She had the *Where*. She had the *When*.

Now she just needed the nerve.

Chapter 26: A Secret Admirer

The next morning, however, nerve was not enough.

Sloane's mind was a battlefield. She had her target—the hidden journal in the library—but she also had her obstacle: Nico, the impassable sentinel. The frustration from her failed probe on the morning walk was a low, simmering fire. She knew a direct approach was useless. She had to be clever. She had to be patient. She had to wait for the perfect opening.

She was in the middle of a grueling session with Katarina, practicing the subtle, aristocratic art of the dismissive glance in a full-length mirror, when her perfect opening was ripped away from her.

A soft chime sounded at the door. A housekeeper entered, carrying a small, exquisitely wrapped velvet box on a silver tray. It was the color of a midnight sky.

"A delivery for you, Mrs. Crestwell," the housekeeper murmured. "As usual it's been scanned for anything dangerous and cleared by the security."

Katarina's eyes narrowed. "From whom?"

"There was no name, ma'am," the housekeeper replied. "The courier said it was from a secret admirer."

Katarina dismissed the housekeeper with a curt nod. She did not leave. She stood there, her hands clasped behind her back, her posture a rigid column of judgment. She was here to watch. To gauge Sloane's reaction. To report back. Sloane was sure of it.

Sloane's heart began a slow, heavy drumbeat. This was not a test from Katarina. This was something else. She knew, with a certainty that was primal, who this was from. The investor. The shark with the kind eyes. This was his move. A probe. An opening salvo in a war she hadn't realized had already begun.

Sloane had a choice: show him the wound, or pretend the blade had missed entirely. The survivor in her, the actress, knew there was only one way to play it.

She walked over to the table, her movements a study in Livia's languid, unbothered grace. "One of Livia's secret admirers, no doubt," she said, her voice light, amused. "They are persistent, aren't they?"

She picked up the box. It was heavy. She lifted the lid.

Inside, nestled on a bed of black silk, were two objects.

On one side, a single, perfect, taxidermied monarch butterfly, pinned under a small, domed piece of glass.

On the other, a small, exquisitely detailed silver locket.

Her mother's locket. *How?! Did Katarina have anything to do with it?*

The sight was a one-two punch to the gut, a physical, breathless blow that seemed to suck all the air from the room. The butterfly, the symbol of her origin wound. And the locket, the last, sacred piece of her mother she had sold for a dream that had turned to ash.

The rage and the grief were a hot, suffocating wave. It was a violation so profound, so intimate, it was a defilement of her very soul. He had not just discovered her secrets. He had curated them. Packaged them. And sent them to her as a gift. He was showing her that there was no corner of her past, no matter how deeply buried, that he could not excavate and own.

Her gaze drifted from the silver locket in her hand to the fresh bouquet of Casablanca lilies on the vanity. They were replaced every three days, always pristine, always blooming. The "coincidence" she'd clung to on her first day—the desperate idea that they were just a generic staple of wealth—shriveled and died.

It wasn't a decorator's choice. It was a data point. The shadowy patron hadn't just studied her filmography; he had excavated her childhood. He knew that for her, the cloying scent of Casablanca lilies was the smell of her mother's funeral. The flowers weren't a gift. They were an invasion. A reminder that even in her most private moments, she was breathing his air.

She wanted to scream. To weep. To hurl the box against the wall.

But Katarina was watching. And through her, *he* was watching. Wasn't he?! Or was her mind playing tricks on her?

Sloane took a deep, steadying, actress's breath. She found the character. The amused, untouchable queen.

She held Katarina's gaze. She let the smile on her face widen, transforming it from amused to delighted. She picked up the locket, letting it dangle from her fingers.

"How lovely," she said, her voice a perfect, musical chime of pleasure. "It's a beautiful replica. Livia had one just like it. A family heirloom. It was lost, years ago, I hear. How thoughtful of someone to remember."

Sloane had done it. The words had come out of her mouth, a perfect, seamless improvisation born of a thousand hours in acting class and a lifetime of hiding her true feelings.

It was a performance exercise, her mind screamed, even as her heart was breaking. *Objective: Deflect. Obstacle: Katarina's watchful eyes. Action: Reframe the threat as a triviality.* She had reached into the character of Livia—the bored, untouchable aristocrat to whom a family heirloom was just another piece of jewelry—and pulled out a perfect line.

She had taken his intimate, surgical strike and re-framed it as a cheap, sentimental imitation. A thoughtful but insignificant gesture. She had given him nothing.

Katarina's eyes narrowed, a tiny, almost imperceptible motion. This was not the reaction she had been sent to observe. She had expected fear. Tears. A breakdown. She had not expected this cool, dismissive, and utterly convincing performance.

"Indeed," Katarina said, her voice clipped. "Very thoughtful."

"Please thank the sender for me, if you discover who it is," Sloane said, placing the locket on the table as if it were a piece of costume jewelry. She turned back to the mirror. "Now, where were we? The dismissive glance. I believe my left eyebrow needs to be a millimeter higher."

It was a dismissal. A clear power play. Katarina broke first. She gave a stiff, formal nod. "As you wish, Mrs. Crestwell."

The moment the door slid shut, Sloane's facade crumbled. She sank onto the chaise lounge, her body trembling. But she did not cry. The hunter had made the first direct attack. And she was still standing.

This surprise attack from the shadowy patron, however, changed everything. He had made abundantly clear that he knew everything about her, and that he could push her buttons anytime he wanted. And yet, she knew nothing about him. She had to go after the secret journal, assuming that it even existed. There was only one way to find out.

Her plan to patiently wait for the perfect opportunity to get into the library was no longer an option. The time for caution was over. He wasn't just a ghost in a journal; he was an active, omniscient presence. He was in her head. She had to get that weapon—the real journal—and she had to get it tonight, before he made his next, more direct move.

***

That night, Sloane did not wait for the house to fall asleep. She waited for it to be distracted.

The shadowy patron's psychological strike had changed the calculus. Patience was no longer a virtue; it was a liability. He was in her head, and the only way to fight back was to get inside Livia's. Tonight.

She waited until the chaotic heart of the evening shift change, a brief, twenty-minute window of noise and movement she had observed for weeks. Doors opening and closing. Staff moving between floors. The low hum of the vacuum cleaner in the main hall covering the sound of her footsteps.

The performance was simple: The Sick Headache. She stumbled from her sitting room, one hand pressed to her temple—a convincing, theatrical display for the corridor cameras. She made it to the bathroom, the door closing behind her, buying her the ten minutes of privacy she needed.

Then she slipped out the suite's secondary service door into the quiet, empty corridors of the west wing. She moved with a silent, purposeful speed, a ghost in her own house, her bare feet making no sound on the polished concrete.

The library door was a massive slab of dark, polished oak. It opened with a silent turn of the handle.

She stepped inside. The lights came on automatically, bathing the room in a soft, warm glow. The air smelled of old paper, leather, and wood polish. It was two stories high, lined from floor to ceiling with thousands of books—a cathedral of knowledge.

Her heart pounded, a frantic drum in the reverent quiet. She forced herself to focus.

Objective: Retrieval. Obstacle: The Eye.

She'd studied the security footage enough to know where the camera was mounted: high upper corner, left of the fireplace. A fixed wide-angle lens. It saw everything, but it lacked depth perception.

She didn't just turn her back to it; she blocked it. She moved to the rolling ladder, positioning her body so that the flare of her silk dressing gown created a curtain between the lens and the shelf. To the camera, she was just a woman browsing for a book. To the shelf, she was a thief.

She climbed. Her bare feet were cold on the brass rungs. She reached the upper gallery. Russian literature. Dostoevsky. Tolstoy. Chekhov.

Her hand stopped. Bulgakov. *The Master and Margarita*.

Her breath caught. This was it.

She pulled the heavy, leather-bound volume from the shelf. She kept it close to her chest, shielded. She reached into the dark, rectangular void it had left behind, her fingers searching the wood.

Nothing.

Panic, cold and sharp, pricked at her. Had she been wrong? Had Katarina found it?

She forced herself to stay calm. Don't break character. She pulled out the next book. *War and Peace*. Reached in. Nothing.

Time was bleeding away. The vacuum cleaner in the hall would stop soon.

She went back to the Bulgakov. She held it in her hands. And then she felt it.

The balance was wrong. The center of gravity was off.

It wasn't a book. It was a prop.

She positioned herself so the volume was shielded by her torso, visible to the camera only as a reader opening a cover. She flipped it open.

The inside was hollow.

Cut out with surgical precision, a perfect, rectangular cavity carved into the pages themselves. A classic dead drop.

Nestled inside, where the story of the devil visiting Moscow should have been, was a thick, black Moleskine journal.

Her hand trembled as she lifted it out. It felt heavy. Dense. It felt like a bomb.

This was the moment. The Transfer.

Still keeping her back to the camera, she let the journal slide from the hollow book directly into the deep, hidden pocket of her dressing gown. It was a sleight-of-hand move she'd learned for a role as a pickpocket seven years ago. Fluid. Invisible.

Snap the book shut. Smooth the silk. Seamless.

She slid the hollowed-out volume back into its original place on the shelf, closing the gap like a wound healing over. It had to look untouched. Perfect.

She descended the ladder, her posture relaxed. She selected a random book from a nearby shelf—Turgenev—and held it casually against her chest as she crossed back toward the door. Just a woman who couldn't sleep, finding something to read. A perfect performance for an audience of one glass eye.

No one saw her. She made it back to her suite just as her window was closing, the sound of the distant vacuum cleaner clicking off.

She locked the door. Leaned against it, the thick journal a block of ice against her skin, its weight a promise and a threat.

She had done it. She had the weapon.

Now, she had to see if it was loaded.

Chapter 27: The War Journal

Her breath came in short, shallow gasps, loud in the silence of the room. She moved to the corner furthest from the vents and the windows, sliding down the wall until she hit the floor.

The Moleskine notebook was a thick, black hole in the immaculate, cream-colored world of her suite. It felt dense, heavy, charged with the weight of a dead woman's secrets.

Her hands were trembling as she opened the journal. The paper was thin, the pages filled with a cramped, frantic, almost illegible scrawl. This was not the beautiful, performative script of the decoy journal. This was the handwriting of a woman who was running out of time. This was Livia's real voice.

The first few entries were a jumble of technical jargon, equations, and data streams. Livia, the cryptographer, was working on a problem. Sloane couldn't understand the specifics, but she understood the tone. The mounting sense of dread.

She flipped back, searching for the beginning of the rot, and found an entry from five years earlier. The handwriting was different here. Still Livia's, but calmer. Colder. The script of an analyst, not a victim.

I found something today. In the estate archives—boxes of old architectural plans from when Argentis was first built. The original owner, a paranoid banker named Müller, constructed a full Cold War-era fallout shelter in 1968. It's marked on the blueprints: beneath the west wing, accessed through what's now a sealed-off storage room in the wine cellar.

The shadowy patron has been busy installing his digital eyes everywhere. I doubt he's ever looked at these old paper plans.

Sloane stared at the page, a chill running through her. Livia hadn't just been paranoid; she had been preparing a bunker.

She flipped forward, skipping over months of equations and observation. Years passed in pages. The handwriting deteriorated, the calm, architectural notes replaced by a jagged, frantic scrawl. The entries jumped forward in time, painting a picture of a slow-motion catastrophe.

Then, years later, the tone shifted completely.

The data outflow is too large. Not a leak. A river. He's pulling terabytes of raw, unanalyzed data from the Core every day. D says it's for market modeling. But the volume... it's too much for that. What is he really building?

Pages later, the suspicion hardened into certainty.

My husband is a genius, but he is a trusting genius. He built a beautiful, open-handed machine. And someone has slipped a knife into its heart. I followed the data trail. It leads not to a financial institution, but to a series of encrypted, untraceable servers. A private network. A shadow.

Panopticon. That's the project name. Found it in a hidden partition. It's not a market predictor. It's a surveillance engine. He's using Damian's predictive models to analyze human behavior, to find weaknesses, secrets, leverage points. It's a machine for blackmail. A global, automated system of control.

Sloane paused. There was a dog-eared page here, referenced back to the early days of their marriage. A confession of what Livia had done to protect the system before she even knew what it was.

Five years ago, when I first began optimizing the kernel, the patron came to me with a problem. He needed to train Damian's machine to predict corruption, but he couldn't do it without real data. And he couldn't feed it his own dirty history without Damian seeing it.

He ordered me to build a Black Box. A secure partition where he could upload "classified intel"—his lies, his bribes, his hits—to train the algorithm. He demanded it be encrypted so heavily that not even the system's architect could read the raw logs.

I did exactly what he asked. I built him the perfect safe. I created the schema to organize his sins. His Dark Ledger. And I locked it with a single, mathematical constant I engineered: the "Root Seed."

I sold it to Damian as "Pure Order"—a concept I knew would appeal to his need for elegance. I sold it to the patron as the ultimate lock. The patron didn't just accept it; he fell in love with it. He declared the Root Seed sacred, believing that changing it would invite chaos. And chaos is the one thing the patron cannot stand.

He thinks he is the only one with the key. He didn't realize I kept a copy.

Sloane's blood ran cold. The vague, paranoid fears had just been given a name. Panopticon. And Livia had built the kill switch into the foundation.

She read on, her breath held tight in her chest. The journal jumped forward again. Livia's entries became more frantic, more terrified. She had begun to compile a list of names, politicians and judges whose public records showed sudden, inexplicable shifts in their voting patterns or legal rulings, all coinciding with data being pulled on them by Panopticon.

Senator Hargrove. Voted against the clean energy bill she co-sponsored. Panopticon had accessed her private emails earlier that month. What did he find? The leash.

Justice Taylor. A surprise, 5-4 ruling on the telecom merger. He was the swing vote. Panopticon had accessed his sealed offshore banking records the week before. Another puppet.

It was a shadow government, a world run by invisible strings, all pulled by the same, unseen hand. The hand of the "patron."

Sloane felt a profound, chilling admiration for Livia. She had not been a passive victim. She had been a hunter, a spy in her own home, using her own formidable skills to map the monster's web.

Then she came to the final, terrifying entries from last year. The weeks before the end.

He knows. I don't know how, but he knows I've been in the system. The backdoors are sealed. I am locked out. And I think... I think I am locked in.

I confronted Damian tonight. I showed him the offshore accounts. I told him about the judges and senators who flipped. He looked at me like I was speaking a foreign language. Then he said: "You're under too much stress. You need rest." And he walked away.

I am married to a man who has perfected the art of not seeing. He can't see the monster standing right beside him because he is too in love with the beauty of his machine. I'm losing him. My marriage is on the brink.

Sloane set the journal down, her hands trembling. She'd thought she understood Damian's grief—the widower who'd lost his wife. But this was different. This was the guilt of a man who'd refused to listen. Who'd walked away from the woman trying to save his life because she was disturbing the peace of his beautiful prison.

D gave me a book today. Alan Turing biography. Said I'd "appreciate the mathematics." But I know him. He doesn't recommend books casually.

I read the first three chapters tonight. It's not about the math. It's about a man who believed his brilliance would protect him. Who thought the institution would value his contributions more than it feared his differences. Who trusted that doing good work mattered more than politics.

He was wrong.

I'm watching Damian with the patron. The way D's face lights up when the patron compliments his algorithms. The way he explains every detail, eagerly, like a student seeking approval. He doesn't see what I see.

The patron isn't D's true mentor. He is his handler.

Turing died at 41. Cyanide apple. "Suicide," they called it.

I will not let Damian become another beautiful mind broken by ugly men.

The next entry was different. Colder. More tactical. A contingency plan.

I have to assume all my communications are compromised. But there is one last, old door. A ghost channel. The circle of trust is VERY small.

I've opened Port 8080 on the weather station's external gateway. To the system, it looks like legacy noise. To us, it's a secure drop.

Route connection to: tempest.argentis.net

Handshake Protocol: The name of the woman who made the deal with the devil. The one who brought you here.

If you are reading this, and you need an ally within Argentis, use this channel. Trust whoever answers.

Sloane's breath hitched. A ghost channel? This was a message from a smart, desperate fighter. A lifeline, hidden within the pages of a dead woman's confession. Livia had just handed her a key. And a puzzle.

Sloane filed the information away, a live wire of hope and terror in the back of her mind, and read on.

I could leak what I have now. The source code. The anomalies. But it's not enough. The patron owns the courts; he owns the news cycles. If I strike and miss, he spins the story, patches the system, and buries the truth along with my body. I only get one shot at a god. It has to be a kill shot.

But the walls are closing in. The patron suspects. If he strikes before I'm ready, the Key cannot be found here. I have to get it off the board. I have to get it out of Argentis.

I have a plan. A vault. A new identity. A final failsafe. I pray to a god I don't believe in that I have enough time.

The final entry was dated December 20th, 2024. A week before they were due to fly to Naples. The handwriting was a barely legible scrawl.

He knows that I'm close. Last night, he "gifted" us a post-Christmas yacht trip out of Naples. A "second honeymoon" for Damian and me. It was not a gift. It was a summons.

Damian presented it to me as a plea, a desperate, heartfelt attempt to save our marriage. He has no idea he's the one leading me into the trap. If I refuse to go, I confirm all of his partner's suspicions and prove to Damian that I am the "paranoid" one. I lose him completely. If I go, I walk into the shadowy patron's territory. But it is one last chance to make Damian see the truth, away from the walls of Argentis.

I have to take the gamble. I believe I can survive this. I have to believe it.

If you are reading this, you know how the story ended.

His name is Roman Lazar.

***

The name on the page was a physical blow. A confirmation so absolute, so final, that it seemed to suck all the air from the room.

Roman Lazar.

Sloane said the name aloud, a harsh, guttural whisper in the silent, luxurious room. It felt like a curse.

The unnamed investor. The man with the kind eyes. The sender of the butterfly and the locket. The killer.

It was all real.

She closed the journal, her body trembling with a violent, silent storm of rage and a grief that was not her own. She was no longer just an actress in a dead woman's clothes. She was the inheritor of a dead woman's war.

Livia had not just left a confession. She had left a battle plan. The vault. A final failsafe.

And she had left the name of the enemy.

Sloane stood up, the thick journal clutched in her hand like a weapon. The fear was still there, a cold, coiling serpent in her gut. But now it had a target. A name.

She walked over to her secure tablet, the one Katarina used for her drills, and opened the gala dossier. She navigated to the investor section and scanned the names, skipping the figureheads at the top until her eyes locked on the fifth name on the list.

Roman Lazar.

She tapped his profile. The dossier entry was sparse, almost insultingly so. *Primary Investor, Crystal Vision SARL. Chairman, The Lazarus Group. Philanthropist.* A few links to charity websites. Nothing more. It was the biography of a ghost.

And where a photograph should have been, there was only a black, featureless silhouette. A standard placeholder icon for a file that was either missing or encrypted.

Sloane stared at the black shape, a man so powerful he didn't even need a face. He was a void. A shadow. The man with the kind, calm, gray eyes that Livia had described existed only in memory and in the pages of this journal. To the rest of the world, he was nothing but a name and a black hole where a person should be.

The lack of a picture was more terrifying than any photograph could have been. It was a statement of absolute control. He didn't just hide in the shadows; he *was* the shadow.

"You don't want to show yourself to me... yet," she whispered to the black silhouette on the screen, her voice a low, venomous promise. "But know this–I'm coming for you."

Chapter 28: The Ghost Channel

The name on the page was a fire in her mind. Roman Lazar.

Sloane stood in the vast, silent suite, the thick journal clutched in her hand like a weapon, her knuckles white around its leather cover. Her heart was a war drum, each beat echoing in her ears with a single, thunderous word: gotcha, gotcha, gotcha.

The elation was a physical thing—a wild, electric surge that made her hands tremble, made her want to laugh or scream or both. She had done it. She had found the ghost. The unnamed investor, the man with the kind eyes and the hundred-million-dollar smile, the architect of Livia's murder—he had a name.

Which meant he could be exposed. Investigated. Stopped.

The feeling lasted for approximately ninety seconds.

Then the cold, hard reality of her situation crashed down on her like a collapsing building, crushing the breath from her lungs. The name was useless. Worse than useless. It was a loaded gun in a locked room. As long as it was trapped in this cage with her, as long as it existed only in her mind and in the pages of a dead woman's journal, it was nothing. Knowing his name didn't give her power. It just showed her how powerless she was.

Roman Lazar wasn't some anonymous monster she could fight in the abstract. He was real. Specific. A man with resources and reach and the kind of power that made governments nervous. A man who'd murdered Livia Crestwell and made it look like an accident. A man who owned this house, owned Damian, owned every inch of surveillance around her.

Knowing his name just meant she knew the exact shape of the cage she was in.

And she would remain his prisoner.

Her first instinct was immediate, visceral: call Manny. She turned toward the fur closet where she'd hidden the burner phone he'd given her, already mentally rehearsing the conversation. *I have his name. Roman Lazar. Call your hacker. I need to know who this man is. Everything. Please, Manny.*

She was three steps toward the closet when a chilling thought froze her in place, her bare feet silent on the plush carpet.

She looked at the ceiling. At the smoke detector that blinked with a rhythm that wasn't quite random. At the motion sensor by the door. At the sleek, glass walls that could vibrate with the sound of a voice.

Manny's voice echoed in her memory, urgent and terrified: *Only use it outside. Away from their eyes.*

But was outside far enough?

She'd called Manny four times since that first night. Each call shorter than the last. Each one heavier with dread. The last time—three nights ago in the garden—she'd heard something that made her blood freeze: a faint electronic whine in the background, growing louder, then cutting out abruptly. Manny had heard it too.

"Hear that? Could be a sweep," he'd whispered. "Hang up. Now."

She'd killed the connection, her hands shaking. Since then, the burner had stayed buried in the closet, a lifeline she was too terrified to use.

Livia's journal confirmed what Manny had suspected: Roman's eyes were everywhere. If she walked out to the garden now, in the dead of night, clutching a burner, would the sensors pick it up? Roman built surveillance systems for nations. He wouldn't just use cameras. He would monitor the airwaves. Radio frequencies. Electronic signatures.

If she dialed out now, and Roman was listening, she wouldn't just be exposing herself; she'd be painting a target on Manny's back.

She backed away from the closet. The risk was too great. One mistake, one miscalculation, and she'd be dead before Manny even picked up the phone.

She needed an ally. But approaching Nico directly was impossible. He was never alone—always shadowed by other security personnel, always within sight of cameras, always performing the role of loyal head of security. Any private conversation would be noticed, recorded, analyzed. And she didn't know if he was ally or enemy. If she approached him and he was Roman's man, she'd be dead by morning.

She needed a way to reach him—or whoever Livia had trusted—without Roman knowing. A way to test allegiances before revealing herself.

Sloane turned slowly, her gaze sweeping across her suite—the elegant furniture, the wall of glass overlooking the black mirror of the lake, the recessed lighting that was soft and flattering and utterly without shadows. Beautiful. Sterile. Perfect. A velvet-lined coffin.

Her eyes fell on the secure tablet sitting innocuously on the antique writing desk—the device Roman himself had given her, encrypted and locked down, supposedly safe. Supposedly hers. But she knew better now. Nothing in this house was truly private. Roman had built Panopticon. He could see through any wall, decrypt any message, trace any connection.

Unless...

Livia's words from the decoy journal flashed through her mind—sudden and sharp.

When all the modern doors are locked, remember: the old ways still work.

An idea sparked, desperate and dangerous. Roman's surveillance was a vast, modern fortress—military-grade encryption and AI-powered monitoring. He was obsessed with the cutting edge.

But maybe, just maybe, there was an old door he'd forgotten to lock. A legacy system buried so deep in the house's digital archaeology that it predated his paranoia.

She grabbed the tablet and settled onto the floor, her back against the wall—the furthest point from the window, from the door, from any obvious camera sightlines. An old habit from her childhood, when small and hidden had meant safe. Her fingers flew across the screen, diving past the sanitized user interface into the system's guts.

The estate's network architecture was a palimpsest—layers upon layers of upgrades and patches and security protocols built over a decade. The top layers were fortress-grade, impenetrable. But underneath, buried like archaeological strata, she found older systems. Legacy protocols. Forgotten doors.

And there, hidden in a subdirectory that hadn't been accessed in years, she found it: an old, text-based chat program. Some ancient admin tool from before the house had been transformed into a digital panopticon. The interface was crude, almost laughably primitive—green text on a black screen, like something from the 1980s. But it was there. Dormant. Waiting.

A ghost channel. The one that Livia had mentioned in her journal, with a built-in loyalty test:

'If you are reading this, and you need an ally within Argentis, use this channel. Trust whoever answers.'

Chapter 29: Down the Rabbit Hole

Sloane leaned back into her chair and stared at the screen.

A tantalizing discovery. A way around the ubiquitous, suffocating surveillance. But was this channel safe?

She pulled up the estate's security protocols. Something she'd learned on the set of Dark Signal—that spy thriller where she'd played a CIA analyst hunting a mole. The technical advisor, Ty Jennings, former NSA, had spent two weeks teaching her how real surveillance worked. "Modern security is layered," he'd said. "They don't just watch video. They monitor every electronic signal. Every device talking to another device leaves a signature."

She scrolled through the monitoring systems. Her chest tightened.

Radio frequency scanning. Active. Covering everything—cell phones, Wi-Fi, Bluetooth, even older wireless bands. The house wasn't just watching through cameras.

It was listening for any electronic whisper.

Her hands went cold. The Ghost Channel was old, buried, forgotten. But the moment she used it, the moment any data moved through it, would the house detect the signal? Would Roman see a ghost waking up in his system?

She didn't know. And not knowing might get her killed.

But staying silent definitely would.

Sloane's breath caught in her throat. Her hands trembled as she opened Livia's journal again, flipping to the page she'd memorized:

The password is the name of the woman who made the deal with the devil. The one who brought you here.

This cryptic entry had made no sense. Until now.

The woman who made a deal with the devil. *Margarita.* It had to be. A chill ran down her spine. Livia wasn't just leaving clues; she was testing the person who found them.

Sloane's fingers hovered over the tablet's bluetooth keyboard. This was a gamble. If she was wrong, if this channel was monitored, if Roman had left this door unlocked as a trap, she was about to walk straight into it.

But she was out of options.

She typed, her fingers shaking:

> Margarita?

She hit send and waited, her heart a frantic metronome, counting the seconds. One. Two. Three. The screen remained dark, empty, mocking her with silence.

Five seconds. Ten.

Nothing.

Despair began to creep in, cold and suffocating. She'd been wrong. The channel was dead, or monitored, or—

The screen flickered.

Green text materialized, letter by letter, like a ghost slowly taking form.

< The Master is waiting.

Sloane's breath escaped in a rush. Someone was on the other end. Someone who knew the password and had passed Livia's loyalty test.

But who? And could she trust them?

Her fingers flew across the keyboard.

> I need help. I have information.

A pause. Then:

< Identify yourself.

Sloane froze. This was the test. Revealing her name felt like stepping onto a landmine, but silence was worse. Anyone else on this channel would be a legacy user—Livia's people. They would have their own codes, their own history. She was the only anomaly in the equation.

She typed, exhaling ever so slowly.

> I'm the new variable. Your turn. Tell me something only you and I know.

The cursor blinked. Once. Twice. Then, the green text scrolled.

< Three push-ups. The fourth one didn't count. Your form was terrible.

A short, sharp chuckle escaped Sloane's lips. It was a dark, jagged sound in the silent room, but it felt real. It was him. The wall. The sentinel.

> Nico?

< Yes. Eyes and ears everywhere. Glad you found the Ghost Channel.

Relief warred with terror. It was him. But whose side was he on?

> Are you his?

The question hung on the screen, stark and dangerous. *His*. She didn't need to say the name.

The response came slowly, each word appearing with deliberate weight.

< No. I was hers. That is why I have access. I failed her. I won't fail you.

Something in Sloane's chest loosened. It could still be a lie. A trap. But he had passed Livia's loyalty test, and he had passed hers.

She made her choice.

> I have his name. The patron. The one who killed her.

Her finger hovered over the keyboard for one last heartbeat. Once she sent this, there was no taking it back.

> Roman Lazar.

The pause on the other end was so long she thought the connection had died. Then:

< Madre de Dios.

Spanish. A crack in his professional armor, shock bleeding through the digital stream. It was him. And he hadn't known.

< You are certain?

> Yes. Her last entry. The day before her trip to Naples. She knew he was going to kill her.

> I need to get this info to my contact in LA. He can build a case.

> I have a burner phone. I can call from the gardens. I did it before.

The response came back at lightning speed.

< DON'T. Not anymore.

> Why?!

< The house is running a constant RF sweep. He's got Damian 'eating his own dog food.' Panopticon is watching the house.

< Every 60 seconds, the system sweeps for unauthorized signals. It flags, geolocates, and analyzes threat patterns. The estate is a live proof of concept for the weapon they are selling at the gala.

< You got lucky before. They've been testing off and on for a week. The full sweep wasn't live yet. As of yesterday, it's active. Using that phone on the property isn't a flare gun, Sloane. It's feeding the monster.

Sloane's stomach dropped. The electronic hiss she had heard during her last call to Manny. It had been an uncomfortably close call.

> Then I'll leave the property. A walk into town.

< You think they'll let you walk to town? Alone? You're Livia Crestwell. You don't take unescorted walks. Deviating from pattern triggers alerts. We need a reason he'll accept. A performance.

A performance. Sloane felt a grim smile touch her lips. Of course. She was an actress. This was just another role.

But she needed to know one last thing.

> If you aren't with him, why are you still here?

The cursor blinked. She needed to understand his stake. What kept a man like Nico Sorrento in a cage he held the keys to?

The reply came haltingly.

< He has leverage.

< My daughter.

< That is all I can say on this line.

< If I become a problem... he has made it clear what happens.

< I am honoring my contract to protect you. But I am also protecting her. She doesn't even know if I'm alive.

< We are both prisoners here.

The confession hit her like a physical blow. A daughter. A teenage girl, used as a leash. The cruelty was breathtaking, the manipulation so perfect it was almost elegant. Roman Lazar didn't just control people. He found the one thing they loved most and held it hostage.

Sloane's fingers trembled.

> I'm sorry.

> We'll get you both out. I promise.

< Don't make promises you can't keep.

He was right. They had to work together.

> Then help me keep this one. Help me destroy him.

Another long pause. Then:

< Okay.

< Tell me what you need.

> A window. An hour or two outside these walls. Somewhere without cameras.

The cursor blinked for a long beat. Nico was calculating.

< I can't authorize that. Only Katarina can. Or Damian.

< You need to give them a reason to open the gate. Use Livia. A memory. A craving. Make it personal.

< I'll handle the logistics. But you have to sell the lie.

> I can do that.

< Good. Now burn this log. Delete the cache.

< And Sloane?

> Yes?

< Be careful. You're playing with fire now.

> I know.

< No. You don't. Not yet.

The connection ended. The screen went dark, the green text fading like a ghost dissolving back into shadow.

Sloane deleted the digital trail as instructed, then swiped back to the dossier Katarina had loaded.

If she was going to get off this mountain, she needed to know her lines.

Chapter 30: The Long Game

Moscow. Winter. 1978.

Katarina had been sixteen years old the night the black Zil limousine pulled up to their apartment building on Komsomolsky Prospekt. Snow falling. Thick and silent. Burying the world.

She'd been doing homework at the kitchen table. Trigonometry. Her father sitting in his chair by the window, reading a report from the Ministry of Foreign Affairs, his wire-rimmed glasses perched on his nose.

The knock came at 10:47 PM.

Not a polite knock. The kind of knock that meant you opened the door immediately or they opened it for you.

Two men in long coats. KGB. You could always tell. The way they stood. The way they didn't bother with pleasantries.

"Andrei Nikolayevich Zimina. You will come with us."

Her father had set down his report. Folded it carefully. Removed his glasses. Looked at Katarina and her mother with an expression she would spend the rest of her life trying to forget.

I'm sorry.

They took him for "re-education." A mistake, they'd said. A misunderstanding. He'd questioned a piece of intelligence in a meeting. Suggested that perhaps the information was flawed. Shown a flicker of principle where only obedience was required.

They never saw him again.

Her mother—Mila Petrovna, a woman of iron wrapped in silk—had waited until the door closed. Until the footsteps faded down the stairwell. Until the Zil's engine growled away into the night.

Then she'd taken Katarina's face in her hands. Her eyes dry. Hard. Empty of tears because tears were a luxury they could no longer afford.

"You will smile," her mother had said, her voice a steel whisper. "You will excel. You will be better than them. You will join them. You will survive. Survival, Katarina, is learning to wear the mask so perfectly that you forget you have a face beneath it."

Katarina had learned the lesson well.

Komsomol. GRU. A career of masks within masks within masks. She'd worn them all. Had worn them so well that sometimes—most times—she didn't know which face was hers anymore.

Forty-seven years of survival since her father was taken.

And she was so, so tired.

***

4:18 AM. Argentis. The security control room.

Twenty-four screens. Twenty-four angles on the same beautiful cage.

Katarina sat at the console, her coffee long cold, watching the fortress sleep.

Screen 12 showed the hallway outside Damian Crestwell's suite. Empty. The door had been closed for five hours. Audio sensors registered the faint, disturbed rhythm of a man thrashing in his sleep. Dreaming. A genius who didn't know he was a puppet.

Screen 7 showed the main living area of Sloane Devereaux's suite. The lights were still on. Sloane was sitting on the floor in the far corner, her back against the wall, a tablet balanced on her knees.

Screen 19 showed the interior of Nico's quarters in the security annex. He was also awake, sitting at his desk, typing on a ruggedized laptop.

Katarina had watched the whole thing. The patterns of their insomnia. The synchronized typing. The covert, digital conversation happening right under the nose of the house AI.

Perfect. Clinical. A masterclass in tradecraft.

Katarina's screen flickered.

A small alert. Barely visible. Easy to miss if you weren't looking.

ANOMALY DETECTED: Legacy Protocol 7 (TextCom) - Active Connection.

Her blood went cold.

The Ghost Channel.

Livia's old backdoor. The one Katarina had helped her set up years ago during a girls' night when they'd both had too much wine and Livia had laughed and said, *What if we need to gossip without the boys listening?*

It should have been dead. Buried in obsolete code. Forgotten.

It wasn't.

Katarina pulled up the live data stream. Green text on black. Scrolling fast.

> *I have his name. Roman Lazar.*

< *Madre de Dios.*

> *I need to get this info to my contact in LA.*

< *Negative. I can't transmit. Roman just installed Level 5 RF Sweeps.*

The soldier. Nico. And the actress.

Forging an alliance in the digital dark.

An alliance against Roman.

Katarina's hand hovered over the keyboard.

Three keystrokes. That's all it would take.

Flag the anomaly. Send the logs to Roman. Activate the response protocol. The Ghost Channel would be shut down within minutes. The two conspirators would be dealt with by morning.

Problem solved.

Her duty was clear. She served Roman Lazar. She had served him for twelve years. Not because she believed in his vision—God, no—but because he held the one thing in the world she still loved.

Her grandson. Dima. Seven years old. Living with his mother in a small apartment in Zurich. Close enough for Katarina to visit twice a month. Close enough for Roman to reach if she ever became... problematic.

Roman had never said it explicitly. He didn't have to. The apartment was paid for by a shell company Roman controlled. The boy's school tuition came from a "scholarship fund" Roman had established. The medical bills when Dima had pneumonia last winter—covered by "insurance" that didn't quite exist.

Invisible chains.

The kind Katarina knew well.

Do your job. Be loyal. Keep your head down. And the boy stays safe.

So why wasn't she typing?

On Screen 7, Sloane looked up from the tablet. Her face was pale in the blue glow of the screen. She looked like Katarina had looked once. Young. Trapped. Trying to decide if she was brave enough to fight or smart enough to survive.

Katarina's father had fought.

He'd died for it.

Her mother had survived.

She'd died inside for it.

And Katarina? She'd spent forty-seven years telling herself that survival was enough. That wearing the mask was the price you paid for breathing. That some battles weren't worth fighting because the powerful always won.

But then why did her hands feel so heavy?

Why did the weight of forty-seven years feel like it was crushing her chest?

The Ghost Channel was still active. Nico and Sloane still typing. Still planning. Still believing—God help them—that they had a chance.

They didn't.

Roman was too smart. Too thorough. Too many steps ahead. Whatever they were planning would fail. And when it did, he would crush them. Slowly. Methodically. As a lesson.

Katarina could stop it now. Save them from themselves.

Or.

She could do nothing.

She could miss the alert. Overlook the anomaly. Let a "technical glitch" slide through. Create the smallest, most deniable gap in Roman's perfect surveillance.

It wouldn't save them. But it might buy them time.

And time... time was the only weapon the powerless ever had.

Her finger hovered over the delete key.

Dima.

Seven years old. Gap-toothed smile. Loved dinosaurs and soccer and his babushka's honey cakes. He called her every Sunday. Asked when she was coming to visit. Told her about his week in that breathless, excited way children had when the world still felt big and full of wonder.

If she did this—if she betrayed Roman—would the boy even understand why she'd stopped visiting? Would his mother tell him the truth? Or would he grow up thinking his grandmother had simply... abandoned him?

Like her father had abandoned her.

No. Not abandoned. Taken.

There was a difference.

Wasn't there?

Katarina closed her eyes.

Breathed.

Her mind flashed back to the security log from a few hours ago. Sloane in the library, high on the rolling ladder. She had angled her body to shield her hands from the lens. A clumsy attempt, but effective. Yet, the behavior was anomalous enough to warrant a deeper dive by the AI—a dive which would surely uncover the empty space behind the books where the journal used to be.

Then her thoughts jumped to the anomaly report from the RF calibration tests three days ago. A single, jagged spike of unencrypted cellular activity from the rose garden. Short. Trembling. A burner phone trying to find a signal in the noise. Roman would dismiss it as "atmospheric interference" during the system tuning. Katarina knew better. It was a lifeline.

If she did nothing, the system would eventually correlate these data points. The AI would connect the library visit to the signal spike to the current chat session.

She made her choice.

She typed three commands, her fingers moving with the muscle memory of a ghost.

purge_alert --id=ACTIVE --cascade

corrupt_archive /video/lib_cam_04 --timestamps<48:00:00 --simulate_codec_failure

rf_config --sensor_drift=random --log_as_calibration_artifact

Technical glitches. System maintenance. A simulated video compression error in the library footage; a "sensor drift" in the RF grid that masked the signal spike as routine calibration noise.

Nothing that would raise flags. Nothing that would point back to her. Just the entropy of a complex machine.

But enough.

Maybe.

She logged out. Stood. Her knees creaked. Sixty-three years old and feeling every single one of them.

On Screen 7, Sloane had put the tablet down. She stood up. Walked to the window. Her reflection ghostly in the glass.

She looked like someone who had just decided to fight.

Katarina smiled. Small. Sad. The smile of a woman who knew exactly how this story ended.

But for the first time in twelve years—maybe in forty-seven years—she didn't feel like a coward.

She felt like her father's daughter.

And if that was enough to get her killed?

Well.

At least she'd die with her own face on.

***

She left the control room. Walked through the silent hallways of Argentis. Past the cameras she knew were watching. Past the listening devices embedded in the walls.

Roman would find out eventually. He always did.

But not today.

Today, two desperate people in a cage had a Ghost Channel they thought was secret. Had a plan they thought might work. Had hope they thought might save them.

It wouldn't.

But Katarina had given them something Roman never expected anyone to give.

A chance.

However small.

However doomed.

She reached her quarters. Locked the door. Sat on the edge of her bed.

Pulled out her phone. Scrolled to Dima's contact photo. That gap-toothed smile. Those bright, trusting eyes.

I'm sorry, she thought. *If this goes wrong. If Roman finds out. If I can't visit anymore. I'm sorry.*

She set the phone down. Lay back on the bed. Closed her eyes.

And for the first time in forty-seven years, Katarina Zimina slept without her mask on.

Chapter 31: The Pattern

Two in the morning. A greasy spoon diner in Van Nuys that never closed. The air smelled of congealed eggs and burnt coffee. Manny slid into a cracked red vinyl booth, the table sticky beneath his elbows, his body aching with a lack of sleep.

He had gotten four more calls from Sloane. All short, tense, whispered—from what sounded like a windy garden in the middle of the Swiss night. The last one, three nights ago, had ended with that sound. A faint electronic whine in the background, then silence. He'd told her to hang up immediately, his heart in his throat.

She hadn't called since.

He stared at the black plastic on the table. He didn't know if she was safe, or if she was just being smart. He had to trust it was the latter.

The burner phone was working. The lifeline was holding. For now.

Across from him, Sarah Jensen took a long, slow drag from a generic cigarette, the cherry glowing in the dim, humming light. In the sanitized Los Angeles of 2025, lighting up indoors was a civic sin, but this was Sal's place. The laws of the state stopped at the door, replaced by the laws of the regulars. Especially after midnight. The waiter didn't object; he just silently slid a chipped bread plate onto the table to serve as an ashtray.

Sarah had been one of the best investigative journalists in the city, a shark with a byline that could topple senators. Then she got too close to a story about a corrupt real estate deal, the kind that built the city, and her career was incinerated. She was a creature of the night now, living in the digital shadows, trading in the kind of information that didn't make the front page anymore.

"You look like hell, Manny," she said, her voice a nicotine-rasped whisper.

"You're a vision, sweetheart," he shot back. He pushed a lukewarm coffee mug toward her."I'm here to offer you a deal."

Sarah laughed, a dry, humorless rasp. "I'm not for sale anymore, Manny. And you can't afford my rates anyway."

"This isn't about money," Manny said, leaning forward, his voice a low, serious growl. "It's about a story. A real one. The kind of story they burned you for, but a hundred times bigger. A private, multi-billion-dollar Swiss corporation, a reclusive genius, and an 'accident' that smells like murder. You help me figure this out, you help me protect my client, and when the dust settles... the exclusive is all yours."

Sarah went very still. He saw it in her eyes—the flicker of the old fire, the ghost of the shark she used to be. An exclusive. The one currency that still mattered to her. Yet, there was a shadow of hesitation in her eyes.

He paused, the usual cynical glint in his eye gone, replaced by something older and more weary. "And maybe," he added, his voice dropping, "it's about making amends. Atoning for a few sins. For both of us."

"I'm listening," she said, and for the first time, she looked like a journalist again.

Manny leaned in with a whisper. "The Lazarus Group. What can you tell me?"

She nodded slowly, exhaling a plume of smoke that curled and flattened against the low ceiling. "A back-room name. The kind that gets whispered after a deal goes bad, not before it's made. Why are you digging?"

"I'm looking for a pattern," Manny said, leaning forward. "A brilliant founder, a meteoric rise, a sudden retreat into seclusion. A beautiful wife who meets with a tragic, convenient accident."

A dark recognition shadowed Sarah's face. Her eyes, hard and knowing, narrowed. She took another drag from her cigarette, but this time she was thinking, her mind a steel trap sifting through a decade of dead-end stories and buried leads. "A story from about ten years ago," she said, her voice dropping. "A hostile takeover. A biotech firm called Helixis. The CEO was a guy named Oliver Harrow. A real fighter. A bulldog, like you. He refused to sell. Said the company's research was too important."

"So what happened?"

"A week after he refused the final offer from some anonymous investment group," Sarah continued, her voice flat, "his daughter, a college kid at UCLA, got into a hit-and-run on Sunset. Freak thing. Left her in a catatonic state. They moved her to a long-term care facility in New Mexico. The driver was never found."

Manny felt a chill that had nothing to do with the diner's rattling air conditioner. He thought of a yacht. A storm off the Amalfi Coast. A body recovered three weeks later.

"A month after the accident," Sarah said, "Harrow is found dead in his study. Gunshot to the head. The cops closed the case in twelve hours. Called it a suicide. Said he was distraught over his daughter."

"And the company?" Manny whispered.

"Two days after the funeral," Sarah finished, crushing her cigarette out in the overflowing ashtray, "Helixis was acquired for pennies on the dollar. By The Lazarus Group."

The pattern. A freak accident to create leverage. A convenient death to close the deal. This was the monster's playbook.

"Find the daughter, Manny," Sarah said, her eyes glinting in the dim light. "He didn't just run her over. He met with her first—tried to use her to pressure Harrow. She sat across a table from the devil. If she can still communicate, she's the only person who can put a face to the ghost."

***

He left the diner and drove. He didn't go back to his office. He didn't go home. He drove through the empty, sleeping streets of the city, the weight of what he had just learned a physical thing in his chest.

He ended up at the Hollywood Forever Cemetery. The gates were locked, but he knew a spot where the fence was low. He was seventy-two years old, a man with a bad tremor, climbing a cemetery fence at three in the morning. He was a goddamn cliché. He didn't care.

He stood in front of a small, simple grave marker, the grass around it still damp from the sprinklers.

SOPHIE GOLDMAN. BELOVED DAUGHTER. 1985-2005.

"I'm in over my head, Soph," he whispered to the stone, the gravelly, showman's voice gone, leaving only the raw, aching voice of a father. "This guy... he's a real monster. He breaks daughters to get to the fathers. And I let our girl walk right into his house."

The shame was a hot, familiar thing. He hadn't found the contract—he'd begged her to burn it. But he hadn't stopped her. He had failed to save her from the desperation that made her say yes. He had been so busy playing the Hollywood game, thinking about comebacks and leverage, he hadn't realized they were in a completely different one.

A game with real bodies.

He reached out, his hand trembling, and traced the letters of his daughter's name.

"I'm gonna find him," he promised the ghost of his child. "I'm gonna put a name to this devil. And I'm gonna give her the weapon she needs to win. Whatever it takes."

He straightened up, his back aching. "This time," he whispered, "I'm not gonna be too late."

He turned and walked away from the grave, his shoulders set, an aging bulldog with a broken heart, ready for the fight of his life. He had a pattern. He had a motive.

Now he needed to see the monster's face. And for that, he needed a different kind of ghost.

Chapter 32: The Heartbeat in the Room

October bled into November, stripping the trees bare and turning the lake from a shimmering blue to a hard, iron gray. The golden light of autumn was replaced by a persistent, drumming rain that walled the estate in sheets of water.

By the time the mornings grew cold enough for fires in the hearth, the house had settled into a fragile routine. Breakfast at seven, Damian's silent presence across the table, his grief a third guest neither acknowledged. Afternoons in the library. Evenings pretending to read while Damian worked, the blue glow of screens the only light under his door.

The routine meant stability. Deviation meant something was wrong.

She found him in his private laboratory at three in the morning, a place she had never been invited. It wasn't the pristine study. It was a chaotic sanctum of humming server racks, whiteboards covered in frantic, beautiful equations, and the cold, clean smell of ozone. He hadn't come to dinner. The routine was broken.

"Damian?" She stood in the doorway. "It's late."

He didn't look up from the screens. His fingers flew across a keyboard, lines of code appearing faster than she could track. "There's an error," he said, his voice tight, brittle. "In the core encryption protocol. A vulnerability I didn't see. If it's there, if I missed it, then everything—" He stopped, pressing the heels of his palms against his eyes. "Everything I built is compromised."

She understood enough to know this wasn't about code. This was about control. About his desperate need for perfect, predictable systems in a world that had taken everything from him. It was a panic attack, expressed in algorithms.

"Can you fix it?" she asked, stepping into the room.

"I don't know." His hands were shaking. "I can't see clearly anymore. Since... since she died, my mind doesn't work the way it used to. Everything is fractured."

Sloane crossed to him. Pulled up a heavy, steel-framed chair. Sat down next to him at the desk where he'd spent years building a digital god.

"Show me," she said.

He looked at her like she was insane. "You're not a cryptographer, are you?"

"No," she said, her voice calm and steady. "But I'm here. And you're spiraling. So show me the problem. Explain it to me like I'm a child. Sometimes just saying it out loud helps."

For a long moment, he just stared at her, his brilliant mind wrestling with the illogical proposal. Then, slowly, as if against his better judgment, he turned back to the screen.

"The vulnerability is here," he said, pointing to a section of code that looked like gibberish. "This function should create a one-way hash, but there's a theoretical attack vector if someone has access to quantum computing. It's a one-in-a-billion chance, but it's there. And if it's deployed as-is..."

He talked for twenty minutes. She understood maybe five percent of it. But she listened. She watched his hands move, sketching patterns in the air. She watched his focus shift from the terror of the problem to the pure, clean beauty of the math. His brilliant mind untangling the knot, thread by thread.

And she saw the exact moment it clicked.

His posture straightened. His hands stilled on the keyboard. A slow breath escaped his lips. "There," he breathed. "That's it. That's the solution."

He typed for another ten minutes, fingers flying, completely absorbed in his world of pure logic. When he finally leaned back, the frantic, hunted tension had drained from his shoulders. He was calm. Centered. The genius back in control of his universe.

"You fixed it?" Sloane asked.

"I fixed it." He turned to look at her, and there was something in his face she hadn't seen before. Not quite a smile. But close. Gratitude. "Thank you."

"I didn't do anything."

"You stayed," he said simply. "Livia used to..." He stopped. Looked away, a flicker of pain crossing his face. "She understood my code better than anyone, but the predictive math... that was a foreign language to her. She dealt in absolutes. I deal in chaos. But she'd sit with me anyway. Said sometimes a genius just needs another heartbeat in the room."

Sloane's chest tightened. She was doing it again. Stepping into spaces that weren't hers. Filling a role she had no right to fill. Becoming the ghost.

But the way he was looking at her—like she was an anchor in a storm—made it impossible to pull away.

"Any time," she said.

And a small, treacherous part of her meant it.

Chapter 33: The Stabilization Protocol

The name was a live wire in her blood. Roman Lazar.

It had been a week since she found it in the journal. Seven days of carrying a grenade with the pin pulled, unable to throw it.

Nico's warning about the RF sweeps had turned the burner phone into a paperweight. She couldn't call Manny. She couldn't transmit the target.

But she couldn't just sit in the silence, either.

If she couldn't send the intel yet, she would refine it. The name was a start, but Manny could use more than just a label on a monster. He could use a map of the damage.

She needed to understand not just who Roman Lazar was, but why he needed Damian stable now. Why the rush? Why pay a hundred million dollars to maintain a ghost?

She opened the tablet again, her fingers flying across the screen. Nico had given her access to the digital archives—the sanitized version of the estate's files, but still more than she'd had before. She began hunting, diving into folders marked "Corporate," "Investors," "Board Documents."

The estate's network was vast, labyrinthine. Most of it was locked behind layers of encryption and biometric gates. But she was learning its geography, its patterns. And patterns, she knew, always had weak points.

She found it buried three levels deep in a subfolder marked "Investor Correspondence"—a title so bland and bureaucratic it practically screamed *nothing interesting here, move along*.

An email. From Roman Lazar to Damian Crestwell. Dated six months ago.

May 15th. Five months after Livia's "accident."

Sloane's blood turned to ice as she read:

From: Roman LazarTo: Damian CrestwellSubject: Stabilization Protocol

Damian,

Your grief is unsustainable. The Q3 board meeting is in 90 days. Your presentation to our primary defense contractor is in 120. You cannot present Panopticon's capabilities while visibly unstable. The optics are catastrophic.

I'm activating a contingency. Trust me.

– R

She stared at the screen, her pulse thrumming in her ears.

Activating a contingency.

You don't draft a contingency *after* a disaster; you prepare it beforehand. Roman hadn't scrambled to find a lookalike in May because Damian was failing. He had the plan ready and waiting.

She wasn't a replacement found in a panic; she was a spare part ordered in advance.

***

Sloane read it once. Twice. Three times, the words rearranging themselves in her mind into a picture so dark, so calculated, it took her breath away.

Your presentation to our primary defense contractor.

Defense contractor.

Panopticon wasn't just corporate espionage. It wasn't just a tool for blackmailing senators and manipulating elections.

It was a weapon being sold to governments.

The implications crashed over her in waves. This wasn't about money—or rather, it wasn't *just* about money. This was about power on a geopolitical scale. Imagine giving a government—any government—the ability to surveil its entire population, to predict dissent before it happened, to identify threats and eliminate them with surgical precision.

It was the panopticon that Bentham and Foucault had theorized about, that Orwell had warned against, made real and perfected and packaged with a bow.

And Damian—brilliant, naive, grief-stricken Damian—was the public face of the sale. The genius inventor, the sympathetic widower, the respectable front for an instrument of totalitarian control.

The timeline snapped into focus with horrible clarity.

Livia had discovered what Panopticon really was. She'd started gathering evidence, preparing to blow the whistle. And Roman had killed her for it.

Why? The gala. The Consortium. The defense contract. The deal had to be worth billions—maybe trillions—to justify murdering his business partner's wife. To justify spending a hundred million dollars just to hire a ghost.

Her eyes dropped back to the email.

I'm activating a contingency.

Sloane felt sick. The contingency was her. She was the solution to Roman's problem—a puppet Livia who would smile and wave and legitimize the enterprise while Damian, kept docile by the illusion of his wife's return, presented the technology to defense contractors who would use it to enslave entire nations.

She had thought she understood the stakes. She had thought she was fighting for her freedom, for justice for Livia, maybe even for a hundred million dollars and a chance to reclaim her career.

She'd been thinking too small.

This wasn't just about her, or Livia, or even Damian. This was about millions of people who would live under the digital eye of Panopticon, their every move watched, their every thought predicted, their every act of defiance crushed before it could take root.

And the gala—the beautiful, elegant, star-studded gala just days away—wasn't a party. It was a product launch. A coming-out party for the surveillance state, with her as the guest of honor.

Sloane sat in the silent, dark room, the tablet's screen casting her face in a pale blue glow, and felt the weight of what she'd just learned settle onto her shoulders like a physical thing.

She took a screenshot of the email. Saved it to an encrypted folder. Then she deleted her browser history, cleared her cache, and powered down the tablet with shaking hands.

She had what Manny needed now. The name. The motive.

Now she just had to survive long enough to get it to him.

She stood, her legs unsteady, and walked to the wall of glass. Outside, the lake was a sheet of black glass under a moonless sky. The mountains were jagged silhouettes against the stars. It was beautiful and cold and utterly indifferent to the war being waged within these glass walls.

Somewhere out there—in a villa across the world, or in a bunker deep underground, or perhaps watching her right now from a screen in this very house—Roman Lazar was waiting.

Somewhere out there, a young girl was living her life, unaware that she was a hostage, that her father's love for her was the chain around his neck. Unaware that her father was even alive.

Somewhere in Los Angeles, Manny was waiting by his phone, terrified and helpless, praying she was still alive.

And here, in this cage of glass and lies, Sloane Devereaux—failed actress, blacklisted has-been, ghost in a dead woman's skin—was haunted by the kind-eyed man who'd given her the role of a lifetime.

But looking at the evidence in her hands, she finally understood the true nature of the part.

She wasn't the leading lady.

She was the bait.

Chapter 34: Becoming Livia

Early November brought frost to the windows each morning. Six weeks of training. Six weeks of bruises. Six weeks of becoming someone else.

Six AM. The gym. Nico circled her on the mat.

"You're dropping your left shoulder."

Nico's voice came from behind her, low and calm, the tone of a man who had done this a thousand times. Sloane adjusted her stance, bringing her shoulder up, her weight shifting to the balls of her feet.

"Better," he said. "Now move."

She lunged. He sidestepped. She pivoted, drove her elbow toward where his ribs should have been, but he was already gone, his hand catching her wrist and twisting just enough to let her know he could break it if he wanted to.

"Too slow," he said. "You're telegraphing. I can see what you're going to do three seconds before you do it."

"Maybe you're just good at reading people."

"Maybe you're just predictable."

She yanked her wrist free and stepped back, breathing hard. They'd been at this for forty minutes. Hand-to-hand combat drills in the estate's private gym, a gleaming space of mirrors and mats and the faint smell of sweat and leather.

Nico looked like he'd barely broken a sweat. He was dressed in a tight black t-shirt and gray tactical pants, his dark hair slightly mussed, his eyes sharp and assessing.

Sloane was in leggings and a sports bra, her skin slick with perspiration, her muscles burning.

"Again," he said.

"I need a break."

"You think Roman's going to give you a break if things go wrong at the gala?"

She glared at him. He stared back, expressionless.

"Again," he repeated.

She moved. This time she didn't telegraph. Didn't think. Just let her body react. Feint left, strike right, low kick to destabilize.

He blocked the strike but the kick connected. Not hard enough to hurt him, but enough to surprise him.

His eyebrows lifted. Almost a smile. "Better."

"High praise."

"Don't get cocky."

He moved before she could react. One moment he was three feet away, the next he was inside her guard, his arm around her waist, his other hand catching her throat—not squeezing, just holding, the threat implicit.

His face was inches from hers. She could feel his breath on her lips. Could feel the heat of his body, the controlled strength, the way he was holding back just enough to make this a lesson instead of an assault.

"If I wanted you dead," he said quietly, "you'd be dead."

"Good thing you don't want me dead."

"Good thing."

They stood like that for three seconds. Five. Long enough for her to notice the way his jaw tightened. The way his eyes flicked to her mouth and then away.

Long enough for her to realize she was breathing faster than the exercise warranted.

He released her. Stepped back. Turned away and walked to the water bottles lined up on the bench.

"That's enough for today," he said, his voice carefully neutral.

"We've only been at it an hour."

"And you're exhausted. Pushing harder just means you'll make mistakes. Rest. We'll do firearms tomorrow."

He handed her a water bottle. She took it, their fingers brushing for a moment.

"You're good at this," Sloane said. "Teaching, I mean."

Something crossed his face. Sadness, maybe. Or regret.

"My daughter." The words came out quiet. Careful. Like he hadn't meant to say them. "Had to teach her a few things. Before."

Before what? Before this job? Before Roman? Before whatever had separated them?

Sloane waited. Didn't push.

"I don't see her anymore," he said finally. His jaw tightened. "It's... complicated. Better for her if I stay away."

The way he said it—like it was killing him—made Sloane's chest tighten. She understood that kind of sacrifice. The choice to become someone else, to bury yourself completely, if it meant keeping the people you loved safe.

"I'm sorry," she said quietly.

Nico looked at her. His eyes were very dark. "So am I."

She wanted to say something. Wanted to ask if he'd felt it too. The moment. The heat. The dangerous gravity pulling them toward something neither of them could afford.

But he was already walking toward the door, his shoulders tight, his movements clipped.

"Nico," she said.

He stopped. Didn't turn around.

"Thank you," she said. "For this. For helping me."

"I'm doing this for Livia," he said, his voice flat. "Because she never got the chance to fight back."

He left before she could respond.

Sloane stood alone in the gym, her body aching, her mind racing, and realized she was in trouble.

Not the Roman Lazar kind of trouble.

A different kind.

The kind that made you do stupid things.

***

The next morning, she found Nico in the firing range.

Argentis had everything. A full gym. A heated indoor pool. A wine cellar that could stock a Michelin-starred restaurant. And, apparently, a private shooting range in the basement, soundproofed and climate-controlled, with targets set at various distances.

Nico was standing at the fifteen-meter line, a Glock 19 in his hands, methodically putting rounds through the center mass of a paper target. Each shot a neat, precise hole. No wasted movement.

Sloane stood in the doorway, watching. He knew she was there—she was certain of it—but he didn't acknowledge her. Just kept shooting until the magazine was empty.

He set the gun down. Pressed the button to bring the target forward. Examined it with the critical eye of someone who had been doing this for twenty years.

"Not bad," Sloane said.

"Not good either." He ripped the target down and clipped a fresh one in place. Sent it back to the fifteen-meter line. Then he turned to face her. "You ready?"

"For what?"

"To learn how to shoot."

She'd fired a gun before. Once. On a movie set, with blanks and a stunt coordinator hovering two feet away. It had been loud and uncomfortable and she'd been relieved when the scene was over.

This was different.

Nico handed her the Glock. It was heavier than she expected. Cold. Real.

"First rule," he said. "Treat every weapon as if it's loaded."

"Is it loaded?"

"Yes."

She almost dropped it. He caught her wrist, steadied her hand.

"Second rule," he said. "Never point it at anything you don't intend to destroy."

"Got it."

"Third rule." He moved behind her, his chest against her back, his hands guiding hers into position. "Shooting is about breath control. Stance. Sight alignment. You don't pull the trigger. You squeeze it. Slowly. Like you're trying not to wake someone sleeping next to you."

His voice was in her ear, low and calm, and she could feel every word vibrate through his chest into her spine.

"Breathe," he said. "In. Out. On the exhale, squeeze."

She did. The gun kicked in her hands. The noise was enormous even through the ear protection. The round went wide, hitting the target's shoulder instead of center mass.

"Not bad," Nico said. "Again."

They did it again. And again. And again. Each time he adjusted her grip, her stance, the angle of her wrists. Each time his hands lingered a fraction of a second longer than necessary.

By the tenth shot, she was hitting center mass consistently.

By the twentieth, she could feel the heat of him like a presence, a gravity well pulling her backward.

She stepped back. Created distance. Her hands were shaking and it wasn't from the recoil.

This was dangerous. Not the guns. Not the training. This. The way her body responded to him. The way she wanted him to touch her again even though she knew he wouldn't. Even though she knew he shouldn't.

Damian trusted her. Was falling in love with her. Or with Livia. Or with whoever she was pretending to be.

And here she was, in a basement with another man, feeling things that had nothing to do with the con.

Focus, she told herself. This is about survival. Not about feelings. Never about feelings.

But her body didn't seem to care what her mind was saying.

"Enough," he said finally, his voice rough.

She set the gun down. Turned to face him. They were close. Too close. His hands were still on her waist, steadying her, and neither of them had moved away.

"You're a fast learner," he said.

"Good teacher."

His eyes were very dark. Very serious. She could see the war happening in them. Desire and duty. Want and consequence.

"We should stop," he said.

"Probably."

Neither of them moved.

"Sloane—"

The door to the range opened. One of the house staff—a young woman whose name Sloane could never remember—stepped in, her eyes widening slightly when she saw them standing so close.

"Excuse me," the woman said, her voice carefully neutral. "Ms. Zimina is looking for you, Mrs. Crestwell. Your language lesson starts in ten minutes."

"Of course," Sloane said, stepping back. "Thank you."

The woman left. The door closed. The spell broke.

Nico turned away, already cleaning the guns, his movements mechanical.

"Same time tomorrow?" Sloane asked.

"Yes."

"Nico—"

"Go," he said, not looking at her. "Katarina doesn't like to be kept waiting."

Sloane left. But as she climbed the stairs back to the main house, she could still feel the ghost of his hands on her waist. The heat of his breath in her ear.

She was in trouble.

And the worst part was, she didn't want to stop.

Chapter 35: The Muse

The snows came in earnest in mid-November. Not just dustings on the peaks, but real, heavy snow that blanketed the estate in a quiet hush, transforming the world outside the glass walls into a monochrome fairy tale. The access roads were plowed but treacherous. The house grew quieter, more isolated. A white cage suspended in the sky.

The gala was now less than three weeks away, a low hum of anticipatory tension in the air.

But the machine wasn't ready.

Sloane could hear it in the way Damian paced the floor of his study at 3 AM. She could see it in the dark circles under his eyes at breakfast. The "stabilization" wasn't holding. He was spiraling again, trapped in a loop of logic he couldn't close.

Katarina had pulled her aside that morning, her voice clipped. "He is tearing apart the core prediction model. Again. He keeps finding 'anomalies' in the behavioral logic and forcing last-minute patches that destabilize the whole system."

She looked at Sloane, her eyes hard.

"We are three weeks from the gala. If he does not authorize the code freeze by Friday, we miss the validation window for the Consortium. And if the final product isn't ready soon..." She didn't finish the sentence. She didn't have to.

If the code freeze failed, the deal died. And if the deal died, her contract was void.

But Roman Lazar wasn't the kind of man who simply asked for a refund. He paid for results. If she couldn't deliver Damian—stable, compliant, code-perfect, and ready to sign—she ceased to be a hundred-million-dollar asset. She became a loose end in a failed conspiracy.

And she knew exactly how Roman Lazar disposed of tools that no longer served a purpose.

Sloane stood at her window, watching the flakes fall. Three weeks had passed since she learned the name "Roman Lazar." Three weeks of silence. She hadn't dared to touch the burner phone—Nico's warning about the RF sweeps had been absolute. She was sitting on the smoking gun, and she couldn't pull the trigger.

She needed Damian to finish the work. And she needed him to trust her enough to take her past the gates.

She heard his door open down the hall. Footsteps. Hesitant. Then the sound of him retreating back into his room. He was stuck. Paralyzed by the ghost of his dead wife and the pressure of a living god.

He didn't need peace. He needed a jolt. A catalyst.

She turned away from the window.

***

She went to him that night.

It was not part of the plan. It was not a performance. Fairweather's words echoed in her mind—*no intimacy, inconsistent with the narrative.*

She went anyway.

The narrative was failing. The machine was stalled. If she didn't unblock Damian's mind, the deal would die. And she would die with it.

She told herself she was just fulfilling the role. A muse had to offer more than just presence. She had to offer a spark.

But as she walked down the silent corridor, she knew that wasn't the whole truth.

Was it because the weight of the lies was crushing her? Because she was tired of performing? Because for one night, she craved something real in this house of ghosts?

Or was it simpler than that? Was it just... want?

She didn't know. The reasons were a tangled, contradictory mess in her own head. All she knew was that her feet were carrying her down the silent corridor, toward his door, and she was helpless to turn around.

The house was silent. The staff asleep. Even the cameras seemed to be looking away—though she knew, logically, they never did.

She stood outside his door in a silk robe, her heart hammering. Last chance to turn back. Last chance to be smart.

She closed her eyes, and in the darkness, two truths coexisted.

She wanted him. Not the performance, not the role—him. The scientist with the beautiful, broken mind who looked at her like she was the solution to an impossible equation. That pull was real.

And she needed this. The trip beyond these walls. The freedom to move through a Swiss village, find a phone booth, make the call that might save her life. That need was also real.

Both things were true. Both things were hers.

She didn't want to separate them anymore.

She knocked.

Soft. Three times.

For a moment, nothing. Then the door opened.

Damian stood there in pajama pants and nothing else, his hair mussed from sleep, his eyes widening when he saw her.

"Sloane?" he said, using her real name without thinking.

She didn't correct him.

"Can I come in?"

He stepped aside. She entered. The door closed behind her.

His room was larger than hers. More lived-in. Books everywhere. Equations scrawled on a whiteboard by the window. The faint scent of coffee and ink.

"Is something wrong?" he asked. "You're trembling."

"No." She turned to face him. "I just... I didn't want to be alone."

He studied her face. Looking for something. Permission, maybe. Or a sign that this was real.

"Are you sure?" he asked quietly. "Because we don't have to—I don't want you to feel like—"

She crossed the distance between them. Put her hand on his chest. Felt his heart beating, fast and hard.

"I'm sure," she said. "I'm not doing this because I think I should. I'm not doing this as Livia. I'm doing this as me."

His hand came up. Cupped her face. His thumb traced her cheekbone, gentle and reverent.

"I don't know who you are anymore," he whispered. "I don't know if you're her or someone else or something in between. But I know I feel more alive when you're in the room than I have in eleven months. And I know I want this. Want you. Whoever you are."

She kissed him.

It was not a kiss of passion or desperation. It was slow. Tender. A kiss of shared sorrow, a quiet exploration in the dark. It felt like a question he had been afraid to ask and an answer she was terrified to give.

His hands slid into her hair. Her fingers traced the muscles of his back. The robe slipped from her shoulders and pooled at her feet.

He pulled back. Looked at her. Really looked. Not at Livia. At Sloane.

"You're beautiful," he said.

"You don't have to—"

"I do. You need to hear it. You're beautiful. And brilliant. And so much stronger than you think you are."

She wanted to cry. Wanted to tell him everything. Wanted to confess every lie she'd ever told him.

Instead, she kissed him again.

They moved to the bed. A tangle of limbs and breath and heat. His hands on her skin, careful and exploratory, like he was trying to memorize every inch of her. Her mouth on his throat, his shoulder, tasting salt and want.

He paused. One hand on her hip, his forehead pressed to hers. "Are you sure?" he asked again. "Really sure?"

"Yes."

"Because if you're not—if this is too much—"

"Damian." She looked into his eyes. Saw the vulnerability there. The fear of losing her again. "I want this. I want you."

That was all he needed.

His hands were shaking when he touched her. Like she was something fragile. Something that might break.

She wasn't fragile. But she let him think it. Let him be gentle. Let him trace the curve of her shoulder, the line of her throat, the hollow at the base of her spine like he was memorizing her.

When he kissed her, she could taste the salt on his skin and the desperation in his breath. When he pulled her closer, she could feel his heart hammering against hers. Twin rhythms. Twin fears.

They moved together slowly. Carefully. Like they were both afraid that going too fast would shatter the moment. Would remind them that this was borrowed time. That after the gala, there would be no escape. No future. No them.

She buried her face in his neck. Breathed him in. Let herself feel it. All of it. The weight of him. The warmth. The way he whispered her name—her real name—like it was a prayer or a promise or a plea.

Afterward, they lay tangled together, his arm around her, her head on his chest, listening to the sound of his heartbeat.

This is real, she thought. *Whatever else is a lie, this is real.*

And that made it so much worse.

"Stay," he murmured, half-asleep. "Don't go."

“I want to stay,” she whispered.

It was the first honest thing she'd said to him in weeks.

***

Afterward, they lay tangled together in the cool silk sheets, the moonlight painting silver stripes across the room. Sloane's mind was a screaming chaos of guilt and a strange, aching tenderness, the truth of her feelings a fresh wound.

She waited for his breathing to slow, to deepen into sleep, her own body a coiled spring of tension. But he didn't sleep. He went very, very still beside her.

Then, in the darkness, he whispered a single word. Not her name. Not Livia's.

"Chaos."

He sat bolt upright in bed, his eyes wide, staring at the far wall as if seeing something she couldn't. "The final variable," he breathed, his voice filled with a stunned, religious awe. "It's not an error. It's a feature."

Before she could speak, he threw back the covers. He was completely oblivious to her, to his own nakedness, to anything but the explosion of insight happening in his mind. He grabbed a tablet from his nightstand, his fingers a frantic blur across the screen.

"But it's not a bug," he whispered, a beatific, terrifying smile on his face. "It's the key. The chaotic, unpredictable, illogical, human variable. It doesn't need to be solved. It needs to be integrated."

Sloane watched him, a cold, sickening realization dawning in the pit of her stomach.

The Muse Protocol had worked. The intimacy, the shared vulnerability, the messy, chaotic, human act they had just shared—it had been the final key. By being real with him, by wanting him genuinely, she had given Panopticon the one thing it lacked: a map of the human heart.

He was already lost to her, his fingers flying across the screen, rewriting the code, his brilliant mind finally whole again. He had found his breakthrough.

She had proven her hundred-million-dollar worth.

And she had just, in a final, devastating act of intimacy, helped him perfect the cage that would hold them all.

Chapter 36: The Morning After

Sloane woke to sunlight and the smell of coffee.

For a moment, she didn't remember where she was. Then it came back in a rush. Damian's room. His bed. His body warm beside hers.

She opened her eyes. He was already awake, propped up on one elbow, watching her with an expression she couldn't quite read.

"Good morning," he said softly.

"Morning."

He reached out. Tucked a strand of hair behind her ear. The gesture was so tender it made her chest ache.

"I made coffee," he said. "Well, I used the coffee maker. I didn't actually roast the beans or anything."

She laughed. It felt good. Normal. "I appreciate the effort."

He got up. Pulled on a t-shirt. Poured two cups from the machine on his dresser and handed one to her.

She sat up, wrapping the sheet around herself, suddenly aware of the cameras. The invisible eyes. The fact that Roman had probably watched the whole thing.

If Damian noticed her discomfort, he didn't show it. He sat on the edge of the bed, his own coffee cradled in his hands.

"I've been thinking," he said. "About after the gala. About what we talked about. Going away. Starting over."

"Damian—"

"I know it's complicated. I know you're still recovering. Still finding yourself. But I thought maybe... maybe we could go to Italy. You always loved Italy. Or we thought you did. Did you?" He paused, suddenly uncertain. "Do you remember loving Italy?"

She should have said no. But that would have broken his self-induced trance. Instead, she heard herself say, "Yes. I remember."

Another lie. Another brick in the wall between them.

"Good." He smiled. That fragile, hopeful smile that broke her heart. "Because I've been looking at villas. Small ones. On Lake Como. Somewhere quiet. Somewhere we could just... be. Without all this."

He squeezed her hand.

"I'll ask Katarina to finalize the paperwork. I want it ready for us. Would you like that?"

"I would," she said. The cruelest lie she'd ever told. "I'd like that very much."

He leaned in. Kissed her forehead. "Then it's settled. After the gala, we disappear. Just the two of us."

"Just the two of us," she echoed.

He stood. Set his coffee down. "I should shower. Get dressed. I have a videocall with Roman this afternoon to go over the final details for the ceremony." He paused at the bathroom door. "Thank you. For last night. For trusting me."

Then he was gone, and Sloane was alone.

She set down her coffee with trembling hands. Stared at her reflection in the window. The woman looking back was a stranger. A liar. A fraud.

She'd just made love to a man who believed she was someone else. Who was planning a future with a ghost. Who had no idea that the woman in his bed was the weapon aimed at his heart.

She wanted to be sick. Wanted to scream. Wanted to run.

Instead, she got dressed. Smoothed her hair. Put on Livia's face like armor.

And walked out into the hallway.

Nico was there. Leaning against the wall opposite Damian's door. His arms crossed. His face a mask.

But his eyes. God, his eyes.

They looked at each other for a long moment. A whole conversation happening in silence.

You slept with him.

Yes.

Did you mean it?

I don't know.

Does he know what you are?

No. He thinks I'm her.

And what am I supposed to do with that?

I don't know. I don't know anything anymore.

"Good morning," Nico said finally. His voice was flat. Dead. Like he was greeting a stranger.

"Nico—"

"Did you fuck him as Livia? Or as yourself?"

The question was a knife. Clean. Precise. Straight to the heart.

"I—"

"Because if you fucked him as Livia, then it's just the job. Just the con. And I can live with that. I knew what this was. What you were."

He took a step toward her. His eyes were burning now. All the restraint finally cracking.

"But if you fucked him as yourself—if you let him see the real you—then I need to know. Because that changes everything."

"I did it for the exit," she whispered, the lie tasting like ash even as she said it. She needed him to believe it was tactical. She needed to believe it herself. "He was stuck, Nico. The algorithm was broken. He needed... a catalyst. A human variable. I gave it to him."

She took a breath, forcing steel into her voice.

"And it worked. He found the solution. He trusts me completely now. He'll take us past the gates. He'll take us anywhere."

She thought this would appease him. She thought he would see the victory.

Instead, Nico looked at her as if she had just confessed to a murder.

He turned away, pressing his palms flat against the wall like it was the only thing holding him upright.

"You gave him the answer," he repeated, his voice hollow.

He looked back at her. His eyes were dry now. Devastated.

"I told myself you were different. That you were still fighting. That underneath Livia's face, you were still Sloane."

His voice dropped to a rough whisper.

"But you just proved me wrong. You didn't just sleep with him. You gave him the weapon. You became exactly what Roman designed you to be. The perfect muse."

He stopped. Shook his head. The realization hitting him like a physical blow.

"And I helped you do it. I trained you. I covered for you. I cleared the path."

He walked past her. Stopped at the top of the stairs.

"Congratulations," he said without looking back. "We both did our jobs."

He was gone before she could respond.

Sloane stood alone in the hallway, the morning sun streaming through the windows.

She was a weapon.

And weapons didn't get to keep the people who remembered they were human.

***

He didn't go to the security office. His feet, moving on autopilot, carried him down to the sub-levels, to the back of the cavernous wine cellar and the hidden door.

He descended the spiral staircase into the cold, concrete silence of the bunker.

This was his sanctuary. Livia's war room. The one place in Argentis where Roman's eyes couldn't see and his own raw, unprofessional emotions couldn't be witnessed.

Her face—the shock, the guilt, the plea in her eyes—was burned into his mind. *It's not complicated.* She had lied. It was the most complicated thing he had ever known.

He walked to the small, locked safe in the corner. His hands were steady now. The tremor of rage and heartbreak had been replaced by a familiar, glacial calm. The calm of an operator assessing a failed operation.

He pulled out the slim, black folder. Livia's "insurance policy." He laid the contents on the steel table. The maps. The schematics. The protocol for her "final retrieval."

A plan that had died with Livia.

He'd read the letter a hundred times, looking for something he'd missed. Some alternate path. Some way to finish what she'd started.

There wasn't one.

He pulled out the letter anyway. A ritual of failure. A reminder of what couldn't be done.

She had pressed it into his hand the night before she left for Naples. The last time he ever saw her.

"To be opened only if I don't come back," she'd said hading it to him a week before her fateful trip.

He'd opened it the night the Ariadne sank. The night he got the call. The night his world ended.

The paper was worn now, creased from the hundred times he'd read it, looking for answers, for guidance, for her.

Her handwriting stared up at him. Precise. Ruthless.

"Nico,

If you are reading this, I have failed. Roman moved faster than I expected, or I made a mistake, or the universe simply decided I didn't get to win this one.

The contingency plan is in the folder. You know what's in the vault. You know what it can do.

I was going to be the one to retrieve it. I was going to be the one to stand in front of the cameras and burn his empire to the ground.

But if I'm gone, the vault is sealed. Behind a live biometric handshake. Not just a code or a key, but a physical presence. It was the only way to ensure Roman couldn't access it.

I trapped the evidence behind my own pulse.

Without me, the plan dies.

Unless you can find a way I haven't thought of.

I know Roman. He won't leave Damian unattended. He'll find some way to maintain control—a handler, a replacement, something. If an opportunity presents itself, use it. Use anything. Use anyone.

But if you ever entrust this mission to another asset, remember: they must be ours, not his. Test them. Break them if you have to. Make sure they aren't compromised. No divided loyalties.

To destroy a monster like Roman, you cannot afford mercy. You cannot afford sentiment. You cannot afford to be wrong about who you trust.

Burn it all down. For your daughter. For Damian. For everyone Roman has destroyed.

No mercy.

—L"

Nico lowered the letter. *A physical presence.*

He looked up at the bank of security monitors mounted on the bunker wall. The hallway feed was empty now. She had moved.

He scanned the grid. Found her on Camera 4: West Wing Suite 2.

The feed was high-definition, infrared-capable. Intrusive. Most clients didn't put cameras in the bedrooms. But Roman Lazar didn't believe in privacy; he believed in ownership.

Sloane was sitting at the vanity, staring into the mirror. She wasn't crying anymore. She was just looking at her own face, touching her cheekbone with a kind of dazed horror, as if trying to recognize the woman staring back.

Through the grain of the black-and-white feed, the resemblance was terrifying.

She wasn't Livia.

But looking at the screen, even he had to blink to see the difference.

Unless you can find a way I haven't thought of.

The idea took root. Cold. Tactical.

What if—

Roman had spent one hundred million dollars to create a key that could fool the world. He hadn't realized he had also created a key that could open his own destruction.

It was possible. Technically, physically, it was possible. Sloane could walk through that door.

But then Nico remembered the hallway. The confession. *"I gave him the weapon."*

Livia's final warning burned in his mind: *Make sure they aren't compromised. No divided loyalties.*

Sloane was compromised. Falling for Damian. Divided loyalties written all over her face.

She had every logical incentive to betray Livia's mission—a life of unimaginable luxury with Damian versus a suicide mission into the heart of the beast. Why would she risk it all to honor a dead woman's wish? From a purely tactical standpoint, she was not a reliable ally. She was a massive security risk.

He slid the letter and the plans back into the folder and locked them away in the safe.

The impossible idea would remain his secret. He would protect Sloane. Maybe even help her escape if he could. But Livia's legacy? The real war? He would not risk it on a woman whose heart was in another man's bed.

He was a sentinel, and his duty was to Livia first.

Chapter 37: The Fragile Truce

The two days that followed their hallway confrontation were a new kind of hell. A cold war, waged in the silent, sterile corridors of Argentis.

Nico was a ghost. He was there, a constant shadow at the edge of her vision, but the man she had just begun to see beneath the sentinel's armor was gone. In his place was the automaton she had first met on the tarmac at Buochs. The sentinel. Cold. Professional. Impassable. Their training sessions in the gym became exercises in silent, brutal efficiency, with no words exchanged beyond clipped commands. The daily walks on the estate grounds were conducted in a profound, suffocating silence that was louder than any argument.

He was punishing her with his distance. And she knew she deserved it. She had chosen the mark over the man who was trying to save her. She was a monster.

But she also knew she couldn't let it stand. He was her only ally. Her only lifeline. And she was losing him.

On the third night, she found him in the library, long after the house had gone to sleep.

He was sitting in one of the leather chairs by the fireplace, a book in his hands he wasn't reading. Just staring at the flames, his face cast in gold and shadow.

Sloane stood in the doorway, suddenly unsure. She'd come looking for him. Needed to see him. Needed to break the killing silence between them.

"Can't sleep?" she asked softly.

He looked up. His expression didn't change, but something in his eyes shifted. "Never can. You?"

"Same."

She crossed the room. Sat in the chair beside his. The fire crackled between them, warm and alive.

"I used her," Sloane said quietly. "I used Livia's memory to bind Damian to me. I used his grief to unlock his mind. And I used you."

"I know."

"And you're still helping me."

"Yes."

"Why?"

Nico was quiet for a long time. When he spoke, his voice was low. Raw. "Because I've watched what Roman does to people. Watched him turn Damian into a ghost. Watched him use Katarina until there's nothing left of the woman she used to be. And I won't watch him do it to you."

"Even if it jeopardizes... your daughter?"

"Especially then." He looked at her, and his eyes were full of something she couldn't name. "Because I want her to grow up in a world where monsters like Roman Lazar don't win. And if I have to die to make that happen, I will."

Sloane looked at him, searching his face. "And her mother? Is she waiting for you too?"

Nico's expression tightened, a shadow passing over his eyes. "No. Oksana died in the Donbas. Years ago. She was a medic—I found her in the rubble of an extraction mission that went sideways in eastern Ukraine. We had a few years of peace before the war caught up to us again. That war almost took Elena, too."

"Is that why Roman threatened her with Mariupol?" Sloane whispered, the geography of the threat finally aligning.

"Exactly. Since I have to stay dead to keep her safe, I can't officially claim her for an Italian passport without alerting my old unit to my survival. She only has her mother's Ukrainian citizenship and Roman's forged Argentine papers. If he pulls the plug on her residency, she's deported back to her home of record—as a ward of the state in a war zone. That's why I made the deal with Roman. I was the only one left to protect her."

The revelation hung between them. He wasn't just a father; he was a widower. A man who had already lost the love of his life.

Sloane reached across the space between them. Touched his face. Felt the rough stubble on his jaw, the warmth of his skin.

"You're a good man, Nico Sorrento."

"No," he said. "I'm a man who's done terrible things and is trying, very badly, to atone."

"Same thing."

His hand came up. Covered hers. Pressed it against his cheek.

"We can't do this," he said.

"I know."

"It's dangerous. For both of us."

"I know."

"And it's not fair to Damian."

"I know."

Neither of them moved.

The fire snapped. Somewhere in the house, a clock chimed midnight.

Sloane leaned in. Slowly. Giving him time to pull away. Time to remember all the reasons this was a mistake.

He didn't pull away.

He met her halfway, his hand sliding from her cheek into her hair, his other hand finding her waist, pulling her closer until there was no space left at all. The careful control they'd both been maintaining shattered like glass. Her fingers gripped his shirt.

Their lips met.

It was a collision. Desperate. Hungry. The kind of kiss that comes from weeks of restraint finally breaking. It was the taste of whiskey and fear and a shared, impossible hope. His mouth was on hers, and for one single, stolen, incandescent second, there was no mission, no Roman, no cage. There was only this.

And then the library door opened.

They broke apart. Fast. Guilty. Katarina stood in the doorway. Her face was unreadable. Not angry. Not disapproving. Something worse.

Disappointed.

"Mrs. Crestwell," she said, her voice carefully neutral. "Your husband is asking for you. He had another nightmare."

Sloane stood. Smoothed her hair. Her cheeks were flushed, and her hands were trembling slightly. Her body was still humming with want.

"Of course," she said. "I'll go to him now."

She walked toward the door. Stopped beside Katarina.

"I know what you're thinking," Sloane said quietly.

"Do you?"

"That I'm making this worse. That I'm hurting everyone. That I'm—"

"I'm thinking," Katarina interrupted, her voice still flat, "that you're playing a very dangerous game. And that people who play dangerous games under Roman Lazar's gaze tend to end up dead."

She paused.

"The cameras in the library malfunctioned tonight. Technical glitch. It happens. But it won't happen again."

She was protecting her. One last time.

"Thank you," Sloane whispered.

Katarina didn't respond. Just turned and walked away.

Sloane stood in the doorway for a moment. Could feel Nico's eyes on her from inside the library. Could feel the weight of what they'd just done. What they'd almost done.

In the hallway, alone, she pressed her back against the wall and closed her eyes.

She was using everyone. Nico's loyalty. Damian's grief. Manny's love. Katarina's quiet rebellion. She had become exactly what Roman had paid for.

A weapon that could be aimed at anyone.

Even the people she was starting to care about.

***

When she reached Damian's room, he was sitting up in bed, his face pale and drawn in the lamplight.

"Livia," he said, relief flooding his voice. "You came."

"Of course I came."

She sat on the edge of his bed. He reached for her hand, held it like a lifeline.

"I dreamed you were gone again," he said. "That you left me. That I was alone."

"I'm here," she said. The lie tasted like ashes. "I'm not going anywhere."

He looked at her with such desperate gratitude that she wanted to scream.

"Stay," he whispered. "Just for tonight. I just need to know you're here."

She should have said no. Should have left. But instead, she lay down beside him, fully clothed, and let him wrap his arms around her.

He fell asleep within minutes, his breathing evening out, his body finally relaxing.

Sloane lay awake in the darkness, staring at the ceiling, trapped between two men she was betraying in different ways.

And somewhere in the house, in the room full of monitors, Katarina watched the feeds.

She saw the intimacy. The desperation. The tactical error of sleeping with the mark.

It was sloppy. It was emotional. It was dangerous.

She reached out and deleted the last hour of the recording buffer.

She told herself it was operational security. Protecting the asset.

But she knew what it really was.

A small mercy.

Chapter 38: Small Mercies

The daylight was dying by four in the afternoon now, the shadows stretching long and distorted across the estate. It was the third week of November, and the mountain was tightening its grip.

The days at Argentis had a rhythm. A careful, orchestrated routine designed to keep her busy, keep her compliant, keep her from thinking too hard about the cage she was living in.

Language lessons with Katarina. Etiquette drills. The endless, grueling work of memorizing the dossiers: the faces, histories, and hidden weaknesses of every powerful guest who would be watching her at the gala. Physical training with Nico. Dinners with Damian, where she performed the role of Livia with such precision that sometimes even she forgot where the character ended and she began.

No. That wasn't quite right.

She didn't *forget* where the character ended. She *chose* not to remember. There was a difference.

Method acting, they'd called it at the studio where she'd taken classes back when she still thought she might be a real actress instead of a professional liar. Become the character. Live in their skin. Think their thoughts. Feel their feelings.

I am Livia Crestwell. This is my home. This is my husband. These are my memories.

She told herself this every morning when she woke up. Every time she looked in the mirror. Every time Damian's eyes found hers across a room and something in them broke open like a wound.

I am Livia. I am Livia. I am Livia.

The lie was easier than the truth.

***

The next morning she found him in the garden, the sun hadn't yet cleared the mountains.

Sloane had been awake for hours. Couldn't sleep. Hadn't been able to sleep properly since the night she'd spent in his bed, an act of cold, tactical calculus that had left her feeling hollowed out and raw. She'd been avoiding him since, taking her meals in her room, letting Katarina fill her days with drills until she was too exhausted to think.

But this morning, insomnia had driven her out of bed and down to the garden, and there he was.

Sitting on the stone bench near the koi pond. A notebook in his lap. Scribbling equations with the fevered intensity of a man trying to outrun his own thoughts.

She should have turned around.

Instead, she walked toward him. Her bare feet silent on the cold stone path. Her silk robe wrapped tight against the morning chill.

"You're up early," she said softly.

He was startled. Looked up. And for one unguarded moment, his face was completely open. Tired. Haunted. Desperate. Then he saw her, and something shifted. His face relaxed. Warmed. Like she was the answer to a prayer he'd been too afraid to speak aloud.

"Livia," he said. The name a barrier and a bridge all at once. "I didn't hear you."

She sat down beside him, close enough to feel the heat of him in the cold morning air.

"Couldn't sleep?" she asked.

"Bad dreams." He closed the notebook. Set it aside. His hands were shaking slightly. "You?"

"Same."

A lie. She'd been awake wrestling with the ghost of what she'd done.

They sat in silence. The koi moved through the water like living calligraphy. Orange and white and gold. The birds were waking in the trees. Tentative songs. Testing the day.

***

"I've been thinking," Damian said finally, his voice careful, measured. "About Küssnacht."

Sloane's heart gave a single, hard kick.

Küssnacht. She had never been. But she had spent hours studying Livia's journal, memorizing the details of the small, picturesque town. The bookstore by the lake. The bakery with the poppy seed rolls. She had the script. Now came the performance.

"The bookstore," she said, her voice a soft, wistful murmur, a perfect echo of Livia's nostalgia. "I remember the little bell over the door."

A real smile, unguarded and boyish, touched his lips. "And the mohnbrötchen. Her favorite." He turned to her, his eyes searching hers, desperate for confirmation. "You remember?"

"I remember feelings," she said carefully. It didn't feel like a lie. The longing was real, even if the memory wasn't. "I remember... feeling happy there. Safe."

Relief flooded his face. He looked away, toward the water, and for a moment she thought she'd passed the test.

Then he spoke again, his voice quieter now. Almost gentle.

"You're very good, you know."

Her breath caught. "What?"

"Livia had a tell." He didn't look at her. Kept his gaze on the koi, on the water, on anything but her face. "When she was nervous, she'd touch her collarbone. Just here." He gestured to the hollow of his throat. "She didn't even know she did it. But I noticed. Every time."

Sloane's heart stopped.

"You," he continued, his voice still soft, still careful, "press your thumb against your index finger. Small. Almost invisible. But it's there."

The world narrowed to the sound of her own pulse in her ears.

He turned to her then. His eyes were gray-green in the dawn light. Sad. Searching. But not accusing.

"I knew," he said, his voice quiet but steady. "From the beginning. Roman showed me your profile. The screen tests. I authorized the... arrangement."

A bitter smile touched his lips.

"I'm a scientist, Sloane. I understand experimental design. Controlled variables. I told myself this was just applied psychology. A stabilizer."

"Damian—"

"But I underestimated the variable." His voice cracked slightly. "I thought I could partition the mind. Keep the knowledge in one part—the rational part—and lock it away. And in the other..."

He looked at her, his eyes raw and desperate.

"In the other, I overwrote the facts with the feeling."

He reached for her hand—slowly, giving her time to pull away.

"You're so close," he whispered. "The voice. The gestures. The way you tilt your head when you're thinking. Most of the time, if I don't look too hard, if I don't think too much..."

His fingers closed around hers.

"Most of the time, I can convince myself it's her."

His fingers closed around hers. Warm. Solid. Real.

"It was the first time in eleven months I felt like a human being instead of a ghost," he said quietly, his gaze fixed on the distant water. "The first time I remembered what it was like to want to be alive."

He turned back to her. His eyes were full of raw, pleading vulnerability.

"Sometimes I feel like I'm living in a dream I'm afraid to wake up from." His voice was barely above a whisper. "Tell me this is real. Even if it's not. Just for now."

Sloane's throat tightened.

He wasn't asking if she remembered being Livia. He was asking her to reaffirm the beautiful lie they were both living. This was the moment she could break the spell. Could say: *I'm not her. This isn't real. Wake up.*

But then she thought of Manny. Of Nico. Of his daughter. Of all the people Roman would destroy if she shattered this man's fragile peace.

She reached out with her free hand and placed it over his. Her touch a steady, grounding anchor.

"It's real," she said, her voice quiet and unwavering. "I'm real. And I'm here."

It was the truest lie she had ever told.

He looked at her for a long moment, searching her face—not for a memory of his dead wife, but for the conviction in the eyes of the living woman beside him.

"Livia was a masterpiece of order," he whispered, his eyes tracing the line of her jaw with a hunger that made her pulse stumble. "Everything about her was precise. Symmetrical. Perfect. But you... you're a masterpiece of chaos. You're vivid, and you're messy, and you're alive."

He leaned in, his forehead coming to rest against hers. "I find myself preferring the difference."

Then he nodded slowly. A single, grateful acknowledgment.

He had found what he was looking for.

Chapter 39: The Sentimental Journey

"I'd like to do it again," Damian said, his voice quieter now. Almost shy. "Go to Küssnacht. Soon. The bakery with the poppy seeds. The clock tower. That dusty little bookstore by the water..."

He looked out at the lake, lost in the memory.

"It was the only place the noise ever stopped," he whispered. "I want to go back there. Just for a short while. Just two people trying to figure out what's real."

Nothing is real, she wanted to say. *This is a con. I'm a weapon. And the moment you sign that contract, everything ends.*

Instead, she heard herself say, "That sounds wonderful."

He smiled. The first genuine smile she'd seen that reached his eyes.

"You're either very brave or very foolish."

"Probably both."

He leaned in and kissed her. It wasn't the heavy, scotch-soaked desperation of their night in his bedroom. It was lighter. Clearer. A kiss not of shared sorrow, but of daylight and delusion.

When he pulled back, his eyes were bright. Almost happy.

"After the gala," he said. "We'll figure it out after the gala. We'll leave. Find somewhere quiet. Somewhere we can be ourselves. No Roman. No contract. No pretending."

"After the gala," she echoed.

It was the cruelest lie of all.

Because she knew—even if he didn't—that there was no "us" in the ending of this script. There was only the signing, the remainder of her six-month term, and the inevitable day she would walk away with her money, leaving him alone with a ghost.

But for now—for this one perfect, terrible morning—she let herself pretend.

She tightened her grip on his hand. "Let's just stay here," she said. "A little longer."

So they did.

Sitting side by side as the sun climbed over the mountains and turned the lake from silver to gold. His hand in hers. His shoulder warm against hers. The cold morning air sharp in their lungs.

Two people who knew exactly what they were doing and why it was impossible.

And did it anyway.

Finding comfort in a lie that felt, for just a moment, like the truth.

***

Later, when they finally walked back to the house, Damian's hand still holding hers, Sloane felt the weight of invisible eyes.

The cameras. The microphones. Roman watching from wherever he watched from.

She wondered if he was pleased. If this was part of his plan. If her falling for Damian—really falling, not just performing—made her a better weapon or a more dangerous one.

She wondered if it even mattered anymore.

Because the truth was this: she was in love with him.

Not with the idea of him. Not with the role she was playing. But with the actual man. The brilliant, broken, desperately hopeful man who knew she was lying and loved her anyway.

And that changed everything.

Because weapons weren't supposed to have feelings.

And con artists weren't supposed to fall for the mark.

But she had. And now she had to figure out what the hell she was going to do about it.

***

She waited until late afternoon... She found Katarina in the main salon, reviewing inventory lists on a tablet, a general inspecting her armory before a campaign.

"Katarina," Sloane said. Her voice was not the fragile, weepy survivor. It was the voice of Livia Crestwell, the concerned partner, reporting a critical development.

Katarina looked up, her expression a mixture of surprise and cool assessment.

"It's Damian," Sloane said, her face a mask of carefully constructed concern. "He's... retreating again. Back into his shell. I saw him in the garden this morning. He was talking about the past, about memories. He's becoming disconnected from the present."

She let that sink in, knowing Katarina's primary function was to monitor Damian's stability. She was not asking for a favor; she was reporting a mission risk.

"He mentioned Küssnacht," Sloane continued, planting the seed. "The old town. The walk by the water. He said it was the only place he ever felt truly at peace."

She walked to the great glass wall, her posture a study in controlled worry.

"This house, this beautiful cage... it's a monument to his grief. If he stays here, surrounded by ghosts, he will break before the gala. We both know it."

Katarina studied her for a long, silent moment, her icy eyes assessing the performance, searching for the flaw. Sloane met her gaze, her own eyes a well of unwavering, strategic concern.

"Security protocols do not permit unscheduled excursions," Katarina said finally, her voice flat. It was a test.

"Then schedule it," Sloane countered, a hint of Livia's steel in her voice. "This isn't about my comfort. This is about the asset. Your primary asset. He needs a connection to a happy memory. He needs a reminder of the world outside this fortress. He needs to feel like a man, not a ghost, if he is to stand in front of The Consortium and be convincing."

She had just used their own cold, clinical language against her. She had framed the trip not as a personal desire, but as a necessary step in the "Muse Protocol."

Katarina's jaw tightened almost imperceptibly. She had been outmaneuvered, not by an emotional plea, but by a superior tactical argument. To refuse now would be to actively sabotage the mission's primary objective.

"Very well," she said, her voice clipped. "I will inform Mr. Sorrento. Two hours in the town. No more. And he will not leave your side for a single moment."

Sloane gave a small, professional nod, the look of a partner whose sound advice has been heeded. "Thank you, Katarina. It's the right move. For Damian."

Chapter 40: The Clean Line

The bookstore smelled of old paper and bergamot tea.

It was a tiny jewel box of a place—narrow shelves of dark wood rising to a pressed-tin ceiling, ladders on brass rails, first editions behind glass, and a reading nook in the corner where afternoon light slanted through leaded windows overlooking the lake. The kind of place that made you believe books were sacred objects, not just products.

Sloane stood at the counter while the elderly woman—Frau Bachmann, according to the small brass nameplate—wrapped a slim volume of Rilke's poems in brown paper with the careful precision of someone who believed books deserved respect.

Behind her, Damian browsed the philosophy section, occasionally pulling down a volume, reading a passage, setting it back. His movements were slower than usual. Calmer. The tight, anxious energy that had defined him for months had loosened. He looked almost... content.

Good, Sloane thought. *That's the point. Keep him stable. Keep him functional. That's the job.*

Frau Bachmann smiled at her—a warm, genuine smile that carried recognition. "It's so good to see you again, Mrs. Crestwell. It's been far too long."

Sloane's heart kicked once, hard, but her face remained perfectly composed. Livia's face. Livia's gentle, pleased smile.

"It has been too long," she said softly. "I've missed this place."

"We have missed you, my dear," the woman's eyes grew misty with genuine emotion. "When we heard about the accident... that you had a long recovery ahead... well. The whole town prayed for you. To see you now, looking so well... it is an answer to those prayers. You are a miracle, Mrs. Crestwell."

The words were a quiet gut-punch. *Miracle.* Sloane felt the weight of the lie, of the performance, settle on her shoulders. She was not a miracle. She was a forgery. But the old woman's belief was so pure, so absolute, that for a dizzying second, Sloane almost believed it herself.

"Thank you, Frau Bachmann," Sloane said quietly, her voice thick with an emotion that was not entirely faked. "That means a great deal."

***

She glanced over at Damian. He was lost, completely absorbed in a heavy volume of philosophy, his back to the counter. He was in his own world.

This was her chance. The window. The reason she was here.

She leaned closer to the bookstore owner, lowering her voice to a conspiratorial whisper. "Frau Bachmann, you'll think me terribly disorganized," she began, her expression a perfect blend of flustered charm. "I've just remembered an urgent family call I must make, and I seem to have left my mobile at the house. And my husband isn't terribly fond of my family's... dramas. I'd rather not borrow his phone."

"Of course, Mrs. Crestwell!" Frau Bachmann brightened, delighted to be part of the small, charming conspiracy. "Just around the corner, by the ferry landing. It still works. My grandson used it just last week."

"You're a lifesaver," Sloane whispered back. She gave a little eye-roll in Damian's direction. "My husband is lost in his books. If he even notices I'm gone, tell him I'll be right back, will you?"

"Of course, my dear," Frau Bachmann said with a knowing smile.

Sloane gave Damian's back one last glance, then turned to Nico, who had been watching the entire exchange, his face a mask of stone. She gave him a small, almost imperceptible nod. It's time.

He gave a single, curt nod in return, his eyes already scanning the street outside. Five minutes.

She squeezed Damian's hand once as she passed—a warm, reassuring touch for the man she was deceiving—and slipped out of the bookstore before he could even look up.

***

Küssnacht was a postcard brought to life.

The afternoon sun turned everything gold. The buildings along the waterfront were painted in soft pastels—rose, butter yellow, pale blue—their shutters dark wood, their window boxes overflowing with late-season geraniums. The cobblestones were smooth and ancient, worn by centuries of foot traffic. A church bell tolled somewhere, its sound carrying clear and pure across the water.

The lake stretched before her like polished glass. Blue-green and impossibly clear, the kind of water you could see ten feet down into, where fish moved like shadows and the rocks on the bottom were visible as dark shapes. The ferry—white with red trim—was just pulling away from the dock, its horn a low, mournful note that echoed off the mountains.

And the mountains. God, the mountains.

They rose on all sides like cathedral walls. Jagged, white-capped, eternal. The Rigi to the east, its peak lost in wisps of cloud. The Pilatus to the west, its silhouette sharp as a knife against the sky. The Alps enclosed this small valley like cupped hands around a candle flame, protective and suffocating all at once.

It was the kind of beauty that made you believe in something larger than yourself. The kind of place where people went to find God, or lose themselves, or both.

Sloane walked quickly but not frantically. A woman on a mission, but not fleeing. Just around the corner, past a café where tourists sat beneath striped umbrellas drinking coffee and eating apple strudel, to the ferry landing where—

There.

The payphone.

A relic from another era. A small glass booth, scratched and smudged with fingerprints, its metal frame green with age. Inside: a heavy black receiver attached to a box with coin slots and push buttons that had probably replaced a rotary dial sometime in the nineties.

Behind it, the lake. Before it, the square. To the left, Nico—twenty feet away, his back to a shop window, his eyes scanning the street with methodical precision. To the right, through the bookstore's front window, Damian browsing peacefully.

And across the square: the obsidian Mercedes. Windows tinted. Motionless.

Watching.

Sloane stepped into the booth. Her heart hammered so hard she could feel it in her throat, her fingertips, the base of her skull.

This was the performance. The con within the con. The lie that would sell the bigger lie.

She picked up the receiver. Cold. Heavy. Smelling faintly of metal and old plastic and a thousand other conversations. She dropped a coin into the slot—the clink of metal on metal satisfyingly analog—and punched in Manny's number.

It rang once.

Twice.

Click.

"Yeah."

Manny's voice. Thick with sleep. Groggy. So familiar it made her chest ache.

"Aunt Carol, it's me," Sloane said, her voice bright and slightly too loud for the benefit of anyone listening. "I'm so sorry I haven't called. Things have been absolutely mad here."

A pause. The sound of shifting sheets. Then his voice changed—the sleep vanishing, replaced by adrenaline.

"Jesus Christ, kid. It's six in the morning. It's been forever since I heard your voice. I was about to charter a goddamn plane."

"I know. Sorry for the wake-up call." She turned her back to the street, pressed herself into the corner of the booth. Lowered her voice. "The security situation changed. They upgraded the surveillance. I can't use burners anymore—not even in the house. Too risky. This is the first chance I've had to get to a public phone."

"Listen, kid, before you say anything else," Manny cut in, his voice urgent. "We found the money trail. Jerry tracked the funding for Damian's companies back to a ghost entity called The Lazarus Group. They've been involved since Damian's first startup. They route everything through a digital fortress in a decommissioned mine in Finland. Untouchable."

"Lazarus," Sloane whispered, a chill running through her.

"And Sarah found the body count," Manny continued, speaking fast. "There's a pattern. Ten years ago, a biotech CEO named Oliver Harrow refused a buyout from them. A week later, his daughter was targeted in a hit-and-run. She's still catatonic in a facility in New Mexico. Harrow died a 'suicide' shortly after, and Lazarus took the company for pennies. It's a playbook, Sloane. They break the family to get the asset."

The intel hit Sloane like a physical blow. The catatonic girl. The leverage. It was exactly what Nico was facing.

"It fits," she whispered, her voice trembling. "I found the name in Livia's secret journal. The man running it. Roman Lazar. "L-A-Z-A-R."

"L-A-Z-A-R," Manny repeated, the connection clicking instantly. "Lazarus Group. That arrogant son of a bitch."

"It's him," she said. "He's the one who ordered the hit on Livia. She named him. In the entry she wrote the day before she died. He's selling Panopticon, a surveillance engine based on Damian's predictive models. To The Consortium."

"The what?" Manny asked.

"Twelve intelligence agencies. CIA, MI6, FSB—the major players. Roman's selling it to all of them at once," she said, the words tasting like poison. "The gala is a cover for their final summit. They need to see Damian looking stable, with his loving wife smiling by his side. That's me, Manny. That's the job."

She heard the sharp intake of breath.

"Manny, listen," she said, her voice urgent. "Roman asked Livia to build a secure 'Black Box' partition to upload 'classified intel' about his deeds. His 'Dark Ledger' to train Panopticon."

She could hear Manny scribbling notes in the background.

"Roman monitors everything," she continued, "but Livia built a secure drop that's invisible to him. Port 8080, handshake 'Margarita', subdomain tempest.a rgentis.net. Livia built it."

"Port 8080, Margarita, tempest.argentis.net. Got it," he said, scribbling furiously. "Okay. I'm on it. Financials, shell companies, connections. I'll find where he bleeds."

"And Manny? Tell your guy about the 'Root Seed'. Livia wrote that she engineered it into the system to lock that partition. She said it's the one thing Roman never changes. I have no idea what it means, though."

"No sweat. My whiz kid Glitch will decode the techno-babble. Root Seed. Got it," he continued scribbling.

"Manny—" Her voice cracked slightly. "Be careful. This man... he makes people disappear. If he even thinks you're digging—"

"Let me worry about that," he cut her off, his voice softening. "You just focus on staying alive. You have any allies in there? Anyone watching your back?"

"The warden is a wall," Sloane whispered, using the coded language they both understood. "But the sentinel... maybe. It's fragile. Lazar has a leash on him. A daughter."

"Jesus," Manny breathed. "Okay. The sentinel is a question mark. Got it. What's our clock?"

"The gala is in two weeks," she said. "That's the big show. After that... I don't know. I don't think he's ever letting me go, Manny."

The unspoken words hung between them: *After the gala, they won't need me to be convincing anymore.*

"Then you run," Manny's voice was a low, urgent command. "The moment that gala is over, you find a window and you run. I'll have an extraction plan ready. I'll—"

"I have to go," Sloane cut in, her voice a tight whisper.

Nico had taken a step closer. A silent reminder that time was up.

"Sloane—" Manny's voice was urgent now, raw. "You hold on."

"I will. I love you, Manny."

"Love you too, kid."

She hung up.

Her hand was shaking. Just slightly. She pressed it flat against the cold metal of the phone box until it steadied.

Then she opened the door and stepped out into the golden afternoon light.

Chapter 41: The Price of Hope

Nico was there. Three steps away. His face a professional mask.

"Finished?" he asked, his voice flat.

"Finished." She gave him a bright, relieved smile that didn't quite reach her eyes. "Thank you for your patience."

His expression didn't change. But something flickered in his eyes—acknowledgment, maybe. Respect. Or warning.

They walked back to the bookstore in silence.

***

Inside, Damian was at the counter with a small stack of books. Philosophy. Poetry. A coffee-table monograph on Bauhaus architecture. His face was lighter than she'd seen it in months. Almost boyish.

"Find everything you needed?" he asked when he saw her, his smile genuine and warm.

"Yes. Thank you for waiting."

He paid for the books—Frau Bachmann wrapped them carefully, her hands gentle and practiced—and they left the shop together. Damian carried the bag, his free hand finding Sloane's as they walked back through the cobblestone streets toward where the Maybach was parked.

The town was beautiful in the late afternoon light. The mountains were turning purple-gold. The lake was burnished copper. Tourists photographed the clock tower. Children fed swans at the water's edge. An accordion player busked near the ferry dock, playing something old and melancholy that drifted across the square like smoke.

It felt like a place where nothing bad could happen. A place outside time. A sanctuary.

It was, of course, an illusion.

As they reached the car, Damian turned to her. His hand squeezed hers—warm, solid, real. His eyes were bright with something that looked dangerously close to hope.

"Thank you," he said quietly, his voice thick with emotion. "For suggesting this. For..." He paused, searching for words. "For letting me remember what it felt like. To be us."

The gratitude in his eyes was unbearable.

Sloane forced a smile, her throat tight. "Of course."

He leaned in and kissed her forehead—gentle, reverent, the kind of kiss you give something precious—and climbed into the car.

Nico held the door for her. As she slid past him, she paused, her hand briefly touching his wrist—a fleeting pressure, there and gone.

"Thank you," she breathed. The words were so quiet they barely existed.

He leaned in, his mouth near her ear.

"I'm doing this for Livia," he said. "And now you are her."

***

The obsidian Mercedes followed them as they left Küssnacht, maintaining a discreet distance but never disappearing entirely. Sloane watched it in the side mirror as the Maybach climbed the winding mountain road back toward Argentis.

The town grew smaller behind them. The clock tower became a white needle against the darkening sky. The lake became a ribbon of silver-blue. The Alps closed in like the walls of a very beautiful prison.

Damian read quietly beside her, occasionally pointing out a passage he thought she might like, his voice soft and hopeful. And Sloane sat there, her hands folded in her lap, her face a perfect mask of calm.

She had won the battle.

She had made contact with Manny. She had given him Roman's name. She had set the bulldog loose.

But she had also weaponized Damian's love. She had used his hope as cover for war. She had let him believe, for one afternoon, that the woman he loved was coming back to him—piece by fragile piece, memory by painful memory.

And the worst part, the part that made her stomach turn with something that felt uncomfortably close to self-loathing, was that she would have to do it again. And again. Until one of them broke. Until the performance became the reality, or until the reality destroyed them both.

She had made a god mortal.

But she had also made a good man hope.

And she wasn't sure which sin would cost her more.

Chapter 42: The Bulldog's Scent

November 20th. In Los Angeles, the Santa Ana winds were blowing hot and dry, kicking up dust in the valley and making the city feel like a tinderbox waiting for a spark.

Manny Goldman sat in his office at 8:47 AM, chain-smoking Marlboros. He wasn't staring at the phone waiting for it to ring anymore. It had already rung, three hours ago, dragging him out of bed with the breakthrough he'd been praying for.

Now, he was staring at the legal pad where he'd scrawled Sloane's whisper-thin intel.

He'd been calling in favors for the past few weeks. Old contacts from the nineties, back when he'd been the guy you called when you needed something untraceable. A passport. A bank account. A new identity.

He'd been clean for twenty years. Built a legitimate talent management business. Represented actors and directors and the occasional musician who needed someone who understood how to navigate the uglier side of Hollywood.

But the old skills never really went away. They just waited. Dormant. Like muscle memory.

He stared at the chaotic collage on his wall. Jerry's financial trail had gone cold at the "Lazarus Group," a fortress of Swiss corporate law. Sarah's historical trail had ended with a catatonic girl and a pattern of death he couldn't prove. He'd gone as far as his street-level network could take him. The shovels he knew were useless against a digital fortress.

But Sloane hadn't just given him a shovel. She'd given him the coordinates of the bodies.

It was time to call in the ghost.

He stubbed out his cigarette and reached for his Rolodex. Yes, he still had a Rolodex. Some things didn't belong in the cloud.

He said "I'm coming, kid" to the empty office like saying it aloud would make it true. But the truth was darker and he knew it.

He was seventy-two years old. Twenty years out of the game. Going up against a phantom whose resources seemed limitless.

The smart play was to walk away. Let Sloane burn. Protect himself.

His hand went to the photo on his desk. Oscar night. Her smile so bright it could light a city. He'd introduced her to the producer who'd blacklisted her. He'd vouched for the manager who'd betrayed her. He had failed to keep her from taking this dangerous contract.

This was his fault.

Walking away wasn't an option. It never had been.

He flipped to the Ps. Found the card he was looking for.

Peters, Doug.

Better known as Glitch.

Technically, the guy was pushing forty—a lanky Korean American with a caffeine addiction and a keyboard for a soul. But with a cursed baby face that still got him carded for beer, he looked like a sixteen-year-old truant.

He was legacy. His father had been a legendary code-breaker and Manny's best friend; his mother, a B-list actress Manny had represented back in the eighties. Manny had introduced them, stood as best man at the wedding, and held Doug at the christening. He'd spent the nineties mediating screaming matches between the rebellious teenage prodigy and his strict father, talking the kid off the ledge more times than he could count.

They didn't do "I love yous." They traded insults like currency. But right now, Manny didn't need a godson. He needed a weapon.

The kid was a digital phantom—a paranoid genius who could walk through the world's most secure firewalls like they were beaded curtains.

Manny dialed from the burner.

The kid answered on the second ring. "Unknown caller. Encrypted signal. You have five seconds to speak before I trace this and brick your phone."

"It's Manny. Calling from my burner."

A pause. The digital hostility vanished. "Jesus, Manny. I thought you were dead."

"Not yet. I need a favor."

"I don't do favors anymore. I do consulting. Very expensive consulting."

"This one's pro bono."

"Why would I—"

"Because a friend of mine is in trouble. And the guy who put her there needs to bleed."

"Give me the layout," Glitch said, the sound of a keyboard clattering to life in the background.

"It's a spiderweb," Manny said, rattling off the intel he'd bled to get. "The billionaire genius Damian Crestwell and his dead wife Livia. The Argentis estate in Switzerland. Crystal Vision SARL. It all traces back to a shell entity called The Lazarus Group. That's the money behind Crestwell's last two exits. They route their primary data through a decommissioned iron mine in northern Finland—a digital fortress buried under a thousand feet of granite. I've got the map, kid, but I can't see the spider."

"And your friend?"

"An actress. Sloane Devereaux. Hired to play the dead wife. She thought it was a gig; turns out it's a cage. She's locked inside Argentis right now, and she's running out of time. But she gathered intel from Livia's journal," Manny said, looking at the legal pad where he'd scrawled Sloane's desperate instructions. "Livia built a secure 'Black Box' for Roman to store the records of his deeds. His 'Dark Ledger'. Sloane also mentioned a secure drop in Argentis. Subdomain 'tempest.argentis.net'. Port 8080. The handshake is 'Margarita'."

The typing stopped abruptly.

"Margarita? Port 8080?" Glitch's voice dropped, sounding impressed. "That sounds like a legacy admin tunnel. Ancient stuff. If that's actually open..." He let out a low whistle.

"Can you use it?"

"I can burn the castle down with it. So who's the king? Who are we targeting?"

"Roman Lazar. L-A-Z-A-R."

"And what's he selling?"

"Panopticon. Surveillance architecture. Global scale. Uses Damian's predictive models to find leverage points—secrets, weaknesses. It's a blackmail engine. Roman's selling it to a consortium of intelligence agencies. Twelve of them. CIA, MI6, FSB—the whole rogue's gallery."

Glitch was quiet for a beat. "Jesus Christ."

"Yeah."

"Okay. If he's playing at that level, he's not just hiding data. He's burying it. Give me a minute."

The line went quiet, but not dead. Manny could hear the clatter of a mechanical keyboard, a frantic, percussive sound like a hailstorm on a tin roof. Glitch had put him on speaker and was already inside, already hunting.

Manny lit another Marlboro, the flare of the match illuminating the deep lines of exhaustion on his face. He paced the small office, the phone pressed to his ear, listening to the sound of the digital war. Click-clack-click. A pause. A muttered curse. More typing, faster this time. It was a language he didn't understand, the sound of a ghost moving through walls he couldn't see.

He took a long drag from his cigarette, the smoke burning his lungs. The silence from Glitch stretched for five minutes, occasionally interrupted by typing. An eternity. Manny's tremor was back, his free hand shaking. He was a man used to kicking down doors, now forced to sit on his hands while someone else picked the lock.

"Jesus Christ," Glitch's voice finally crackled back onto the line, a breathless, horrified whisper. "Manny, this is... you know who this guy is, right?"

"I know he's rich. I know he's dangerous. I know he murdered a woman named Livia Crestwell and got away with it."

"He's not just rich. He's connected. You were right—the guy has intelligence agencies and billionaires on speed dial. But his digital footprint is... it's like he doesn't exist. And the parts that do exist are locked behind encryption I've never seen before."

"Can you crack it?"

"I don't know. Maybe. It's going to take time."

"We don't have time."

The line was silent for a beat. Then Manny heard a sharp, excited intake of breath on the other end. The weariness in Glitch's voice was suddenly gone, replaced by a low, humming, electric energy.

"So it's a speed run," Glitch said, and Manny could practically hear the feral grin spreading across his face. "Okay. I'm in. But Manny? If this goes sideways—"

"It won't."

"—you never called me. We never had this conversation. And if I end up dead in a ditch somewhere, I'm haunting your ass."

"Deal."

"One more thing," Glitch added. "I'm not sending anything directly to your laptop. No attachments, no pings, nothing traceable."

Manny exhaled. "I'm listening."

"You'll get a link to the vault. End-to-end encrypted, no persistent logs, burns after access. Anything I find goes there, and you pull it down on your end. Cleaner that way."

"All I heard was 'vault.'" Manny nodded, cigarette tip glowing orange as he waved off the techno-babble. "Good. Keep it clean."

"You know me," Glitch said. "I don't leave footprints. And after this call, I'm switching to my burner."

The line went dead.

Manny looked at the photo of Sloane on his desk. The one from Oscar night, when she'd been on top of the world. Before the fall. Before Argentis. Before she'd become someone else's weapon.

"I'm coming, kid," he whispered to the empty office. "Hold on just a little longer."

He lit another cigarette, the flare of the match illuminating a face that had suddenly shed twenty years of soft, Hollywood living. The agent was gone. The fixer was back.

He had made a mistake. He had let himself get old. Complacent. He had assumed the monsters of his past were a bygone era.

He hadn't known there were still ghosts out there who made the predators of Hollywood look quaint.

But the bulldog was loose now.

And he was hungry for blood.

Chapter 43: The Daughter

Manny's phone rang at 2:18 AM.

He was still awake. Still working. The office smelled like burnt coffee and desperation. Three empty Pepto-Bismol bottles lined his desk like soldiers who'd already surrendered. His hands shook—the Parkinson's worse at night, or maybe just the fear.

The caller ID said "Unknown." He answered anyway.

"Manny." It was Glitch. His voice tight with something electric. "I found her."

"Found who?"

"Roman Lazar's daughter."

The words hung in the smoke-thick air.

Manny sat up straighter, suddenly very awake. "What daughter?"

"Katya Lazar. Born 1981. Died 2004." Glitch's fingers were flying across a keyboard—Manny could hear the rapid clicks through the phone. "She was twenty-three. A journalist in Moscow. The real deal. Investigative reporter."

A notification pulsed on Manny's screen — the vault link Glitch had promised. He clicked it, entered the passphrase, and a single image loaded.

A young woman stared back at him. Dark hair pulled into a careless ponytail. Sharp, intelligent eyes. She was holding up a press badge, grinning at the camera like she'd just won something.

There was something fierce in that smile. Something that said she believed truth was a weapon.

"She'd just published her first major investigation," Glitch continued. "Oligarch embezzlement. Ties to the Kremlin. Money laundering through London shell companies. The whole package. It was brilliant work, Manny. Fearless. Two years out of college."

Manny's chest tightened. "Past tense."

"Yeah." Glitch's voice went flat. "Three days after publication, someone threw her from her apartment balcony. Eighth floor. Her editor found her body on the pavement the next morning."

"Jesus Christ."

"Police ruled it suicide. Case closed in forty-eight hours. No investigation. No witnesses. Just a dead girl and a very convenient conclusion." Glitch paused. "The oligarch she exposed? He went dark. Deep underground. Vanished into the global gray zone. The official story was that he took his billions and retired to a non-extradition haven where no one could touch him."

Manny stared at the photo. The girl's smile. The press badge held up like a shield that hadn't protected her from anything.

She'd died for the truth.

And someone had made sure it looked like she'd jumped.

"Where was Roman when this happened?"

"London. Business trip. He flew back the moment he heard." Glitch's typing slowed. "Then he disappeared for six months. Complete breakdown. The records say he checked into a private psychiatric clinic in Vienna. It wasn't his first visit. He went straight there. Like he was returning... home."

Manny lit a cigarette with hands that wouldn't stop shaking. "What did the shrinks say?"

"That's where it gets interesting." Glitch's voice changed. Became quieter. "I got into the clinic's files. Klinik Weisswald. Very exclusive. Very discreet. The kind of place that treats wealthy people who've had very public disasters."

"And?"

"Roman kept repeating the same thing. Over and over. For weeks." Glitch paused. "'If I'd known. If I'd been watching. If I'd seen the threat coming.'"

The cold clarity hit Manny like a fist.

Roman Lazar wasn't building Panopticon because he was evil.

He was building it because his daughter died and he couldn't save her and he'd decided the only way to stop it from happening again was to watch everyone. Know everything. Make sure no threat could ever hide.

"Maybe he wasn't always this," Manny murmured, his voice a low, rough thing, full of a conflict he didn't want to feel. "Maybe the monster is just... what grief left behind."

Manny's eyes were full of a weary, ancient sadness, thinking of Sophie. "He's a grieving father, kid. A grieving father who decided that the only way to make sure no one ever felt his pain again was to burn down the world's privacy to build a monument to his dead daughter. And God help me, for one sick second... I almost understand it."

"Bingo," Glitch's voice came back over the line, grim and sharp. "He thinks he's the hero. He's weaponized his grief. Turned it into a crusade."

"Which makes him more dangerous."

"Exactly. A villain who thinks he's saving the world? That's the kind who never stops. Never compromises. Never questions whether the cure is worse than the disease."

Manny stared at Katya's photograph. She'd been younger than Sloane. Younger than Sophie had been when—

He crushed that thought before it could finish.

"The therapist's notes are pretty clear," Glitch continued. "Patient exhibits profound grief and rage. Fixates on the idea that his daughter's death could have been prevented with better information. With total surveillance. States repeatedly that he intends to build a world where secrets cannot exist. Where no one can hide. Where the powerful cannot escape justice."

"Except he became the powerful one," Manny said. "He became exactly what killed his daughter."

"Yeah. Funny how that works." Glitch's laugh was bitter. "And that oligarch who supposedly retired? He didn't make it to any island. Roman hunted him down six months after leaving the clinic. Made it look like a heart attack. Clean. Professional. Untraceable."

"Revenge."

"Justice. At least that's how Roman would see it." Glitch paused. "But that was just the beginning. After Katya died, everything changed. He liquidated half his legitimate assets. Turned them into ghost companies. Started building the infrastructure for Panopticon. He's been at this for over two decades. Using dirty money the whole time. The initial versions had mixed success, and were unstable. Some even said it was a fool's errand. But Roman was relentless. He realized that he needed a young genius to solve the unsolvable. And more money than God. And time. And then he would solve it. For his Katya."

"Jesus..." Manny whispered. "Twenty years."

"Roman was nothing if not patient. He built a labyrinth of shell companies, invested in promising startups. Multiplying his money, scouting talent. That's how he found Damian."

"The wunderkind," Manny said.

"Two companies public before he turned twenty-three. Roman knew he'd found his architect. But here's the problem—Damian was young, brash, and already one of the richest men in the world. You can't buy a guy like that. You can't intimidate him. So what do you do?"

Manny's hand tightened on the cigarette. "You give him a mission."

"Exactly. Roman identified Damian at seventeen—a prodigy launching a company from his dorm room. He played the grand mentor with the grander vision. Groomed him for eight years. Through both IPOs. Both exits. Both disillusionments.

"And when Damian was twenty-five, lost and searching for meaning? Roman made his move. Convinced him to leave Silicon Valley, move to Switzerland, build his magnum opus. That's how Crystal Vision SARL was born.

"But here is the kicker, Manny. Damian threw out everything Roman gave him. The old Panopticon architectures, all of Roman's failed attempts from the nineties—junked. He built it from scratch. New math. New code. Everything."

Glitch's voice carried an edge of reluctant admiration. "Took him two years just to lay the foundation. Then another decade refining it. Brick by brick. The guy's a genius."

"Was stable," Manny said quietly. "Past tense."

"Yeah. He was close a year ago. Then Livia died. Damian fell apart. Dark despair, total isolation. Wouldn't see anyone. Wouldn't work. Roman's twenty-year investment was about to collapse because the architect lost his wife. The irony?" Glitch snorted softly, "Roman's the one who had her killed, jeopardizing his own investment. Presumably because she had dirt on him."

Manny exhaled smoke. "So Roman hired an actress to play her."

"Yep. That's where your friend came in. To stabilize Damian. To have him go the last mile and release the perfect product to The Consortium. The culmination of what began with Roman's dirty money and body count to boot."

Manny was quiet for a beat. "The Twelve don't know."

"The intelligence agencies he's partnering with? They think he's clean. A tech billionaire with a vision for a safer world." Glitch's typing picked up speed again. "They have no idea they're signing a deal with someone who's murdered, bribed, and extorted his way to this moment. Either that or they couldn't care less as long as they get what they want. Wouldn't be the first time they've dealt with a monster."

"That's the irony," Manny said. "He thinks he's building a system to stop the powerful from escaping justice. But he's the powerful one now. The one who kills to protect his empire."

"Welcome to the human condition. We become what we hate." Glitch's voice cracked slightly. "I'm sending you everything I found. Katya's investigation. The police report. The psychiatric records. Roman's financial transactions after her death. It's all there."

"How much?"

"Not much. Maybe fifty megabytes. Medical files, mostly. Some news articles. The police report. I'm uploading it to the vault now."

On Manny's screen, a notification pulsed—a new file added to the vault.

He clicked the link, the encryption handshake blooming across the display, and the dossier opened. He began to read.

And realized he was looking at the key to understanding Roman Lazar.

Not just his crimes.

His why.

"Glitch," Manny said. "This is good work."

"It's not enough to stop him," Glitch replied. "This tells us why he's building Panopticon. It doesn't prove he's a criminal. Grief isn't illegal. Revenge murder from two decades ago? Good luck proving it."

"So we keep digging."

"Already on it." Glitch paused. "Manny, listen. I tripped something when I accessed those psychiatric files. Not a local alarm. Something bigger. The clinic's security is way beyond standard medical privacy protocols. Someone paid serious money to protect those records."

"Roman."

"Has to be. Which means he knows someone broke in. He's probably already tracking the intrusion. I covered my tracks, but..." Glitch trailed off.

"But you're worried."

"I'm always worried. That's how I've stayed alive this long." A pause. "There's more to find. I can feel it. Something bigger. Something that ties everything together."

"Then find it," Manny said. "But be careful, kid. This guy doesn't leave witnesses."

"Neither do I." Glitch's attempt at bravado fell flat. "I'll call you when I have something."

The line went dead.

Manny sat in the silence of his office, staring at Katya Lazar's photograph. The young journalist who'd believed truth mattered. Who'd died for it.

Her father had turned her death into a weapon.

And now that weapon was about to be sold to twelve of the world's most powerful intelligence agencies.

Manny closed his laptop. Lit another cigarette. His hands were still shaking.

Somewhere in the digital dark, Glitch was hunting for more evidence.

Somewhere in Switzerland, Sloane was trapped in a nightmare.

And here, in a shitty office in Los Angeles, Manny Goldman held a file that explained why a grieving father had decided to destroy privacy itself.

It wasn't enough.

But it was a start.

He got back to work.

Chapter 44: The Final Test

Late November brought a biting frost that encrusted the windows in intricate, fractal patterns of ice.

Ten weeks of fire had forged a new weapon. The woman who had collapsed after three push-ups was a ghost. In her place was someone leaner, harder, colder. Her hands no longer shook when she held the Glock. Her breathing stayed calm under pressure. Her body was no longer a stranger's; it was an instrument she had learned to play with brutal precision. Nico had rebuilt her from the inside out.

The gala was less than a week away. The final preparations were a low hum of activity throughout the estate. But for Sloane, the real work was happening in the silence and the violence of her training.

She found Nico in the gym at dawn. He was standing in the center of the vast, empty room, a dark, motionless figure in the gray, snowy light. He had been different since their conversation on the Ghost Channel. The professional distance was still there for the cameras, but in the quiet moments, there was a new, shared intensity. A partnership forged in secrets.

"The training is over," he said, his voice quiet. "This is the final test."

She shed her warm-up jacket, leaving her in a simple black tank top and leggings. She moved to the center of the mat. Her body was different now. Ten weeks of relentless, brutal work had burned away the softness. She was lean, hard, and coiled. The woman who had collapsed after three push-ups was a ghost.

"Three minutes," Nico said. "Full contact. Everything I've taught you. You don't have to win. You just have to survive."

She nodded.

He came at her not like a teacher, but like an enemy. Fast. Efficient. Brutal. She reacted on pure, screaming instinct, the hours of muscle memory taking over.

Block. Parry. Pivot.

She ducked under a sweeping kick and drove her elbow toward his ribs. He absorbed the blow, his hand clamping onto her arm, using her momentum to twist her off-balance. She hit the mat. Hard.

"Get up," he growled.

She got up, her side a symphony of pain, and came at him again. Feint left, strike right. She was faster than she had ever been. Stronger.

At ninety seconds, she landed a solid kick to his thigh. He stumbled back a step, a flicker of genuine surprise in his eyes. He smiled. A rare, dangerous, feral thing. And he came back harder.

***

The next minute was a blur of pain and adrenaline. He was a professional killer. She was an actress who had learned how to fight. It was not an equal contest.

At two and a half minutes, he had her. Pinned to the mat, his forearm pressed against her throat, his body a dead weight. She was trapped. Defeated.

"Time," she gasped, ready to tap out.

"There is no 'time' in a real fight," he said, his voice a harsh whisper in her ear, the pressure increasing just enough to make her see stars. "There is only winning. Or dying. Find a way out."

Panic flared. She was going to black out. He wasn't stopping.

She stopped fighting his strength. She did the one thing he hadn't taught her. The one thing a street fighter from Oklahoma would do.

She bit him.

Her teeth sank into the flesh of his forearm. Hard. She tasted salt and blood.

He roared, a sound of pure, shocked pain, his arm recoiling.

It was the opening she needed.

She twisted, bucked, and threw all of her weight in one explosive movement. She was free. She scrambled to her feet, gasping for air, her fists raised, ready to go again.

Nico stood a few feet away, breathing hard, looking not at her, but at the deep, bleeding bite mark on his forearm. A slow, incredulous, and deeply impressed smile spread across his face.

He looked at the gym's clock. Three minutes and five seconds.

He looked back at her, at the defiant, terrified, and utterly unbreakable woman standing before him. The actress was gone. In her place was a warrior.

"You're ready," he said.

Sloane nodded, her breath coming in ragged gasps. She left the gym, her body aching, her mind sharp.

***

The rest of the day passed in a fugue state of high-stakes choreography. Final fittings for the emerald gown under Colette's critical eye. A tactical walkthrough of the ballroom with Katarina, mapping sightlines and exits. A quiet, tense dinner with Damian where they spoke of everything except the future. Sloane moved through it all on autopilot, her performance flawless, but the warrior underneath was waiting.

It was nearly midnight when she finally retreated to her suite. She stood in the center of the room, surrounded by the silence of the snow-muffled house. She waited for the familiar prickle of eyes on her skin. The invisible weight of Roman's attention that she had felt for weeks.

But tonight, the air felt different. Lighter. Empty.

The red light on the smoke detector didn't blink. The motion sensor in the corner seemed dormant.

It wasn't relief she felt; it was a cold, sinking dread.

He wasn't watching.

Which meant he didn't need to anymore. Roman Lazar didn't guard his prisoners. He just built cages so perfect he knew they could never leave.

She washed away the exhaustion of the long day and crawled into bed, telling herself it was just paranoia. Telling herself she was safe.

She closed her eyes, embracing the dark.

But she was wrong. The dark wasn't empty.

It was waiting.

Chapter 45: The Serpent on the Screen

She didn't know how long she slept. An hour? A minute?

She woke to darkness.

Not the normal darkness of a room at night. Something else. Something *wrong*.

The walls were moving.

Sloane's eyes snapped open. She sat up in bed, heart already hammering before her brain could catch up, and tried to understand what she was seeing.

The walls weren't walls anymore.

They were *static*. Black and white pixels that writhed and pulsed and *breathed* like something alive. All four walls. The ceiling. Even the floor beneath her bed was glowing with that sick, organic movement.

She was inside it. Inside the static. Inside the nightmare.

The room was cold. Had the temperature dropped? Or was that just her blood turning to ice?

And then the voice came.

Not from one direction. From *everywhere*. From the walls, from the ceiling, from beneath the floor, from the air itself. Surround sound. Perfect acoustics. Calm. Cultured. Kind.

"Hello, Sloane."

***

She couldn't move.

Couldn't breathe.

The static was *everywhere*. Covering every surface. Pulsing in rhythm with the voice. Like the room itself was speaking. Like the house had grown a mouth.

And underneath the static—barely visible, like something seen through deep water—a shape on the ceiling. The outline of a man. Sitting in darkness. No features. No details. Just a silhouette. A void where a person should be.

"I thought it was time we had a conversation."

The voice was coming from above her. Behind her. In front of her. She couldn't locate it. Couldn't pin it down. It was *omnidirectional*. Like God speaking from the clouds.

"You've been so busy lately." The silhouette on the ceiling shifted. Leaned forward. The static parted slightly around it, but revealed nothing. "Reading things that don't belong to you. Planning things you shouldn't plan. Making alliances with people who can't save you."

Sloane's throat was closed. Her mouth was open but no sound came out.

This wasn't real. This couldn't be real. She was dreaming. She had to be dreaming.

She pinched her arm. Hard. Hard enough to bruise.

Nothing changed.

The walls kept breathing.

The voice kept speaking.

And then she understood. This wasn't a dream. It wasn't a hallucination. The walls weren't walls. They were screens. The entire room—every surface—was a seamless, high-resolution display.

This was a video call. A projection. He had turned her bedroom into a 360-degree screen, and she was trapped inside it with him.

She could feel her heart hammering against her ribs. Could taste copper in her mouth where she'd bitten her tongue.

"I want you to understand something." Still calm. Still reasonable. Like a teacher explaining a simple concept to a struggling student. "I don't enjoy causing pain. I'm not a cruel man. But I am a *thorough* man. And thoroughness requires demonstrations."

The static glitched.

Every wall at once. A violent, disorienting burst of color and noise that felt like needles behind her eyes. She gasped. Tried to look away. But there was nowhere to look. It was on every surface. Surrounding her. Swallowing her.

When the image stabilized, the walls showed something different.

Manny.

But wrong. All wrong.

On all four walls. Four angles of the same grotesque illustration. Not a photograph—something rendered. Stylized. Like a panel from a dark graphic novel where human faces were drawn with too many lines, too much shadow, angles that didn't quite make anatomical sense.

Sitting in a chair in a concrete room. Hands bound behind his back. Face bruised in colors that were too saturated—purples too deep, reds too bright, yellows too sickly. One eye swollen shut and leaking something black—not blood, but ink. A single overhead bulb casting shadows that fell in impossible directions, making him look less like a man and more like a sketch of suffering.

The style was immaculate. Professional. Like someone had hired a manga artist to illustrate torture.

He looked up at a camera he couldn't see. His eyes—God, his eyes—were defiant. Angry. But underneath, rendered in obsessive, loving detail, she could see the fear.

The image wasn't real. But the threat was. This is what Roman could do. This is what he was planning to do. This was a preview. A promise. A threat wrapped in art.

"No," Sloane whispered. Her voice barely audible. "No, no, no—"

The images dissolved. Not like digital corruption. Like ink in water. The four versions of Manny bleeding across the walls—his illustrated face stretching, warping, mouth opening impossibly wide in a silent scream—before pooling at the floor like spilled paint and vanishing back into the breathing static.

"Your friend is comfortable," the voice said. Coming from everywhere. Coming from inside her head. "For now. Fed. Watered. Unharmed. But I wanted you to see the storyboards for the alternate ending. Beautiful work, isn't it? The artist I commissioned captured his fear perfectly. See how the pupils dilate? How the mouth tenses? That's real research. Real observation. I know exactly what your Manny looks like when he's afraid."

A pause. The static breathed.

"I know what you look like when you're afraid, too."

Sloane scrambled out of bed. Her legs tangled in the sheets. She fell. Hard. Knees hitting the floor—the floor that was now a writhing sea of static that made her eyes hurt to look at.

The door. She needed the door. Needed to get out. Needed—

The static pulsed. Faster now. Like a heart rate accelerating. Like something getting excited. Like it was enjoying this.

Another image materialized.

This one worse. Worse because it was even more beautifully rendered. Worse because someone had spent hours on the shading. Worse because it showed care.

Not a photograph. On all four walls. Eight feet tall. Inescapable.

Another illustration. The same dark style. Hyper-detailed. Almost loving in its precision.

A young girl. Fifteen. Dark curls. An awkward, hopeful smile, a glint of silver braces. Standing outside a school gate. Yellow backpack slung over one shoulder. The style made her look both more innocent and more vulnerable—eyes too large, posture unguarded, shadows falling across her like she was already haunted.

Completely unaware that a camera was watching her.

Nico's daughter?

But beside her—in three of the four wall-versions—was a second panel. The same girl. Different scene. Mouth open in a scream. Hands reaching. The yellow backpack torn. The school burning behind her.

Not real. Not yet. But rendered with the same obsessive care. The same attention to detail. The same artistic talent put to monstrous purpose.

On the fourth wall, just text in elegant, hand-lettered script: "Chapter One: Before" and "Chapter Two: After."

Like a storyboard. Like a graphic novel. Like Roman had commissioned a proof of concept for her destruction.

"Mr. Sorrento has been very loyal to you," the voice said. The image of his daughter—four versions of Before, three versions of After—surrounded her. "Admirable, really. I wanted him to know I've been thinking about her. Studying her routine. Her school. Her friends. Her walk home. I had an artist render several possible outcomes. This is just one. Would you like to see the others?"

The three "After" panels started to change. Flickering through variations. Different scenarios. Different horrors. All rendered in that same beautiful, terrible style.

"Loyalty is a lever, Sloane. And every person you care about is another lever I can pull. But more than that—every person you care about is another story I can commission. Another panel I can draw. Another chapter I can write."

The images started to bleed.

On all four walls at once.

The digital ink ran like fresh blood. The illustrations melted, dissolving into abstract horror—geometric patterns that vibrated, fractals that seared her retinas, colors that shouldn't exist pooling into shapes that looked like mouths. Like hands. Like something trying to claw its way out of the walls—

Sloane made a sound. Not a word. Not a scream. Something broken. Something animal.

She was crawling now. Hands and knees on the static floor that pulsed and moved beneath her palms. Crawling toward the door. Toward escape. Toward anything that wasn't this.

The walls returned to static. All of them. The ceiling. The floor. The silhouette above her like a dark angel.

"I know everything," the voice said.

The static pulsed with each word. Fed on them. Grew darker. Heavier. The bass so deep she could feel it in her chest. In her bones.

PULSE. The room shook. Or maybe that was just her.

"That desperate, shivering call from the payphone in Küssnacht."

PULSE. Louder. Deeper. The subwoofers were weapons.

"Did you really think a few coins in a slot could buy you privacy? You didn't find a lifeline, Sloane. You just painted a target on an old friend's back."

PULSE. Her ears were ringing.

"Your feelings for Damian."

The walls flickered. All four at once. Showed an image: the garden. Dawn light. The two of them on the bench by the koi pond. His hand holding hers. The moment before the kiss.

"The way you looked at him in Küssnacht. At that little bookstore. The way you touched his face in the garden. That wasn't you playing Livia. That was *you*."

The image dissolved back into static.

PULSE. Her heart was trying to escape her chest.

"And I know about Nico."

New image. The library. His hands in her hair. Her body pressed against his. His mouth on hers.

"The library. 2:47 AM. The way you and Nico flew apart when that door opened. Guilty children caught stealing. You were so frantic to separate—his hand still tangled in your hair, your breath still on his lips. Katarina didn't even need to say a word."

A pause. The static breathed. "Tell me, Sloane. Was that method acting too? Or do you just have a weakness for broken men in glass cages?"

The image began to burn. Pixels turning to ash.

PULSE. The floor was vibrating.

"And of course, I know about Damian's room. Two weeks ago. His bed. The way you whispered his name when you—"

"Stop," Sloane gasped. "Please. Stop."

"Why? You didn't stop. You didn't think about the consequences. You didn't think about the fact that every kiss, every touch, every whispered word belonged to *me. I* was there. I'm always there."

PULSE. PULSE.

Sloane sank to her knees, her hands clawing at her own arms as if she could scrape his gaze off her skin. The memory of Damian's touch—the one thing she had told herself was real—turned rancid in her mind. It wasn't a memory anymore; it was footage. Content. A scene she had performed for an audience of one.

Bile rose in her throat, hot and acidic. A jagged, wet sound tore out of her chest—not a sob, but a rejection of the air in the room.

"Oh, Sloane," his voice softened to a whisper. Intimate. Disgustingly soothing. "Don't look so shattered. I hired you to be Damian's muse, and frankly? The improvisation in his bed... it was a masterclass. The vulnerability. The desperation. That is exactly the level of commitment I paid for.

"And look at the return on my investment. You didn't just comfort him; you unlocked him. You gave him the missing variable he's been hunting for months. Thanks to your... performance... the code is finally perfect. Panopticon is awake."

The static wall in front of her shifted. A vague shape leaned closer.

"Bring that same passion to the Gala. Make The Twelve fall in love with you just like Damian did. But no more secrets. Or else—"

PULSE. PULSE. PULSE.

The room screamed.

Sloane reached the door. Grabbed the handle with both hands. Pulled.

It didn't move.

She pulled again. Harder. Desperate.

Locked.

No. No, it couldn't be locked. This was her room. She lived here. She should be able to—

"Where are you going?" the voice asked. Amused now. Coming from directly behind her head even though there was nothing there when she whipped around to look.

The silhouette on the ceiling was standing now. Rising. Growing. Filling the entire ceiling with its formless mass.

"Sit down, Sloane," the voice said. Gentle. Patient. Like speaking to a child. "We're not finished talking."

"Let me out." Her voice was shaking. Breaking. "Please. Please let me out."

"You might wonder," the voice continued, ignoring her plea entirely, "why I'm telling you this. Why reveal the extent of my knowledge. It's because I believe, fundamentally, that you are one of the smartest people in this equation besides myself."

The silhouette was moving across the ceiling. Flowing like smoke. Like liquid. Getting closer to where she huddled by the door.

"And I believe that once you understand the stakes—your friend's life, the girl's life, your own—you will make the logical, rational choice."

Sloane pressed her back against the door. Slid down to sit on the floor. Her hands were covering her ears but she could still hear him. The sound was *inside* her head now. Vibrating through the door, through the floor, through her bones.

"You will perform at the gala, Sloane."

The static began to pulse faster. Faster. Faster. All four walls. The ceiling. The floor. Everything moving in sync.

"You will be flawless."

PULSE.

"You will smile."

PULSE.

"You will stand beside Damian."

PULSE.

"And you will get him to sign the documents I place in front of him."

PULSE. PULSE. PULSE.

The pulsing reached a crescendo. The room became a storm. The walls a violent chaos of black and white and impossible colors. Shapes that moved wrong. Patterns that made her eyes water and her brain scream for it to *stop*, please God, please make it *stop—*

"And if you do this—" The voice was louder now. Not shouting. Just *present.* Unavoidable. "—if you follow my very simple instructions—everyone you love stays alive."

The static was screaming. A high-pitched whine from the speakers that felt like glass in her ears.

"But if you disappoint me—"

The walls were closing in. Not literally. But it felt like it. The static pressing down. Suffocating. Drowning.

"—if you betray me—"

Closer.

"—if you run—"

Closer.

"—if you try to warn anyone—"

The whine was unbearable. Her hands were over her ears but it didn't matter. It was coming from *inside* the room. Inside the walls. Inside her skull.

"—then I will take them apart piece by piece—"

Closer.

"—while you—"

CLOSER.

"—watch."

The storm reached its peak. The room was pure sensory overload. Visual chaos. Audio assault. Physical vibration so intense she thought her teeth might shatter. Colors that hurt. Sounds that cut. Patterns that made her brain feel like it was being *pulled apart—*

And then.

Silence.

Complete silence.

Every wall went black at once. The static disappeared like it had never existed. The speakers cut out. The temperature normalized. The lights came back on—soft, warm, normal bedroom lights.

The room looked exactly like it had when she'd gone to sleep.

Walls were walls. Ceiling was ceiling. Floor was floor.

Nothing was breathing. Nothing was moving. Nothing was wrong.

Except her.

Chapter 46: The Aftershocks

Sloane sat on the floor by the door.

Her body shaking so violently her teeth were chattering. Her nightgown soaked with sweat. Her hands still pressed over her ears even though the sound was gone.

Had it been real?

It had felt real. The static. The voice. The images. Manny. Nico's daughter. The colors that shouldn't exist.

But the room was normal now. Peaceful. Innocent. The walls were just plaster and paint. The mirror was just glass.

Maybe she'd imagined it. Maybe she was losing her mind. Maybe the stress was finally breaking her and—

A soft, cheerful chime sounded. The house AI's notification tone.

Sloane froze.

The wall facing the bed—the one that had just been a screaming mosaic of Manny's face—flickered. A single, crisp line of text appeared in the center, glowing in a gentle, ambient white.

Sleep well, Sloane. The big day is nearly upon us.

It held there for five seconds. Just long enough to be read. Just long enough to prove he was still in the operating system.

Then it faded.

The room was dark again.

Her legs gave out.

She collapsed onto the floor, curling into a fetal position on the cold carpet.

It had been real.

All of it.

He'd done that. Roman Lazar. The faceless man. The void. The shadow.

He'd turned her room into a nightmare. Had locked her inside it. Had made her watch while he showed her exactly how powerless she was.

And then he'd let her go.

Because the cage was never really locked. She could leave whenever she wanted.

She just had nowhere to go.

The walls had eyes. The ceiling had ears. The floor had memory.

And Roman was everywhere.

She tried to breathe. Couldn't. Her chest was too tight. Her throat was closing. She was drowning on dry land.

Manny. Tied to a chair. Beaten. Alone.

Nico's daughter. A child who didn't know she was a hostage.

Damian. Who thought she loved him. Who had no idea he was sleeping with a weapon.

And her. Failed actress. Blacklisted has-been. Ghost in a dead woman's skin.

Trapped in a house that was really a mouth.

Being slowly swallowed.

She couldn't do this. She couldn't—

The bathroom.

The only room in her suite without cameras. Without screens. Without eyes.

She rolled off the bed. Hit the floor. Crawled—couldn't stand, couldn't trust her legs—across the carpet that had been static minutes ago.

Reached the bathroom door. Pulled herself up. Stumbled inside.

Locked the door.

The only lock in her entire prison that actually meant something.

She turned on the shower. Hot. As hot as it would go. Steam filled the room immediately. Thick. Choking. Good.

She stepped under the spray fully clothed. The silk nightgown plastered to her skin. The water so hot it should have burned but she couldn't feel it.

All she could feel was the weight of his eyes.

Still watching.

Always watching.

She slid down the tile wall. Pulled her knees to her chest. Let the water hammer down on her head while her mouth opened and—

She screamed.

Finally.

Let it out. All of it. The terror. The rage. The helplessness. The knowledge that she was trapped and watched and owned and there was nothing—*nothing*—she could do about it.

She screamed until her throat was raw. Until her voice gave out. Until the only sound left was the water and her own ragged breathing.

And then she just sat there. In the steam. In the heat. The only space in this entire house where Roman Lazar couldn't see her.

Or was he here, too?

She stared at the vent in the ceiling. The gap behind the mirror. Was there a pinhole in the grout? A sensor in the glass? She squeezed her eyes shut, but the prickle on her skin didn't stop. She felt naked, not just in body, but in soul.

Except that it didn't matter.

Because he didn't need cameras to watch her.

He was in her head now. In her memories. In her nightmares.

I know everything.

The words played on loop. Over and over. A mantra. A curse.

I know about the call from the payphone. I know about your feelings for Damian. I know about Nico. I know. I know. I know.

She pressed her forehead to her knees.

How?

She'd been so careful. So precise. Every move calculated. Every secret buried.

But did he know the rest?

The journal? The Ghost Channel? Manny's hacker?

Was there no safe space left?

There was only Roman. And his eyes. And his voice.

Everywhere and nowhere.

The water kept falling. She kept breathing. Barely.

Time became meaningless. Minutes. Hours. She didn't know. Didn't care.

Eventually the water ran cold. Eventually her body stopped shaking. Eventually the only thing left was a numb, hollow acceptance.

He was everywhere.

And there was nowhere—nowhere—she could hide.

***

When she finally turned off the water, the bathroom was silent. The mirror completely fogged. She couldn't see her reflection.

Good.

She didn't want to see what she'd become.

She peeled off the soaked nightgown. Left it in a heap on the floor. Wrapped herself in a towel and stood there, dripping, staring at nothing.

The door was still locked. She'd locked it herself. From the inside.

But suddenly she was afraid to open it.

What if the room was static again? What if she opened the door and the walls were breathing and the voice was waiting?

What if this was the rest of her life?

Locked in a bathroom. Afraid of her own bedroom. Prisoner in a cage made of architecture and light.

She put her hand on the doorknob. Her fingers were trembling.

One. Two. Three.

She opened it.

The bedroom was normal. Peaceful. Soft lamplight. Cream-colored walls. Hardwood floor. The bed with its rumpled sheets.

No static. No voice. No nightmare.

Just a room.

A beautiful, expensive, comfortable prison.

She walked to the bed on legs that felt like they belonged to someone else. Sat on the edge. Stared at her hands.

Sloane Devereaux.

Thirty years old.

Failed actress.

Blacklisted has-been.

Ghost in a dead woman's skin.

And now—as of tonight—officially broken.

She lay back on the bed. Pulled the covers up to her chin. Stared at the ceiling.

The ceiling where, just an hour ago, a silhouette had been watching her.

She closed her eyes. Not to sleep. She knew sleep wouldn't come. Just to not see the ceiling. Not see the walls. Not see the room that had tried to eat her alive.

But closing her eyes didn't make him go away.

In the darkness behind her eyelids, she could see him. Somewhere. In a room she would never find. Sitting in a chair she couldn't see. Watching a bank of monitors where her misery played out in high definition.

She imagined him leaning forward. Watching the rise and fall of her chest. Watching the tremor in her hands.

And she could feel his smile.

It felt like a drop in temperature. Cold. Satisfied. The quiet nod of a craftsman realizing the tool finally fits the hand.

She belonged to him.

Every breath. Every thought. Every secret hope.

His.

Tomorrow she would wake up. Put on Livia's face. Sit through Katarina's lessons. Smile at Damian over breakfast. Pretend everything was fine.

Because that was the performance.

And the show had to go on.

Even if the audience was a monster.

Even if the stage was a cage.

Even if the applause was just the sound of her own heart breaking.

She lay in the darkness and waited for dawn. Knowing—knowing—that the walls were watching. That the ceiling was listening. That the room itself belonged to him.

And that tomorrow, when she woke up, she would smile.

Because Roman Lazar had just taught her the most important lesson of all.

Resistance was futile.

Hope was a lie.

And the only way to survive was to become exactly what he'd always known she was.

A weapon.

His weapon.

Perfect. Obedient. Aimed at Damian's heart.

She opened her eyes one more time. Looked at the ceiling. At the invisible lens she knew was there.

She whispered into the darkness.

"I understand."

Two words.

Surrender wrapped in acceptance.

And somewhere in the dark, she knew Roman heard her.

And smiled.

Chapter 47: The Gala Dossier

Sunday morning broke over the Alps with the cold, sharp clarity of a blade.

The mist had vanished. The mountains stood exposed against a hard blue sky. In thirty-six hours, the doors would open, and the world would walk in.

Katarina stood at the front of the small conference room, her expression as cold and precise as a surgeon. She didn't need to look out the window to know the enemy had arrived.

Across the dark water of Lake Lucerne, the lights of the Bürgenstock Resort glittered like a diamond necklace draped over the opposing mountain.

"The Consortium is in residence," Katarina said, her voice flat. "The Twelve arrived at the Bürgenstock three days ago. Their technical teams have spent the last seventy-two hours running red-team simulations against the prediction engine. Feeding it adversarial data. Edge cases. Chaos. They tried to blind the algorithm. They failed. It saw everything. Now, they are satisfied the weapon works."

She tapped the screen, bringing up the timeline.

"Tomorrow night is the Gala. It is not a celebration. It is a viability assessment. The lawyers have spent two years drafting a multi-trillion-dollar deal. The code is ready. The money is ready. The only variable left is Damian."

Sloane looked at the dossier on the table. Twelve names. Twelve people who could buy and sell countries. Not investors. Spies.

"The deal includes a 'Stability Clause,'" Katarina continued. "The Consortium needs to know that the machine's architect is sane enough to run it. If Damian cracks, if he looks grief-stricken or erratic, the deal dies in the room."

"So I'm not just a wife," Sloane said. "I'm the insurance policy."

"You are the proof of life," Katarina corrected. "They need to see him happy. They need to see him whole. You are the glue holding a multi-trillion-dollar house of cards together."

She swiped the screen, changing the display.

"But the Consortium is only the primary threat. There is a secondary audience. Smaller, but sharper."

"Livia's friends," Sloane said.

"Emotional landmines," Katarina agreed. "Damian's therapists thought it would be beneficial for his 'recovery' to include them. I pruned the guest list aggressively, but I couldn't eliminate them entirely without raising suspicion. A Livia Crestwell with zero friends is a red flag. So a few remain. For optics."

She looked at Sloane, her eyes icy. "The Consortium is looking for business stability. The friends are looking for *Livia*. They know her tics. Her history. Her soul. If you can fool them, you can fool anyone."

Sloane's stomach tightened. "And the inner circle?"

"Roman's lieutenants," Katarina said, tapping the screen again. Two faces appeared. "Kovac Sokolov, his head of security. A ghost. You won't see him unless he wants you to. And Violet. She runs the financial side of the Lazarus Group. She is ambitious, intelligent, and utterly loyal to Roman. He calls her his 'Viper.' Avoid her at all costs."

"Study their files," Katarina commanded. "Memorize every detail. Your life depends on it."

"Understood."

Katarina closed the tablet. "All of them will be watching. The spies for weakness. The friends for recognition. The viper for blood. Give them nothing."

"I won't."

"Good." Katarina's expression softened. Barely. For just a moment. "You're stronger than you think, Sloane. Stronger than Livia was. If anyone can survive this, it's you."

It was the first time Katarina had used her real name.

Sloane didn't know what to say.

Katarina turned away. "That's all. Get some rest. Tomorrow will be very long."

***

Later that night, a soft chime at her door. It was Katarina.

"Walk with me," she said, her voice a low, conspiratorial murmur that made the hairs on Sloane's arms stand up. It was not a request.

Sloane followed her not to the main salon, but out onto a small, private balcony she had never seen before, a stone ledge that overlooked the vast, dark expanse of the lake. The air was cold and sharp.

Katarina lit a long, thin cigarette, the flame briefly illuminating her stark, angular features. "I know what you are," she said, her voice a low, dangerous murmur as she exhaled a plume of smoke into the night air.

Sloane's heart hammered, but she kept her face a neutral mask. "I'm Livia Crestwell."

"No," Katarina said with weary contempt. "You are a weapon. And you are beginning to aim yourself."

She took another drag from her cigarette, the cherry glowing bright in the darkness. "I have watched you with Mr. Sorrento. The stolen moments in the library. The charged silence in the gardens. I see the way he tracks your movements—not like a bodyguard protecting a client, but like a man watching the only thing that matters. Those brutal sessions in the gym? That isn't just training. That is intimacy disguised as violence. You aren't just forging an alliance. You are recruiting a soldier."

Sloane was silent. It was not a denial.

"You are going to try to run," Katarina stated simply. "And you are going to try to hurt Roman on your way out."

"That's a dangerous accusation." The denial was automatic, but hollow.

"Please," Katarina said, her voice laced with weary contempt. "I've been playing this game since before you were born. I see what the machine doesn't. I see the human variable." She took another drag from her cigarette. "Do you know what he did to Livia? She wasn't just my employer. She was... family. I've spent a year waiting for someone strong enough, crazy enough, to finish what she started."

"Can I trust you?" Sloane asked, the question a stark, simple thing in the cold air.

"That," Katarina said, and a faint, dangerous smile touched her lips, "is the question, isn't it? I could be Roman's final test, feeding you false hope before crushing you. Or I could be exactly what I appear to be: a woman who wants to see the man who destroyed her family burn."

"So which is it?"

"At the gala, watch for a woman in a blood-red gown. Near the champagne fountain. If the glass drops, you have your answer. If she drinks from it, you have a different answer."

Sloane's breath caught. "Violet," she realized. "You're using his own lieutenant as the trigger?"

Katarina's expression was unreadable in the moonlight. "Yes. She will be there. Watching. As she always does." A pause. "But the signal is not about her. It is about me. About whether I am still... free to act."

"And if she drinks?"

"Then you know I cannot help you." Katarina's voice was cold. "And you are alone."

Sloane's mind raced. "Why not just—"

"Because he is watching." Katarina cut her off, her voice dropping to a whisper. "Me. You. Sorrento. Everyone. If I signal you directly, you are dead before the champagne bubbles pop." She flicked her cigarette over the balcony rail. "The woman in red is noise. Background. A ghost at a party full of ghosts."

A pause. The wind carried smoke between them.

"And because you need to learn." Katarina's eyes were hard. "You are still too trusting. You want allies. You want certainty. That will kill you. Question everything. Everyone. Even me. Especially me."

Sloane's mind raced, probing for the flaw. "And if she doesn't show up at all?"

Katarina looked out at the black, sleeping lake. "Then it means I'm already compromised," she said quietly. "And you have bigger problems than whether you can trust a ghost."

She turned and walked back inside, leaving Sloane alone on the balcony, the cold biting at her skin.

She stared at the closed door, her mind reeling. The gala. A woman in red. A glass of champagne.

Everything depended on whether it shattered.

Chapter 48: The Dark Night

She woke at 3:00 AM. Couldn't go back to sleep. The waiting was over. The day had arrived. Tonight, she would walk into a room full of the world's most dangerous people and smile.

She sat up in bed. Stared at the ceiling. The ceiling where, two nights ago, Roman's silhouette had watched her.

Was he watching now?

Probably. Always.

She got out of bed. Walked to the bathroom. Turned on the shower. Hot. As hot as it would go.

But she didn't get in.

Instead, she slid down the tile wall. Sat on the cold floor. Pulled her knees to her chest.

And realized she was thinking about walking away.

Just walking. Out the door. Into the woods. Into the snow. Let the cold take her. It would be an ending. A quiet one. No more performing. No more fear. No more watching Damian look at her like she was salvation when she was just another lie.

Just... peace.

It was the closest she had ever come to giving up.

Then she thought of Manny, under siege in Los Angeles. She thought of Damian, a prisoner in his own home. She thought of Nico, a father chained by love for a daughter he couldn't protect.

And the whisper of surrender was drowned out by a familiar, stubborn rage.

Roman Lazar would not win. Not like this. Not without a fight.

She had no plan. No physical weapon. No allies she could safely contact.

But she knew how to read a character.

Roman played the role of a god—cold, omniscient, untouchable. But gods didn't need to watch everyone. Gods didn't need to build fortresses or terrorize women with storyboards of loss.

Only broken men did that.

He was afraid of something. Chaos. Surprise. Loss. Somewhere in his past, the world had hurt him, and he had built an all-seeing machine to make sure it never happened again.

He wasn't a machine. He was a man with a wound.

And wounds could be pressed.

She turned off the water, dried herself, and got dressed.

She walked to the mirror. Stared at the woman looking back. Pale. Exhausted. Terrified.

But not broken. Not yet.

"Tonight," she whispered to her reflection, "I walk into that room. I smile. I play my part. And I wait for the monster to blink."

She moved to the window. The darkness was absolute. No stars. No moon. Just the black glass of the lake below.

The rehearsal was finished. The real performance—the one that bled—was about to begin.

There was no going back.

Chapter 49: The Serpent's Gaze

Eight o'clock. Showtime.

The descent down the grand, floating staircase was like walking on air. The emerald Valentino gown, Livia's armor, felt like a second skin, cool and heavy against her own. Every eye in the room turned to her—hundreds of the world's most powerful, critical, and influential people, watching.

Sloane felt their collective gaze as a physical force. Curiosity. Skepticism. Awe. She was not just a woman in a beautiful dress. She was a ghost walking in the light, a miracle, a myth made flesh.

The ballroom was a stage set for the end of the world.

Crystal chandeliers hung overhead like frozen explosions. Marble floors reflected hundreds of beautiful, dangerous people in formal wear. In the corner, a string quartet played Vivaldi—background music for people who could buy countries before dessert.

Sloane recognized faces from the dossiers. Consortium members. Roman's lieutenants. Livia's friends.

They weren't guests. They were an audience that could destroy her with a single wrong note.

Sloane reached up to tuck a stray lock of hair behind her ear, her finger grazing the cold, invisible plastic of the micro-receiver molded deep inside her canal. It was silent for now, but open. A direct line to the woman who was pulling the strings.

She located the three points of her compass.

She felt the familiar, electric hum of stage fright, but it was sharper now. Cold. In Hollywood, she had spent the last five years begging for a spotlight. Now she was stepping into one that could burn her alive. There would be no second take tonight. No director to call "Cut" if she missed her mark. Just a live audience of predators waiting for her to stumble.

At the bottom of the stairs, her anchor, her scene partner, the sun around which her counterfeit world had to orbit: Damian. He was waiting for her, his face a mask of pure, worshipful, and tragic adoration.

To the southeast, near a towering ice sculpture of a swan, was her grounding reality: Nico. He was a dark, silent shadow in his perfectly tailored suit, a glass of water in his hand, his posture relaxed but his eyes constantly in motion, scanning exits, tracking threats. He was not watching the crowd. He was watching her.

And across the room, by the champagne fountain, was the answer she was waiting for.

The woman in the blood-red gown.

It wasn't just red. It was the color of a fresh wound, a sheath of crimson silk so dark it was almost black in the shadows, shimmering under the chandelier light as if wet. She was young, beautiful, her dark hair falling in a sleek, straight cascade down her back, her smile a polite, surgical incision.

Sloane recognized her instantly from Katarina's dossier. Violet. The Viper.

Positioned precisely as Katarina had described.

The woman held a delicate crystal flute, the bubbles rising in a slow, golden stream. She lifted it slowly, elegantly to her lips.

Sloane's heart, which had been a steady, professional drum, gave a single, hard kick of dread. She's going to drink it.

Then you know I cannot help you.

The memory of Katarina's voice was cold and final.

And you are alone.

Then the woman paused. Her eyes, dark and intelligent, found Sloane's across the crowded ballroom. And deliberately, almost in slow motion, she let the glass slip from her fingers.

It shattered on the white marble floor with a bright, crystalline sound. Champagne spread across the stone like liquid gold. Several guests turned to look at the minor disturbance, then dismissed it as a clumsy accident even as a steward materialized to erase the mess.

But Sloane saw the spectacle for what it was. A signal. A promise.

Across the room, half-hidden behind a marble pillar, Katarina stood watching. Her face was a mask, unreadable, cold. But her eyes met Sloane's. And she gave the slightest nod. Almost imperceptible.

She was in.

Sloane felt something loosen in her chest—not relief, exactly, but a definitive shift in the odds. One more ally. One more piece on the board.

She gave a single, almost imperceptible nod back, and then she turned her full, dazzling focus to the man at the bottom of the stairs.

She caught a glimpse through the ballroom's glass doors of the private conference room on the mezzanine level. It was dark, a quiet void above the chaos of the party. But the man inside, holding the high ground, wasn't the silver-haired architect she expected.

It was a man built like a concrete pillar in a tuxedo that couldn't conceal his brutality. Kovac. The ghost from Katarina's dossier. Roman's shadow.

He held an open dossier in his hands, a polite fiction for anyone glancing up from the floor. But his eyes never dropped to the page. He was dissecting the crowd. He simply marked her position, catalogued her presence, and turned his attention back to the perimeter.

The cage was locked.

She turned away, her heart hammering against her ribs.

Her eyes scanned the crowd, picking out the faces from the dossier. The woman in Chanel by the window was the deputy director of the CIA's Special Activities Center. The man with the silver beard was MI6's director of operations. They and the other ten representatives of The Twelve moved through the room with practiced ease, but Sloane could see the calculations behind their polite smiles. These weren't investors. They were predators. And they were here to buy a weapon.

They circulated with the confidence of people who owned the world, orchestrating introductions, smoothing conversations, positioning themselves on the human chessboard. But there was a tension in the air. An expectation. They were waiting for their king.

Her performance began.

***

As she reached the final step, Damian took her hand, his own trembling slightly. His eyes were locked on hers with an intensity that made her chest ache. He looked like a man seeing a vision. A man seeing salvation.

"Livia," he whispered, the name a prayer, a confession, a plea. "You are... breathtaking."

Sloane gave him the small, intimate smile she had practiced a thousand times in the mirror, the smile that said you and I are the only two people in this room. She let her fingers tighten around his, a gesture of reassurance, of conspiracy, of love.

"Am I?" she replied, her voice a soft, amused murmur that only he could hear. She let a hint of Livia's particular brand of self-deprecating wit color the words. "I just put on the first old thing I could find."

A ripple of warm, appreciative laughter moved through the guests closest to them. The tension broke like a soap bubble. She was a charming, witty hostess. A woman very much alive. The room erupted in polite, welcoming applause.

Damian's eyes shone. He brought her hand to his lips, a gesture so tender and so full of raw, unguarded emotion that Sloane felt something crack inside her chest. Guilt. Sharp and hot and impossible to ignore.

This was not a role. This was war, waged on a stage of marble and champagne. And the curtain had just gone up.

Chapter 50: A Masterclass in Deception

For the next two hours, Sloane was a supernova. She moved through the glittering crowd on Damian's arm, a flawless, radiant Livia, her every word, every gesture, a masterclass in deception. But this was not the cold, technical performance she had planned. It was something far more dangerous, fueled by the complicated, genuine emotions churning inside her.

Her audience was not the crowd.

It was Damian.

With every witty remark, with every shared, knowing glance, she was playing directly to him. She was performing the part of the brilliant, captivating woman he was falling in love with, the woman she had been in his arms just a few nights ago, surrendering to a raw, consuming heat. And the guilt of it was a sharp, constant pain beneath the triumph of her performance. His adoration was not for a ghost anymore. It was for her, for the artist who was crafting this beautiful, poisonous lie. And he was drinking it down like a healing tonic.

Katarina's voice was a cool, steady presence in her ear, a river of data feeding her the lines she needed, a director giving notes from the wings. The earpiece was so small, so perfectly molded to her ear canal, that it was invisible. A technological miracle. A leash disguised as assistance.

"On your right, the man with the red pocket square. That is Heinrich Wolff, CEO of Bayer Quantum Systems. Livia found him boorish but necessary. At the

Vienna Summit last year, you mocked his yacht, calling it 'a floating testament to insecurity.' He found it hilarious."

Sloane turned, her smile dazzling, and caught Damian's eye. She leaned in close, her voice a conspiratorial whisper. "Watch this."

She glided toward Wolff, a large, florid man with the confident bearing of someone who had never been told no. "Heinrich, darling!" she said, her voice warm, her arms outstretched. "I see you survived your latest adventure on that magnificent boat of yours. Tell me, have you finally added the helipad? Or are you still making your guests arrive by jet ski?"

Wolff let out a booming laugh that turned heads across the ballroom. He was utterly captivated. "Livia! My God, you haven't changed a bit. Still the sharpest tongue in Europe." He embraced her, a bear hug that smelled of expensive cigars and scotch.

Sloane gave a tiny, private eye-roll in Damian's direction, a shared joke, a moment of intimate conspiracy. His face broke into a genuine, boyish grin. The kind of smile that transformed him from a haunted genius into something younger, lighter, hopeful.

The intimacy of that moment was a small, sharp knife twisting in her gut.

As she turned away from Wolff, the gorgeous woman in the blood-red gown stepped smoothly into her path, blocking her return to Damian.

Violet.

"Mrs. Crestwell," the woman said, her voice a low, European purr. "How lovely to see you recovered. Roman speaks so highly of your... resilience."

"Thank you," Sloane said carefully, her own performance clicking back into place.

Violet's smile didn't reach her eyes. She reached out and straightened a crystal pin on Sloane's shoulder strap. Her fingers lingered near Sloane's throat, cold and deliberate.

"You're wearing the Valentino," Violet noted, her eyes drifting over the bodice with clinical precision. "Livia hated this dress. She told me the silk chafed her skin. You seem remarkably comfortable in it."

Sloane's heart skipped a beat. It was a trap. A lie designed to rattle her. To check for flaws in the merchandise.

But Sloane remembered the video in Fairweather's office. The emerald gown. The Parisian gala. The diamond necklace. Livia hadn't looked uncomfortable; she had looked radiant. She had looked like a queen.

Sloane let a small, indulgent smile play on her lips—the look one gives a forgetful child.

"Nonsense," she said, her voice a cool, melodic chime. "It's my favorite. I wore it to the gala in Paris—with the diamond necklace, remember? I felt like a million dollars that night."

She leaned in, dropping her voice to a conspiratorial whisper, turning the knife. "Perhaps your memory is playing tricks on you, Violet. Or perhaps you're just projecting your own... discomfort."

Violet held the stare for a second too long, her expression tightening as the trap snapped shut on her own fingers.

Then she was gone, gliding back into the crowd like a serpent disappearing into tall grass.

Sloane stood frozen. That wasn't just a greeting. It was a warning shot.

Later, while Sloane was trapped in a conversation with a tedious Belgian diplomat, she looked across the ballroom at Damian. He was talking to a group of men in expensive suits, explaining something with his hands, his face animated in that way it got when he was lost in his beautiful, abstract world. He looked happy. Whole.

One of the men—she recognized him from the guest list as the FSB deputy chairman—said something that made Damian laugh. Even from across the room, she could almost hear his earnest explanation, a version of the speech she had heard a dozen times. She could practically read his lips: *"No, no, Panopticon isn't surveillance, it's prediction. We prevent conflicts before they begin. Humanitarian applications, disaster response, ethical resource allocation..."*

Damian still believed in his beautiful utopian dream, even as the men who were preparing to turn it into a global nightmare nodded and smiled.

She felt something crack in her chest. He still believed. After everything, after all of Livia's warnings that he had surely dismissed, he still believed in the goodness of his creation.

"Approaching now, Countess Annelise von Hess," Katarina's voice continued, relentless, efficient. "Austrian aristocracy. Her son, Klaus, was just arrested for embezzlement in Prague. Show sympathy, but with an edge of condescension. Livia believed the boy was a spoiled fool who would never amount to anything."

Sloane pivoted smoothly, her expression shifting from playful to concerned in a heartbeat. The Countess was a thin, elegant woman in her sixties, her face a mask of aristocratic composure barely concealing deep embarrassment.

"Annelise, my dear," Sloane murmured, taking the Countess's hands in her own. Her touch was warm, her expression a perfect blend of sympathy and steel. "I was so terribly sorry to hear about Klaus. Boys will be boys, I suppose. Though one does hope they'll learn to balance a checkbook before they turn forty."

The Countess's laugh was surprised, grateful, tinged with relief. She had expected judgment. Instead, she had received understanding wrapped in wit. It was a masterclass in social navigation. The kind of skill that took decades to cultivate.

Or eleven weeks of brutal training and an Oscar-winning talent for total embodiment.

It was intoxicating. Sloane was not just playing a part. She was wielding a power she had never known. The power of status, of wealth, of a name that commanded respect and fear in equal measure. Men who had blacklisted actresses like her for a single wrong word now hung on her every syllable. Women who would have sneered at the girl from Oklahoma now leaned in to hear her opinions on art, on politics, on the state of the world.

She was a ghost, an imposter, a complete and total fraud.

And she had never felt more real in her life.

Every few minutes, her gaze would sweep the perimeter of the room, instinct pulling her attention to the shadows, to the places where danger lived. And every time, she would find him.

Nico.

He was a constant presence. Lethal, yet strangely comforting. A dark planet in the corner of her eye. He moved through the room like smoke, always at the edges, always watching. His tuxedo fit him like a second skin, elegant and dangerous. His face was carved from stone, revealing nothing. His hand never strayed far from the weapon she knew was holstered beneath his jacket. He was working, scanning faces, tracking exits. A predator in a room full of predators.

Each time their gazes met, it was a jolt. A grounding shock of reality that cut through the perfumed air of the party. He was a reminder of the real stakes, of the cold, hard world of threats and angles that existed just beyond the champagne and polite laughter.

The memory of his raw, desperate kiss in the library was a stark, brutal counterpoint to the elegant, intellectual fantasy she was weaving with Damian.

One was a beautiful, tragic poem. The other was a cold, hard, and terrifying truth.

She was caught between them, a performer playing two roles at once, and she knew, with a certainty that chilled her to the bone, that the fallout was going to be devastating.

Chapter 51: The Chill

She was in the middle of a charmingly dismissive conversation with a British lord—something about the decline of the modern art market and the insufferable pretension of the Venice Biennale—when she felt it.

A shift.

Subtle. Almost imperceptible. But unmistakable.

The energy of the room changed. A quiet, almost imperceptible parting of the crowd, the way a school of fish might move to make way for a shark. A sudden drop in the room's temperature, a pocket of stillness in the swirling chaos. The air grew colder. Thicker. The laughter around her seemed to dull, as if someone had turned down the volume on the world.

And then she saw him.

He was standing across the ballroom, by the tall glass doors that led to the terrace, as if summoned by her darkest thoughts.

She had never seen his face. Not in the dossier, not online, not in Livia's videos. He was a ghost without an image. But she knew him instantly.

Mid-sixties. Silver hair swept back from a high forehead. An impeccably tailored charcoal suit that made the tuxedos around him look like costumes. He radiated a calm, absolute authority that made the powerful men around him look like children.

Kind eyes. A grandfather's smile. Everything about him was designed to project warmth, benevolence, trustworthiness.

But the reality of him was something else entirely.

His stillness was the first thing that registered. In a room full of motion—people talking, laughing, gesturing, moving—he stood perfectly still. He was speaking to a U.S. Senator, a man Sloane recognized from the news, and his posture was one of deep, attentive interest. Listening. Engaged. But underneath that polite attention was something else. Something that made every animal instinct in Sloane's body scream.

The apex predator.

The crowd around him seemed to sense it too. Not consciously. But there was a subtle, unconscious parting. A buffer of empty space that surrounded him like a force field. People gave him room. Deferred to him. Orbited him at a safe distance.

He must have felt her gaze.

He looked up. His eyes found hers instantly, unerringly, across the sea of faces and champagne flutes and glittering jewels.

The world went silent.

The music, the laughter, the clinking of glasses—it all faded away to a distant, muffled hum, as if someone had wrapped the entire ballroom in cotton. There was only the two of them, connected by a single, invisible line of pure, predatory focus.

His famous, kind smile did not falter. But his eyes...

His pale, winter-sky gray eyes went utterly, terrifyingly dead.

The mask of the philanthropist dropped. Not for long. Just a single, shocking second. But it was enough. Sloane saw the void beneath. The absolute, chilling emptiness of a man who felt nothing. A black hole in human form.

He held her gaze. It was a violation. A silent, brutal acknowledgment of their shared secret. He was not looking at Livia Crestwell, the tragic beauty miraculously returned. He was looking at Sloane Devereaux, the girl from Oklahoma, the actress, the pawn in his game.

And he was enjoying her terror.

Then, as if a switch had been flipped, the warmth returned to his eyes. The mask snapped back into place. He was once again the benevolent philanthropist, the concerned friend, the kindly grandfather. He said something to the Senator, who laughed, and then he turned his attention back to the conversation as if nothing had happened.

But Sloane knew.

She had just been seen. Catalogued. Claimed.

Katarina's voice materialized in her ear—flat, cold, and utterly precise.

"Visual confirmed. Roman Lazar. Southwest quadrant. He is establishing dominance before he approaches. Hold your ground, Sloane. Do not give him the satisfaction of seeing you run."

But it was too late.

Roman was moving. Not toward her. Not yet. He excused himself from the Senator with a gracious nod, then turned and walked slowly, unhurriedly, toward the terrace doors. He moved like water. Like smoke. Effortless. Inevitable.

As he walked, his gaze swept the room, a king surveying his court.

Sloane saw his eyes pass over Violet, still holding her position near the champagne fountain. The shards were long gone, the marble wiped flawless, but Roman's gaze cut to the exact spot where the crystal had shattered. A flicker of something—annoyance? calculation?—crossed his face before it was gone. He had noticed the "accident." And in his world, nothing broke without permission.

Then his gaze continued, finding its true anchor.

He looked past Sloane, locking eyes with the man standing sentinel against the far wall. Kovac. The shadow from the mezzanine. He had descended from the high ground and was now waiting in the wings, a silent, brutal statue in a sea of silk and laughter.

Roman gave a slight jerk of his head toward the terrace's other entrance. Kovac nodded once, then detached himself from the wall and began to move through the crowd, a silent, implacable shark parting a school of fish.

Her stomach tightened. He was positioning his rook. He was turning the terrace into a cage.

Only then, with his enforcer in motion, did Roman pause just before stepping through the doors. He turned his head and looked back at her.

And gave a single, subtle nod.

Come here.

It was not a request. It was a command. A summons. A king calling his subject to the throne.

Sloane felt her blood turn to ice. Every instinct screamed at her to run. To grab Damian's hand, to turn to Nico, to cause a scene and flee into the night, consequences be damned.

All it would cost was her soul.

And then she thought of Livia, murdered for the truth. She thought of Manny, moving heaven and earth in Los Angeles to save her. She thought of Elena, the innocent collateral in Nico's war.

They didn't need a victim. They needed a weapon.

Roman believed intelligent people always chose survival.

He was wrong.

"Livia?" Damian's voice cut through the haze. He was looking at her, his brow furrowed with concern. "Are you alright? You've gone pale."

"I'm fine," she said, but her voice sounded thin, distant, like it was coming from very far away. She forced a smile. Livia's smile. Warm. Reassuring. "I just... I see an old friend. I should say hello."

"Would you like me to come with you?" His hand was on her arm, protective, worried.

"No," she said quickly. Too quickly. She softened her tone. "No, darling. Stay. Enjoy yourself. I'll just be a moment."

She leaned in and kissed his cheek, a gesture of intimacy, of trust, of the lie they were both living. His hand lingered on hers for a moment, reluctant to let her go.

Then she pulled away.

She began to move through the crowd. It parted for her, guests stepping aside, offering polite smiles, unaware that they were clearing a path for a woman walking to her own execution. The music swelled around her, violins and cellos building to something that sounded like a requiem.

Her eyes flickered to the side. Nico was no longer at his post by the wall. He was moving, a shadow at the edge of her vision, paralleling her path. His hand disappeared into his jacket, a smooth, practiced motion. He was preparing for the worst. His face was a mask, but his eyes were locked on her, dark and full of a silent, furious warning.

Don't.

But she had no choice.

Katarina's voice cut through the earpiece—a cold command clipped with military precision.

"Mrs. Crestwell. Focus. You are drifting. Do not engage. You are not ready for him. Turn around. Now."

Sloane reached up with one hand, as if adjusting her hair, and slipped the tiny earpiece out. She dropped it into her clutch. The voice stopped. The director had left the building. She was alone now.

She reached the terrace doors. The glass was cold beneath her palm as she pushed them open. The night air hit her like a slap, crisp and sharp and smelling of pine and ice. The music from the ballroom faded to a distant, muffled murmur.

She stepped onto the terrace.

Roman Lazar was standing at the railing, his back to her, looking out at the view. Below them, the lake was a sheet of black glass. The distant lights of Lucerne glittered across the water, a smear of cold diamonds nestled against the dark mass of Mount Pilatus. The Alps rose around them like the walls of a cathedral built by gods.

They were alone.

He didn't turn around. He just stood there, perfectly still, his hands resting lightly on the railing. Waiting.

Sloane's heart was a frantic, wild thing in her chest. Every muscle in her body was screaming at her to run. But her feet carried her forward. One step. Then another. The sound of her heels on the stone was the only noise in the vast, cold silence.

She stopped a few feet behind him.

"Hello, Sloane," Roman Lazar said, his voice a low, cultured murmur that carried easily in the still night air.

He used her real name.

The world tilted beneath her feet.

He turned to face her. The kind smile was still there. The gentle, grandfatherly warmth. But his eyes were dead. Empty. A winter sky with nothing behind it.

"I've been looking forward to meeting you," he said. "Shall we have a chat?"

Chapter 52: A Lesson in Ownership

The cold was immediate. Sharp. It cut through the thin silk of the Valentino gown and settled into Sloane's bones—then vanished.

Invisible, high-intensity infrared emitters recessed in the overhang found her, bathing her in a silent, artificial warmth. It was unnatural. Controlled.

Damian might hold the deed, but Roman held the dominion. He didn't just control the house; he terraformed the air around him.

The terrace was vast, cantilevered out over the mountainside. Above, a waxing gibbous moon hung bright and pitiless over the Alps, turning the lake below to hammered silver. Everything was visible. Exposed. The light left nowhere to hide.

Below them, the drop was sheer—five hundred meters of empty air before the mountain plunged into the water.

The lake gleamed black and silver, waiting like a promise.

Roman Lazar stood at the railing, his posture relaxed. He looked like he owned the mountain, the lake, the sky itself.

He turned his gaze on her. It was slow, deliberate, traveling from the hem of her gown to her eyes with the proprietary air of a collector inspecting a new acquisition.

"I must admit," he said, his voice a soft, appreciative hum. "I was worried the cameras might be flattering you. The resolution of the projection system in your suite is excellent, of course—I saw every tear, every tremor the other night—but digital feeds lack... texture."

He stepped closer, invading her space without touching her.

"In the flesh? You are even more vivid. More... real."

He smiled, satisfied.

"You're doing very well," he said, his voice conversational. "The performance is flawless. The Consortium is mesmerized. You haven't just charmed them; you have reassured them. They see a stable genius anchored by a loving wife, and that was the final variable needed to close the deal. Even I am almost convinced. Looking at you... it is as if she never stepped onto the *Ariadne* at all."

Sloane didn't flinch. She didn't feign confusion. She let the mask of Livia Crestwell drop, revealing the cold, hard stare of the woman beneath.

"I'm a professional," she said, her voice stripped of Livia's accent, flat and dangerously calm. "I'm delivering the product you paid for."

"Oh, I paid for more than a product," Roman said softly. "I paid for a history."

He took a step closer, his eyes locking onto hers, dissecting her.

"Sloane Devereaux," he recited, the name tasting like a curse in his mouth. "Born in Tulsa. Clawed your way to Hollywood on nothing but hunger. Won an Oscar at twenty-two. Said 'no' to the wrong man at twenty-five. And paid the price."

Each fact was a nail in a coffin. He wasn't revealing her identity; he was itemizing his property.

"You were starving when I found you," he continued. "Erased. A ghost in your own life. That is why I chose you. Not just for the face. But for the desperation."

Sloane's throat closed.

The butterfly jar. The locket. The walls of her bedroom coming alive with illustrated horror.

She could still see the rendered torture. Still hear his voice coming from everywhere and nowhere: *I know everything.*

And now here he stood. In the flesh. The architect of her nightmares, smiling like a grandfather.

"Why are you telling me this?" Her voice came out thinner than she wanted. Brittle. "You've already made your point."

She wouldn't name the violations. She wouldn't give him the satisfaction.

"Because reminders," Roman said, his voice dropping to something intimate, almost tender, "are necessary. Because I want you to understand your situation. Clearly." He reached into his jacket with the casual ease of a man reaching for a wallet. "Completely."

The phone appeared. Small. Sleek. Innocent.

He tapped the screen. Turned it toward her.

Sloane's stomach dropped before her brain could process what she was seeing.

Two photographs. High-definition. Side by side.

The left: Manny. Her Manny. Standing on a Los Angeles sidewalk, squinting in the afternoon sun. He looked tired, the familiar crease in his forehead deep with worry. The timestamp in the corner read 13:52 PST.

Today.

The right: A young girl—fifteen, dark curls, yellow backpack—standing outside a school in Buenos Aires. Warm, golden evening light. It was summer there. She was laughing at something a friend had said.

"Pictures taken within the last hour," Roman said pleasantly.

Sloane felt bile rise in her throat, hot and acidic. "If you hurt them—"

"Hurt them?" Roman sounded genuinely puzzled. "Why would I hurt them? They are leverage, not targets. As long as you and Mr. Sorrento do exactly as I say, Mr. Goldman and Elena will live long, happy lives."

He swiped a finger across the glass, zooming in on the girl's smile.

"But if the terms of our arrangement are violated..." His tone didn't change. Still pleasant. Still kind. That was what made it obscene. "Then Elena's residency documents get exposed as forgeries. She gets arrested. Detained. And then I'll make sure she's deported to Ukraine. To Mariupol."

He looked up. His gray eyes—those kind, grandfatherly eyes—found hers.

"To a war zone where the life expectancy of a fifteen-year-old girl is measured in days."

The words landed like physical blows. Sloane's hands began to shake. She tried to stop them. Couldn't. The tremor moved up her arms, into her shoulders, her chest. Her whole body rejecting what she'd just heard.

She clenched her fists so hard her nails bit into her palms. The pain helped. Grounded her.

"You're a monster," she whispered. The words came out broken. Barely sound.

"I'm a businessman," Roman said, pocketing the phone with the casual finality of someone closing a ledger. "And you, Sloane, are an asset. A very expensive asset. One hundred million dollars invested to stabilize Damian. And it worked. The technical briefings this week were a masterpiece. The Consortium is mesmerized. The deal is all but done."

"The deal," she repeated.

"Five trillion dollars," Roman said, his voice a low purr. "Twelve intelligence agencies. Damian's technology will reshape global power. And in eight days, he will sign the documents that transfer operational control to me."

He stepped closer, his scent of mint and ozone overpowering the fresh mountain air.

"After the signing, Damian remains as my chief engineer. And you? You remain by his side. Permanently."

Her stomach dropped. "The contract said six months."

She'd done the math every morning.

"I've been counting," she whispered, her voice cracking. "Eleven weeks down. Fifteen to go. That was the deal."

"The contract," Roman said, his voice sharpening like a scalpel, "was a recruitment tool. The hundred million dollars? A pleasant fiction. But you were never leaving. You know too much. You're not an employee, my dear. You're a replacement part. And replacement parts don't retire—they function until they break."

The words were a physical blow. The promise of freedom had been the biggest lie of all.

"Argentis was always a one-way trip," Roman said. "You have two choices: live here as Mrs. Crestwell for as long as you're useful, or die here when you're not. Those are your only exits."

Sloane tried to remain calm, but an involuntary shiver ran through her. Roman saw it.

"You think this is cruel," he said softly. "It is not. Cruelty is random. Cruelty is chaos. This..." He gestured to the silent, sleeping world below them. "This is order. And order requires structural integrity. You are a load-bearing wall now, Sloane. You don't get to move."

He leaned back, his gaze analytical. "The choice is simple. You can be a forgotten ghost in a world of chaos, or you can be a queen in a world of order. My world."

Roman gave a single, satisfied nod. "Here are your instructions. The legal teams require a week to finalize the operational transfer documents—twelve agencies, twelve jurisdictions, all coordinated through Swiss banking protocols. A necessary delay. It gives us time to properly entertain our guests—let them experience the primal spectacle of the Klausjagen before we conclude our business.

"So, next Tuesday, you will stand beside Damian at the signing ceremony in Bürgenstock. You will smile. You will be the perfect, supportive wife. And if you do exactly as I say, everyone you love stays alive. But if you disappoint me, Manny dies first. Then Elena."

He leaned closer, his voice dropping to an intimate whisper.

"In eight days, Sloane Devereaux will cease to exist. And you're going to smile and thank me for it."

The words hit her like a physical blow. She couldn't breathe. Couldn't think. The terrace, the drop, the stars—everything narrowed to his pale eyes and that patient, grandfatherly smile.

He straightened, his expression shifting to something almost jovial. "Oh, come now. Don't look so glum." His tone was mock-comforting, the sadist offering sympathy for the wound he'd just inflicted. "Think of it this way—when the ink dries next Tuesday, Damian becomes the world's first trillionaire. And you get to be the queen of that empire."

He gestured around the terrace, encompassing the luxury, the power, the altitude.

"Isn't this infinitely better than that miserable North Hollywood apartment, waiting for an agent who'd given up on you?"

The cruelty of it—the casual reminder of how low she'd fallen, how desperate she'd been—made her stomach turn.

"Now," he said, his voice hardening. "Show me the face of the queen."

With Herculean effort, Sloane forced the corners of her mouth to lift. It was a brittle, hollow thing, but it was a performance. And it was enough.

Roman gave a single, satisfied nod.

He offered his arm, a perfect gentleman. "Now. Let's return to the party before Damian starts to worry. You have guests to dazzle."

She took his arm. Her hand was shaking. But she let him guide her back toward the glass doors, toward the music and light and the beautiful lie she would now have to live for the rest of her life.

They had taken only three steps when a figure emerged from the ballroom, moving fast, urgent. Damian.

His eyes found hers and his face went pale. He crossed the terrace in four long strides.

"Livia." His voice was tight with worry. He barely acknowledged Roman. "What's wrong? You look—"

"Damian," Roman interjected smoothly. "Your wife and I were just admiring the view. Catching up on old times."

But Damian wasn't listening. His hands framed Sloane's face, his thumbs brushing her cheekbones, and she realized with horror that there were tears on her face.

"You're crying," Damian said, devastatingly gentle. "What did he say to you?"

The lies came, automatic, desperate. "Nothing. It's just... the party. It's overwhelming."

"You're shaking." His arms went around her, pulling her against his chest, positioning his body between her and Roman.

Over Damian's shoulder, Sloane caught Roman's expression. He was watching them with mild, clinical interest. Like a scientist observing mice in a maze. This was exactly what he'd paid for. Damian's absolute devotion.

And she was the instrument of his destruction.

Chapter 53: The Scar

Damian's arms were a fortress around her, his body a physical shield between her and Roman. He held her tight, his heart hammering against her back, a frantic, protective rhythm.

"Come inside," Damian murmured against her hair. "Let me take you upstairs. You need to rest—"

"No." She pulled back, forced Livia's brave smile through the tears. "No, I'm fine. Really. Just a moment of emotion. Seeing everyone again after so long."

"You don't have to be strong all the time," he said softly, and the tenderness in his voice made her want to scream. "Not with me. Never with me."

She reached up, cupped his face in her hands—hands that in eight days would belong to Livia Crestwell, not Sloane Devereaux—and lied directly into his trusting eyes. "I know. That's why I love you."

The words tasted like ash. But he believed them. God help her, he believed every single one.

Roman stepped back, checking his watch with the casual authority of a man whose time was infinitely valuable. "I should circulate. The Consortium has been remarkably patient with the briefings, but I suspect they've had their fill of algorithms. They need to be entertained now, not educated." His pale eyes found Sloane's. "I wouldn't want to monopolize the guest of honor."

The words were gracious. The subtext was steel.

"Of course," Damian said, his arm still protective around Sloane's waist.

Roman's gaze lingered on her for one more beat—a silent reminder of everything he'd said, everything he controlled, everything he could destroy. Then he turned and walked back toward the ballroom, his silver hair catching the light, his posture regal.

But he didn't disappear into the crowd. Through the glass doors, Sloane could see him stop near the bar, positioning himself with a clear sightline to the terrace. Talking to a man in a dark suit. Watching. Always watching.

The message was clear: I'm giving you space. But I'm not giving you freedom.

For a moment, neither of them moved. Damian held her, his heart beating steady and strong against her cheek, and she thought: *In eight days, Sloane Devereaux will cease to exist. And I'm going to smile and thank him for it.*

She could feel Roman's gaze on her back like a physical weight. The careful distance he'd created—twenty feet, maybe thirty—was somehow more oppressive than his presence had been. He was demonstrating control. She could stand here with Damian, could feel safe in his arms, could pretend for these few stolen moments that she had autonomy.

But they both knew the truth.

Roman was directing this scene, too.

"Livia."

The new voice made them both turn. A woman in midnight blue was approaching from the ballroom, her expression warm but concerned.

Dr. Mona Acosta.

Sloane recognized her instantly from the dossier. Livia's college roommate. Her maid of honor. The neuroscientist who mapped neural pathways for a living. Katarina had positioned her on the far side of the ballroom with the diplomatic delegation, creating a buffer zone of bodies and distance.

But the buffer had failed.

Sloane's blood ran cold. There was no warning in her ear—the device was still in her clutch, cold and useless. She was flying blind. Katarina had calculated the psychology, positioned the handlers, and built the walls.

And Mona had walked right through them.

This was the emotional landmine—and no amount of planning could stop a best friend from wanting to see her friend's face one more time.

But it was too late.

Mona reached them, her smile faltering slightly as she took in the tension, the coiled energy radiating from Sloane. She looked from Sloane to Damian, her scientist's brain clearly processing, analyzing, cataloguing anomalies.

Then she turned to Sloane and opened her arms.

"My God," Mona said, her voice thick with emotion. "It's really you."

She pulled Sloane into an embrace. It was warm, genuine, full of relief and joy and a thousand unspoken things. Sloane stood frozen for a moment, then her body remembered its training. She hugged back. She made the appropriate sounds of delight and surprise. She was Livia again.

When Mona pulled back, her hands stayed on Sloane's shoulders, her eyes searching Sloane's face with a scientist's precision.

"You look..." Mona began, then paused. Something flickered across her expression. Confusion. Concern. "You look exactly the same. But your eyes... they look so sad."

Damian stiffened beside her. Sloane felt it—the subtle shift in his breathing, the way his hand found her waist again. Protective. Possessive. Anchoring her to this performance.

"Mona," he said, his voice carefully warm. "It's good to see you."

"Damian." Mona's smile was polite but distant. Then her attention snapped back to Sloane, her voice dropping lower, full of genuine, worried intimacy. "Livia, darling, are you alright? You seem... rattled."

Her gaze dropped. To Sloane's left hand. Which was gripping the cold metal railing. Her knuckles were white.

The theatrical wax Katarina had applied to mask the ridge of the scar had begun to peel under the heat of the ballroom lights an hour ago. Sloane had rubbed the residue away in the powder room, gambling that the dim terrace lighting would hide the truth.

She lost the bet.

And there, on her palm, clearly visible in the ambient light from the ballroom, was the scar.

Mona frowned. "Wait," she said, her voice laced with sudden, sharp confusion. "When did you get that scar on your palm? I don't remember you ever having—"

The world stopped.

It was the one detail she couldn't fake. The one piece of her real life she couldn't hide. The butterfly jar. The broken glass. The emergency room in Tulsa when she was nine years old.

Sloane's mind went blank. Every line she had ever learned, every piece of Livia's carefully constructed history, evaporated. There was only the scar, a bright, damning piece of evidence under the cold Alpine stars.

Through the glass doors, she saw Roman turn slightly. Still talking to the man in the dark suit. But his eyes had found her. And on his lips was the faintest, cruelest smile she had ever seen.

He was watching her squirm on the hook.

And he was enjoying it.

She had to say something. Anything.

"Oh, this?" she said, forcing a light, dismissive laugh. She held up her hand, turning it over as if inspecting it for the first time. The performance was back. Desperate. Sloppy. But it was all she had. "A silly gardening accident. Last month. A rose bush fought back."

It was a flimsy lie. Pathetic. And they both knew it. Livia didn't garden. Livia hired people to garden.

Damian's hand on her waist tightened. Not protective now. Confused. She could feel the question forming in his mind, the brilliant quantum computer beginning to process the anomaly.

Mona looked from the scar to Sloane's eyes. Her brow furrowed. Her brilliant, analytical mind was refusing to let go of the anomaly. She opened her mouth to press the issue, to ask more questions.

But Sloane cut her off. She turned her body, creating a physical barrier, claiming the moment as her own.

"Mona, darling, I'm so sorry, but I feel a terrible headache coming on," Sloane said, pressing her fingers to her temple in a perfect gesture of pained fragility. "Too much champagne, I'm afraid. Can we catch up properly tomorrow? Lunch? Promise me."

Mona looked at her. Really looked at her. And in those intelligent eyes, Sloane saw suspicion beginning to bloom. But Mona was a friend. A loyal friend. She nodded slowly.

"Of course, Livia," she said, her voice soft with concern. "Of course. We'll have lunch. Get some rest."

She embraced Sloane one more time, a quick, reassuring hug. Then she turned and walked back toward the ballroom, glancing back once over her shoulder, her face troubled.

As Mona disappeared into the crowd, Sloane felt rather than saw Roman moving. Not toward them. Just... repositioning. A subtle shift to maintain his sightline. She didn't need to look to know he was still watching. Still waiting.

Still in complete control.

Damian turned her to face him, his hands gentle on her shoulders, his expression a careful mix of concern and something else. Something that looked like doubt.

"Livia," he said quietly. "Are you sure you're—"

One of Roman's assistants appeared at the glass doors. He caught Damian's eye and gave a subtle, insistent nod toward the interior. The Consortium was waiting to be charmed.

Damian's jaw tightened. He looked torn, caught between the woman he loved and the work that defined him.

"Go," Sloane said softly. "Dazzle them. I'll be fine. I just need a moment."

"I don't want to leave you—"

"I'm fine," she insisted, forcing Livia's brave smile. "Really. Just too much champagne and too many ghosts. Give me five minutes to breathe, then I'll come find you."

He studied her face, and she saw the cognitive dissonance warring behind his eyes. Not suspicion—he knew exactly who she was. This was the struggle to maintain the illusion. The scar. The headache. Mona's concern. They were intrusions of reality. Cracks in the perfect illusion he was desperate to believe.

He could have acknowledged them. He could have let the fantasy shatter right there.

But he wanted to believe. God, he wanted to believe.

"Five minutes," he said finally. He kissed her forehead, a gesture so tender it made her chest ache. "Then I'm coming back to get you."

He walked back into the ballroom, pausing once to look back at her, his face unreadable in the golden light.

And then she was alone.

***

The cold wind bit at her skin. She looked down at her palm. The scar. The one piece of evidence she couldn't fake.

Roman knew. Of course he knew. He knew about the butterfly jar. He knew about Tulsa.

And now he knew that Mona had seen it.

Sloane's stomach turned to ice. She thought of Oliver Harrow. The CEO who resisted. The daughter in the facility in New Mexico. The people who became inconvenient variables in Roman's equation.

Mona had just become a loose end.

And Roman never left loose ends.

Through the glass doors, she found him in the crowd. He was talking to a gray-haired man in an expensive suit, laughing at something, playing the gracious host. He didn't look at her. He didn't need to.

He had already made his point.

The message was clear: I saw what just happened. And I will deal with it when I am ready.

Below, the black water waited. And somewhere in the distance, a clock was ticking.

Eight days.

But looking at Roman's smile through the glass, Sloane knew the truth.

Mona didn't have eight days.

Chapter 54: Collateral Damage

The rest of the gala passed in a haze of pure, adrenaline-fueled performance. Sloane was no longer acting; she was surviving. She returned to the party, a flawless, smiling automaton, her mind a screaming chaos of Lazar's whispered word and Mona's suspicious eyes.

She slipped the receiver back into her ear, desperate for Katarina's cold, calculated guidance to navigate this luminous jungle.

She found Damian, clung to his arm like a drowning woman, and let his oblivious adoration be her shield.

Katarina's voice in her ear was a cold, steady metronome, guiding her through the final hour of social obligations. "Breathe, Mrs. Crestwell. Compose yourself. The Israeli finance minister is approaching. He is a gossip. Show no weakness."

Sloane did as she was told. She smiled. She laughed. She was a perfect, beautiful, glittering lie. But underneath the emerald gown, her skin was crawling. She felt like an animal in a trap, a trap whose walls were shrinking with every passing minute.

She kept scanning the crowd for Mona, a knot of dread tightening in her stomach.

She found her in a quiet corner near the terrace doors. With Damian.

Sloane couldn't hear them from across the ballroom, but she could see Mona's face. No longer just concerned. Alarmed. Mona's hands moved urgently—pointing, gesturing, pleading. Damian stood perfectly still, his back to Sloane.

Sloane didn't need to hear the words to know: her carefully constructed world was being dismantled in real-time.

Then Damian reached out, touched Mona's arm briefly, and walked away.

Mona stood there, staring after him, her face stricken.

She looked like someone who had just realized she was standing on a trapdoor.

Damian turned and began to make his way back through the crowd. He moved mechanically, his face a perfect, porcelain mask that gave nothing away. He reached Sloane's side, and his hand found the small of her back—reflexive, possessive, or perhaps just to keep himself upright.

Sloane felt a wave of dizziness so profound she had to grip his arm to steady herself. The game was up. The moment the party ended, Damian would confront her. The illusion would shatter.

And then what? What happened to the counterfeit when she was no longer useful?

The party finally bled out around 2 AM. Sloane stood with Damian at the grand entrance, a perfect, porcelain doll, smiling as she bid farewell to the last of the world's most powerful people.

Mona was in the final group to leave. As she passed, her eyes, cold and analytical now, met Sloane's for a fraction of a second. There was no warmth in them. Only a chilling, appraising curiosity.

She completely ignored Sloane and turned to Damian, pulling him into a brief, tight hug. "You call me," she whispered to him, her voice urgent and protective. "If you need anything. Anything at all."

She pulled back, gave Sloane one last, unreadable look, and then said a single, quiet word, meant only for her.

"Intriguing."

Then she was gone, her small figure disappearing into the cold, Swiss night. The word was not a compliment. It was a diagnosis. It was a promise that she was not done with this puzzle.

***

She sat in the window of her suite, still in the Valentino gown, watching the dawn break over the mountains. She was a condemned woman, waiting for the executioner's knock on the door.

She expected Katarina. She expected Nico. She expected Damian, his face a mask of rage and betrayal.

But no one came.

The house settled into an eerie, post-party stillness. The silence pressed against her eardrums like water. She could hear her own heartbeat, the rush of blood through her veins, the mechanical click of the wall clock marking seconds that felt like hours.

The waiting. The not knowing. It was a new kind of torture.

She had to know what Mona had said to Damian. She had to know if her cover was blown.

Her hands were ice-cold as she retrieved the tablet Nico had given her—the one with access to the security feeds. It was a massive risk. But staying blind was a greater one.

The screen glowed to life in the dim room, casting her face in pale blue light. Her reflection looked back at her from the black glass—a ghost in emerald silk.

She found the archives from the gala. A grid of silent, black-and-white video feeds from the dozens of hidden cameras that had recorded every moment of the party. Her fingers moved too fast, fumbling, scrolling through timestamps. 11:47 PM. 11:52 PM. There.

The conversation in the corner.

She tapped the feed. The image expanded, high-definition and soundless. Two figures in the frame: Mona, small and urgent, and Damian, his back to the camera.

She zoomed in. There was no audio, but she didn't need it. She was an expert in reading the silent language of the body.

Mona's hands moved with desperate precision. Pointing to her own palm. Gesturing back toward the terrace.

Sloane didn't need audio. She could read the lines.

Look at her hand. The scar. It's not the same. She's not Livia.

Damian stood perfectly still. A man made of stone.

Then he asked something. A single question. His head tilted slightly, and Sloane's breath caught.

Mona answered, holding up her own hand, pointing to her palm. The scar. She was telling him.

Damian turned slightly—just enough. His face came into profile for a single, devastating moment.

It was not the face of a man discovering a shocking betrayal.

It was the face of a man having his deepest, most terrifying fears confirmed.

He looked... broken. Resigned. Lost.

He placed a hand on Mona's arm—a gesture that managed to be both comforting and dismissive at once. His mouth moved. Short. Final. Sloane could read the shape of it even without sound: *I know*.

Mona's face crumpled. Her mouth opened in protest, but Damian was already turning away. Shutting her down. Shutting it out.

He had chosen the lie.

Even when confronted with the truth from his wife's best friend, he had chosen the beautiful, comforting illusion over the ugly, inconvenient reality.

A wave of something—relief? pity? contempt?—washed over Sloane. Her cover was not blown. Damian was a willing participant in his own deception. He didn't want to know. He wanted the ghost. He wanted the fantasy. He was a weaker, more broken man than she had ever imagined.

She had collapsed into bed around three in the morning. Her body had won the war her mind had been waging, pulling her under into a dark, restless sleep plagued by fractured images: Mona's smile, the terrace railing, the sound Roman said a body made hitting rock.

She woke just past ten to cold sunlight streaming through the windows. Her first thought was Mona. Her second was the news.

She made coffee she couldn't drink and sat in the window seat overlooking the lake, tablet in hand, refreshing the local news sites. Waiting. Dreading. Knowing.

The alert came at 11:14 AM.

It was from a local Swiss news outlet. The headline, in German, was stark.

Prominente Neurowissenschaftlerin bei tragischem Unfall am Vierwaldstättersee ums Leben gekommen.

Sloane's German was rudimentary, but she didn't need a translation. She knew the words *tragisch, Unfall, ums Leben gekommen*.

Tragic. Accident. Killed.

Her fingers went numb. The tablet nearly slipped from her hands.

She tapped the link. The page loaded with agonizing slowness—a grainy photo of a car, a late-model Mercedes, twisted and mangled at the bottom of a ravine. Metal bent like paper. Glass scattered like diamonds across rock.

And a professional headshot of the victim.

Dr. Mona Acosta, 38, brilliant neuroscientist, beloved wife to David, loving mother to Sofia (7) and Marco (5), died tragically in a single-vehicle accident on a mountain road outside Küssnacht...

The words blurred. Sloane's vision tunneled. The room tilted.

Sofia. Seven years old. Marco. Five.

The names were a fresh stab of pain. Children. She had to see them. A frantic, morbid curiosity took over. Her fingers, slick with a cold sweat, flew across the tablet's keyboard, typing Mona Acosta's name into a social media search bar.

Her profile was public. Of course it was. She had been a person who lived in the light.

And there they were. The first photo. Mona, her arm around a smiling man. And in front of them, two small children. A girl with her mother's dark, intelligent eyes. A boy with a bright, gap-toothed smile. The caption read: *My whole world.*

Sloane's stomach lurched. She barely made it to the bathroom before she was violently, wretchedly sick.

She knelt on the cold marble floor, her body trembling, her mind a screaming void. This wasn't a game anymore. This wasn't a performance. This was a war, and real, innocent people were dying. People whose only crime was getting too close to the truth.

And it was her fault.

The thought was a shard of ice in her gut. If she hadn't come here, if she hadn't been playing this grotesque part, Mona would still be alive. Her presence in this house was a catalyst, a poison.

She pulled herself up, staggered to the sink, and splashed cold water on her face. Her reflection in the mirror was a ghost—hollow-eyed, pale, broken.

But as she stared at her own reflection, at the haunted woman looking back, the grief that was a vast, black ocean threatening to pull her under began to recede. And beneath it, something else began to form. Something hard and cold and ugly.

Rage.

A rage so pure and so absolute it burned away the tears, the guilt, the fear. A rage for Mona and her children. A rage for Livia. A rage for the catatonic girl in New Mexico. A rage for herself, for the terrified girl in the Malibu house, for the broken woman who had pounded on her steering wheel after an audition for hemorrhoid cream.

She had had enough.

She was done being a pawn. She was done being a victim. She was done being afraid.

She stood up, her movements stiff, precise. She looked at her own reflection in the mirror, at the hollow-eyed woman staring back. The actress who'd played grief at the gala, who'd manufactured tears, had burned away. What was left was colder. Cleaner.

Operational.

She was no longer just trying to survive. She was no longer just trying to expose him.

She was going to destroy him.

The door to Damian's Sanctum was locked. Damian himself was the key. And she now knew, with a chilling, absolute certainty, that she had to see his face. She had to watch his eyes when she said Mona's name. She had to know if there was anything human left in there to turn.

She walked toward his study.

***

The room smelled like leather. and wood smoke. Damian sat at his desk, tablet in his hands, knuckles white. The news report glowed on the screen. He was staring at it like it was written in a language he could no longer read.

She didn't knock.

The door swung open under her hand. He looked up—startled, guilty, caught.

"Damian."

She didn't use Livia's melodic lilt. She used her own voice—flatter, harder, the vowels of Oklahoma and the grit of North Hollywood. She dropped the posture, let her shoulders fall, stood there without the ghost's grace.

She stood there as Sloane.

He flinched at the sound of a stranger in his room. "I saw."

"She was your wife's best friend," Sloane's voice came out raw. Unpolished. "She saw this." She held up her left hand, the scar catching the firelight. "She saw me. The real me. And for that, Roman had her killed."

Damian stared at her palm. His throat worked. She watched his face like a sniper watching a target.

For a long, terrible moment, he looked like a man on the edge of a cliff. She saw it flicker in his eyes—the knowledge, the guilt, the terror.

He knew.

"Damian, look at me," she said, stepping closer, her voice stripped of every careful affectation. "Not at the ghost. Look at me. I'm Sloane Devereaux. I'm a real person. I'm from Oklahoma. I had a life before this. And I'm telling you—Roman is a murderer. Please." Her voice cracked. "Wake up."

Then he closed his eyes. A slow, deliberate lowering of a curtain. When he opened them, the man was gone. The machine hummed back to life.

"It was a tragic accident." His voice—that cold, clinical, dead thing—hit her like a scalpel. He looked directly at her. His eyes, those high-performance instruments built for perfect recognition, cataloged the truth. He processed the raw vowels of Oklahoma. He measured the fracture in her posture. He saw Sloane.

And then, he performed a manual overwrite.

"These mountain roads are treacherous. You're overwrought, Livia." The name was a scalpel, precise and cutting. "Your... trauma... is making you see patterns that aren't there."

The use of the name felt like a slap. Like being buried alive.

She understood then. He knew. He'd always known, on some level, that she wasn't Livia. But knowing required consequences. Required guilt. Required him to face what he'd helped create. Easier to see the ghost. Safer to call her by a dead woman's name and pretend the woman in front of him didn't exist.

Calling her Livia was his choice. His anesthetic. His final act of cowardice dressed as sanity.

Her heartbeat slowed. The hot rage cooled and hardened into something else.

Clarity.

She looked at him and saw what Livia must have seen in those final weeks. Not a man. A machine. A beautiful, broken machine that had decided blood was an acceptable lubricant for its gears.

He was beyond saving.

She stopped trying.

She'd seen this story before. Read it in a dozen scripts, studied it on a hundred stages. The brilliant king, convinced by a trusted advisor to destroy the one person who told him the truth. The noble general, whispered to by a loyal friend until his love turned to poison. It always ended the same way. In blood and ruin.

You can't reason someone out of a delusion they need to survive. And Damian needed Roman's vision the way a drowning man needs air, even if the air is poison.

She finally understood. She could not save him. She could only try to survive the final act.

"Of course," she said, and the words came out in Livia's voice again. The mask sliding back into place because survival demanded it. "You're right. I'm just... emotional."

She turned and walked out, her footsteps echoing on the marble. Loud. Final. He didn't call after her.

The house felt different now. Bigger. Emptier.

But there was one person who'd never lied to her. One person who'd seen the truth from the beginning. One person who had always called her Sloane.

Nico.

She knew where to find him.

Chapter 55: The Alliance of Ghosts

She found Nico in the main salon.

He was standing in the shadows near the window, disassembling a handgun with the mechanical, rhythmic clicks of a man who found comfort in cold steel. The moonlight caught the edge of his profile—sharp jaw, watchful eyes, the coiled tension of a man who never truly relaxed.

He saw her approach. His posture shifted. The professional sentinel assessing a new variable. Then he saw her face. Whatever he read there made his hands still. It wasn't surprise. It was a dark, weary recognition.

"It's over with Damian," she said. Her voice was flat. Dead. A clinical report from a battlefield. "Roman's hold on him is absolute. He chose the lie."

"You sound surprised," Nico said, his voice a quiet rumble. Then, gentler: "You had to try."

"I thought I could reach him," she admitted, the words tasting like ash. "I thought if he saw the truth, the real, brutal truth of Mona's murder, he would break free."

"Livia died trying to save him, too," Nico said, finally looking at her. Something in his eyes was unbearably sad. "He welded that door shut from the inside. You can't rescue someone who has fallen in love with their kidnapper. Some people can't be saved, Sloane. They can only be survived."

Sloane looked at him, a new understanding dawning. The pity was gone, replaced by the same cold clarity that lived in Nico's gaze. "What does that mean?"

"Roman didn't recruit him with facts," Nico said quietly. "He recruited him with belonging. Purpose. Protection from a world Damian couldn't navigate. The promise that his genius mattered." He paused. "Groomed him for a dozen-plus years. That's not logic. That's a trauma bond."

"It's a cult of one," she whispered, the pieces clicking into place. Roman had given Damian what he craved most—the illusion of being understood. And that need had become a chain stronger than any cage.

The slide of the Glock hissed home—a sharp, metallic snap that sounded like a gavel.

"Exactly," Nico said. "To admit Roman is a monster is to admit his entire life was a con. Everything he built. Everyone he lost." He looked at her. "Damian won't make that trade. Not for you. Not for anyone."

Sloane finally understood. The man she had started to fall for, the brilliant, broken man in the garden—he was the architect of his own haunting. And he would never leave it willingly.

She closed the distance between them. "In her journal," she said, her voice quiet but unrelenting, "Livia mentioned a bunker. A place you knew about."

His eyes cut to hers. This was it. The final move.

"The war has started, Nico," she pressed, her voice a fierce whisper. "Mona is dead. The signing is in a week. We are out of time. So you are either going to help me execute Livia's real plan, or you are going to get out of my way."

He saw it then. The actress was gone. The victim was gone. The compromised asset was gone. The woman standing before him was the weapon Livia had foreseen. Not a counterfeit wife, but a successor.

She had passed the test.

He gave an almost imperceptible nod. "Phase Two was never meant for Livia," he murmured.

"Come with me."

***

He led her through the house like a shadow.

Down the grand staircase. Through the portrait gallery where dead Crestwells watched them pass with oil-painted eyes. Into the cavernous wine cellar that smelled like oak, damp earth, and the rich, complex breath of aging vintage.

The temperature dropped. Sloane's bare feet were cold now. She could see her breath.

Nico moved past rows of dusty bottles—vintages older than she was, labels in French and Italian and German. He stopped at the back wall. Ancient stone. Rough-hewn. The kind of masonry that predated electricity by several hundred years.

He ran his hand along a section of wall.

"Here," he said.

His fingers found something. A seam in the stone. A crack that looked like natural weathering but wasn't.

He pushed.

The wall moved.

A section of stone—three feet wide, seven feet tall—swung inward on silent hinges. Beyond it: a small, sterile antechamber. And waiting inside, the brushed-steel doors of a private elevator.

Nico pressed his thumb to a biometric pad hidden in the rock. The steel doors slid open with a whisper of displaced air.

"The one place he can't hear us," he said.

He ushered her inside. The interior was modern, lit by a soft, amber strip along the floor. No buttons. Just a destination.

The descent was fast and smooth—a stomach-dropping glide into the earth. There was no mechanical grinding, only the faint hum of magnetic motors.

Sloane counted the seconds. Ten. Fifteen. Twenty.

How deep did this go?

The doors slid open. At the bottom, Nico stopped in front of a heavy steel door. Military surplus. The kind designed to seal against blast waves and radiation.

He pulled it open.

The hinges groaned.

And Sloane stepped into Livia's war room. The bunker.

Müller's fallout shelter. The words from Livia's journal made concrete.

Livia hadn't just found a paranoid banker's 1968 blueprints; she had resurrected them. She'd taken a "sealed-off storage room" from a forgotten era and turned it into a war room.

This wasn't just a hideout. It was an ambush that had been waiting fifty years for the right woman to trigger it.

***

Fifty feet square of reinforced concrete, organized with military efficiency. Sleeping quarters in the corners. Along one wall, a kitchenette and floor-to-ceiling pantry stacked with supplies. Deep in a soundproofed alcove, a massive backup generator sat silent, waiting for the grid to fail.

It wasn't just a hiding place. It was a habitat. Livia hadn't just planned a meeting; she had prepared for a siege.

The walls were lined with copper mesh—a fine grid that covered every surface like metallic wallpaper.

"Livia was right," Nico said, his voice echoing in the concrete chamber. "Roman is so obsessed with his digital eyes, he never bothered with the old paper blueprints. To him, the house starts where his network ends." He gestured at the reinforced walls. "To his sensors, this room doesn't exist. It's an analog ghost."

He gestured to the stocked pantry.

"We spent six months making it operational. Leeched power from the municipal line upstream of Roman's sensors. Filtration. Supplies. As far as his systems know, this space is a void."

Sloane ran her hand over the copper mesh. It felt cool. Real. The tiny squares pressed against her palm like chainmail.

"It's a Faraday cage. No signals in or out," Nico continued. "No electromagnetic radiation. His surveillance can't penetrate a Faraday cage. This is the only room in the entire estate where we can speak freely."

Sloane turned slowly, taking it in.

A steel table dominated the center—military surplus, scarred and dented. Maps covered its surface. Zurich. The surrounding mountains. Train routes. Highway access roads.

A computer hummed quietly in the corner. Older model. Air-gapped. Not connected to any network.

And on the far wall: a corkboard.

Sloane moved toward it like a sleepwalker.

The board was chaos. Photographs. Handwritten notes. Strings connecting faces to names to locations. Red ink. Black ink. Livia's handwriting everywhere—precise, controlled, increasingly frantic as the dates progressed.

Roman's face in the center. Arrows radiating outward.

Shell companies. Offshore accounts. A web of connections that looked like a conspiracy theorist's fever dream.

Except it wasn't a fever dream.

It was the truth.

"She was preparing for this," Sloane whispered.

"She was ten steps ahead of him." Nico's voice carried a note of profound grief. Pride mixed with loss. "Her endgame wasn't just to escape. It was a counter-strike."

Sloane turned from the board. "What kind of counter-strike?"

"A dead man's switch." Nico moved to the table. Pulled one of the maps forward. Zurich city center. A building circled in red ink. "The Helvetica Privatbank. Vault seven. In a safety deposit box."

His finger tapped the circle.

"She stored everything there," Nico said. "The source code for Panopticon. The Master Key. The structural maps of Roman's empire. She didn't steal the crimes, Sloane. She engineered the Black Box where Roman hides them, and she kept a copy of the key."

"Why Zurich?" Sloane asked, looking at the map. "Why not hide it here, in the bunker?"

"Because the bunker is still under Roman's watch," Nico said. "Damian owns the deed, but Roman controls the sensors. If he ever got suspicious, if he ever swept the estate with ground-penetrating radar, he'd find it. He'd destroy it."

He tapped the red circle on the map.

"But the Bank? That is sovereign territory. Different jurisdiction. Attorney-client protections. Roman is powerful, but he doesn't own the Swiss banking system. And Livia had legitimate reasons to be in Zurich—she had previous accounts there. Plenty of friends and previous business associates. She hid the trip in plain sight. She put the weapon in the one place his money couldn't reach."

The sheer audacity of it hit Sloane like a physical blow.

Livia hadn't just been documenting Roman's crimes.

She'd been building a bomb.

Unbeknownst, Manny and Glitch were trying to replicate the same feat in their own way.

Chapter 56: The Zurich Protocol

"It's the weapon that burns his entire world to the ground," Nico said quietly.

Sloane stared at the map. At the red circle. At the careful notations in Livia's handwriting along the margins—guard rotations, security protocols, vault access procedures.

"Why haven't you told me this?" Her voice came out sharp. Accusatory. "I've been here for eleven weeks. Fighting in the dark. And you knew this the whole time?"

Nico turned from the map. His face was a mask of conflict.

The sentinel was gone.

What was left was just a man. Tired. Angry. Jealous.

"Because Livia's final order was clear," he said. His voice low. Rough. "'Do not trust the asset with the endgame until she has proven she is ours, not his. No divided loyalties.'"

He held her gaze.

"I saw you with him, Sloane. In the garden. At the piano. In his bed." The words came out like broken glass. "I saw you looking at him like—" He stopped. Shook his head. "I couldn't risk the mission on a woman whose heart was divided."

The memory flashed through her mind. The hallway confrontation. His raw, jealous question: *Did you fuck him as Livia? Or as yourself?*

This wasn't just about the mission.

This was personal.

Sloane looked at him. Really looked at him. At the loyal soldier bound by duty to a ghost. At the jealous man who'd been hurt. At the person who'd been watching her fall for someone else while he stood in the shadows and said nothing.

She understood.

The high-EQ actress in her—the part that read people's emotional subtext like sheet music—saw the whole picture. His conflict. His pain. His impossible position.

"My heart is not divided," she said. Her voice was steel. "Not anymore."

Nico searched her eyes. Looking for the lie. The hesitation. The small crack that meant she wasn't sure.

He found nothing.

The break was clean. Final. Whatever she'd felt for Damian—whatever illusion she'd been nursing—had died in that study when he'd chosen the beautiful lie over the brutal truth.

Nico gave a single, slow nod. Acceptance. "Okay," he said. "Then it's time you saw the whole board."

***

He turned back to the table, his demeanor all business. "Livia's plan was always a two-phase operation. Phase One was the escape—she had routes mapped, a car stashed, fallback positions prepared. She was ready to run when the moment came." He paused, his jaw tight. "That moment never came for her. But we have something she didn't."

His finger traced a route on the map of Küssnacht. "Klausjagen. Three days from now. We use the festival chaos as our cover—the diversion she never had. You convince Damian to take you. A romantic, sentimental journey to see the tradition. Once we're in the town, in the crowd, in the fire and the noise, we create our own chaos and slip away. There's an old chapel by the square—service door in the back leads to an unguarded alley. Livia stashed a car there a year ago. I'll verify it's still operational and load our gear."

Sloane followed his finger, her heart pounding. It was a clean, audacious plan. "And Phase Two?"

Nico's expression hardened. He tapped a second map of Zurich's financial district. "Phase Two was the counter-strike. Livia has a safe deposit box at the Helvetica Privatbank. It contains her Master Key—the Root Seed—and the siphoned logs she managed to pull before the patron locked her out."

He paused, the gravity of the mission settling in. "She had the trigger, but she was waiting for a complete picture of the crimes to make the indictment stick. She died before she could finish it. She put the trigger to his destruction in a vault, waiting for a pulse to wake it up."

He sighed, a sound of profound, weary defeat. "But that plan required Livia." He looked up, his eyes dark with the finality of a mission failed. "With her dead, that door is closed. Phase Two is impossible. The weapon is gone forever."

He started to fold the Zurich map, ready to put it away. Ready to settle for just survival.

"Wait," Sloane said.

Nico paused, his hands on the map.

"If the account is still active," Sloane said slowly, a wild, audacious, and utterly insane idea blooming in her mind, "why couldn't I do it?"

Nico looked at her, his brow furrowed in confusion. "What are you talking about? You can't walk in there. You're not her. The biometrics, the signature..."

"I have her face. I have her voice. I've practiced her signature a thousand times. I can do this."

He stared at her, his expression unreadable, a long, silent moment stretching between them in the cold concrete room. Sloane held his gaze, refusing to look away, letting him see the defiant, desperate fire in her eyes. She wasn't asking for his permission. She was stating a fact.

She watched him process it. Watched the flicker of disbelief in his eyes war with something else. A slow, analytical reassessment. He was looking at her not as the fragile asset he'd been assigned to protect, but as a new, unpredictable variable in Livia's equation.

A muscle worked in his jaw. Then, a slow, almost imperceptible nod, not of agreement, but of dawning, reluctant acknowledgment. He had seen something. He had made a calculation.

Understanding, followed by a flicker of something that might have been a grim, dangerous hope, crossed his face. "Sloane," he said, and his voice was a low, awed whisper, "that's not a retrieval anymore. That's a felony... It's a heist."

"So it is. A heist." A small, dangerous smile touched her lips. "I've played a few of those. Never for real, though."

"This isn't a movie!" Nico's voice was a low, urgent growl. "This is insane. They'll catch you. You'll spend the rest of your life in a Swiss prison."

"What's the alternative?" she shot back. "We run? We disappear and let Roman win? Let him get away with murdering Mona, endangering Manny, and selling a weapon that will enslave billions? No. Not anymore." She leaned forward, her hands flat on the table, claiming the mission as her own. "We are not running. We are fighting back. We are executing Phase Two."

He stared at her, at the woman who was proposing a suicide mission with a terrifying, exhilarating calm. The actress he thought he was protecting had just become the most dangerous person in the room. He saw the logic. The desperation. The sheer, insane courage of it. And he saw that they had no other choice.

"Okay," he breathed, the word a surrender to her will. "Okay. A heist. I'll double-check on their security protocols to see if we are missing anything."

He unfolded the Zurich map again, his focus now sharp, analytical. "But if we're going to do this," he said, a new, grim energy in his voice, "then you need to become her completely."

He slid a Swiss passport across the table. The photo showed Livia with auburn hair and glasses—a disguise she'd used to open the account. The name read: Helena Baros.

"Helena Baros," Nico said. "Livia's ghost identity. With the right wig, glasses and makeup, you can pass for her. The safe deposit box is registered under this name. From now on, that's you."

He moved to a locked steel cabinet against the wall and opened it. He pulled out a sleek, black Glock 19. He chambered a round and held it out to her, butt first.

"This isn't practice," he said, his voice deadly serious. "This is for the mission."

Sloane took the gun. The weight was familiar, but the finality of it was a shocking, brutal reality.

He held her gaze. "This is Act Three. And in Act Three, the hero gets a weapon."

The cold metal in her hand was a promise. The shared mission in his eyes was another. The air in the bunker felt thick. Charged. Like the moment before a thunderstorm breaks. All the walls between them—duty, jealousy, grief, suspicion—had finally collapsed.

There were only two people left in the world. Standing on the edge of a suicide mission. With three days until everything burned.

Nico didn't say a word.

He just closed the distance between them.

***

The kiss was a collision.

Desperate and raw and angry. A release of weeks of unspoken fear and desire. His hands were in her hair, her fingers gripping his shirt, and it wasn't about romance. It was about affirmation.

I am here. You are here. We are real.

Sloane felt his heartbeat against her chest. Felt the heat of his skin through his shirt. She pushed him back against the steel table, maps crinkling beneath them. Her hands found the hem of his shirt, pulled it up, felt the ridged muscle beneath. Scars. So many scars.

"Sloane—" His voice was ragged.

She pressed closer, needing to lose herself, needing to forget the odds for just one minute.

But Nico caught her wrists.

He didn't push her away. He just held her there, his forehead pressed against hers, both of them breathing hard, their bodies humming with a kinetic, unspent energy.

"No," he whispered. The word was a rough rasp. "Not here."

Sloane looked up at him, her eyes searching his. "We might not get another chance."

"We will," he said, and the fierceness in his voice made her believe him. He lowered her hands, interlacing his fingers with hers. "I am not taking you on a metal table in a bunker like we're already dead. I am not making you a secret."

He kissed her forehead, a gesture of profound, aching restraint.

"We survive this," he said. "We get out. And then... we do this right. When we're free."

Sloane let out a shaky breath, the adrenaline slowly ebbing into a different kind of strength. He was right. To give in now was to admit they might die. To wait was a bet on their future.

"Okay," she whispered. "When we're free."

They stood there in the silence, holding onto each other, the promise hanging in the air between them—heavier and more real than any weapon in the room.

***

Later, they sat side by side on the concrete floor, backs resting against the heavy steel legs of the table. Sloane's head rested lightly on his shoulder, a quiet intimacy that felt heavier than the passion from before. The maps were still scattered above them.

"Three days," Sloane whispered. "Until Klausjagen."

"Three days." Nico's voice was a low rumble against her hair. "Until we burn it all down. Or go down in flames."

She lifted her head. Looked at him in the dim light.

"Manny," she said suddenly.

Nico's expression shifted. "What about him?"

"I haven't been able to reach him since Küssnacht. Since the call from the payphone." Sloane's voice carried an edge of frustration. "The ledger is the weapon, but Manny is the shield. He has the journalists, the legal reach, the ability to make the truth stick. Besides," she added, her eyes narrowing as she recalled the journal, "his hacker might be able to find a digital path to the ledger."

"He's the multiplier," Nico said, his voice a low, tactical hum. "He ensures the impact is permanent. Without him, we're just throwing pebbles at a tank."

Sloane nodded. "And we're just casualties waiting to happen. If we can't transmit the truth... we just run until Roman catches us. We need a line out."

Nico was silent for a long moment. Thinking.

"What?" Sloane asked.

"There's a way." The corner of his mouth quirked up. "To reach him. Securely." Nico's expression was carefully neutral.

"How?" Sloane's voice carried disbelief. "Roman is watching everything. Every phone line. Every internet connection. Every—"

Nico's smile was dark. Amused.

"Not everything," he said. He stood, walked over to a locked steel case in the corner, and placed his hand on the keypad.

Chapter 57: The Lifeline

In the secret bunker beneath Argentis, Sloane held her breath as Nico's fingers moved across the keypad. The lock released with a soft click. The case opened with a soft hiss.

Inside, nestled in dense foam padding, was a sleek black device. Military-grade hardware with a small digital display and a thick coiled cable attached.

"Livia's last resort," Nico said, lifting the device carefully.

Sloane stared at it. Then at the copper mesh lining the walls around them.

"Wait." Her voice carried sharp intelligence. "Didn't you say this bunker is a Faraday cage? I'm no physicist. But I'm pretty damn sure that no signals can travel in or out of it. So how can this phone work from here?"

Nico smiled. It was a rare expression—genuine, almost proud.

"Very perceptive," he said. "You're absolutely right. A functioning Faraday cage blocks all electromagnetic signals. Radio waves. Cell signals. Satellite communications. Everything." He held up the device. "Which is why this isn't a standard satellite phone. It's a base station. And the signal doesn't originate from inside the cage."

He pointed to the wall behind the steel case. In the shadows, barely visible, was a small armored port. Reinforced steel. The kind designed to survive anything.

"See that port?"

Sloane moved closer. Examined it. "What is it?"

"A hardwired connection. That port is linked by armored fiber-optic cable to an active antenna hidden half a kilometer up the mountain. The cable runs through bedrock. Through old utility conduits from the original construction."

His voice carried weight. Memory. "Livia and I spent weeks snaking that line. Bit by painful bit. We had to move through the service tunnels in complete darkness to avoid detection."

Understanding dawned on Sloane's face. "So the bunker stays sealed. But the antenna outside—"

"Transmits the signal," Nico finished. "The phone connects to the antenna through the cable. The electromagnetic waves never enter or leave this room. Just data traveling through a physical line. As far as the Faraday cage is concerned, nothing is being transmitted."

"And Roman can't detect it?"

"The antenna is hidden inside the old weather vane on top of the boathouse," Nico said.

Sloane's eyes widened. "That's why you stopped me that day. On the path."

"I couldn't let you draw attention to it," Nico confirmed. "The cable runs through the old drainage conduits from here to the water. Roman's surveillance systems catalog the boathouse as 'derelict structure.' It's his blind spot."

Sloane looked at the device with new respect. "Jesus. Livia thought of everything."

"She had to." Nico took the thick black cable from the phone base and connected it to the wall port.

Click.

A small green light on the device blinked to life.

"It's active," he said quietly. "Encrypted end-to-end. Untraceable. Roman's systems have no idea it exists."

Sloane stared at the glowing green light. At the device that represented weeks of dangerous, meticulous work. At the lifeline Livia had built in secret while living under the eye of a monster.

A way to reach Manny.

A way to make sure the evidence didn't die with them.

A way to fight back.

"How long do we have?" she asked.

"Minutes," Nico said. "It's a clean line, but physics is physics. A weather station pulses; it doesn't stream. Keep the line open too long, and the pattern stands out against the noise. Make it count."

He handed her the handset. The plastic was cool and heavy.

Sloane looked at the keypad. She hadn't spoken to Manny since the payphone in Küssnacht. It had been a long silence while she played house and he hunted ghosts in Los Angeles.

"If I make this call," she said, looking at Nico, "I might be leading Roman right to his door."

"He's already at the door, Sloane," Nico said, his voice grim. "Manny has been poking the bear for weeks. The only way he survives is if we give him the weapon to kill it."

She nodded, the decision settling in her bones. Defense was no longer an option. The only way out was to attack.

She dialed.

The phone rang.

Once.

Twice.

She held her breath.

***

Sloane's heart hammered against her ribs. She could hear it—her own pulse, too loud in the concrete silence of the bunker. Could Nico hear it too?

Her finger tightened on the device. The green light blinked steadily. Active. Encrypted. Untraceable. But what if Manny didn't answer? What if Roman had already gotten to him? What if—

The third ring lasted an eternity.

Click.

"Yeah?" Manny's voice. Rough as gravel. Wary. Alive.

The relief hit her like a wave. She closed her eyes. Exhaled. "Manny, it's me."

A sharp intake of breath on the other end. Then a muffled curse—creative, profane, utterly Manny. "Jesus Christ, kid. Where the hell are you? I thought—"

"Secure line. But still risky." She cut him off. Her words came fast, urgent, no time for reunion. "What have you found on Lazar?"

"We found his 'why', kid. It's a daughter," Manny said, his voice dropping into a somber register. "Katya Lazar. Moscow, 2004. She was a reporter, a real firebrand. Someone threw her off an eighth-floor balcony to bury a story. Roman had a breakdown, checked into a psychiatric clinic in Vienna, and spent the next twenty years building a machine to ensure no one could ever hide a secret from him again. He isn't just a billionaire, Sloane. He's a man who turned his grief into a global cage."

Sloane gripped the handset, Livia's journal entries about Roman's 'kind eyes' suddenly taking on a chilling new dimension. The grieving father was the most dangerous version of the monster.

"First, the psychological weapon," Sloane began, her mind already moving past the 'why' to the kill-shot. "Your guy found the daughter. That's good, but may not be enough. Is that his origin wound? The first trauma? The thing that made him *capable* of this? Tell Glitch to dig into Vienna. What really happened in his past, before Moscow? I want you to find the first body he buried."

"We're ahead of you," Manny said, his voice grim but satisfied. "Glitch has been scraping the dark web for weeks. He kept finding dead links leading back to a clinic in Austria. Scrubbed files. Sealed police reports. He sensed a ghost in Vienna. We'll dig deeper. What's the second mission?"

"The 'how'," Sloane replied. "In her journal, Livia confirmed a 'Dark Ledger'—a complete record of his crimes, encrypted and hidden in his system. I need Glitch to find it and see if there's any way in."

"That explains the partition," Manny muttered, the pieces clicking into place. "Glitch found a massive, black-boxed sector on Roman's private server. He's been sitting at the front door. If that's the Ledger... he's ready to breach."

She paused. "Manny, this is a two-front war. Which brings me to Path B. Livia left something in Zurich. A backup. We're planning to retrieve it from a bank vault."

"Absolutely not," Manny growled. "You're begging to rot in a Swiss prison. If that's the Ledger, Glitch is already at the door. We don't need whatever's in that vault if we can crack the encryption from here. Let us try first."

"Manny, we have no other move—"

"Yes, you do!" he implored. "Me and the kid! You are trapped in a cage, we are not. Let us do our jobs. If the Ledger exists digitally, Glitch can pull it. We don't need a physical key if we hack the lock. He's the best there is. Just give us time."

Sloane closed her eyes, weighing the two impossible paths. A digital ghost hunt versus a physical suicide mission. "We don't have time," she whispered.

"The Klausjagen festival starts Friday night. It's our only window to escape from Argentis."

"Then give us until then," Manny pressed. "If I don't have ironclad proof in your hands by Friday evening, you do your crazy thing. Promise me."

Sloane looked at Nico, who gave a single, almost imperceptible nod. It was a long shot, but it was their only shot at a clean win. "Three days, Manny," she said, her voice tight. "To find the origin wound and the Ledger. After that, we're going to Zurich."

"I hear you," Manny said, a new, frantic urgency in his voice. "We'll find it before then. I promise."

A pause. Longer this time. When Manny spoke again, his voice carried something she wasn't used to hearing from him. Vulnerability. "Sloane, baby. Are you safe?"

She thought about lying. About giving him the reassurance he needed. She couldn't.

"No," she said honestly. The word felt like broken glass in her throat. "But I'm close to the end. Call back on this number if you want to get in touch. Stay alive, Manny. I need you on the other side of this."

"You too, kid." His voice cracked slightly. "You too."

The line went dead.

Sloane lowered the phone. Stared at it. The green light was still blinking, a tiny, hopeful pulse in the dim room. But the connection was gone.

She looked up at Nico. He was watching her, his expression unreadable. He had heard everything.

She handed him the phone. Their fingers brushed. The contact lasted a second longer than necessary. "It's done," she said quietly. "The bulldog's on the scent."

Nico disconnected the cable from the wall port. The green light died. He placed the phone back in its foam cradle. Locked the steel case with a soft click that echoed in the concrete chamber. "Now what?" he asked.

Sloane turned to the steel table. To the maps spread across its surface. Zurich city center. The Helvetica Privatbank. Vault seven. The circle drawn in Livia's careful red ink.

"Now," she said, her voice a low, steady thing, "we assume their plan will fail. And we prepare for the heist."

Chapter 58: The Origin Wound

Glitch called the same night at 3:47 AM.

Manny was asleep in his office chair, head on his desk, drooling on a legal pad. The phone's buzz made him jerk awake so hard he knocked over his coffee mug. Cold coffee spread across yesterday's notes.

"This better be good," he growled into the phone.

"It's better than good." Glitch sounded breathless. Manic. The voice of someone who hadn't slept for days and was running on adrenaline and Red Bull. "I found the origin wound."

"The what?"

"The thing that broke him before Katya. The first trauma. The reason he was already twisted when his daughter died."

Manny sat up straighter. "Talk to me, kid."

"Your girl had a good instinct about Vienna. I hit the jackpot there," Glitch began. "Turns out he's a 'loyal customer.' I went back into the Weisswald servers—but this time, I drilled down into the '90s cold storage. I pointed every bot I have at their deep encryption. And I found it. Lazar's 'Rosebud.'"

"His what?"

"His weakness," Glitch explained. "His origin wound. The one file the clinic protected more obsessively than any other patient record—buried under encryption that goes way beyond standard medical privacy. Someone paid them serious money to hide this."

Manny leaned forward, pen hovering over a fresh legal pad. "What's in it?"

"Psychiatric evaluations from when he was sixteen. 1976. Right after his family fled Russia." Glitch's voice dropped. "His parents died, Manny. House fire in Vienna. The official story is it was an accident. Electrical fault. The whole family asleep. Roman was the only survivor."

"Survivor's guilt."

"Maybe. Or maybe something worse." Glitch paused. "The therapist's notes are... let's just say they raise questions."

"What kind of questions?"

"The kind where a sixteen-year-old boy sits in a psychiatrist's office and can't explain why he woke up before the smoke alarms went off. Can't explain why he was already dressed when he ran outside. Can't explain why the fire started in his parents' bedroom, not the kitchen or the living room."

Manny's blood went cold. "They suspected him."

"The police ruled it an accident. No investigation. Case closed in a week." Glitch's typing was frantic now. "But the insurance company? They fought the payout for two years. Hired investigators. The arson specialists found accelerant residue in three locations. All in the parents' bedroom. All inconsistent with electrical fire."

"Jesus."

"It gets better. Or worse, depending on your perspective." Glitch's voice took on that clinical tone he used when the information was particularly dark. "Roman's family wasn't just wealthy Russian nobility. They were thieves on a historical scale."

He paused, letting that sink in. "His father was a high-ranking KGB colonel who spent decades exploiting his position to systematically loot state museums. Fabergé eggs. Religious icons. Old Master paintings. A treasure trove of a nation's history, smuggled piece by piece to Vienna through diplomatic channels. By the time the family defected in 1976, he'd assembled one of the most significant collections of stolen art in the Cold War. We're talking lost masterpieces that museums and governments are still searching for."

"Fifty million dollars if they'd liquidated everything through a fire sale. In 1976." Glitch's typing stopped. "That wasn't just 'fuck you' money, Manny. That was 'reshape the world' money. And Roman inherited every last piece when his parents died in that house fire. At sixteen."

"That's how he built his empire," Glitch continued, his voice a low, chilling rasp. "Stolen art from dead parents who may or may not have been murdered by their own son."

Manny lit a cigarette with hands that wanted to shake but wouldn't let themselves. He inhaled the smoke like it was oxygen. "What did the shrink say?"

"Dr. Emil Kurtz. Very expensive. Very discreet. The kind of therapist who treats the children of oligarchs and doesn't ask too many questions." Glitch's voice was grim. "His notes are fascinating. And terrifying."

"Read them."

Glitch cleared his throat. When he spoke again, his voice changed. Became quieter. Like he was reading something he wished he could unread.

"Patient exhibits profound dissociation when discussing the night of the fire. Memory gaps. Inconsistent timeline. When pressed about why he woke before the smoke alarms, patient becomes agitated. States: 'I knew something was wrong. I always know when something is wrong. I see patterns others don't see.'"

Manny exhaled smoke. "He was already paranoid."

"Gets better. Listen to this: 'Patient expresses no grief over parents' death. When asked how he feels, patient responds: They were going to leave me. They were planning to abandon me in Vienna while they returned to Russia. I heard them arguing about it. They said I was too much trouble. Too difficult. That I frightened them.'"

"Did they actually say that?"

"Who knows? The therapist notes that he can't verify the patient's claims. The parents are dead. No one else heard the arguments." Glitch paused. "But here's the kicker. The therapist writes: 'Patient may have acted in perceived self-defense. If patient believed abandonment was imminent, and if patient's attachment issues are as severe as observed, the fire may have been a desperate act to prevent separation. However, patient shows no remorse. No acknowledgment of wrongdoing. Patient appears to believe the outcome was justified. Possibly even necessary.'"

The silence on the line was heavy.

"So he killed them," Manny said finally.

"Maybe. Or maybe he just let it happen. Maybe he woke up, smelled smoke, and decided not to wake them. Decided to let the universe make the choice for him." Glitch's voice was hollow. "Either way, he was sixteen years old and his parents died and he walked away with fifty million dollars and zero consequences."

"And that's when it started."

"The surveillance obsession? Yeah. According to the notes, Roman told Dr. Kurtz that he was going to build systems. Create order. Make sure he always knew what was coming. The therapist writes: 'Patient expresses grandiose plans to monitor environments, predict threats, control variables. Patient states repeatedly: I will never be surprised again. I will never not know. I will see everything before it happens.'"

Manny closed his eyes. "He was already building Panopticon in his head. At sixteen."

"But he couldn't build it in the seventies," Glitch said. "The tech didn't exist. So he played the long game. He took that fifty million in stolen art money—his seed capital—and spent the next twenty-eight years turning it into an empire."

"He was building a war chest," Manny murmured. "Fifty million in blood money."

"Which he turned into five hundred million. Then five billion. Then who knows how much. And then came the trigger." Glitch's voice dropped. "2004. Roman is forty-four years old. He has the money. He has the obsession. And then Katya dies."

Glitch's typing stopped, the silence on the line heavy.

"That was the perfect storm, Manny. He realized money alone couldn't save her. He didn't just want to be rich anymore; he needed to be omniscient. That's when the concept became a crusade."

"And the shrink?"

"He predicted it all the way back in '76," Glitch said. "Dr. Kurtz recommended long-term institutional care. He wrote that the patient was a danger to himself and the fabric of society. Roman refused treatment after six months. He left Vienna and disappeared into the digital world to build the cage that would keep him safe."

Manny stared at his legal pad. The notes he'd been taking looked like a profile of a serial killer, not a tech billionaire.

"This is good work, kid."

"It's not enough to stop him," Glitch replied. "This tells us he's a psychopath. It doesn't prove he's committed crimes we can prosecute. Patricide from five decades ago? Even if it was murder, he was a minor. The case is closed. The evidence is gone."

“How about the murder of the oligarch who killed Katya?”

“Different jurisdiction. Twenty-eight years between bodies. And it contradicts the ‘official’ report. Wouldn’t be the first time a shady oligarch dropped dead of ‘natural causes’ anyway.”

"And the hit on Livia?" Manny pressed.

"A dead woman's journal entry against a billionaire's word? In court, that's hearsay, not a smoking gun."

"So we keep digging."

"We don't have to dig for the motive anymore," Glitch said, his voice changing, becoming urgent. "The shrink notes confirm exactly what Sloane told you. We go after the hard evidence."

"Livia's 'Dark Ledger'," Manny said, testing the weight of the words.

"Roman called it his 'Gospel' in therapy. A meticulous record of every action, every decision, to prove he was always right. Livia was right, Manny. She saw the shape of it before anyone else. He didn’t just document his crimes; he turned them into a dataset."

"And fed them to Panopticon," Manny added, the pieces clicking together with a sickening thud. "He used his own history to train the machine. He’s teaching the algorithm how to find everyone else’s secrets by modeling his own."

"Exactly," Glitch said, his voice dropping to a chilling register. "He’s building a digital god out of his own sins. So the Ledger exists, Manny. We just have to find the vault it's buried in."

"That's the problem. A man this paranoid doesn't leave his gospel on a laptop. He buries it deep." Glitch paused, his fingers hovering over the keyboard. "But I found the thread that ties it all together. The financial backbone," Glitch said, his voice dropping. "Twenty years of bribes, wire transfers, shell companies. Every transaction has metadata. Timestamps. IP addresses. Coded references to other files. It's the Rosetta Stone."

"What are you saying, kid?"

"I'm saying the Ledger isn't a *thing* to be found," Glitch explained, his typing picking up speed. "It's a jigsaw puzzle to be assembled. If I can get into his core financial server, I can use the transaction data to trace backwards. Vienna connects to Moscow. Moscow connects to the *Ariadne*. The *Ariadne* connects to Harrow. I can compile the Dark Ledger myself."

“Did you say ‘compile’?” Manny sat up upright.

"Yes. I can scrape every isolated transaction and bind them into a single file. And if I can put it together, Roman Lazar is finished. But Manny?" Glitch's voice cracked. "If I'm right, he's going to know someone's coming for it. And he's going to do everything in his power to stop us."

"Jesus. How can I help?"

"I can't do it from here. My perimeter alarms are already tripping. They're tracing the echoes of my probes." Glitch's voice was tight, breathless. "This is too big. Too loud. This isn't a sneak-and-peek; it's a smash-and-grab on his central fortress. If we don't hit them today, Manny, we don't hit them at all. I need a clean location. A secure, hardwired system. I can package it all on a USB drive if you have a way of getting it to Sloane."

Manny thought for a moment. "Leave that to me. I'll call an old friend who can help."

"Good. Because I'm scrubbing my rig now. I'll be there at 1 PM. Your office?"

"No. I feel eyes on me, too. Come to Gable & Crane. I'll get us the private room. It has a hardwired ethernet port. Remember the place?"

"I do," Glitch paused. "And Manny? Pack a bag. After this, we both disappear for a while."

The line went dead.

Manny sat in his office, smoking, staring at the notes he'd just taken.

Roman Lazar had killed his parents at sixteen. Lost his daughter at forty-four. And spent his entire life building a machine to make sure nothing ever surprised him again.

Now that machine was about to be sold to twelve intelligence agencies.

And the only thing standing in the way was an aging fixer with Parkinson's and a hacker kid who was probably about to get himself killed.

Manny crushed out his cigarette.

Today.

The endgame.

He started packing.

Chapter 59: The Ledger

The back room of Gable & Crane smelled like old leather and expensive cigars and the electric ozone tang of overworked electronics.

Glitch had arrived at 1 PM with a duffel bag and the sunken eyes of someone who hadn't slept in three days and knew he might not sleep again. He'd set up his equipment on the private room's table—three laptops, external hard drives, a mess of cables that looked like electronic spaghetti.

Manny watched from the corner, drinking scotch he couldn't taste, his hands shaking so badly he had to hold the glass with both palms.

"You look like shit," Manny said.

"You look like shit's grandpa." Glitch didn't look up from his screens. His fingers flew across the keyboard. "How much Pepto have you had today?"

"Not enough."

"There's not enough Pepto in the world for this." Glitch's laugh was brittle. "By the way," he said, typing a rapid string of commands. "I pinged the address Sloane gave you. The 'Margarita' protocol. She was right. It's an ancient text-based admin tunnel. Totally invisible to modern sweeps. I've established a secure uplink. If we need to dump anything fast, that's our chute."

"Good," Manny grunted. "Now fill it."

Glitch looked up. "This is the big one. No turning back after this. You ready?"

"No."

"Good. Neither am I. Let's do it anyway."

The central screen showed lines of code scrolling past at impossible speed. Glitch was inside something. Somewhere dark and heavily guarded.

"Where are you?" Manny asked.

"Roman's personal servers. The fortress. The place he keeps everything that matters." Glitch's eyes never left the screen. "I've been mapping his security for a week. Learning the patterns. Finding the weak spots."

"Is there a weak spot?"

"There's always a weak spot. You just have to be crazy enough to exploit it." Glitch's grin was feral. "And baby, I am certifiably insane."

The screen changed. A single file was isolated in the center of the screen, its name simple and arrogant: INDEX.LEDGER.

"That's it," Glitch whispered, his voice a note of pure, unadulterated awe. "The master index. The Rosetta Stone. The secret schema that Livia created. Roman's Dark Ledger."

"What the hell does that mean?" Manny growled.

"Three weeks I've been chasing him. He compartmentalizes everything," Glitch explained, his fingers flying as he initiated a complex script. "The Livia contract is in a file codenamed 'Ariadne.' The Harrow blackmail is in 'Helixis.' The psych evals are buried in his family's 'Estate Archives.' They're scattered across a dozen servers, each behind its own wall of encryption."

"So it's useless," Manny said, his hope deflating.

"It was," Glitch countered, a feral grin spreading across his face. "But the Ledger... Roman built a map for himself. It's the index that links them all. And I'm using it to pull everything into one beautiful, terrible package right now."

"Why would he even create an index?" Manny asked. "It's insane."

"No," Glitch said, his voice dropping. "It's essential. Panopticon is a predictive engine. It can't predict the future if it doesn't know the past."

He pointed at the screen. "The algorithm has to know that the bribe in Zurich connects to the murder in Naples. It needs the full dataset to learn. Without this index, Panopticon is just a bunch of isolated cameras. With it, it's omniscient."

Manny felt sick. "He built a master key because the weapon required it."

"Exactly. And he thought his encryption made it untouchable." Glitch's grin turned feral. "But he forgot about the devil."

"So we're about to play God," Manny said, his voice grim.

"Something like that."

Glitch hit ENTER.

Two progress bars appeared on the screen. "Split stream," Glitch muttered. "Pulling from his servers, piping to two places at once—USB drive in my hand, and the Ghost Channel back at Argentis. One local, one remote. If they smash this laptop, the Swiss server still has it. If they jam the signal, the drive survives. Redundancy is life."

Both bars started at 1%.

"Wait," Glitch said, his euphoria vanishing instantly. He tapped a key, and a preview window opened showing streams of garbled, chaotic static.

"Let me guess. It's encrypted," Manny said, lighting a cigarette.

"Worse. It's Root Seed encryption. A custom algorithm. Roman's signature. I can download the files, Manny, but I can't read them. I have the lock, but I don't have the key. Without Livia's drive, this is just terabytes of noise. It would take a supercomputer a hundred years to crack."

Manny stared at the screen. The realization hit him like a physical blow.

"Livia," Manny whispered. "The journal. She said she engineered the Root Seed. She didn't leave evidence in that bank vault, Glitch. She left the decoder."

"Then we have to get this 'noise' to Sloane," Glitch said, his fingers flying. "She has the one thing that can turn this garbage into a gun."

Manny's stomach dropped. If they needed Sloane to finish this, that meant she had to survive long enough to get to Zurich. To break into a bank. To decode seventy gigabytes of evidence while Roman hunted her.

"She's not ready for this," Manny said.

"She's all we've got," Glitch replied, not looking up from the screen. "And she's got Nico. That's gotta count for something."

Manny thought of Sophie's grave. Of the promise he'd made. *Keep her safe.*

He was about to break it.

"When this is done, we won't just have a bullet," Glitch muttered, staring at the climbing numbers. "We'll have the whole goddamn arsenal. Roman scattered the pieces. I put them together. This is mine."

4%... 7%...

The fan on Glitch's laptop whirred louder. The machine was working at full capacity, pulling down seventy gigabytes of damnation.

Manny's heart was a drum against his ribs. "How long?"

"Seventy gigabytes. Compressed. Maybe thirty minutes. Maybe less." Glitch's hands were shaking now too. "The download is fast, but the re-encryption for transport takes time."

He glanced up, his face pale.

"Bad news. The moment I accessed this folder, I tripped every alarm in his system. He knows someone's inside. He's already mobilizing."

Manny stared at the screen. "We already have the Vienna psych reports. We have the police file on Katya. We know *why* he's a monster. Why do we need this?"

"We have the smoke," Glitch corrected. He pointed to the progress bar downloading the massive encrypted file. "But this? This is the fire. This is the raw data Roman fed into the Black Box. The Dark Ledger. The actual orders. The money trails. The proof."

11%... 15%...

The door to the back room was locked. But Manny could hear the restaurant beyond. The low hum of conversation. The clink of glasses. The world continuing like nothing was wrong.

Manny wondered how many of those people out there were on Roman's payroll. How many were watching without knowing they were watching.

22%... 28%...

"What else is in there?" Manny asked.

"Everything," Glitch said quietly, reading the directory tags as they streamed in. "I can see the structure. The Consortium. Payments to intelligence officials. Bribes. Blackmail. He's been building leverage for years. Judging by the file sizes, we're looking at hundreds of millions spread across dozens of officials. The categories are specific: some took money, some took favors, some just took the promise that Panopticon would give them power."

35%... 41%...

Manny lit a cigarette. His hands wouldn't stop shaking.

"There's more," Glitch continued. "Twenty years of crimes. Murders. Extortion. Money laundering. Politicians disappeared. Witnesses recanted. Journalists went silent. He's funded the whole operation with blood money. And he documented it all. Because in his mind, it's justified. It's necessary. It's the price of building a better world."

48%... 54%...

"He's insane."

"He's logical. That's worse." Glitch's eyes were locked on the progress bar. "Insane people are chaotic. Unpredictable. Roman is neither. He's a machine. Every crime calculated. Every risk assessed. Every decision backed by data."

61%... 67%...

Manny's phone lit up. He looked at the screen.

Unknown number.

He didn't answer.

It rang again. Same number.

"Don't," Glitch said. "It's him. Or his people. They're trying to trace us."

Manny powered the phone off and dropped it on the table.

73%... 79%...

Glitch's hands never stopped moving. Code scrolled. Files compressed. The upload to the Ghost Channel ran parallel to the USB download, a digital insurance policy being written in real time.

84%... 89%...

"Come on, come on," Glitch whispered.

93%... 96%...

The progress bar crept forward with agonizing slowness.

98%... 99%...

Time stretched. The fan whirred. The world held its breath.

Then:

100%

DOWNLOAD COMPLETE.

The second progress bar hit 100% a heartbeat later.

UPLOAD COMPLETE.

Glitch hit a final sequence of keys, verifying both transfers. "It's done," he said, his voice hollow with exhaustion and triumph. "The encrypted Ledger is uploaded to the Ghost Channel. It's a locked box, Manny. If Sloane doesn't find the key in Zurich, this was all for nothing."

"She'll find it," Manny said.

He took another drink. This time, he tasted it. Smoke and peat and victory.

Chapter 60: The Arsenal

"It's done," Glitch said, his voice a sharp exhalation of relief. "Upload complete. The Ghost Channel has the package."

He unplugged the tiny USB drive—the physical backup—from his machine. "The whole damn thing. It's all on there. But it's a brick without the Key."

He held it out. Manny took it, the small piece of plastic feeling like a sacred relic in his palm. They had done it. They had stolen the bomb. Now Sloane just had to find the detonator.

"Holy shit, you did it, kid," Manny hugged Glitch and planted a wet kiss on his forehead.

"Woah, gramps. Go easy," Glitch said, though he looked proud. "There's still work to be done. She has to open it."

"Now what?" Manny asked.

"Now we burn the logs," Glitch said, his fingers already a blur across the keyboards. "Scorched earth. In five minutes, these rigs will be expensive paperweights. I was never here."

"And you? Where do you go?"

Glitch didn't look up, but a faint, tired smile touched his lips. "I've got a locker waiting at LAX. Tomorrow, I'm a freelance coder in Portland with a passion for artisanal coffee. Doug Peters is dead."

"I owe you, kid," Manny said, his voice thick.

"Just nail the bastard," Glitch replied. "That's payment enough."

"I've got to call her," Manny said, his hands shaking as he pulled out the satellite phone. "I have to tell her we have the gun."

Glitch nodded, his screens filling with cascading deletion scripts. "Make it quick, old man. The ghosts are coming."

Manny dialed. The encrypted line clicked, hissed, connected.

***

The satellite phone in the bunker buzzed, a harsh, jarring sound in the concrete silence. Sloane snatched it up, her heart hammering. "Manny?"

"We got it, kid." His voice was a triumphant, breathless roar. "Glitch just pushed the upload to the Ghost Channel. Seventy gigabytes of compressed damnation. It's the whole rotten empire. The Ledger, the contracts, everything."

Sloane's legs gave out. She sank onto a crate, a choked sob of relief escaping her lips. "You have it?"

"We have the box," Manny said, his voice urgent. "But I was wrong, kid. Digital wasn't enough. It's locked down tight. Root Seed encryption. Glitch says it's a custom algorithm—unbreakable without the master key. We can't read a single word of it, and neither can the Feds."

"Root Seed," Sloane whispered. The journal entry flashed in her mind. *'I convinced Damian that the architecture needed a soul. A single, mathematical constant that would never change, never update, never shift.'*

Livia hadn't just found the flaw. She'd engineered it.

"But we found the other thing you asked for," Manny continued, his voice dropping into a darker register. "Vienna. Glitch went back to 1976. Roman was sixteen. His parents died in a house fire—wealthy Russian defectors with a fortune in stolen art. KGB colonel's family. Fifty million in looted masterpieces."

Sloane's breath caught. Sixteen. A house fire. Stolen art.

"The insurance investigators found accelerant residue," Manny said. "Three locations. All in the parents' bedroom. Police ruled it an accident, but the psychiatric notes tell a different story. The kid woke up before the smoke alarms. Was already dressed. Showed no grief. Just kept saying his parents were going to abandon him, that he had to see everything coming, that he'd never be surprised again."

A cold certainty settled in Sloane's chest. "He killed them."

"And spent the next twenty-eight years turning their blood money into an empire. That's your psychological weapon, kid. A sixteen-year-old murderer who built Panopticon because he's terrified of losing control."

Sloane closed her eyes, the pieces assembling into a horrifying picture. A boy who killed for control. A father who lost control when his daughter died. A man who built a global surveillance system because he couldn't save either of them.

"The origin wound," she whispered.

"Yeah," Manny said. "Now you know what you're fighting."

He took a breath, the gravity of the situation settling in. "We built the gun, Sloane. But you have the firing pin. You have to go to Zurich. You have to get Livia's Key. It's the only way to turn this static into an indictment."

"I will," she whispered, the words a prayer. "I promise."

"In my hand," he said, looking at the USB drive, "is the physical backup. Just in case. My contact is wheels-up for—"

***

Back in Gable's, as Manny was speaking, Glitch was on the final deletion sequence—forty seconds left—when a sharp, authoritative knock rattled the back room door.

Glitch's head snapped up from his work, his finger frozen over the ENTER key. "Manny."

"Manny?" Sloane's voice, small and hopeful, crackled from the phone in his hand. "Manny, what was that?"

The door splintered, bursting inward. Two men in tactical vests spilled into the room, guns raised. "FBI. Hands up!"

Manny's world stopped. He was still on the phone with Sloane.

"Manny?!" Her voice was a scream of terror now. "What's happening?!"

He looked from the agents' dead eyes to the USB drive in his other hand. Through the doorway, he caught a flash of movement—Glitch, diving through the bathroom window into the alley. The agents hadn't seen him. They only had eyes for Manny.

Good kid. Run.

It was over. But the upload had finished. She had the file.

"I love you, kid," he whispered into the phone, his voice a raw, broken thing. "Now go be a superstar. Finish the scene."

He didn't end the call.

The phone was a witness; he had to leave it behind. The drive was the weapon; he couldn't let them find it.

With a practiced sleight of hand from his old card-playing days, Manny lowered his arm below the table edge. He slid the phone onto the velvet cushion of the booth, face up, pushing it deep into the shadows beneath a discarded napkin.

Then he stood up abruptly, knocking his chair back, drawing every gun and every pair of eyes in the room directly to him.

"Easy, fellas," Manny wheezed, raising his hands high, ensuring they looked at his face, not the table. He tried to summon one last shred of his trademark bravado, even as his heart hammered. "Watch the face. I'm too goddamn handsome for the rough stuff."

The agents swarmed him, slamming him against the wall beside the booth.

"Emanuel Goldman," the lead agent boomed. "You're being arrested on federal charges of accessing, possessing, and distributing child pornography."

The bravado died instantly.

The words were a physical blow, a punch to the gut that knocked the air from his lungs, the fight from his soul.

Child. Pornography.

The world went silent. The sounds of the restaurant faded away to a dull, white noise. He looked at the agent's dead, pitiless eyes, and he finally, truly understood the nature of the monster they were fighting. This wasn't just a frame. This was a soul-murder. A lie so vile, so monstrous, that it didn't just destroy your life. It defiled the very memory of you.

"That's... that's not possible," Manny stammered, his mind reeling, the words tumbling out loud enough for the phone to catch. "That's a mistake. I would never... I had a daughter..."

The agent's face was stone. "You're done." He yanked Manny's arm behind his back.

The cold, hard steel of the handcuffs clicked around his wrist. The sound was deafeningly final.

And Sloane heard it all.

They hauled him out of the room, leaving the phone in the darkness of the booth, the connection still open.

As they pushed him toward the door, through the stunned, silent crowd of diners, he saw it. A news van, parked across the street, its camera light a single, red, unblinking eye. They weren't just arresting him. They were executing him, live, for the world to see.

As they shoved him toward the car, he saw a storm drain by the curb.

In one last, desperate motion, he let the USB drive slip from his cuffed hands. It fell, unseen, into the darkness of the drain.

The Feds wouldn't get the evidence. Roman wouldn't get it back.

It was all up to Sloane now.

They shoved him into the back of the sedan. As the door closed, sealing him in the darkness, he looked out the window, at the camera, at the city he had loved.

He thought of Sloane, alone in that house of horrors, waiting for a weapon that would never arrive.

He was not her protector. He was a stain. A disgraced, disgusting old man whose name would now be a poison.

He had failed her. Just like he had failed Sophie.

The car pulled away from the curb, and Manny Goldman, the last honest man in Hollywood, leaned his head against the cold glass of the window and began to weep.

***

Switzerland. The bunker.

Sloane sat frozen on the crate, the satellite phone pressed tight against her ear long after the voices had faded to background murmur at the other end of the line.

She had heard the crash. The struggle. The joke about his face.

And she had heard the charge.

Child pornography.

It was a lie so distinctive, so specifically designed to destroy a reputation beyond repair, that it could only have come from one mind.

"Sloane?"

Nico's voice was a distant echo. He was standing, moving toward her, his face a mask of concern.

She didn't look at him. She couldn't. She was seeing Manny's face. She was feeling the weight of the "stain" Roman had just painted on him.

"They took him," she whispered. The words had no air behind them. "They framed him. And they destroyed him."

Nico knelt in front of her, his eyes searching hers. "The data? Did he send it?"

Sloane nodded, tears finally spilling over, hot and fast. "It's in the Ghost Channel. But it's locked. He... he sacrificed his life just to get us the encrypted file."

She looked past Nico, her gaze falling on the steel table. On the maps of Zurich. On the detailed schematics of the Helvetica Privatbank.

Manny had done his part. He had caught the grenade.

"He said we have to finish it," she said, her voice hardening into something cold and sharp. A new kind of steel. "He said we have to get the Key."

It was no longer a backup plan. It was no longer just a heist.

It was a rescue mission for the truth.

"We go to Zurich," she said. "And we burn them all."

Chapter 61: The News Report

The silence where Manny's voice had been was a ringing abyss. Sloane sat on the cold concrete floor of the bunker, the dead satellite phone still clutched in her hand, her mind replaying the last thirty seconds on a screaming loop. The splintering door. The shouts. *FBI.* Manny's last, broken words.

"He's gone," she whispered to the empty room. "They got him."

Nico knelt in front of her, his face a grim mask. "The Dark Ledger?"

"He had it in his hand," she confirmed, the words a death sentence for the physical backup.

"But he said the upload finished," she added, her voice trembling. "The encrypted Ledger is waiting on the Ghost Channel. Manny kept his word."

She looked at the dead phone.

"He sacrificed himself to arm us, Nico. Path A is gone. Now it's up to us to pull the trigger."

She didn't know how long they sat there in the humming silence, two soldiers surveying the wreckage of a battle they had just lost. Eventually, Nico's hand on her shoulder, firm and steady, pulled her back to the present. "We need to move," he said. "Before the house realizes that we are missing."

She returned to her suite in a daze, the luxury of it a mocking insult. She collapsed onto the bed, fully clothed, and let the darkness pull her under into a shallow, fitful sleep plagued by the ghost of Manny's voice.

A soft chime at her door jolted her awake.

At 2 AM.

The door slid open, and Katarina Zimina stood there. She was not in her usual severe, gray dress. She was wearing a simple, black silk robe, her silver hair down. She was holding a tablet.

"I thought you should see this," Katarina said. Her voice was the same flat instrument, but her eyes... her eyes held a flicker of something that looked almost like recognition.

She held out the tablet. On the screen was a live news feed. The chyron read: HOLLYWOOD AGENT ARRESTED IN FEDERAL CHILD PORNOGRAPHY STING.

Sloane didn't flinch. She had heard the battle. This was just the official, public execution. She stared at the image of Manny, his face a mask of horror, being shoved into a car.

"Roman is very thorough," Katarina said quietly. "He doesn't just remove the piece from the board. He burns the square it stood on."

"He's a monster," Sloane whispered, her voice a raw, broken thing.

"Yes," Katarina agreed. "But he is a monster who has made a mistake."

Sloane looked up. "What?"

"He left him alive." Katarina tapped the screen, her fingernail clicking against the glass. "He chose humiliation over elimination. He wants Mr. Goldman to suffer. But as long as he is breathing, he can be exonerated."

She looked at Sloane, and for a second, the mask slipped. Sloane saw the shadow of an old, deep wound in the Russian woman's eyes—a memory of another man taken away in the night by men in long coats.

"Grief is a cage," Katarina said, her voice dropping to a whisper. "Do not sit in it. Use it."

"I need to be alone," Sloane whispered.

Katarina gave a single, almost imperceptible nod. "Then be alone. But be ready."

She turned and left the room as silently as she had entered it.

***

The footage was raw, shaky, shot from a news van across the street. It showed Manny being led out of Gable & Crane, his beloved, sacred space, his kingdom.

His hands were cuffed behind his back. His face, the kind, funny, fiercely loyal face that had been the one constant in her chaotic life, was a mask of pure, uncomprehending horror.

He looked old. Broken. A seventy-two-year-old man, his flamboyant silk shirt rumpled, his gold jewelry looking cheap and tarnished in the harsh, flashing lights of the police cars.

A reporter's voice, sharp and predatory, narrated the scene. "...Emanuel Goldman, a veteran Hollywood agent, was taken into custody by the FBI just moments ago. Sources say the arrest is the culmination of a months-long investigation into a high-level child pornography distribution ring..."

Lie. The word was a silent scream in Sloane's mind. *It's a lie. It's a frame.*

She watched as the agents shoved him into the back of a black sedan. Just before the door closed, Manny looked up, his eyes finding the news camera. His face was a raw canvas of despair and a desperate, urgent warning. He mouthed a single, silent word, a final, desperate plea to the one person in the world he knew would be watching.

Run.

The car door slammed shut. The sedan pulled away from the curb and disappeared into the Los Angeles night.

The news report cut to a talking head, a "legal analyst," his face grave and self-important, already dissecting the "sordid details" of the case, already pronouncing Manny guilty in the court of public opinion.

Sloane stared at the screen, at the space where Manny had been. He was gone. Lazar had not just arrested him. He had not just stopped him. He had taken him, this loud, loving, fiercely decent man, and he had painted him as a monster. He had destroyed his life, his legacy, his very name, with a single, perfectly aimed, and utterly diabolical lie.

It was a fate worse than death. It was a soul-murder.

***

Sloane stood alone in the center of the vast, silent suite. The news report was over, but the images were burned onto the back of her eyelids. Manny's face. The handcuffs. The desperation in his eyes.

The hope that had been a roaring fire in her chest just hours ago was now a pile of cold, dead ash.

She had done this.

The thought was a shard of ice in her gut. She had been the one to activate him. She had pushed him. She had sent him into a war against a god, armed with nothing but his loyalty and his fists. And she had gotten him captured. Destroyed.

Lazar hadn't just been playing with her. He had been playing with both of them. He had let them think they were winning. He had let them get their hands on the prize, let them taste the victory, just so the fall would be that much more devastating.

The grief was a physical thing, a crushing weight on her chest that made it impossible to breathe. Manny. Her Manny. The only person in the world who had never asked for anything from her, who had loved her unconditionally. And she had led him to the slaughter.

The silence of the room was a scream. The luxury was an insult. The beautiful, panoramic view of the Alps was a mockery.

She looked around the room, at the priceless art on the walls, the elegant, minimalist furniture, the silk and cashmere that surrounded her. It was all a lie. A beautiful, expensive, and utterly soulless lie.

And she was a part of it.

She had made a deal with the devil, and the price had not been her own soul. It had been Manny's.

The thought broke her.

The cold, hard resolve, the rage, the defiance—it all shattered, leaving only a vast, black, empty void.

She lied down, staring at the ceiling.

***

Sleep, when it finally came, was not a respite. It was a descent. Sloane fell into a dark, churning abyss, her mind a chaotic theater replaying the horrors of the last few weeks on an endless, looping reel.

She was back in the Sanctum, the download bar glowing a mocking green—*complete, useless.* Manny's voice crackled through the static—*they're here*—before the line was choked by the words of the frame-up that turned his name into poison. Roman's laughter wasn't a sound; it was the floor dissolving beneath her.

She was on the terrace at the gala, the cold alpine air sharp in her lungs. Mona Acosta's kind, concerned face was crumbling into confusion as she saw the scar on Sloane's palm. *When did you get that scar, Livia?* The question was a gunshot, echoing in the silent night, a sound that was followed by the screech of tires and the sickening crunch of metal.

She was in her apartment in North Hollywood, the eviction notice a stark, white flag of surrender on her counter, and the serpent crest on the envelope was a living, breathing thing, coiling and uncoiling, its silver eyes watching her with a cold, reptilian intelligence.

And then, the dream shifted.

***

She was drowning.

The water was black, cold, and impossibly deep. It was the water of Lake Lucerne, and it was pulling her down, down into the silent, lightless abyss. The beautiful, emerald Valentino gown she had worn at the gala was a shroud, its heavy, crystal-beaded fabric wrapped around her legs like an anchor, dragging her deeper.

Her lungs were on fire. She clawed at the water, her movements frantic, useless. She looked up. The surface was a shimmering, silver ceiling, a million miles away. The moon, a perfect, white disk, hung in the sky like a disinterested god.

Panic was a wild, screaming animal in her chest. This was it. The boating accident. The freak storm. The end of the story.

Then she saw another figure in the water beside her.

It was Livia.

She was not struggling. She was floating, serene, her eyes closed, her dark hair a cloud around her pale, beautiful face. She looked like a tragic, sleeping princess from a fairy tale. As Sloane watched, Livia's eyes fluttered open. They were not the warm, intelligent eyes from the videos. They were empty. Hollow. The eyes of a ghost.

Livia looked at Sloane, and a small, sad smile touched her lips. She reached out, her fingers trailing through the dark water, and touched the scar on Sloane's palm, a gesture of silent, sorrowful acknowledgment.

Then, the dream shifted again. The water vanished.

***

They were in a vast, empty ballroom. The floor was a polished, black and white checkerboard, stretching to an infinite horizon. The only light came from a single, bare bulb hanging from a cord, casting long, distorted shadows.

Sloane was on one side of the room. Roman Lazar was on the other. He was dressed in the simple, dark clothes of a chess grandmaster. He sat at a small, elegant table, a single chessboard between them.

"Your move," he said, his voice the same calm, reasonable murmur from the recording.

Sloane looked down at the board. The pieces were not chess pieces. They were small, perfectly carved, living figures.

There was a tiny, terrified Manny, his hands bound. A hollow-eyed Damian, clutching a sheaf of papers that were burning in his hands. A stoic Nico, a gun in his hand but aiming it at himself. A weeping, catatonic girl who had to be Oliver Harrow's daughter.

And on her side of the board, there was only one piece. A single, solitary queen, carved in her own likeness.

"This isn't a game," Sloane said, her voice a raw, angry whisper.

"Of course it is," Lazar replied, his kind, gray eyes full of a gentle, paternal pity. "Everything is a game, Sloane. You simply have to learn the rules." He gestured to the board. "The rule is simple. You can save one. Who will it be? The loyal friend? The broken husband? The brave soldier? The forgotten girl?"

It was a monstrous, impossible choice. A choice designed to shatter her.

"I won't choose," she said, her voice shaking.

"You have to," he said, his smile patient, understanding. "That's the game. Inaction is also a choice. And if you refuse to move, I simply take all the pieces. One by one."

He reached out, his long, elegant fingers closing around the small, weeping figure of Manny. He lifted it from the board.

"No!" Sloane screamed.

She lunged across the board, her hands outstretched, to stop him. But the floor gave way beneath her. The black and white tiles dissolved into nothing, and she was falling again, plunging back into the cold, black, silent water.

This time, when she looked up, she saw two figures standing at the surface, their silhouettes black against the moon. Roman Lazar. And next to him, a man she had thought was her ally.

Nico Sorrento. He was looking down at her, his face a mask of cold, professional indifference, as she drowned.

***

Sloane woke with a strangled gasp, her body drenched in a cold sweat, the silk sheets tangled around her like a shroud. The scream was trapped in her throat, a silent, jagged thing.

She was in her suite. The first, pale light of dawn was filtering through the vast glass wall. The house was silent.

The dream.

It was just a dream.

But it felt real. The cold of the water. The weight of the gown. The impossible, monstrous choice. And the final, devastating betrayal.

Nico.

Her rational mind knew it was just a dream, a chaotic projection of her deepest fears. Lazar was inside her head. He had planted the seeds of paranoia with the new camera, with his final, taunting message. And her own subconscious had watered them, grown them into this terrifying vision of betrayal.

But the feeling... the feeling was real. The cold, sick certainty that she was utterly, completely alone. That she could trust no one.

Nico had taken her into the dark. He had handed her Livia's secrets—an act of apparent deep trust.

But what if that, too, was part of the game? A move designed to win her confidence, only to lead her into a more final, more perfect trap?

She threw back the covers and went to the window, wrapping her arms around herself, the silk of her pajamas doing little to ward off the chill that was coming from inside her. The sun was rising, painting the snow on the distant peaks in shades of blood and gold.

The choice was clear. She could succumb to the paranoia. She could let Roman's games fracture her mind, turn her against the one person who might be her ally. She could let the ghost of her dream, the vision of Nico watching her drown, become her reality. She could drown in the fear.

Or she could fight.

She would not drown. She would surface.

And she would pull Roman Lazar under.

Chapter 62: The Winter Garden

The choice had been made in the cold, gray light of dawn. A choice to fight. A choice to trust.

But a choice was just a thought. Despair was a weight.

She stood in the shower for half an hour that morning, the water as hot as she could stand it, and seriously considered just walking out of the house. Just walking. Into the woods. Into the snow. She could let the cold take her. It would be an ending. A quiet one.

The thought was seductive. No more fighting. No more fear. No more performing. Just... peace.

It was the closest she had ever come to giving up.

Then she thought of Manny, sitting in a cell, his name poisoned, his life destroyed for refusing to betray her. She thought of Damian, a prisoner in his own home, a puppet who didn't even know the strings existed. She thought of Nico, a father chained by love for a daughter he couldn't protect.

And the whisper of surrender was drowned out by a familiar, stubborn rage.

Roman Lazar would not win. Not like this. Not without a fight.

She turned off the water, dried herself, and got dressed. There was work to do.

She felt empty. A hollowed-out shell.

She didn't know how long she sat on the floor of the suite, a broken doll in a dead woman's clothes. An hour. Two. Time had lost its meaning. The house was a tomb, and she was its newest ghost.

Eventually, a cold, chilling thought pierced through the fog of her despair. Lazar had done this. He had orchestrated Manny's fall with surgical precision.

And he was watching. He had to be. He would be savoring this. Her breakdown. Her absolute, crushing despair. This was the victory he had wanted all along. Not just to stop her, but to break her.

The thought was a spark in the void. A tiny, defiant flicker of her old rage.

She would not give him the satisfaction.

With a strength she didn't know she possessed, she pushed herself up from the floor. Her body ached. Her head throbbed. She looked at her reflection in the dark glass of the window. A wreck. A ghost with a tear-streaked, blotchy face.

She walked into the master bathroom and turned on the cold water, splashing it on her face again and again, the shock of it a welcome, clarifying pain. She stared at her reflection in the mirror. *He will not break me,* she thought, the words a silent, desperate vow. *He will not win.*

But what was left to fight for? The proof was a digital brick—seventy gigabytes of encrypted static sitting in the Ghost Channel that she couldn't read and the world couldn't see. Without the key from the Zurich vault, it was just noise. Manny was gone. The only man who knew how to make the truth stick was in a cell, his name poisoned by the very monster she was trying to kill.

She was alone, trapped, and utterly outgunned.

She needed to think. She needed air.

***

She left her suite, a ghost gliding through the silent, sleeping house. She didn't know where she was going. She just needed to move. Her feet carried her down the grand staircase, through the main salon, its cavernous space filled with the phantom echoes of the gala.

She found herself in the winter garden.

The vast, three-story glass atrium was dark, the only light the faint, ethereal glow of the moon filtering through the glass ceiling, painting the exotic, pale-colored flora in shades of silver and gray. The air was cool and humid, thick with the scent of damp earth and night-blooming jasmine. It was a beautiful, haunted place. Livia's sanctuary.

Sloane walked through the silent, indoor jungle, her bare feet cold on the slate floor. She trailed her fingers over the soft, velvety petals of a ghost orchid. This was Livia's favorite flower. A beautiful, ephemeral plant that thrived in shadows, clinging to the bark of other trees while taking nothing—a master of the illusion of belonging.

A perfect metaphor for her own existence in this house.

The rage she had felt in her suite began to bubble up again, hot and acidic. The injustice of it all. The sheer, monstrous arrogance of Roman Lazar. He sat in his invisible castle, moving people around like chess pieces, destroying lives with a whisper, and for what? For order? For power?

She saw a crystal vase on a small table, filled with the same white Casablanca lilies that had haunted her since she arrived. Fresh. Damp with mist. As if they had been placed there specifically for her to find among the orchids. Her mother's favorite.

They weren't flowers anymore. They were Roman's signature on a death warrant. They were the floral scent of her own erasure. Another one of his sick, little games, left here to taunt her—to tell her that no matter how hard she fought, he would always be three steps inside her head.

With a guttural cry, she picked up the heavy crystal vase and hurled it against the far stone wall.

The sound was a catastrophic explosion in the silent house, a shattering, splintering crash that echoed through the vast space. The vase exploded into a thousand glittering shards. Water and flowers sprayed across the floor.

It felt good.

She wasn't done. She grabbed a delicate, porcelain sculpture of a bird from a pedestal and threw it to the ground, where it shattered into dust. She swept a row of orchids from a shelf, their pots cracking, soil spilling across the clean, slate floor.

She was screaming now, raw, wordless sounds of fury and grief. She was a hurricane, a whirlwind of destruction in this pristine, perfect, and soulless house. She was tearing down the beautiful lie, piece by piece. She was showing him, the man she knew was watching, that she was not a passive specimen in his cage. She was a wild, untamable thing.

She grabbed a stone bench and heaved it over, the heavy object crashing onto its side with a deafening thud. Her hands were raw, her knuckles bleeding. She didn't care. The pain was real. It was hers.

She finally collapsed onto the dirt-and-shard-strewn floor, her body heaving with ragged, exhausted sobs. The destruction was all around her. A beautiful room, ruined. Just like her.

She had nothing left. No plan. No hope. No fight. She was just a broken woman in a broken room, waiting for the end.

***

She didn't know how long she sat there, a ghost in the ruins of her own making. The rage was gone, the adrenaline had faded, leaving only a vast, hollow emptiness.

The first rays of dawn were beginning to filter through the glass ceiling, painting the wreckage in a soft, gray light, when she heard a sound.

A single, soft footstep on the slate floor.

She looked up. A figure stood in the doorway, a dark silhouette against the light of the main hall.

It was Nico.

He didn't move. He just stood there, his face unreadable in the dim light, taking in the scene of absolute devastation. The shattered vase. The broken sculpture. The overturned bench. And her, a small, broken heap in the middle of it all.

In the wreckage of the lilies, she saw his mask finally crack. There was no judgment in his expression. Only a dark, quiet understanding.

He entered slowly, his footsteps careful among the shards of glass. He sat down on the one remaining, undamaged bench, a few feet away from her. He didn't try to comfort her. He didn't offer a hand. He just sat there, a silent, watchful presence in the ruins. A sentinel, standing guard over her despair.

They sat in silence as the sun rose higher, filling the winter garden with a gentle, forgiving light. The silence was not the oppressive, engineered silence of the house. It was a shared silence. A human silence.

After an eternity, Sloane's voice, hoarse and broken, cut through the quiet.

"He took Manny," she whispered. "He'll take Elena next. He won't stop. He's never going to stop."

She looked up at Nico, her eyes dry and terrifyingly clear.

"I'm going to kill him."

It was not a threat. It was a statement of fact. The last, single, flickering ember of her will to fight.

Nico was silent for a long moment, his gaze on the distant, snow-capped peaks glowing with morning sun.

Then he turned to look at her, his dark eyes steady. She saw the ghost of the man beneath the soldier. As trapped. As haunted.

"No," he said. His voice was quiet. Absolute. "We are."

Chapter 63: The War Room

They got back to the bunker. Their world, their sanctuary, their church. The despair that had crushed Sloane after Manny's arrest had been burned away, leaving a core of cold, hard, diamond-like purpose. They were no longer grieving. They were preparing for war.

With thirty-six hours left until the Klausjagen festival.

Nico was in his element. Her teacher. Her handler. Her drill sergeant. He gave her a crash course in the tradecraft of a ghost.

"Never walk in a straight line," he told her, sketching a diagram on a white-board. "Always use reflections. Shop windows. Car mirrors. The screen of your phone. Assume you are always being watched by at least two sets of eyes."

He taught her how to create a "legend," a cover story for her "Helena Baros" persona in Zurich.

"You already know how to do this," Nico said, a faint smile touching his lips. It was the first time he had explicitly acknowledged her talent without a tactical caveat. "Method acting is just tradecraft with an audience. But at the bank, the audience is looking for a reason to lock the vault. Favorite color?"

"Burgundy," Sloane said without hesitation. "First pet was a tabby named Schubert. Attended the American School in Vienna. My father was a diplomat."

"Good. Now make me believe you actually miss that cat."

Sloane let her shoulders drop. She didn't just give an answer; she let a flicker of genuine, soft nostalgia cloud her eyes. "He used to sleep on my father's piano," she murmured, her voice losing its edge. "I'd find him there every morning, curled up on the sheet music."

Nico studied her for a long beat. The silence in the bunker stretched, no longer cold, but heavy with a new kind of recognition. "That's the part the scanners can't see," he said quietly. "The details you don't plan. Keep building her."

They ran through weapons drills that felt different from the early weeks. He wasn't teaching her the mechanics of the Glock anymore—she could field-strip and reassemble it in under thirty seconds in total darkness. He was teaching her the calculus of chaos.

"Threat assessment. Escape routes. Knowing when to squeeze the trigger and when to run." He set a timer, making her navigate the bunker's tight sectors—using the floor-to-ceiling pantry racks and the generator alcove as a lethal maze—while he played the aggressor. She moved with a fluid, predatory grace now. The weapon was no longer a foreign object; it was a physical extension of her resolve.

"You're ready," he said after she'd successfully disarmed him in a close-quarters drill. There was a note of pride in his voice that made her pulse jump more than the exercise had.

In those long, quiet hours, the partnership deepened into something ironclad. The professional distance had been a casualty of the war they were starting. She wasn't an "asset" or a "counterfeit" in this room. She was his teammate.

One night, after a particularly brutal drill, they sat side by side on the concrete floor, backs against the reinforced wall. The air in the bunker was stale, smelling of gun oil and sweat, but for the first time since she'd arrived in Switzerland, Sloane felt like she was breathing.

His hand found hers in the darkness. He didn't say anything. He didn't need to. They were two ghosts building a mission that might kill them both, but as his fingers interlaced with hers, the risk felt like a price worth paying.

The survivor and the sentinel. They weren't just executing Livia's plan anymore. They were writing their own.

***

"The Zurich Protocol," he said, his voice pulling her from a half-trance as she field-stripped the Glock for the twentieth time. He had cleared the corkboard and replaced it with a massive, satellite-image map of Zurich's financial heart. He began to lay out the heist with the cool, dispassionate precision of a surgeon.

"The bank is the Helvetica Privatbank headquarters," he said, tapping a grand, 19th-century stone building on the map. "Old-world institution with new-world security. And it's a nightmare."

He detailed the layers of the fortress they had to breach. "Layer one is access. The private vault section is by appointment only. I've handled that. Helena Baros has an appointment on the Monday after the festival weekend finishes. Ten AM. That gets you in the door."

"Just me?" Sloane asked, her stomach tightening.

"Just you," Nico confirmed, his gaze steady. "I'll be your overwatch. On the street, with communications. But once you're inside, you're on your own."

The thought was a jolt of cold fear, but she pushed it down. This was the mission.

"Layer two is the vault room itself," he continued. "Biometric facial recognition. It will scan you against the file photo Livia used to open the account. Your resemblance is a statistical miracle, but it's not a perfect match. A machine might see the difference."

"I fooled the sensors at Argentis on day one," Sloane said, a flash of pride in her voice.

"That system was calibrated to ninety-four percent match threshold—designed for training," Nico said, his gaze steady. "The bank demands ninety-nine. You have to be better than you were at Argentis. You have to be flawless."

Sloane absorbed this. A higher bar. Harder security. But not impossible.

"So it really is the role of a lifetime," she whispered.

"There are no retakes," Nico said simply. "But you aren't that rookie anymore. You've had eleven weeks to fully become Livia. I know you can do this."

He changed the image on the screen, showing a close-up of the deposit box face itself. "Layer three is the box. Triple-lock protocol. First, the bank officer's master key. Second, the client key—which Livia left me. And the third..." He zoomed in on a small, glowing biometric pad. "The handprint scanner."

"Livia's right handprint is on file. Yours is not," he said, stating the mission-killing fact. "This is the one thing we can't fake."

Sloane stared at the glowing image of the scanner, a knot of despair tightening in her chest. They had come so far, only to be stopped by a single, insurmountable wall. A dead woman's handprint.

"Wait," she said. Her mind flashed to a dusty soundstage in Burbank. A cheap TV pilot. A role as a spy. A week with a CIA technical advisor.

A piece of her old, broken life, a skill she had thought was useless, was about to become the key.

"My hand can be her hand," she said, the excitement rising in her voice.

Chapter 64: The Hand and the Heart

Nico stared at her. "How?!"

She shook her head. "All I need is a high-resolution photograph of Livia's right hand."

"You don't say," his voice dripped with sarcasm. "Let me get right to getting you a perfect picture of the dead woman's hand."

"I'm serious. And I'll need some specialized materials."

"The materials, I can get couriered to a dead drop," Nico said. "But how do we get her handprint?"

They spent the next hour scouring the Livia archives. They found hundreds of photos, thousands of hours of video. But nothing was right. Despair began to creep back in, cold and suffocating.

It was a fool's errand.

Sloane was about to give up when she saw it. It wasn't in the photo archives. It was in a folder of scanned documents, buried deep in Livia's personal files.

It was a scanned document from her old life. A security clearance vetting form from her time contracting with intelligence agencies. A "Biometric Enrollment Record." And at the bottom of the form, required for Tier-1 access, were two perfect, high-resolution scans of Livia's hands. Both palms. Both sets of fingerprints.

Sloane let out a shaky, triumphant laugh. "Thank God you were a hoarder," she whispered to the ghost of Livia Crestwell.

Nico leaned in, eyes scanning the high-resolution ridges of the scans. "Intelligence contractor habits," he murmured. "Never throw away your own vetting documentation. These are one-to-one scale, Sloane. They're perfect."

They had it. All the pieces. The plan was no longer a desperate hope. It was a machine.

***

Nico leaned over, saw the image on her screen, and a slow, incredulous smile spread across his face. Livia, even from beyond the grave, had left them the key.

The triumphant energy in the bunker slowly faded, replaced by a tense, focused silence as they began to plan the final, logistical steps of the heist. But as Sloane watched Nico at the computer, mapping their exfiltration route, she saw him pause. His hands hovered over the keyboard, then stilled.

His gaze drifted to the locked steel case in the corner of the room. The one that held the satellite phone.

The soldier was gone. In his place sat a man being crushed by the weight of years.

"You should call her," Sloane said softly.

He didn't look up. Didn't acknowledge she'd spoken. Just kept tracing that button, his jaw working, his breathing shallow.

"I can't," he finally said, and his voice was barely audible. "It's not just the signal. The deal with Roman was absolute: I stay dead. That was the price of her safety. If I reach out, if I create a trail, the people who killed her mother... they might find her."

"Nico." Sloane moved closer, her voice gentle but firm. "Roman is the threat now. And he's already threatening her. The silence isn't protecting her anymore. It's just hurting her."

His hand closed around the phone. Knuckles white. Tendons standing out like cables.

"She deserves to know you're alive," Sloane pressed. "Even if it's just for five minutes. Even if this is the last time."

That broke something in him. His head dropped. His shoulders curved inward.

The war raged behind his eyes—operative versus father, survival versus love, fear versus desperate, aching need.

The father won.

He powered on the phone with a soft click that sounded like a gunshot in the concrete silence. He dialed from memory.

It rang.

Once.

The sound was hollow, digital, bouncing off satellites somewhere in the cold black between earth and space.

Twice.

Nico's breathing had stopped. His entire body was rigid, frozen, waiting for a voice he hadn't heard since she was a seven-year-old girl standing on a porch in the Donbas, holding up a crooked bead bracelet and making him swear he'd never take it off.

Three times.

Sloane saw his lips move silently. A prayer, maybe. Or just her name.

Then a click. A breath. And a girl's voice—young, uncertain, fragile as spun glass.

"¿Hola?"

Spanish. The unmistakable, melodic cadence of Buenos Aires—rhythmic and sharp. Wary. She didn't recognize the number.

Nico opened his mouth. Nothing came out. His throat had locked. Eight years of silence, and now, with her on the line, he couldn't find his voice.

"¿Hola?" the girl said again, about to hang up.

"Elena." It came out as a rasp, broken, barely a word.

Silence on the other end. Not empty silence. The kind of silence that's full of the world stopping, full of the ground dropping away, full of a heart trying to understand something impossible.

"¿Papá?" The word was a whisper. A question. An accusation. A desperate, terrified hope. "Papá, is that... is that really—"

"Sí, mija." His voice cracked completely. "It's me. It's really me."

The sound that came through the speaker was somewhere between a gasp and a sob and a laugh and a scream. Pure, undiluted shock giving way to something that might have been joy or grief or both at once.

"Oh my God. Oh my God, Papá, they told me you were—" Her voice shattered. "They said you died. They said there was an explosion in Bogotá and you were— Tia Sofia cried for three days, she couldn't even— I thought you were gone, I thought I'd never—"

She was crying now. Huge, wracking sobs that tore through the phone line and hit Nico like physical blows.

"I'm not dead, mija." He was crying too, silent tears streaming down his face, his voice thick and raw. "I'm alive. I'm here. I'm sorry, I'm so sorry I couldn't call, I couldn't let you know, it wasn't—"

"Where are you?" Her voice was higher now, younger, the teenager giving way to the child underneath. "Where have you been? Why didn't you call? Do you know what it's been like, thinking you were—"

"I know." The words broke on the way out. "I know, Elena, and I'm sorry, I'm so very sorry—" He pressed his palm against his eyes, trying to hold himself together. "I couldn't risk it. I had to stay dead. That was the price of keeping you safe. If I reached out, if I made a sound... the violence from before might have found you again."

"Found me?" Her voice trembled. "Papá, are we in danger?"

Nico looked at Sloane, his face a mask of anguish. She nodded slightly. *Tell her what she needs to know. Not all of it. Just enough.*

"I'm working on something," he said carefully, his voice steadying slightly, the operator coming back online even as the father remained. "Something dangerous. And I had to disappear for a while to ensure it didn't touch you."

"Is it safe now?" Elena's voice was small. Terrified. "Can you come home?"

Nico looked around the bunker. At the weapons on the table. At the maps of Argentis. At Sloane, who was watching him with eyes that understood exactly how much this cost.

He gave his daughter the truth.

"No," he said, and the word was stripped bare, honest, brutal. "It's not safe. Not yet. But I'm calling anyway because I—" His voice broke again. "Because I can't do this anymore. I can't miss any more of your life. Even if it's just five minutes on a phone. Even if this is all I get."

The silence on the other end was thick, heavy, full of Elena trying to process what he was saying, trying to be brave, trying to be older than fifteen.

Chapter 65: The Armor

"I got into the arts program," she said finally, her voice small but laced with shy, fragile pride. "At UCLA. The pre-college summer intensive. Tia Sofia said you'd be proud."

Nico's face crumpled. He covered his mouth with his fist, trying to hold back the sound that wanted to escape.

"I know," he whispered. "I heard. I've been... I've been keeping track. From far away. And Elena, I am so proud of you, I can't even—" He stopped, breathing hard. "You're the most brilliant person I know. The strongest. The best thing I ever did in this life."

"I still have it, you know," Elena said suddenly, her voice dropping to an intimate whisper. "The bracelet. One of the two we made when I was seven. The ugly one with the weird blue and yellow beads. I'm looking at it right now."

Nico's free hand moved unconsciously to his own wrist. To the faded, cheap plastic beads—chipped and worn, the elastic stretched too tight on his adult wrist. Blue and yellow. Crooked. Made with clumsy child hands and an excess of glitter glue that had long since flaked away. The identical twin to the one his daughter was holding a thousand miles away.

He'd worn it through the shelling in the Donbas the day Oksana died—the beads pressed against his pulse while he tried, and failed, to dig her out. Through Medellín firefights and black site interrogations. Through every cold, surgical shadow-op he'd executed since to pay the interest on his bargain with Roman Lazar. The clasp had broken twice; he'd fixed it with wire. The elastic was frayed; he'd reinforced it with fishing line.

It was the most valuable thing he owned.

"I'm wearing it right now," he said, his voice thick, rough, barely holding together. "I've never taken it off, mija. Not once. It's my armor. My reminder of what I'm fighting for. Of who I'm fighting for."

There was a long pause. Then Elena's voice, very small: "When are you coming home, Papá?"

It was the question he'd been dreading. The one he didn't have a good answer for. The one that, if he answered honestly, might break them both.

Nico's face crumpled completely. The ghost, the soldier, the hardened operator—all gone. Burned away. In their place was just a father. Just a man on the other side of the world from his child, knowing he might never see her again, knowing this phone call might be the last time he heard her voice.

"Soon, mija," he said, and his voice broke completely, dissolved into something raw and bleeding. "I promise you, I'm going to come home soon. I just have to finish this first. I have to make sure you're safe. That no one can ever—" He stopped, breathing hard, his hand pressed against his chest like he could hold his heart in. "I love you so much, Elena. So much. You have to know that. Whatever happens, you have to know that."

"Papá, you're scaring me." Her voice was shaking now. Terrified. "You're talking like—like you're saying goodbye. Like you're not coming back."

"I'm coming back," he said fiercely. "I swear to you, I'm coming back. But if I don't—if something happens—"

"*No.*" Elena's voice was sharp, young, desperate. "Don't say that. Don't you dare say that."

"*If something happens,*" Nico continued, his voice steady now, deliberate, the father making sure his daughter heard this even if she heard nothing else, "you remember that I loved you. That everything I did, every choice I made, was to keep you safe. That you were the best part of my life. The *only* good part. You remember that, *¿entiendes?*"

Elena was crying openly now. Hard, gasping sobs. "I don't want to remember. I want you here. I want you to come home."

"I know, baby. I know." Nico was crying too, silently, tears streaming down his face and dripping off his jaw onto the table. "I want that too. More than anything."

"Then come home," Elena begged, her voice breaking. "Please, Papá. Please just come home."

"Soon," he whispered. "I promise. Soon."

There was a long silence. Just breathing on both ends. A father and daughter, thousands of miles apart, holding onto each other across satellite signals and encrypted channels and the vast, terrible distance that war creates.

"I love you, Papá," Elena finally whispered.

"*Te amo, mija,*" Nico replied, the Spanish words torn from somewhere deep in his chest. "*Te amo más que todo en el mundo. Siempre.*" I love you more than everything in the world. Always.

"*Siempre,*" Elena echoed, and the word was a vow and a prayer and a goodbye.

The line went dead.

Nico sat there, the phone still on speaker, the line dead in the sudden silence. He stared at it. Didn't move. Didn't breathe.

Then his hand slowly reached out and ended the call.

The silence that rushed in was suffocating.

For a long moment, he just sat there, perfectly still, his head bowed, his hands flat on the table. The bracelet on his wrist caught the harsh fluorescent light—cheap blue and yellow beads, faded and cracked, a child's craft project held together with wire and fishing line and desperate love.

Then his shoulders started to shake.

It started small. Just a tremor. Then his breath hitched—once, twice—and the sound that came out of him was something broken, something animal, a grief so profound it had no shape, no language.

He folded forward, his forehead hitting the table, his hands coming up to cover his head, and he *sobbed*. Huge, wracking, silent sobs that tore through his entire body, that shook him like something was trying to break its way out of his chest.

Sloane didn't move. Didn't speak. Didn't reach out.

She just sat there, watching, bearing witness to something private and terrible and sacred.

She'd seen him as a sentinel. As a teacher. As a soldier.

Now she was seeing him as a man.

A man who had just given his daughter what might be his last goodbye.

A man who had just shown her the profound, terrifying, beautiful thing he'd been hiding from the world.

The fuel that drove him. The thing he would die for.

The reason he couldn't afford to lose.

The sobs slowly subsided. His breathing evened out. But he didn't lift his head. Didn't move. Just stayed folded over the table, broken and empty, a soldier who'd finally run out of strength.

"We're going to win," Sloane said quietly. Fiercely. "You hear me, Nico? We're going to burn his empire to the ground, and you're going to go home to her. That's not hope. That's a fucking promise."

Nico didn't respond. But his hand moved slowly across the table.

Found hers.

And held on.

***

The call left a fragile, human silence in the bunker. It was a reminder of the real, tangible lives that were at stake, a universe away from the cold tactics on their maps.

Later that night, while Nico was packing their go-bags—minimal gear, maximum mobility, everything they'd need to disappear, Sloane sat at the computer, using a heavily encrypted browser to scan the fringes of the internet. She was hunting for any scrap of news about Manny, any sign of life.

She found a grainy photograph on a tabloid website. Manny in an orange jumpsuit, being led down a hallway in the Metropolitan Detention Center. He was thinner. Grayer. His left arm was clamped tight against his ribs, his shoulder hiked high in a rigid, unnatural posture she recognized instantly. He was trying to pin the hand to his side, a desperate attempt to hide the tremor she'd noticed months ago from the cameras. He was vibrating apart from the inside out. The stress was killing him.

She stared at the photo until her vision blurred. Then she kept scrolling.

And found a ghost from her own past.

It was a small, insignificant detail on a tabloid website. A banner ad for a new, high-end talent agency that had just opened in Beverly Hills. *Phoenix Artists Group. Rising from the ashes.*

And at the bottom of the ad, a list of their new agents. The first name on the list was Barry Feldman.

Her old agent. The one who had dropped her the second the blacklist whispers started. The one who had fed her to the wolves.

Sloane stared at the name, and the timeline clicked into place with a sickening, ugly certainty. This wasn't a coincidence. It was a land grab.

With Manny framed and removed, there was a vacuum in the industry. A client list up for grabs. Office space available. Roman hadn't just destroyed Manny; he had cleared the board for the vultures.

It was the ultimate proof of Roman's worldview: Loyalty was a weakness to be punished. Opportunism was a strength to be rewarded.

She thought of her old life. Of the compromises. Of the men like Mitchell Carver and Barry Feldman. It wasn't just a game she had lost. It was a rigged system. And Roman Lazar was the man who owned the casino.

A new, colder fire settled in her soul. She closed the browser. The time for grief was over. The time for anger was over. All that was left was the cold, clean work of demolition.

She walked over to where Nico was working.

"Show me the Zurich schematics again," she said, her voice devoid of all emotion. "Every camera angle. Every guard rotation. Every possible point of failure. I want to know it all."

Nico looked up, saw the new, hard, diamond-like edge in her eyes. He didn't ask what had happened. He just nodded and turned to the monitors.

They worked until the bunker's air grew stale and the digital clock on the wall marked the death of the afternoon.

Chapter 66: The Serpent's Heart

By the time she emerged from the sub-levels, the light in the corridors was turning gold and blood-red. The sun was dipping below the peaks, pulling the shadows long across the estate.

Tomorrow night was Klausjagen. Which meant she had to convince Damian tonight. Right now. She had one chance to make him believe taking her to the festival was his idea.

Sloane paused outside the winter garden, gathering herself. She smoothed the silk of her dress—Livia's dress, cream cashmere that draped like water. Her hands were steady now. The tremor was gone.

She pressed her palms flat against her thighs, not to calm herself, but to center the performance. She needed to find the character. Livia. Wistful. Nostalgic. Yearning.

She pushed the doors open and stepped into the winter garden.

***

Damian stood by the glass wall, staring out at the lake. A statue of a man. He looked thinner, translucent, like something was eating him from the inside.

"Damian," she said softly.

He turned, a flicker of raw, unguarded hope in his eyes before the mask fell back into place. "Livia."

She moved closer. "I've been thinking," she said, her voice Livia's—warm, thoughtful, a little sad. "About the Klausjagen festival. Do you remember? We went, years ago. You hated the crowds, but I dragged you anyway."

She invented the memory on the fly, filling it with the sensory details she'd read about.

"The bonfires," she continued, her eyes distant. "The chaos. I felt so alive that night. I want to go again. I need to. To remember what it felt like. To feel something other than this... quiet."

He hesitated. "Küssnacht will be a sensory assault, Livia. The torches, the noise... after the accident, the intensity could trigger a setback. You're still so fragile."

"I am fragile because I'm a specimen in a jar, Damian," she said, her voice dropping to a fierce, weaponized whisper. She took his hand. "I used to be the one who led you into those rooms, remember? I was the one who translated the world for you."

She stepped into his shadow, her breath warm against his jaw. "You saved me from the water, Damian."

He flinched as if she'd struck him. She saw the ghost of the Ariadne surge in his eyes—the raw, agonizing guilt of the man who hadn't been fast enough. For a second, the cognitive dissonance threatened to shatter his composure.

"Don't let me drown in the isolation of this house instead," she pressed, her voice a soft, relentless prayer that gave him the absolution he'd been starving for. "Help me find my way back to the woman you loved. Just for one night."

Damian studied her face, searching for the beautiful lie he wanted to believe.

"Katarina will object," he said finally.

"Katarina is a soldier," Sloane replied softly, her hand sliding up his chest to rest over his heart. "And I am your wife. I'm asking you to take me on a date, Damian. Not for the cameras. Not for the board. For old times' sake. For me."

Something in him broke. "Okay," he breathed. "Yes. Let's go."

The victory felt hollow. A trap closing around them both.

***

Dinner that evening was a careful performance. After, he led her to his study. The sound of a cello filled the space—Bach, mournful and beautiful. He poured them both a scotch.

They sat by the fire. He in his leather chair, she on the sofa. Close but not touching.

"He's a very persuasive man," Damian said quietly, his gaze on the fire. "Roman. He doesn't command. He convinces you. Makes you believe his vision is your own." He looked up, his eyes desperate, pleading. "When you're alone in a world that doesn't speak your language, a vision like that is a powerful thing."

He was confessing. Trying to explain why he'd chosen the lie.

"You're not alone now," she said softly. It was the lie he needed.

He reached across the space between them and took her hand. "There's something I should tell you," he said, his voice a low, confessional murmur. "About Roman. Something Livia once asked me about."

Sloane's pulse kicked. She kept her face neutral. Concerned. Attentive.

"He has a weakness," Damian continued. "One thing in this world he truly loves. Not a person. A thing. A music box. Eighteenth-century. It was his mother's. The one thing that survived the fire that killed his family when he was a boy."

Sloane's mind sharpened. Focused. This was intelligence. Real intelligence.

"It's called 'The Serpent's Heart,'" Damian said. "He keeps it with him. Always. Livia thought it was sentimental. But I've seen the way he looks at it. It's not sentiment. It's worship."

The Serpent's Heart.

The name hit her with the force of a physical blow. Her mind flashed back to the hot, dusty apartment in North Hollywood. The heavy cream envelope. The shimmering silver crest embossed in the corner—a serpent entwined.

She had stared at it then, feeling a vague, instinctive dread. She had seen it on the tablet Fairweather handed her. On the gates of Argentis. On the documents she'd signed.

Now she understood. It wasn't a corporate logo. It was an altar. The symbol of the fire that made him, stamped on everything he owned.

Including her.

A cold sweat broke across her skin. The room suddenly felt very small, the air too thin to breathe.

"Why are you telling me this?" she asked, her voice a brittle whisper, straining to hold back a shudder of pure dread.

Damian looked at her, his eyes wet. "Because you are fighting him, in your own quiet way. And I think... I think Livia would have wanted you to have a weapon."

Then he leaned forward. And kissed her.

For one terrible, tempting moment, she let him. His lips were gentle. Tentative. The kiss of a man terrified of breaking something precious. The taste of scotch and solitude and a heartbreaking, impossible hope.

Then she thought of Nico. In the bunker. Waiting. Trusting her. His words: *No. Not here... We get out. And then... we do this right. When we're free.*

She pulled back.

"Damian," she whispered, her hand on his chest, creating a space between them. "I... I can't. Not yet. I'm sorry."

His face fell. Confusion, hurt, and fear flickered across his features. "Did I do something wrong?"

"No." She forced herself to meet his eyes, to give him the lie gently, to save the mission. "It's not you. The gala. Mona. I just... I need time. To feel like myself again. After everything."

It was the perfect excuse. Livia, still recovering. Still fragile.

He wanted to argue. She could see it. But he was too afraid of breaking her. "Of course," he said finally, his voice thick with disappointment. "I'm sorry. I shouldn't have pushed."

"You didn't push." She squeezed his hand, a final, gentle performance. "Tomorrow. The festival. Let's just have that. Something normal. Something good."

She stood. Smoothed her dress. "Goodnight, Damian."

She left before he could ask her to stay. She walked down the corridor, her heart a frantic drum against her ribs. She had the intel. She had secured the mission.

She had won.

So why did it feel like she was leaving a part of herself behind in that room?

Chapter 67: The Day Of

The last day was the longest. The house was charged with a new, anticipatory energy. Tonight was the Klausjagen. Tonight was the escape. The air itself seemed to vibrate with the weight of their secret, with the silent, ticking clock counting down the final hours to a moment that would change everything.

Sloane moved through her final day at Argentis in a state of heightened, almost painful awareness. Every detail, every sensation, felt freighted with a final, poignant significance. The way the morning sun slanted through the glass walls of the winter garden. The taste of the impossibly strong, black coffee the staff prepared for her. The feel of the cold, alpine air on her skin during her last, silent walk.

She was a ghost, haunting the last hours of a life that had never been hers.

She feigned a headache in the afternoon, sequestering herself in her suite, a necessary seclusion to make her final preparations.

She laid out the pieces of her plan on the vast, empty bed. The Helena Baros passport, a masterpiece of forgery. The slim, black tactical outfit she would wear under her festival clothes. The small, powerful Glock 19.

She checked the action on the weapon one last time. Racked the slide. Ejected the magazine. It was heavy, cold, and real. The only prop in her life that wasn't a lie.

As dusk began to settle over the mountains, painting the sky in shades of bruised purple and blood orange, she knew she had to see him one last time before she stepped onto a stage where a single missed cue would mean their end.

***

The bunker was a haven of cold, hard reality in a house of illusions. Nico was at the steel table, a satellite map of Küssnacht's winding, medieval streets spread out before him. He was cleaning his weapon, his movements economical, precise, a ritual of deadly meditation.

He looked up as she entered, his dark eyes intense. "You shouldn't be here," he said, his voice a low rumble. "It's too close to the mission. Too risky."

"I had to," she said simply. She sat down opposite him, the table between them. The air was thick with a shared, unspoken tension. The adrenaline of the coming battle. And something else. Something more fragile and more dangerous.

"We go over it one last time," he said, his voice all business, a retreat into the safety of tactics. "The signal. The rendezvous. The route."

They went through the plan, their voices a low, conspiratorial murmur in the concrete room. They were soldiers on the eve of battle, their focus absolute. But as they spoke of kill zones and exfiltration routes, their eyes kept meeting across the map, and a different, more personal conversation was taking place. A conversation of fear, of hope, of a shared, terrifying future.

When they were done, a heavy silence fell between them. The plan was as perfect as they could make it. Now, there was nothing left to do but wait for the clock to run out.

"If we survive this," Sloane said, the words a quiet, fragile thing in the silence, "what will you do?"

Nico was silent for a long moment, his gaze on the map, on the small town where their fates would be decided. "See Elena," he said, his voice a rough, quiet murmur. "Even if it's just from a distance. Just to know she's okay."

"And then?"

He shook his head. "There is no 'and then.' For men like me, the mission is never over. There's always another monster. Another ghost to hunt." He finally looked up at her. "What about you? You'll have the money. You'll be free. What will you do?"

"I don't know," she said, and the words were the truest thing she had said in months. "I've been someone else for so long... I'm not sure who Sloane Devereaux is anymore." She looked at him, at his hard, beautiful, and profoundly lonely face. "Maybe I'll find her."

The unspoken words hung in the air between them. *Maybe we'll find her together.*

He stood up and walked over to a small, locked cabinet. He opened it and took out a bottle of Wild Turkey 101—a high-proof American bourbon that was hilariously out of place in this world of vintage Bordeaux and single-malt Scotches. He poured two fingers' worth into two small, clean glasses.

"Livia kept this here," he said, handing her a glass. "For emergencies. I think this qualifies."

Sloane took the glass. The whiskey was harsh, fiery, and completely real. It burned a clean, straight line down to the cold, knotted place in her stomach.

They stood there in the silent bunker, drinking in a quiet, shared communion. They were so close she could feel the heat radiating from his body. She could see the faint, white line of the scar at the corner of his mouth. The exhaustion in his dark eyes.

"Nico," she whispered.

He looked down at her. The air in the room crackled, charged with a voltage that was more than just adrenaline, more than just the intimacy of shared purpose. It was a raw, undeniable, and profoundly dangerous connection.

"When this is over," she whispered, "what happens to us?"

His gaze dropped to her lips. She saw the soldier, the ghost, the disciplined operative, have a brief, silent, and violent war with the man.

"We get a real life," he said, his voice a rough, ragged thing. "Not someone else's."

She leaned in, closing the small, infinite distance between them, her heart a wild, frantic drum. She was rising on her toes, her lips just inches from his.

He met her halfway, his hand coming up, his fingers warm and rough against her cheek, cupping her face—

And then he stopped.

His thumb traced the line of her cheekbone, a gesture of profound, aching restraint. His eyes were full of a deep, unbearable sadness.

"Not yet," he said, his voice a raw whisper that was almost a plea. "Not here. Not in this house of ghosts. When we're free. When we're real."

She wanted to argue. To kiss him anyway. To have this one, real, human moment in the face of all the lies and all the death. But she understood. He was a man of honor. A man of a code she was just beginning to comprehend. This place was poisoned. Their first kiss would not be a stolen, desperate act in the darkness. It would be a choice, made in the light.

"Promise me," she whispered, the word a fragile breath.

"I promise," he said.

He held her gaze for a moment longer, a silent, binding contract passing between them. Then he stepped back, the spell broken, the professional mask sliding back into place.

"It's time," he said, his voice all business again. "You need to go. They'll be expecting you to dress for the festival."

Sloane nodded, her body still thrumming with the ache of the surrender they had denied themselves.

At the door of the bunker, she turned back. He was standing by the table, his back to her, already clearing the maps, erasing the evidence of their meeting, becoming a ghost once more.

"Nico," she said.

He turned.

"Be careful," she said.

A faint, almost imperceptible smile touched the corner of his mouth. "You too," he replied.

She stepped back into the private elevator, leaving the cold, concrete world of the war room behind as she rose back into the beautiful, treacherous world of the performance. But this time, she was not alone. She was carrying a promise.

Chapter 68: The Enigma

The final hours before the festival were a study in controlled, silent chaos. Sloane was back in her suite, a ghost in the machine of her own deception. The confrontation with Damian had left her shaken, raw. She had plunged a knife into his heart, a necessary, brutal act of emotional surgery, but she was not a surgeon. She was just a woman trying to survive, and the cost of this war was rising with every passing minute.

Now, there was only the performance left.

She stood before the full-length mirror as Colette, the severe French stylist who had fitted her for the gala, returned to armor her one last time. This time, she wasn't alone. A young, silent assistant knelt at Sloane's feet, adjusting the hem, while Colette worked the intricate lacings of the bodice with surgical precision.

It was a traditional Swiss dirndl, but a version so exquisitely made, so luxurious, that it whispered wealth rather than shouted it. The bodice was a deep, forest-green velvet, the blouse a delicate, hand-embroidered silk, the apron a shimmering, silver brocade. Livia's clothes. Livia's life.

But beneath the heavy, voluminous skirt, lay a secret Sloane had guarded fiercely. She had donned her underlayers alone, behind a locked bathroom door, before summoning the women to drape the heavy fabric over her. She wasn't wearing stockings. She was wearing thermal tactical leggings and boots with a grip sole—hidden by the hem, ready for the run. Strapped to her right thigh in a compression holster, the Glock 19 sat heavy and invisible—a cold weight of steel and polymer hidden beneath the brocade. She was a soldier dressed as a doll.

"The weather will be unforgiving tonight, Madame," Colette murmured, taking a heavy, fur-lined velvet cloak from her assistant. "This will keep the wind out."

She draped the cloak over Sloane's shoulders and fastened the silver clasp at her throat. It was warm, heavy, and enveloped her completely—perfect for hiding the warrior beneath, and the fear.

Sloane looked at her reflection. Warm. Armored. Ready.

She was dressed for a party she had no intention of attending. Her mind was a million miles away, in the narrow, cobblestone streets of Küssnacht, on the dark, winding smuggler's road, in a cold, sterile vault in Zurich.

She was so lost in her tactical calculations that she didn't hear the door to her suite slide open.

"Colette, leave us," a voice said—a voice of cold, quiet authority.

Sloane's eyes snapped up, meeting a pair of icy, gray-blue eyes in the mirror. Katarina Zimina.

The stylist gave a small, nervous bow, signaled her assistant, and they scurried from the room, leaving the two women alone in the silence.

Katarina walked slowly into the room, her presence a sudden drop in the atmospheric pressure. She was not in her usual severe, gray uniform. She was dressed for the festival, in a simple, elegant, and impeccably tailored black wool coat.

She stopped behind Sloane, her reflection a stark, grim counterpoint to Sloane's festive, colorful attire in the mirror.

"You are going to do it tonight, aren't you?" Katarina said. It was not a question. It was a statement of fact.

Sloane's blood went cold. She did not turn. She met Katarina's gaze in the mirror, her own face a mask of practiced, Livia-esque calm. "I don't know what you mean," she said, her voice a light, musical thing.

"Do not," Katarina said, her voice a low, dangerous hiss, "insult my intelligence. I have seen you with Mr. Sorrento. I have seen the planning in your eyes. I have seen the new, hard light in you since the news about your friend, Mr. Goldman. You are not the broken woman you've been pretending to be. You are a soldier, preparing for battle."

Sloane was silent. The game was up.

"He will kill you," Katarina stated simply. "Lazar. He will not let you leave this mountain alive. He has men everywhere. You will not make it to the end of the street."

"Then I'll die trying," Sloane said, her voice her own now, stripped of all artifice, hard as steel.

Katarina was silent for a long moment, studying Sloane's reflection with a strange, analytical intensity, as if she were trying to solve a complex equation.

"Livia said that once," she whispered, her voice a raw, unguarded thing. It was the first time Sloane had ever heard a crack in her icy composure. "The day before she left for Naples. I told her he would kill her. She said, 'Then I'll die trying.'"

Katarina stepped closer, her hand reaching out to brush an invisible speck of lint from the shoulder of Sloane's heavy velvet cloak. The gesture was fussy, maternal, and heartbreakingly sad.

"She was a fool," Katarina murmured, her eyes on the silver embroidery. "Brave, and brilliant, and one who I would die for. But a fool nonetheless. She thought she could fight a god with nothing but her own righteousness."

She pressed a hand flat against her chest, feeling the hard, round outline of the metal disc hidden in her inner breast pocket. Her true north.

She looked up, locking eyes with Sloane in the mirror.

"But you... you are not righteous. You are angry. And you are armed."

She turned, and the mask snapped back into place, but Sloane had already seen the fracture—the raw, profound grief of the woman who had watched her world burn.

"So tell me," Katarina asked, her gaze cutting through the room like a blade. "What do you actually have to fight him with?"

"A plan," Sloane said, her voice dropping an octave. "And Nico."

"Mr. Sorrento is a capable operative," Katarina conceded. "But he is one man. Lazar has an army. It is not enough."

"Then what do you suggest I do, Katarina?" Sloane shot back, her own frustration boiling over. "Stay here? Wait for Roman to have me disposed of like all the others?"

Katarina walked over to her, stopping so close that Sloane could smell the faint, cold scent of her Chanel No. 5. She reached out, and her fingers, cool and dry, adjusted the laces of Sloane's dirndl bodice, her touch surprisingly clinical, efficient.

"I suggest," Katarina said, her voice a low, conspiratorial whisper that made the hairs on Sloane's arms stand up, "that you do not go to the chapel."

Sloane's heart stopped. The chapel. The exit point. How could she possibly know about the chapel?

"The moment you separate from Mr. Crestwell," Katarina continued, her eyes locked on Sloane's in the mirror, "Lazar's men will follow you. The chapel will be a kill box. You and Mr. Sorrento will be dead before you reach the altar."

It was a trap. Their entire, brilliant plan was a trap. Lazar had been listening. He had to have been. The bunker wasn't safe. Nothing was safe.

"How do you know this?" Sloane whispered, her voice a raw, choked thing.

Katarina's face was a mask of stone. "Because I am the one who designed their protocols," she said simply. "I know how they think. I know how they hunt."

Sloane stared at her, her mind a screaming chaos of confusion. Was this a trick? A final, brilliant mind game to make her abort the mission? Or was it... a warning? An act of alliance?

"Whose side are you on, Katarina?" Sloane breathed.

Katarina's gaze was a deep, cold, and profoundly sad ocean. "I am on Livia's side," she said, her voice a low, dangerous murmur. "And I serve people who clean up the messes men like Roman leave behind. We have been watching him for a very long time."

She reached into the pocket of her coat and pulled out a small, encrypted satellite phone, a military-grade device that was far more sophisticated than Nico's. She pressed it into Sloane's hand, her fingers closing over Sloane's with a surprising strength.

"The smuggler's road is compromised," she said, her voice a rapid, urgent whisper. "They will be waiting for you. If you escape from Klausjagen, Lazar would expect you to run for Zurich. He has the highways locked down. So you will go where he is not looking."

She leaned closer. "There is an old service tunnel, a kilometer past the town's eastern edge. It leads to a private airstrip. A jet will be waiting. It will take you to a private airfield just over the border with Germany. From there, Nico knows a safe house in Singen. It's a major rail hub. Easy to disappear from."

"Germany?" Sloane whispered.

"You must break the containment," Katarina replied. "Leave the country. Let his trail go cold. Then, when the heat dies down, you cross back into Zurich on your own terms to finish the job."

"When you are clear of Küssnacht city limits," she continued, "you use this phone. You call the only number in its memory. You say the words, 'The serpent is broken.' Help will come."

She pulled out a folded paper map from her other pocket and pressed it into Nico's hand. "Three safe houses in Zurich," she said, pointing to three green dots marked on the map. A red dot marked the Helvetica Privatbank. "Memorize the addresses and entry codes on the back. Then burn this. Leave no trail. These are for your return. Each safe house is stocked—food, supplies, two separate internet connections, and a clean car in the garage. Livia's exfiltration plan."

She tapped the map. "However, plans fail. The jet will wait in Germany for seventy-two hours. But if you cannot make it back across the border..." She pointed to the green dot nearest the red one. "This safe house is closest to the bank. If anything goes south in Zurich, take refuge there and don't leave."

Her eyes met Sloane's. "Your transport is a black BMW, staged in the ravine at the tunnel exit. The trunk contains one hundred thousand euros, a trauma kit, and thermal layers. I will ensure your bags are waiting inside."

She leaned in, her voice dropping to a final, hard command. "The key is inside the fuel door. Do not stop for anything."

It was a new plan. A complete, fully-formed escape route, delivered in a whisper, from the one person Sloane had believed to be her enemy. Not just information—but practical, tangible help. Money. Equipment. Shelter. Katarina had been preparing this for days, perhaps weeks.

"Why?" Sloane asked, her mind reeling. "Why are you doing this?"

Katarina's hand dropped from hers. She turned to leave, the moment of intimacy, of conspiracy, over. At the door, she paused, her back to Sloane.

"Livia didn't know you," she said, her voice a flat, dead thing. "But she knew Roman. She calculated that he would find a replacement. A counterfeit to keep the illusion alive."

She looked over her shoulder, and her pale, gray eyes were full of a cold, hard, and utterly implacable fire.

"She turned her own legacy into a trap, waiting for the stranger who would wear her face. You are the weapon she anticipated. I am merely... aiming you."

And then she was gone.

***

Sloane stood in the silent room, the dense, black device in her hand, her mind a battlefield of conflicting truths. Katarina—the warden, the traitor, the ally—had just given her a map to the exit.

A chime sounded at her door. Damian.

Sloane slipped the phone into the deep inner pocket of her velvet cloak. It vanished into the heavy folds, invisible against her side. She looked at her reflection one last time. No fear. No hesitation. Just the mask.

She opened the door. Damian stood there, his face a mask of tragic, hopeful love.

"You look beautiful," he whispered.

"Thank you," she said, her voice a perfect, cool, and steady Livia.

And she walked with him into the fire.

Chapter 69: Klausjagen

The drive down the mountain to Küssnacht was a descent into another world. The sleek, silent Maybach, a hermetically sealed capsule of modern luxury, glided down the winding roads, leaving the cold, sterile perfection of Argentis behind. As they neared the town, the first sounds of the festival reached them—a faint, rhythmic, and deeply primal pounding of drums that seemed to vibrate up through the floor of the car.

Sloane sat in the back, a silent, beautiful doll in her exquisite dirndl, Damian at her side. He was nervous, his hands fidgeting in his lap, a man of quiet order about to be plunged into a sea of chaos. Nico was in the front passenger seat, a dark, coiled spring of a man, his eyes constantly scanning, his face a mask of professional calm that did not quite conceal the electric, high-stakes tension radiating from him.

The plan had changed. Everything had changed.

Before they left, Sloane had found a way to have a brief, silent, and terrifying conversation with Nico. She dropped an earring in the main foyer. As he knelt to help her find it, their heads close together, she whispered the words, a frantic, desperate message.

"Katarina. She knows. The chapel is a trap. The smuggler's road is compromised. New plan. Service tunnel, east of town. A BMW. A jet."

Nico did not flinch. His expression did not change. He simply found the earring, placed it in her palm, and said, his voice a low, calm murmur, "Thanks. I'll get the specifics from Katarina." But his eyes, when they met hers, were a blaze of new calculations, of redirected plans, of a shared, terrifying uncertainty.

Now, they were driving into a trap they knew was waiting for them, armed with a new, untested escape route from a source they did not fully trust. Was Katarina saving them? Or was she leading them into a more sophisticated, more final ambush?

Every instinct Sloane had screamed that Katarina's warning was real. The cold fury in her eyes, the raw grief... it had been too genuine to be a performance. But in this world of masks, of ghosts and counterfeits, certainty was a luxury she couldn't afford.

The car could go no further. The narrow streets of Küssnacht were a surging river of humanity. Nico got out, his hand resting almost casually on the small of his back, where Sloane knew his weapon was holstered. He opened the door for them.

"Stay close," he commanded, his voice a low growl meant only for them.

The moment they stepped out of the car, the chaos enveloped them. It was a full-body sensory assault. The air was thick with the smell of woodsmoke from dozens of torches, the sweet, spicy scent of mulled wine, and the smell of thousands of packed bodies. The sound was deafening—a bone-rattling, polyrhythmic pounding of drums and the deep, resonant clang of massive cowbells being shaken by men in terrifying, horned masks.

And the light. The light was a frantic, flickering thing. The town was on fire. Torches lined the streets, their flames casting long, dancing shadows. And moving through the crowd were the Iffelen, the men in the giant, illuminated bishop's hats, each one a six-foot-tall, glowing lantern, painted with intricate, beautiful, and demonic scenes.

It was a nightmare carnival. A beautiful, terrifying, medieval rave.

"It's... louder than I remember," Damian said, his voice tight, his eyes wide with a mixture of awe and panic.

Sloane took his arm, her touch both a comfort to him and an anchor for herself. "It has to be," she shouted over the din, leaning close to his ear. "That's the tradition. They use the noise to drive out the spirits. To purge the valley of darkness."

Damian looked at her. The panic in his eyes softened into a raw, naked hope.

"Then let them shout," he whispered, gripping her hand. "Let them drive it all away."

Sloane forced a smile, her heart breaking. He thought the ritual was for him. He didn't know he was standing next to the thing that was about to turn his world upside down.

Nico moved in front of them, a human shield, clearing a path through the dense, surging crowd with a quiet, authoritative pressure that people seemed to obey without realizing why. They made their way toward the mayor's chalet, a beautiful, timber-framed building with a balcony overlooking the main square.

Sloane's mind was a frantic, whirring machine, her senses on high alert. She was not just an actress anymore. She was an operative, scanning, processing, analyzing. She saw them almost immediately. Lazar's men.

They were not hard to spot if you knew what to look for. They were the ones who were not looking at the parade. They were the ones whose eyes were scanning the crowd. They wore dark coats, simple beanies, and a professional, bored indifference that was a stark contrast to the festive chaos around them. They moved in pairs, communicating through subtle, invisible earpieces.

She saw one pair by the fountain. Another by the entrance to the alley that led to the chapel. The kill box. Katarina had been right.

Sloane met Nico's gaze over the heads of the crowd. He gave a single, almost imperceptible nod. *I see them too.*

They reached the chalet and were escorted through a private entrance, up a narrow staircase, and into a warm, crowded room that smelled of wine and wealth. The mayor, a stout, florid man, greeted them with an obsequious reverence.

They were led to the balcony. Below them, the main square was a sea of heads, a writhing, cheering mass of humanity. The main procession was beginning, a river of fire and noise. The Trychlers, the men in the horned masks, were at the front, their massive bells clanging in a deafening, hypnotic rhythm.

Sloane stood at the railing, Damian at her side, Nico a silent, watchful presence behind them. She smiled. She waved. She was a queen on her balcony, surveying her kingdom of chaos.

But her eyes were not on the parade. They were on the square below. She was mapping the battlefield. She could see Lazar's men taking up their positions. Two by the alley. One near the chapel door. Another across the square, a sniper's overwatch position, though he had no clear shot through the crowd. They were closing the net, waiting for her to make her move.

The main procession of the Iffelen began to enter the square, their glowing hats a beautiful, ghostly armada floating through the darkness. The roar of the crowd intensified.

Nico's hand rested on her shoulder, a light, almost imperceptible pressure. Three quick, firm taps.

The signal.

It's time.

***

Sloane took a breath, the roar of the crowd fading to a dull hum in her ears. One lie to rule them all. One final, perfect performance to buy their freedom.

She turned to Damian, her face a mask of sudden, pale distress. She swayed slightly, her hand flying to her forehead. "Damian," she whispered, her voice a weak, breathy thing. "I... I don't feel well. The heat. The noise. It's too much."

"Livia?" he said, his face instantly a mask of concern. He put his arm around her. "You're pale. Let's get you inside."

"No," she said, shaking her head. "I just need... some air. Some quiet." She looked desperately around the crowded room. "The chapel. The little chapel on the square. It's quiet in there, isn't it?" She was feeding him the lines, leading him to the trap she had no intention of walking into.

"Of course," he said, all concerned. "Nico, escort us to the chapel."

"That may not be wise, sir," Nico said, his voice a low, professional warning, playing his part in the charade. "The crowd is very thick."

"Just get us there," Damian commanded, his concern for his "wife" overriding all other logic.

This was it. The moment of separation.

They moved back into the crowded chalet, Nico once again clearing a path. But this time, Sloane did not stay close to Damian. She let the surging bodies of the partygoers create a small, momentary gap between them.

As they reached the back of the room, near the staircase, a new wave of the procession entered the square below. A massive, deafening roar went up from the crowd, accompanied by a sudden, explosive burst of drums.

In that single, chaotic, disorienting moment of sensory overload, Sloane made her move.

She did not go left with Damian and Nico toward the main exit. She went right, slipping behind a thick velvet curtain that led to a small, private service corridor.

She was gone. A ghost, disappearing in plain sight.

She ran down the narrow corridor, her heart a wild, frantic bird in her chest. She could hear Damian's voice, distant and panicked, calling her name. *"Livia! Livia, where are you?"*

She didn't stop. She burst through a door at the end of the corridor and found herself in a small, dark alley behind the chalet. The sounds of the festival were a muffled, chaotic roar here.

A figure stepped out from the shadows.

Nico.

He had created his own diversion, peeling off from Damian in the chaos.

He didn't speak. He just grabbed her hand, his grip like steel, and pulled her into the darkness.

"They'll be looking for us at the chapel," she said, her voice a breathless gasp as they ran.

"I know," he said, pulling her into another, even narrower alley. "Let them."

They were two ghosts, running through a maze of fire and shadows, the sound of the hunt beginning behind them, the promise of freedom a cold, terrifying, and beautiful thing, waiting for them on the other side of the mountain.

Chapter 70: The Escape

The alleyways of Küssnacht were a labyrinth, a maze of cobblestone and ancient, leaning timber-framed houses. The air was cold and smelled of damp stone, woodsmoke, and the faint, sweet scent of mulled wine. The deafening, primal roar of the Klausjagen festival was both their cover and their enemy, a wave of chaotic sound that masked their footsteps but also hid the sounds of their hunters.

Nico ran with a silent, economic grace, his hand clamped around Sloane's wrist, pulling her along in his wake. He was not just running; he was navigating, his mind a GPS of the escape route they had memorized, his senses on a high-alert razor's edge. He moved like a predator, a ghost in his own element.

Sloane ran, her lungs burning, her traditional Swiss festival dress a clumsy, absurd costume for a spy. The adrenaline was a fire in her veins, burning away the fear, leaving only a pure, crystalline focus. This was it. The point of no return.

They burst out of one narrow alley and had to cross a wider, torch-lit street. For a moment, they were exposed, silhouetted against the firelight.

"Nico!" a voice shouted from behind them.

They didn't stop. They didn't look back. They plunged into the darkness of the next alley, the sound of running footsteps echoing on the cobblestones behind them. Lazar's men. They had realized the chapel was a feint. The hunt had begun.

The alley was a dead end. A high, brick wall blocked their path.

"Nico!" Sloane gasped, her heart seizing with panic.

He didn't break his stride. "Up," he commanded, pointing to a rusty fire escape ladder on the side of the building.

He gave her a boost, his hands strong and sure at her waist, and she scrambled up the cold, wet metal rungs. She could hear the shouts of their pursuers, closer now, echoing in the narrow space. She reached the first landing and turned, her hand outstretched to help him.

But he was already there, having scaled the first ten feet of the wall like a spider, his movements fluid and impossibly fast. He vaulted onto the platform beside her.

A gunshot, a soft, muffled *phut*, splintered the wood of the building just inches from her head. Silenced. Deadly.

They didn't wait. They ran, up another flight of stairs, onto the slick, wet rooftops of the old town.

***

The world was a dizzying, terrifying panorama of fire and shadow. Below them, the Klausjagen festival was a river of light and chaos. Above them, the sky was a black, starless void. They ran across the steeply pitched, tiled roofs, their footsteps muffled by the roar of the crowd.

It was a nightmare ballet. They leaped across the gaps between buildings, their movements desperate and athletic. Sloane's stage combat training, the years of choreographed fights and falls, kicked in. Her body knew how to do this. How to balance. How to land without breaking an ankle.

They saw two of Lazar's men emerge onto a rooftop a hundred feet to their left, dark figures silhouetted against the torchlight. Another silenced shot whizzed past Nico's head.

Nico pushed her down behind a chimney stack. "Stay here," he commanded.

He drew his Glock 19, the movement a single, fluid, and terrifyingly practiced motion. He leaned out from behind the chimney, fired twice—two quick, controlled shots. The sound was not the deafening blast of the movies, but a sharp, hard crack that was almost lost in the din of the festival.

One of the men on the other rooftop crumpled and fell, his dark figure disappearing into the shadows below. The other one dove for cover.

"We need to move," Nico said, grabbing her arm. "Now."

They ran, a mad, desperate scramble across the treacherous, uneven terrain of the medieval rooftops, moving not west toward the smuggler's road, but east, deeper into the labyrinth of the old town.

"This way!" Nico yelled over the roar of the festival, pulling her down a steep, tiled roof and onto the narrow ledge of a lower building.

Headlights swept the alley below them. A black Audi, Lazar's men, already sealing off their original path.

"They're boxing us in," Sloane gasped.

"She said a kilometer past the eastern edge," Nico said, his voice a low, urgent growl. "We just have to get to the street."

They reached the final rooftop. Below them was a narrow, dark street, away from the main festival chaos. It was a thirty-foot drop. Too far to jump.

"There," Nico said, pointing to a large, canvas awning over a bakery two floors below. It was their only shot.

He didn't wait for an answer. He grabbed her, wrapping his body around hers, and leaped.

***

The impact was a brutal, jarring thud as they hit the thick canvas. The awning ripped from its mountings with a screech of tearing fabric, collapsing into a makeshift slide that dumped them in a bruised, tangled heap onto the cobblestones below.

For a moment, Sloane just lay there, the air knocked from her lungs, her body a symphony of aches. The sounds of the festival were a distant, muffled roar.

Nico was already on his feet, pulling her up. "Are you hurt?" he asked, his hands checking her for broken bones.

"I don't think so," she gasped.

"Good," he said. "The tunnel is this way. We run."

They ran, a clumsy, stumbling flight through the dark, silent backstreets. The sounds of the festival faded behind them, replaced by the sound of their own ragged, desperate breaths and the slap of their shoes on the stone.

They found it exactly where Katarina had said it would be: a rusted, corrugated metal fence at the end of a dead-end service road. Behind it, obscured by a thick curtain of ivy, was the dark, circular maw of an old service tunnel.

Nico stopped. He drew his own Glock 19 from his waistband. Sloane reached under the heavy velvet of her skirt, her fingers finding the release on her thigh holster. She pulled her weapon free—warm from her body heat—and handed it to him.

He took it without a word, sealing both guns in a heavy-duty waterproof bag from his kit. He wedged the package into a gap between the tunnel's stone wall and a drainage pipe, then covered it with loose rocks.

"GPS marked," he said, his voice tight. "Can't cross the border with hardware. But if we come back..."

"When," Sloane corrected.

He nodded once.

Nico tore the fence aside. As Sloane scrambled into the cold, damp darkness of the tunnel, she looked back. Headlights were flooding the far end of the street. They had been found.

"Go!" Nico commanded, shoving her forward as he followed, pulling the ivy back into place behind them. They were plunged into an absolute, pitch-black silence, the sounds of the hunt sealed away behind them. They had made it to the ghost road.

Chapter 71: The Ghost Road

The service tunnel was a forgotten artery in the mountain's stone heart. It smelled of damp earth, cold stone, and a deep, ancient silence. Nico switched on a small, powerful tactical flashlight, its beam cutting a sharp, white cone through the oppressive darkness. They moved quickly, half-running, their footsteps echoing in the claustrophobic space. The roar of the Klausjagen faded behind them, swallowed by the sheer weight of the mountain.

Sloane's body was a symphony of aches. The jump from the roof, the crash through the pine branches, the hard landing on the cobblestones—the adrenaline had masked the pain, but now it was a screaming chorus. A sharp, throbbing fire had started in her right ankle. She ignored it, gritting her teeth, her only focus the bouncing circle of light ahead of her and the steady, iron grip of Nico's hand in hers.

"How far?" she asked, her voice a breathless whisper that was loud in the suffocating quiet.

"Half a kilometer, maybe," Nico replied, his voice a low, urgent murmur. "Katarina's instructions said the car would be there."

If Katarina was telling the truth, Sloane thought, the chilling possibility of a double-cross a fresh spike of ice in her gut.

The tunnel was not straight. It curved, dipped, and rose, following some long-forgotten geological logic. The air grew colder, thinner. Water dripped from the stone ceiling, each drop a percussive, echoing splash in the darkness. Twice, they heard the scuttling of unseen things in the shadows just beyond the flashlight's beam, and Sloane had to fight down a primal scream. This was a place for things that did not like the light.

The pain in her ankle flared, white-hot, and she stumbled, crying out as she fell to one knee on the rough, uneven floor.

Nico was there in an instant, his light swinging around, his body a shield between her and the darkness behind them. "Sloane? What is it?"

"My ankle," she gasped, the pain a nauseating wave. "I think I twisted it in the fall."

He knelt, his expression a mask of grim, professional concern. He ran his fingers gently but firmly over her ankle, his touch surprisingly sure. She hissed as he probed a tender spot.

"It's not broken," he said, his voice a quiet, factual assessment. "Sprained. Badly." He looked up, his eyes meeting hers in the harsh glare of the flashlight. "Can you walk?"

"I have to," she said, her jaw tight. It was not a question.

He nodded once, a gesture of respect. He reached into a pocket and pulled out a roll of medical tape and a blister pack of ibuprofen from the small kit he carried.

He popped two pills into her palm. "Take these," he said. "For the swelling."

Then he unrolled the tape. "This is going to hurt," he said, not as an apology, but as a statement of fact.

In the cold, damp darkness of the forgotten tunnel, he expertly wrapped her ankle, his movements quick and efficient, creating a tight, functional brace. The intimacy of the moment was a strange, sharp contrast to the brutal reality of their situation. His focus was absolute, the soldier taking care of his partner.

"Okay," he said, finishing the wrap. "On your feet."

She stood, testing her weight on the ankle. It held, the pain now a dull, manageable throb. "Thank you."

"We take care of each other," he said simply. He took her hand again, his grip now not just pulling her, but supporting her. "Let's go."

***

They reached the end: a heavy, steel maintenance hatch, rusted shut. Nico produced a small, carbon-fiber pry bar from his jacket. With a grunt of effort and a screech of protesting metal that seemed to echo for miles, he forced it open.

Cool night air flooded the tunnel. They emerged into a small, rocky ravine, hidden from the main roads by a thick stand of pine trees. The moon was a sliver of silver in the black sky. And there it was. A black BMW, its keys tucked in the gas cap. Katarina's efficiency was terrifyingly real.

They scrambled into the car. The smell of clean leather and new plastic was an absurd luxury after the primeval damp of the tunnel. The engine started with a low, predatory hum. Nico pulled onto a deserted access road, his eyes scanning the darkness.

"We're clear of the town," he said, his voice a low, urgent growl. "Make the call."

Sloane pulled the heavy satellite phone from the secret pocket of her cloak. Her hands were shaking, caked with dirt from the rooftops and the tunnel. She powered it on. There was only one number in its memory, labeled simply 'Exfil'.

She pressed the call button. It rang once, a strange, digital tone.

A synthesized, unidentifiable voice answered. "Go."

Sloane took a breath, her heart hammering. This was it. The leap of faith. She was betting their lives on Katarina's word.

"The serpent is broken," she said, the code phrase feeling strange and powerful on her tongue.

There was a beat of silence on the other end. Then the synthesized voice replied with a single word.

"Acknowledged."

The line went dead.

A moment later, the phone chirped. It was a text. A single set of GPS coordinates and a five-digit access code. Nothing more.

Nico took the phone and entered the coordinates into the car's navigation system. A route appeared on the screen, a red line snaking through a black, featureless landscape of forests and hills.

"Thirty kilometers," he said, flooring the accelerator. "Twenty minutes."

The drive was a tense, silent race through unlit country roads. Every flicker of a distant farmhouse light, every shadow that darted across the road, was a potential threat. Sloane sat with the Glock in her lap, her eyes scanning the darkness, her new soldier's instincts on a razor's edge.

They finally saw it. The coordinates led them to a high, chain-link fence topped with razor wire, a featureless, military-style barrier in the middle of a dense, dark forest. An access panel was set into one of the concrete pillars.

Nico stopped the car. "Stay here," he commanded.

He got out and walked to the panel, punching in the five-digit code from the text. For a long, heart-stopping moment, nothing happened. Sloane's hand tightened on her weapon. *It was a trap. It was always a trap.*

Then, with a low, electronic hum, two massive steel gates slid silently open, revealing a long, perfectly paved runway, lit by a single, ghostly line of blue lights.

Nico got back in the car and drove through. The gates slid shut behind them, sealing them in.

A single, sleek Gulfstream G650 sat at the far end of the tarmac, its cabin lights a warm, inviting glow in the cold, German night. Standing at the bottom of the stairs was a single, impassive figure in a pilot's uniform.

"She did it," Sloane breathed, a wave of profound, disbelieving relief washing over her.

But Nico didn't relax. "Wait," he said, his voice a low growl. He slowed the car to a crawl. "Something's not right."

"What is it?"

"Too quiet," he said. "No ground crew. No security. Just one pilot?" He killed the engine a hundred yards from the jet. "Stay here. Lock the doors. If he makes a move, you drive. You don't wait for me. You understand?"

"Nico, no—"

"That's an order, Sloane," he said, his voice hard as steel.

***

He got out of the car, his hand disappearing into his jacket, and walked slowly, deliberately, across the tarmac toward the jet. Sloane's heart hammered against her ribs. This was it. The final trap. She watched, her hand on the ignition, ready to execute the order she prayed she wouldn't have to.

Nico stopped fifty feet from the plane, a lone, dark figure in the vast, empty space. He and the pilot stood in a silent, tense standoff. She saw them exchange a few, inaudible words. Then, the pilot gave a curt nod and gestured toward the open door of the jet.

Nico turned back to the car and gave Sloane the all-clear sign.

She got out, her legs unsteady, the cold night air biting at her skin. Nico walked back to meet her, his eyes scanning the treeline. He popped the trunk, pulled out two duffel bags, and slung them over his shoulder.

"What was that?" she asked.

"Just confirming our flight plan," he said, his voice calm, but she saw the tension coiled in his jaw.

They walked together across the tarmac and climbed the stairs and stepped into the luxurious, cream-leather interior of the jet. The pilot followed them in, closing and sealing the heavy door behind him. The sound was a solid, satisfying thud.

"Welcome aboard," the pilot said, his German accent thick. "Short flight. We will be on the ground in Donaueschingen in twenty minutes." He turned and went into the cockpit.

Sloane sank into one of the plush seats, the sheer, impossible reality of their escape finally crashing down on her. They had done it. They were safe.

She looked at Nico. He was staring out the small, oval window as the plane began to taxi, his face a mask in the flashing lights of the runway.

"What did he really say?" she asked softly.

Nico turned from the window. His dark eyes were grim. "He said, 'She sends her regards. And a warning.'"

Sloane waited.

“The serpent is wounded, and raging,” Nico quoted, his voice a low, hard rasp. “He’ll burn the world to get to you. Move. Now.”

The jet's engines roared to life, a powerful, relentless sound, pressing her back into her seat. The plane accelerated down the runway, a blur of blue lights. They were free. They were flying.

But Katarina's warning was a cold, chilling prophecy. They had escaped the cage. But the serpent was already hunting.

Chapter 72: The Piano Ghost

The house was too quiet.

Damian Crestwell stood in the main salon at 3:47 AM, a glass of sixty-year-old Macallan in his hand—1926 vintage, worth more than most people earned in a lifetime—and felt nothing.

The glass was crystal. Baccarat. The scotch was amber perfection. The room was temperature-controlled to exactly 20.5 degrees Celsius, the optimal environment for preserving the Fazioli. But the instrument sat silent, a massive, hollow shell in the center of the room. He couldn't look at the ebony lid without seeing Sloane—without remembering the way she had traced the wood grain that first night with a tenderness that wasn't in her script. The piano had been the first thing she brought to life in this house; now, it was just another cold, precision-engineered relic.

Numbers. Precision. Control.

All meaningless.

Livia was gone. Again.

No. Not Livia.

Never Livia.

His mind—that ruthless, pattern-seeking engine that had made him a billionaire by twenty—had finally accepted what his heart had been screaming for weeks.

The woman who'd walked these halls, who'd played "Chopsticks" on this piano, who'd looked at him with those searching, vulnerable eyes—

She had been someone else entirely.

Sloane Devereaux. An actress. A ghost wearing his wife's face.

And he had known.

Some part of him had always known.

The way she held a fork. The cadence of her laugh. The tiny hesitation before she said his name, like an actress finding her mark.

He'd seen it all. Catalogued every discrepancy. His mind was built for pattern recognition—it was what made him dangerous, what made him valuable to men like Roman Lazar.

And he had chosen to ignore it.

I find myself preferring the difference, he'd told her that morning in the garden. He'd looked into her eyes—Sloane's eyes—and admitted that the counterfeit was better than the original.

God help him, he'd meant it.

The real Livia had been perfect. A Stradivarius—flawless, precise, irreplaceable. But cold. Always slightly out of reach, even when she lay beside him.

Sloane had been chaos. Warmth. Imperfection incarnate.

And he had wanted her anyway.

Even knowing she was a lie.

Especially knowing she was a lie.

Damian walked to the piano. Set his glass on the closed lid. Ran his fingers across the smooth ebony.

Livia's piano. She'd played Chopin, Debussy, Rachmaninoff. Mathematical perfection translated into sound. She'd played the way she lived—technically flawless, emotionally remote.

Sloane had played "Chopsticks."

Like a child. Like someone discovering music for the first time.

He'd loved her for it.

His hand trembled as he lifted the lid. The keys gleamed in the low light. Eighty-eight ivory teeth, grinning at his weakness.

He pressed middle C.

The note hung in the vast room. Clear. Perfect. Lonely.

"I should have listened to you," he whispered.

Not to Sloane. To the real Livia. The ghost he'd buried a year ago.

She'd tried to warn him about Roman. In her careful, mathematical way. Leaving breadcrumbs. Hints. Concerns wrapped in the language of efficiency and risk assessment.

The surveillance architecture has no natural limits, she'd said one night, months before she died. *Once deployed at scale, there's no mechanism for constraint. It's a runaway equation.*

He'd dismissed her concerns. Called them philosophical. Abstract.

Roman had been so persuasive. So clear in his vision.

"The world is chaos," Roman had said. "Both of us were broken by the systems that should have anchored us. Your parents were lost in their theorems; mine were lost in the fire. And then I lost Katya."

He'd leaned in. "Different wounds, same lesson: the world is a slaughterhouse for the unguarded. We're building Order. A system that sees the blade before it touches the skin."

And Damian, the lonely genius who'd never quite fit into the world, had believed him.

Had *wanted* to believe him.

Because Roman offered something more valuable than money: purpose. Belonging. A vision large enough to fill the void where human connection should have been.

He pressed another key. D. Then E. Random notes. Discordant.

The sound of a man breaking.

His mind—that beautiful, terrible curse—showed him the math now. The equations he'd been avoiding.

Panopticon wasn't about preventing chaos.

It *was* chaos. Weaponized. Monetized. Sold to the highest bidders.

And he had built the quantum encryption that made it unbreakable.

He had solved the lattice-based cryptographic problem that everyone said was unsolvable.

He had created the perfect lock for a prison that would hold billions.

His hands moved across the keys. Still not a melody. Just fragments. Broken pieces.

F sharp. G. B flat.

The glass of scotch sat untouched on the piano lid. Dark amber. Silent.

The Panopticon deal. The culmination of twelve years.

He hadn't taken a sip.

Now it tasted like ashes in his mouth.

The house was too big. Twenty-three bedrooms. Forty-thousand square feet of marble and glass and precisely controlled emptiness.

He was worth 622 billion dollars. A number meaningless to him. And that figure was primed to quadruple with the flick of a pen when the deal with 'The Twelve' was signed on Tuesday. He wouldn't just be the richest man in history; he would become a sovereign state with a human face.

He owned homes on three continents.

He owned a portfolio that defied the conventional laws of physics.

He owned a machine that could see the soul of the world.

And he was utterly, completely alone.

Livia was dead.

Sloane was gone.

Roman was a monster he'd helped create.

His hands stilled on the keys.

The silence rushed back in. Suffocating.

If she comes back...

The thought crystallized. Hardened into something like purpose.

Sloane—no, he should call her by her real name now, even in his thoughts—Sloane had run for a reason.

She and the bodyguard. Nico. The man who'd looked at her with something Damian recognized because he'd felt it himself.

Love.

They'd run because they were going after Roman.

Had to be. Why else disappear during Klausjagen? Why else take the risk?

Damian's mind spun through the probabilities. The evidence Livia had been gathering. The banker's boxes in her study. The encrypted files she'd hidden.

Sloane had found them. Had to have. That's what this whole elaborate con had been about.

She was going to use Livia's evidence to destroy Roman.

And she would fail.

Because she didn't understand the full scope of what Roman had become. The defenses. The contingencies. The network of power he'd built.

She needed help.

If she comes back to fight him...

Damian closed the piano lid. The soft thud echoed in the empty room.

"I will help her," he said aloud. To Livia's ghost. To the cold, listening house. To the god he no longer believed in.

"I will pay the price I should have paid a long time ago."

He needed to understand. What had she found? What had driven her to run?

He walked to Sloane's room. The room where she had impeccably played Livia's role, lived the lie.

The bed was made. Perfectly. As if she'd never been there at all.

But his breath hitched as he saw the chaise lounge. The emerald Valentino gown was draped across the velvet—a shimmering, hollow skin Sloane had left behind like a discarded soul. The crystal beads caught the morning light, glowing with a cold, spectral fire. It looked like a woman who had simply evaporated into the mountain air.

Nestled in the deep, green silk of the bodice sat the black Moleskine journal. Sloane hadn't hidden it; she had staged it as an altar. Resting on the cover was a single, heavy piece of cream-colored stationery—Livia's personal correspondence card.

Damian traced the loops of the letters, his mind automatically running the comparison. The slant was exact. The pressure on the downstrokes was perfect. It was the sharp, mathematical script he'd recognize anywhere—and yet, his heart didn't recognize it at all.

He knew Livia was a year in her grave. He knew the ink on this card was too fresh, the scent of the paper too new to be a relic. This wasn't a ghost reaching from the past; it was a masterpiece of counterfeit grace. He could almost see Sloane sitting at the desk, her brow furrowed in concentration, her hand cramping as she obsessively mastered the one voice he had allowed her to have.

She hadn't written it as herself. She had used the mask he'd paid for to deliver the truth he deserved:

For D. Read everything. —LC

The perfection of the forgery was the most honest thing she had ever given him. It was a map drawn in a dead woman's hand, pointing him toward the living man's fire.

Damian's hand trembled as he picked it up. He recognized it immediately—the cover, the weight, the small embossed initials on the corner: L.C.

Livia's private journal. The one he'd never been allowed to read. The one she'd kept locked away, even from him.

Sloane had found it. Had read it. And had left it behind.

He sank onto the edge of the bed and opened it.

The words came at him in fragments, each one a blade:

—locked out. And I think... I think I am locked in—

—I confronted Damian tonight. I showed him the offshore accounts—

—He looked at me like I was speaking a foreign language—

—"You're under too much stress. You need rest."—

—a man who has perfected the art of not seeing—

His vision blurred. He forced himself to keep reading.

—the patron isn't D's true mentor. He is his handler—

—Turing died at 41. Cyanide apple. "Suicide," they called it—

—I will not let Damian become another beautiful mind broken by ugly men—

—Damian presented it to me as a plea... He has no idea he's the one leading me into the trap.—

—If you are reading this, you know how the story ended.—

The journal slipped from his hands. Fell to the floor.

She'd known. She'd seen everything. She'd tried to warn him.

And he'd walked away.

He'd called her stressed. Paranoid. Told her to rest.

He'd killed her with his willful blindness as surely as if he'd driven her off that cliff himself.

No. Roman had killed her. But Damian had handed him the knife.

He picked up the journal with shaking hands. Held it against his chest. A relic of the woman he'd failed. A record of warnings he'd refused to hear.

And now Sloane—the counterfeit who'd worn Livia's face—was out there somewhere, trying to finish what his wife had started.

He stood. The journal felt heavier than it should. He carried it to his study, placed it on his desk where he could see it. A reminder. A witness to what came next.

He understood with perfect, crystalline clarity what he had to do.

His eyes drifted to the locked drawer. Bottom right. The one he hadn't opened since late-January.

A month after Livia's death. The nadir of his grief. He had written it in a scotch-fueled fugue state—a digital suicide note. He had decided then: if his life had no meaning without her, his creation didn't deserve a future.

Inside lay a single, matte-black drive. It looked like nothing—a sliver of cold plastic—but it sat in the tray with the heavy, radioactive silence of an unexploded bomb.

He had named it Chaos.

It was the mathematical inverse of Panopticon. If the machine was Pure Order, this was Pure Entropy.

He'd never finished it. He'd locked it away when the darkness receded, terrified of what it could do.

But now—

Now it wasn't a fear. It was a solution.

He unlocked the drawer.

***

His mind was already working. Calculating. Planning.

He had resources. Access. And he knew the machine better than the man who thought he owned it.

And he had something else. Something more valuable than all his billions.

Guilt.

The kind of guilt that could only be redeemed through sacrifice.

He picked up the glass of scotch. Sixty thousand dollars. Sixty years old.

He poured it down the bar sink. Watched the amber liquid disappear.

He didn't deserve expensive scotch.

He deserved whatever came next.

But first, he had to set the final board. He walked to his study, the room now feeling like a tomb of his own making, and sat at his terminal. His fingers, which had played only discordant notes on the piano, now moved with a familiar, fluid grace across the keyboard.

He navigated through layers of his own quantum encryption, deep into the core architecture of his digital estate. He initiated a final, encrypted sync between the two hearts of his creation: the Sanctum, the live data center humming here beneath his feet, and its perfect, hidden mirror—the Ghost—a dormant, secondary facility whose location was his most closely guarded secret.

He knew he might not survive what was coming. He needed a final contingency. A dead man's switch.

He created a new master control protocol, one that would govern the Ghost. He linked it to a biometric signature that was not his own. He pulled up the high-resolution file from her employment contract, the one he had stared at for hours. Her face. Her name.

Sloane Devereaux.

If his own security check-in—a simple heartbeat confirmation from his watch—failed to register for ninety-one consecutive days, all access, all control, would fail-over to her. It was a profound act of trust. A final, desperate bet on the one chaotic variable he had come to believe in.

He saved the protocol, logged out, and wiped the command log. The digital ghost was in the machine.

He had one final piece of insurance to place on the board. He opened a separate, secure terminal and composed a short, cryptic message. It was addressed to one person. The lead programmer on his remote team. His brilliant, designated successor. Dr. Alice Wrangler.

To: A.Wrangler@crystalvision.ioSubject: second life

The Serpent is in the garden. He has corrupted the equation.If the system goes dark, trust the variable. Not the constant.— D.C.

He scheduled it for delayed delivery—enough time for Sloane to make her move, but not so long that Roman could bury the truth entirely. It was a message in a bottle, a final, desperate hope that the one person who truly understood the machine would also understand how to help dismantle its corrupt shadow. He had just told his prodigy to trust the ghost who wore his dead wife's face.

Now he could help Sloane Devereaux burn down the monster he'd helped build.

Even if it cost him everything.

Especially if it cost him everything.

The piano stood silent behind him.

A relic of a woman who'd tried to warn him.

And a ghost who'd shown him the truth wrapped in a beautiful lie.

Both gone now.

But their echoes remained.

And Damian Crestwell, lonely genius, soon-to-be-trillionaire, builder of cages, was finally ready to listen.

He picked up the secure, encrypted phone from his desk. He dialed a number from memory—the direct line to his private solicitor in Zurich, a man who had handled the Crestwell family's affairs for thirty years.

The old lawyer answered, his voice thick with sleep. "Damian? Is everything alright?"

Damian looked out the window at the black, sleeping lake. "Everything is fine, Wilhelm," he said, his voice perfectly calm, perfectly clear. "I need to make an update to my will. Activating the contingencies that we had discussed."

Chapter 73: The Safe House

The Gulfstream G650 landed with a whisper, a ghost settling onto a black scar of tarmac in the middle of a sleeping German forest. The moment the engines spooled down, a profound silence descended, broken only by the frantic, high-pitched ringing in Sloane's ears.

The heavy cabin door hissed open, and the cold, damp air of the German night rushed in, smelling of pine and wet earth. The pilot emerged from the cockpit, his face impassive. He handed Nico a single, unmarked keycard for the safe house.

"There is a car in the hangar," the pilot said, his German accent clipped and professional. "A blue Volkswagen Golf. The coordinates for the safe house are in the navigation system. It is fueled. My mission is now complete. If you need another ride after you conclude your business, call the same number two hours in advance. Get here at your earliest, and you'll get a safe passage to anywhere in Western Europe. Good luck."

He didn't wait for a reply. He turned and went into the cockpit, leaving them alone on the silent, empty airstrip.

"Let's go," Nico said, his voice a low, rough thing. "The clock is ticking."

Sloane followed him down the stairs, her sprained ankle screaming in protest. Every muscle in her body was a canvas of deep, throbbing bruises from the rooftop chase and the brutal fall. Her beautiful dirndl was a ruined, torn thing, stained with dirt and pine needles. She was a fairytale princess who had just survived a war.

The Volkswagen was as anonymous as the pilot's promise. It was clean, functional, and utterly forgettable. A ghost car for a ghost city. They slipped inside, the simple cloth seats a world away from the Maybach's plush leather. Nico started the engine, and without turning on the headlights, he navigated them out of the hangar and onto a dark, unlit service road.

The drive to Singen took nearly an hour—a slow, deliberate crawl through the skeletal, frost-dusted pines of the Black Forest. Nico didn't race; speed was a signature they couldn't afford. He kept the Volkswagen in the right lane of the A81, blending into the sparse rhythm of late-night freight trucks, his eyes fixed on the road as a fine, crystalline snow began to dance in the headlights.

The silence in the car was heavy, but no longer jagged. The adrenaline was a dying fire, leaving behind the cold ash of bone-weary exhaustion. The heater hummed, struggling against the December chill, the rhythmic sweep of the wipers the only heartbeat in the cabin. For the first time in months, there was no one watching them through a lens, no algorithm predicting their next move. There was only the mist and the dark.

Sloane leaned her head against the cold glass, watching Nico's profile in the dim glow of the dashboard. To the world, he was a machine—a creature of pure, functional purpose designed to survive the unthinkable. But she knew the truth now. She had heard his voice break on a satellite phone. She had seen the man beneath the sentinel: the father, the widower, the ghost who was finally beginning to haunt his own life.

***

The safe house was a small, anonymous apartment in Singen, a gray, industrial German train town just across the border. It was clean, spartan, and utterly forgettable, one of a thousand identical doors in a concrete block building overlooking the train yards. The air smelled of diesel and steel, and the distant rumble of freight cars was a constant, low hum. Katarina's, and Livia's, paranoia had been a gift.

Nico unlocked the door with the keycard, and they slipped inside, two shadows returning to a home they had never seen. The air inside smelled of fresh paint and disinfectant, a place scrubbed clean of all identity. There was a cheap sofa, a small kitchenette, and a single bedroom with two twin beds. It was a place to disappear.

Nico dropped the backpack with their gear on the floor and went straight to the window, peering through a crack in the blinds at the quiet, empty street below.

"We're clear for now," he said.

Sloane leaned against the closed door, the last of her strength finally giving out. The adrenaline that had sustained her since the tunnel was gone, and the ibuprofen Nico had given her in the dark was losing its war against the inflammation. Her ankle, still tightly bound in his tactical tape, was throbbing with a rhythmic, sickening heat that made her vision swim.

Nico turned from the window, his eyes immediately finding her feet. "The field wrap isn't holding the swelling anymore."

"It's getting tight," she admitted, her voice a dry rasp. She tried to take a step, but her knee buckled as the joint refused to anchor.

Nico was there before she could hit the floor. He caught her by the waist, his grip firm and steady, and guided her toward the cheap sofa. "The adrenaline is a liar, Sloane. It makes you think you're whole until you stop moving. Now that we've stopped, the body is going to collect the debt."

He knelt at her feet, his movements stripped of their usual lethal aggression. He didn't ask permission; he carefully cut away the blood-stained tactical tape from the tunnel, his fingers moving with a focused, clinical grace. As the pressure released, the joint bloomed—swollen, distorted, and stained a deep, angry purple.

"The high sprain I flagged in the tunnel?" he murmured, his thumbs tracing the bone to check for new displacement. "It's worse than I thought. You've been running on sheer will for three hours."

"I had a good motivator," she whispered, looking down at him. "And a good sentinel."

He didn't look up. He reached into the military-grade first-aid kit, snapped a chemical ice pack to life, and began the process of a proper rest-and-recovery wrap.

As he worked, his fingers brushing against her skin, the air between them became thick with a new, different kind of tension. This was not the adrenaline of the chase. It was the quiet, profound intimacy of two people who had survived a battle together, who had seen the raw, vulnerable truth of each other. She could feel the heat radiating from him. She could smell the scent of his skin—a mixture of sweat, pine, and something uniquely, elementally him.

When he finished applying the dressing, he didn't pull away immediately. He kept his hand anchored on her calf for a second too long, a silent acknowledgment of the weight they were both carrying.

"Thank you," she said, her voice a low, rough murmur.

"We're partners," she replied, the word feeling solid, real. "We take care of each other."

"We're targets," he corrected, but he didn't pull away. He looked at the clock. It was nearly 4:00 AM on Saturday. The bank didn't open until Monday. "We have forty-eight hours to become invisible. We use them to sleep. We eat. We recover. Because on Monday morning, we have to be perfect."

He pointed to the beds. "No watches. No drills. Just sleep, Sloane. That's an order."

She changed out of her ruined dirndl and into the clean, black tactical gear that had been left for them. The simple, functional clothes felt like a uniform, a second skin.

She went to the small bathroom and scrubbed the heavy theater makeup from her face until her cheeks were raw. She looked at her reflection, then down at the scar on her palm—not as a biometric flaw, but as her own history. She had to take a respite from being Livia. She needed to be Sloane for a moment, or she would disappear entirely.

***

Saturday was a blur of heavy, dreamless sleep and the smell of industrial diesel from the train yards outside. They didn't speak of Roman or the Ledger. They existed in a bubble of silence, punctuated only by the changing of bandages and the application of ice to Sloane's swollen ankle.

Nico proved he was human by collapsing for twelve hours straight. When he finally woke, his movements were less like a machine and more like a man carrying the weight of a decade. He made pasta from a box in the pantry, and they ate it in silence on the small sofa, their knees touching. For those few hours, they weren't ghosts; they were just two people hiding from a storm.

By evening, the adrenaline debt was paid in full. But the void it left behind was worse than the exhaustion.

***

Saturday night, the silence became unbearable.

Sloane lay in the narrow twin bed, staring at the ceiling, her body exhausted but her mind still running on emergency protocols. Every creak of the building was a footstep. Every distant siren was coming for them. Her ankle throbbed with each heartbeat, a metronome of pain that kept her tethered to consciousness.

"Sloane." Nico's voice came from the other bed, quiet in the darkness. "You're not sleeping."

"Neither are you."

A pause. The sound of him shifting in the narrow bed. Then: "Come here."

She didn't question it. She didn't overthink it. She got up, her ankle protesting, and crossed the small space between the beds. He pulled back the thin blanket, and she slid in beside him. The bed was too small for two people, forcing them close. His arm came around her, solid and warm, and she pressed her face against his chest.

The scent of him—sweat, soap, something indefinably human—grounded her in a way nothing else could.

"We're alive," he whispered into her hair.

"We're alive," she repeated, the words a talisman against the dark.

His heart beat steady beneath her ear. Strong. Reliable. For the first time since the tunnel, she felt safe. Not because they were hidden, but because she wasn't alone. Because this man—this sentinel who'd guarded her through hell—was still here. Still breathing. Still fighting.

She felt his hand move, stroking her hair with a gentleness that seemed impossible from someone so lethal. "Sleep, Sloane. I've got you."

And she did. She fell asleep like that—his arms around her, her hand resting over his heart, two ghosts finding comfort in the only warmth left in the world.

***

Sunday morning, Nico woke first. The gray light of dawn filtered through the thin curtains. Sloane was still pressed against him, her breathing deep and even—the first real sleep she'd had in days. He didn't move, didn't want to wake her.

But the clock was ticking.

When she finally stirred, her eyes opening slow and confused, he said quietly: "We need to move to Zurich today."

She blinked, still half-asleep, her body warm against his. "Today?"

"We get to Zurich, prep the disguise, rest tonight, hit the bank tomorrow morning." He looked down at her. "Can you walk?"

She pulled away slightly, tested her ankle—still swollen, but the ice and tape had done their work. The sharp, screaming pain had dulled to a persistent ache. "I can walk."

"Then we leave in two hours. I'll get us to the station. From there, we disappear into the Sunday crowd."

She nodded, then looked up at him. Their faces were inches apart. She could see the exhaustion in his eyes, the weight he carried. On impulse, she reached up and touched his face—just her fingers against his jaw, a gesture of gratitude and something deeper she didn't have words for.

"Thank you," she whispered. "For last night. For... this."

His hand covered hers, held it there for a moment. "We take care of each other," he said, echoing her words from the night before. "That's the deal."

Then he pulled away, the moment breaking. Back to business. "Two hours. Pack light. We're not coming back here."

Chapter 74: The City of Ghosts

Sunday, late morning. They boarded the regional train from Singen under a low, gray sky that threatened snow. The weekend travelers—families with strollers, university students with backpacks, elderly couples heading to Sunday lunch—gave them perfect cover. Just two more anonymous faces in the Sunday crowd.

Sloane wore simple clothes: jeans, a dark sweater, a scarf that hid half her face. Nico had found her a pair of cheap sunglasses. She looked like a thousand other women on a Sunday morning. Forgettable. Invisible.

It was a slow, crowded, local service that made a dozen stops before crossing the border back into Switzerland. It was anonymous. Public. The last place Roman's men, who would be watching the highways and the high-speed expresses, would think to look.

They were two anonymous figures in a crowded carriage, hiding in plain sight. As the train rumbled through the German countryside, its rhythm a slow, steady heartbeat, Sloane felt a strange, new sense of calm.

But as they neared the border, the calm evaporated, replaced by a cold, prickling dread. Her hand rested on her handbag, where the Helena Baros passport felt like a block of ice. Every time the train slowed for a stop, her body tensed, her eyes scanning the platform for the dark green uniforms of the Swiss Grenzwache, the border guards.

She half-expected the doors to slide open and for them to step aboard, their eyes methodically checking every face, their hands resting on their sidearms. She rehearsed the lines in her head. Helena Baros. Art dealer. Visiting for business. A flimsy story that would fall apart under the slightest pressure.

But no one came. The train rumbled on, crossing an invisible line in the landscape without ceremony. One moment they were in Germany, the next, Switzerland.

They were ghosts, re-entering the graveyard. And no one had even bothered to check their papers.

***

Zurich was a city of quiet, disciplined beauty. It was a city built of gray stone, money, and secrets. As their taxi drove across the Quaibrücke bridge, the afternoon sun glinting off the calm, blue-green water of Lake Zurich, Sloane was struck by the city's profound, almost aggressive sense of order. Trams glided by, silent and electric. Pedestrians waited patiently for the walk signals, even on empty streets. It was the architectural and cultural opposite of the chaotic, sprawling, and beautifully messy Los Angeles she had left behind.

This was a city that did not tolerate mistakes.

"His eyes are here," Sloane murmured, scanning the passing faces. "I don't know where, and I don't know who. But Roman... he casts a long shadow."

"He doesn't need to be here to pull the trigger," Nico said, his gaze cutting through the crowd with lethal precision. "Roman is a king. And kings don't bloody their own hands. They send the headsman."

"And if the headsman finds us?"

A faint, dangerous smile touched Nico's mouth. "Then we stop running. And we start fighting."

They had the taxi drop them near the university district, blocks away from their real destination. They doubled back on foot to the address Katarina had marked on the map. The Zurich safe house.

It was a nondescript, gray stone building in a quiet, residential neighborhood. A place of old-world charm and, more importantly, total invisibility. Livia had chosen it well.

Nico punched the code into the keypad. The door clicked open.

The apartment was more substantial than Singen—a proper two-bedroom flat with a small living room, a functional kitchen, and windows that looked out onto a quiet street lined with chestnut trees. The furniture was simple but clean. The air smelled of lemon cleaner and time.

Livia had prepared for a longer stay here.

Nico checked the windows, tested the locks, and cleared each room with professional efficiency. "We're good," he said finally. He set down their bags and checked his watch. "I'm heading out to pick up the materials from the dead drop. I should be back in an hour or so."

He looked at her, his expression serious. "Lock it behind me. Three knocks, pause, two knocks. Don't open it for anyone else."

"Three, pause, two," Sloane repeated. "I'll be here."

She watched him leave, the lock clicking home with a solid, heavy thud. She was alone in Zurich, the heartbeat of the enemy's world, waiting for the tools to build a ghost.

***

Nico was back by five. He set two heavy shopping bags on the kitchen table with a purposeful thud.

"The dead drop was clean," he said, breathing out the winter chill. He began to unpack the bags with the methodical care of a bomb technician.

Sloane watched as the anatomy of a heist materialized on the formica tabletop. First, the industrial supplies: a bottle of premium liquid prosthetic latex and a canister of specialized molding agent. Then, the precision tools: a set of fine-tipped sable artist's brushes and a small, high-intensity UV curing lamp.

Next came the technology. Nico opened a small, foam-lined case to reveal six impossibly thin heating strips—each no thicker than a human hair—and a micro-battery the size of a postage stamp. Then a small tube of fine-milled graphite dust. Finally, he produced a small, unmarked glass jar filled with a translucent, shimmering powder.

"CV Dazzle," Nico said, tapping the jar. "Computer Vision dazzle. It's an infrared-reflective pigment. To the banker, it looks like standard high-end foundation. To the vault's depth-mapping scanners, it scatters the light, flattening the geometry of your cheekbones just enough to match Livia's baseline file. It's digital camouflage for your face. The graphite is for the hand," he added. "Latex is too translucent; under the vault's near-infrared scan, it would look like a plastic toy. The dust provides the internal opacity of living tissue, scattering the beam so the machine sees flesh instead of a glove."

He laid out the final piece: the high-resolution, one-to-one scale photograph of Livia's right hand.

"The transfer has to be perfect," Sloane said, her fingers hovering over the photo. "If the latex is too thick, the scanner won't pick up the ridge detail. Too thin, and it'll tear."

"It's a standard inverse transfer," Nico said. "By painting the latex directly onto this positive image, the whorls of her fingerprints will be embossed into the material. When you flip it onto your hand tomorrow morning, the orientation corrects itself. You don't need to mirror the file, but you do need to eliminate every microscopic air bubble."

Sloane took a breath, centered herself, and picked up the finest brush. The performance had moved from her voice to her fingertips.

She worked by lamplight while the city quieted outside. She painted the first layer of liquid latex over the photograph, working the material into every ridge and valley of the fingerprints. By nine o'clock, she'd mixed the graphite into the final structural layers, turning the material from a milky translucent to a dull, flesh-toned matte. It was a painstaking, silent dance. Nico sat on the sofa, cleaning his weapon, providing a silent, steady anchor in the room.

"Favorite color?" he asked around seven o'clock, his voice a low rumble.

"Burgundy," Sloane said, her hand never wavering. "First pet?"

"Schubert. He used to sleep on the sheet music." She didn't just recite the fact; she let a flicker of genuine nostalgia cloud her eyes, letting the memory ground her to the role.

Nico studied her. "Good. Stay in that skin. That's the detail the algorithm can't see."

Once the latex had cured, Sloane spent the next hour using a pair of surgical tweezers to embed the heating strips. She laid them in a specific pattern—one along each finger and two across the palm—mimicking the heat signature of arterial blood flow. She connected them to the micro-battery at the wrist.

At 10:15 PM, she finally peeled the prosthetic from the photograph. It was a ghostly, translucent replica of a dead woman's skin. She fitted it over her own hand for a momentary test.

As the battery hummed, the latex reached thirty-seven degrees Celsius.

"Thirty-seven degrees," she whispered, touching the warm, fake skin. "The temperature of living blood."

"To the scanner, the ghost is breathing," Nico said.

She carefully peeled the prosthetic back off and laid it in a silk-lined case. "I can't wear it tonight. If I roll in my sleep, the strips could shift."

"Smart," Nico said. He stood and reached into the kit, pulling out a fine-grit emery board. "One more thing. The nails."

Sloane looked at her hand. "They're already short."

"Short isn't enough. If a single edge is sharp, it'll puncture the latex from the inside the moment you grip the tablet. File them down until they're perfectly rounded. No snags. No accidents."

She spent ten minutes meticulously smoothing her fingernails while Nico watched. It was a strange, meditative ritual—the final calibration of a weapon.

"Promise me something," she said quietly as she finished.

"Anything."

"If it goes wrong tomorrow—if I get caught—you run. You finish this."

"No, Sloane." His voice was steel. "We started this together. We end it together. Now sleep. That's an order."

They fell into bed at 11:00 PM without discussion—her back against his chest, his arm draped over her waist. Two ghosts finding the only warmth left in a cold city. They slept deeply, a dreamless, necessary recovery before the storm.

***

Monday morning arrived with frost on the windows. Sloane woke at six, feeling the unusual weight of a full night's sleep. The adrenaline debt was paid; she felt cold, clear, and dangerous.

Nico was already up, making coffee in the small kitchen. He handed her a cup without a word. "Two hours until we leave," he said. "You need to become Helena."

While Nico slipped out into the city to prep the getaway car, Sloane began the transformation. She showered, letting the hot water wash away the last of the fear, then wash-dyed her hair to a sophisticated auburn red. She applied the contouring makeup to subtly alter her bone structure, changing the shape of her eyebrows to a sharper, more severe line.

When Nico returned, he stopped in the doorway and stared. Sloane sat at the small vanity, wearing the simple, elegant navy blue dress and the heavy, tortoise-shell glasses.

"Wow," he breathed.

"It's just a costume," Sloane said, but her voice already carried the aristocratic distance of the art dealer.

Nico approached, setting down the small, unmarked jar of shimmering powder he had set aside for her the night before. "The final touch. CV Dazzle."

Sloane looked at the jar, then at his reflection in the mirror. "First the graphite for my hand, now this for my face. I'm starting to feel like I'm more pigment than person."

"The graphite was for biology," Nico said, his voice dropping to a tactical hum. "CV dazzle is for the geometry. It scatters infrared light to scramble the depth-mapping. It'll flatten your cheekbones and widen your ocular spacing just enough to match Livia's baseline file. It's the only way to make the algorithm accept the counterfeit."

Sloane took the brush and dusted the powder across the bridge of her nose and the high points of her cheeks. "War paint," she whispered.

"Digital camouflage," Nico corrected.

He handed her the rugged black tablet, now loaded with the encrypted payload Manny had siphoned from Finland. "This goes in your bag. And the hand?"

"The very last step," she said. She sat at the table and carefully applied the medical adhesive to her skin before sliding her right hand into the latex prosthetic, ensuring the perfectly filed nails didn't snag the material. She adjusted the micro-battery at her wrist, feeling the artificial thirty-seven-degree warmth blossom against her skin. She flexed her fingers; the seam was invisible, the transition flawless. To any thermal sensor, she wasn't wearing a glove. She was radiating life.

Nico handed her the small, almost invisible earpiece. "I'll be on the street. Ninety seconds to get out if the alarm trips. Haunt them, Sloane."

"I intend to," she said.

***

They stepped out into the Zurich morning. The air was a sharp, bracing cold that tasted of the lake and ancient stone. Monday morning was beginning to pulse—the rhythmic chime of trams, the focused stride of bankers in wool coats, the smell of roasted coffee.

Sloane walked with the measured confidence of a woman who owned the sidewalk. Her ankle, still tightly wrapped, throbbed with a dull pain she refused to acknowledge. Nico was a ghost in the crowd a block behind her, a shadow that felt more like a shield than a tail. They moved with their senses dialed to the maximum, scanning every passing face, every tinted window for the obsidian-black Mercedes they had been taught to fear.

"Anything?" Sloane whispered into the invisible microphone.

"Clean," Nico's voice crackled back, low and steady. "The perimeter is quiet. No signatures. No tails. Roman is looking for us at the border crossings and the airports. He's blinded by the exit."

Sloane felt a dangerous flicker of relief. The streets felt orderly, almost indifferent. The city was a masterpiece of discipline, and right now, they were simply part of the brushstroke. They reached the financial district without a single shadow crossing their path.

"We're ghosts today," she breathed.

"Almost there," Nico replied. "You belong here, Helena. Walk through the front door."

She reached the bank. The massive, granite building loomed over her, a temple of money and secrets. She took one last, steadying breath, stepped up the stone stairs, and pushed through the heavy bronze doors.

She left the sunlight behind and entered the silent heart of Livia's war, unaware that the eyes she feared were already inside.

Chapter 75: Helena Baros

The main hall of the Helvetica Privatbank was a cathedral built to the god of money. The ceilings were impossibly high, vaulted and ornate, the floors a gleaming, soundless expanse of polished marble. The air was cool, still, and smelled of old paper, leather, and a century of quiet, disciplined wealth. The only sound was the soft, reverential whisper of hushed conversations and the distant, rhythmic click of a teller's stamp.

Sloane walked across the vast, intimidating space, her heels making a soft, confident clicking sound on the marble. She was Helena Baros. Art dealer. Bored. Rich. Here on a tedious but necessary errand. She channeled the effortless, aristocratic ennui she had seen Livia deploy so many times. She did not look at the soaring ceilings with awe. She did not look at the stern-faced bankers with fear. She looked straight ahead, her expression one of polite, unassailable impatience.

She approached the private banking desk, a massive, mahogany monolith at the far end of the hall. A severe-looking woman with perfectly coiffed gray hair looked up, her eyes cool and appraising.

"Can I help you?" the woman asked, her English perfect, her accent a faint, musical German.

"I have an appointment," Sloane said, her voice a perfect, cool Helena. "Ten o'clock. With Herr Ziegler. The name is Baros. Helena Baros."

She adjusted the strap of her oversized Hermès bag. Inside, hidden beneath a silk scarf and her compact, the tablet hummed in sleep mode. The locked safe, waiting for Livia's combination.

The woman's expression did not change, but a flicker of recognition registered in her eyes. "Of course, Frau Baros," she said, her tone shifting from dismissive to deferential. "Herr Ziegler is expecting you. If you'll please come this way."

She led Sloane through a discreet, unmarked door and into a different world. The grand, public space of the bank gave way to a series of quiet, wood-paneled corridors, the air even stiller here, the silence even more profound. They were in the heart of the machine now. The inner sanctum.

***

Herr Ziegler was a small, neat man in his late sixties, with a fringe of white hair and a kind, grandfatherly face. He wore a perfectly tailored suit and a polite, professional smile. He was the friendly, human face of an inhumanly secure system.

"Frau Baros," he said, standing to greet her in his plush, antique-filled office. "A pleasure to see you again. I trust your trip from Paris was pleasant?"

The first test. Livia's file for the Helena Baros alias listed her primary residence as Paris.

"As pleasant as any flight can be," Sloane replied with a small, weary smile. "The coffee at Charles de Gaulle is still a tragedy."

Ziegler laughed, a soft, polite sound. "Indeed. A crime against the senses." He gestured to a chair. "Please. Now, you are here to review the contents of your holdings. I have your file right here."

He sat behind his desk and produced a thin, leather-bound folder. He opened it. "Locker number 28714. Opened in 2022. The contents of your safe deposit box have not been accessed in... almost a year." He looked up at her over the top of his spectacles. "Everything is in order."

"Excellent," Sloane said. "Then if I could just..."

"Of course," he said. He stood up. "If you'll follow me."

***

He led her from his office, down another silent corridor, to a heavy, steel-grilled gate. He swiped a keycard, and the gate slid open with a soft, electronic hum. They stepped into a small, sterile antechamber. Before them was a round, vault-like door, made of what looked like a foot of solid, polished steel.

"The first checkpoint," Ziegler said, gesturing to a small, wall-mounted panel. "ID check and thumbprint."

Sloane's heart gave a single, hard kick. A thumbprint. This was not in Nico's intel. The plan was already going wrong.

She fought back the surge of panic, her face a mask of calm. She reached into her handbag and produced the Helena Baros passport, handing it to Ziegler. Her mind was racing. *What do I do? What do I do?*

Ziegler took the passport and slid it into a slot in the panel. He then placed his own thumb on a small, glass scanner. A green light pulsed. He was authenticating himself as the bank officer.

"Now you, Frau Baros," he said, gesturing to the scanner.

This was it. The end of the line. The latex prosthetic was on her right hand, for the final vault scanner. Her left thumb was her own. The moment she placed it on the scanner, the machine would know. The alarm would sound. The game would be over.

She looked at the scanner. She looked at Ziegler's polite, expectant face.

And then she saw it. The scanner was a simple, older model. It was not a full-print reader. It was just a pressure-plate authenticator, designed to confirm that a second person was present. A two-man rule. It was not scanning her print. It was just confirming her presence.

It was a piece of security theater.

She took a breath, a silent, shuddering intake of air. She placed her left thumb on the scanner.

A green light pulsed. The heavy, steel-grilled gate in front of them slid open.

She had passed the first test.

***

The corridor beyond was short, leading to another, even more imposing door. This one was a single, seamless slab of titanium. There was no handle. No visible lock. Just a small, black camera and a laser grid projector set into the wall beside it.

"The second checkpoint," Ziegler said, his tone still politely conversational. "Biometric facial recognition."

This was the one Nico had warned her about. The machine that could see a thousand different data points. The one that could spot the lie in her bone structure.

"Please stand on the marked spot, Frau Baros," Ziegler said, pointing to a small circle on the floor.

Sloane stepped into the circle. She took a breath.

She was not Sloane. She was not Livia. She was Helena.

A soft, red laser grid swept over her face, mapping every contour, every millimeter of her bone structure. The small, black camera lens stared at her, an unblinking, analytical eye.

The seconds stretched into an eternity. Sloane held her breath. She did not blink. She was a statue. A perfect, beautiful lie.

She could feel her heart hammering against her ribs, a frantic, terrified drumbeat. She prayed the machine couldn't hear it. *Breathe*, she told herself. *You are Helena Baros. You belong here.*

A soft, female voice echoed from a hidden speaker. "Identity confirmed. Welcome, Frau Baros."

Did it sound like Aura? Was she powered by... Panopticon? Sloane shuddered, pushed the thought away, and looked ahead with a thin Mona Lisa smile.

The titanium door slid silently into the wall.

Sloane let out a breath she didn't realize she had been holding. She had done it. She had fooled the machine.

***

The room beyond was the heart of the fortress. The vault room. It was not a room of steel and alarms. It was a quiet, beautiful, wood-paneled library of secrets. Floor-to-ceiling walls of safe deposit boxes, each with a small, brass door and a keyhole.

"Your box, Frau Baros," Ziegler said, leading her to a section in the far wall. "Number 28714."

He took a key, a long, antique-looking brass key, from his pocket. "As you know, the protocol requires two keys. My key, and your key."

This was it. The final act.

Sloane reached into her handbag and produced the single, antique-looking brass key that had been packaged with her Helena Baros passport. A gift from Katarina's invisible network. It felt impossibly fragile in her hand.

Ziegler inserted his key into the upper lock and turned it. *Click.*

"Your key, Frau Baros," he said.

Sloane's hand was surprisingly steady as she inserted the key into the lower lock. She turned it. *Click.*

Ziegler then gestured to the final security measure. A small, glowing glass plate next to the box. The handprint scanner.

"And finally," he said, "for the record."

Sloane took a breath. This was it. The final, high-tech gatekeeper.

Sloane looked at her right hand, the hand that was not her own. Beneath the seamless, invisible layer of liquid latex was a masterpiece of deception. A ghostly replica of a dead woman's skin, mixed with theatrical-grade graphite dust to scatter any infrared scan. Along the palm lines, Nico had helped her embed six impossibly thin heating strips, powered by a wafer-thin battery taped to her wrist. The prosthetic was not just a copy; it was a living, breathing lie, warm to the touch.

She pressed her palm flat against the cool glass plate.

A brilliant blue light from within the scanner swept across her hand, from the base of her palm to the tips of her fingers, reading not just the lines and whorls, but the heat signature and pulse.

The final moment of truth.

Ten seconds. The longest ten seconds of her life. She could feel her own pulse, a frantic, panicked thing, throbbing in her wrist. She could feel a bead of sweat trickle down her temple.

The machine was silent. The light went out.

Failure.

Her mind screamed. It had failed. The alarm would sound. The doors would lock. It was over.

Then, a soft, green light pulsed from the scanner. And with a final, satisfying, and impossibly loud CLUNK, the lock on box 28714 disengaged.

Ziegler smiled his polite, grandfatherly smile. "There you are," he said. He opened the small, brass door. "I will leave you to your business. Please press the call button when you are finished."

He turned and walked out of the vault room, leaving Sloane alone with the fruits of her impossible, terrifying victory.

She was in.

Chapter 76: The Livia Key

The moment the heavy vault room door whispered shut, leaving her in the hushed, reverent silence, Sloane's knees almost gave out. The tension, the adrenaline, the sheer, terrifying weight of the performance—it all hit her at once in a dizzying wave. She leaned against the wall of cold, brass-fronted boxes, her breath coming in short, ragged gasps, her heart a wild, frantic drum against her ribs.

She had done it.

She had walked through the belly of the beast, passed through a gauntlet of locks and lasers and lies, and she had won. The feeling was a potent, intoxicating cocktail of terror and triumph.

She looked at her right hand. The latex prosthetic still clung like a ghostly, second skin. A brilliant, desperate gambit that had actually worked. She felt a surge of hysterical laughter bubble up in her chest, and she had to bite her lip to keep it from escaping.

Break a leg, she had told the young actress at the hemorrhoid commercial audition. She had just given the performance of a lifetime, and her only audience was a series of unblinking machines.

But there was no time for relief. The clock was ticking. She didn't know if the vault room was monitored. She had to assume it was. She had a role to play, even here. Helena Baros, the wealthy art dealer, reviewing her holdings.

She turned to the open safe deposit box. Number 28714. It was deeper than she expected, a long, narrow metal container. She pulled it out. It was surprisingly heavy.

She carried it over to a small, private viewing desk in the corner of the room, a discreet, elegant space with a single chair and a soft, overhead light. She sat down and placed the box on the polished wood surface.

Her hands were trembling now, the adrenaline crash beginning. She took a deep, steadying breath. *Finish the scene*, she told herself.

She lifted the lid of the box.

Her breath caught. Inside was not a chaotic jumble of files. It was Livia. Her mind. Her vengeance. All perfectly, meticulously organized.

On top was a single, slim, black hard drive. Labeled simply: ROOT.

Sloane wasted no time. She pulled the rugged black tablet from her bag—the one holding the encrypted file Manny had sacrificed himself to send.

She plugged Livia's drive into the tablet's USB port.

The screen flickered. A prompt appeared: BIOMETRIC HANDSHAKE REQUIRED.

Sloane leaned in. She hesitated, then reached up and removed the heavy, tortoise-shell glasses—the anchor of the Helena disguise. She needed the machine to see the mask behind the mask.

The tablet's camera scanned her face—Livia's face. Her heart hammered against her ribs.

A soft chime. IDENTITY VERIFIED.

Sloane didn't have to touch a key. Livia's ghost took the wheel.

Lines of green text scrolled rapidly across the black screen:

> HYDRA PROTOCOL: INITIATED> TARGET: [ENCRYPTED_PAYLOAD.DAT] LOCATED> KEY: [ROOT_SEED_INVERSE] VERIFIED> STATUS: INTEGRITY CONFIRMED> ARCHIVE: EXTRACTING... 100% [COMPLETE]> PAYLOAD SIZE: 115GB (EXPANDED)

The screen flashed, shifting from code to a stark, red interface.

Glitch's raw data met Livia's decryption key. The noise turned into words. The static turned into a smoking gun.

A progress bar appeared. DECRYPTING: DARK LEDGER...

0%... 5%...

Sloane watched it, her pulse racing. Every second felt like an hour. She was sitting in the fortress of Livia's choosing, marrying Livia's key to Glitch's ledger, weaponizing the evidence that would destroy Roman.

20%...

Footsteps in the hallway outside. She froze.

50%...

She forced herself to breathe. In through the nose. Hold. Release. The file was massive—years of transactions, communications, surveillance records.

85%...

A knock at the door.

"Frau Baros?" Herr Ziegler's voice.

Sloane stared at the screen. 92%.

"Just a moment," she called out, her voice steady, pure Helena. "I am just finishing up."

98%... 99%...

DECRYPTION COMPLETE.

The screen changed. Files appeared—thousands of them. Readable. Unlocked. Names. Dates. The order to execute Katya's killer. The bribes to the Consortium. All in a master folder, organized with Livia's meticulous precision.

Sloane reached out and gently disconnected Livia's hard drive. The metal was warm. She pressed it briefly to her lips—a silent prayer of thanks to the ghost who had just handed her a sword. She slipped it into the bottom of her Hermès bag.

Then, she reached into her bag and pulled out a slim, silver USB drive—a blank slate Nico had insisted she carry.

She plugged it into the tablet. Selected the decrypted master folder. Hit copy.

The progress bar appeared:

COPYING TO EXTERNAL DRIVE...

One hundred fifteen gigabytes of evidence—the smoking-gun contracts, surveillance footage, wiretap recordings. The Dark Ledger of Roman's crimes, extracted and exposed.

ESTIMATED TIME: 3 MINUTES.

Three minutes she didn't have.

She left the tablet working on the desk and turned back to the box. Next to where the drive had been sat a thick, leather-bound ledger. Handwritten. Sloane opened it. The pages were filled with Livia's elegant, looping script. It was a list of names, dates, and corresponding bank account numbers. A manual backup. An analog weapon in a digital war. Livia, the brilliant, paranoid cryptographer, had left nothing to chance.

Sloane slipped the ledger into her bag.

Beneath it was a single, sealed manila envelope. On the front, in Livia's hand, was one word: *Nico.*

Sloane's heart ached. This was it. His exit. The trust fund for his daughter. The letter Livia had written, the one that contained the final, devastating twist of her plan. The key to the real life he had promised himself, the life Livia had ordered him to live. She placed it reverently next to the ledger.

The box was not empty. There was one last item at the bottom.

A single, old Polaroid photograph.

Sloane picked it up. It was a self-portrait, taken in what looked like a hotel bathroom mirror. Livia. But not the glamorous, confident Livia from the videos. This woman was exhausted. Her hair was a mess. There were dark circles under her eyes. But her gaze, in the reflection, was a thing of pure, unyielding, defiant fire. It was the face of a soldier on the eve of her final battle.

Sloane turned the Polaroid over. On the back, in Livia's frantic, urgent handwriting, were two short lines.

The first read: *To whoever finds this: You are braver and stronger than I was. Finish it. — L.C.*

Sloane felt a chill, an intimate, ghostly connection to the dead woman who had predicted her, who had believed in her.

Then she read the second line, which looked like it had been added later, a final, wry, and heartbreaking piece of advice.

P.S. — Don't trust the pretty ones. Especially the ones with kind eyes.

Sloane let out a short, choked, tearful laugh. It was a direct, venomous, and perfect shot at Roman Lazar. Even from beyond the grave, Livia was sharp, funny, and utterly, brilliantly herself.

She pocketed the Polaroid, a sacred relic, a message from her ghost-commander. She slid the empty safe deposit box back into its slot and closed the small, brass door.

A soft chime came from the desk.

Sloane turned. The tablet screen glowed green.

TRANSFER COMPLETE.

Sloane disconnected the silver USB drive. She slipped it into the deep pocket of her wool trench coat, keeping it tight against her body—separate from the bag, just as Nico had asked. *'Separate the assets. If you lose the bag, you don't lose the war.'*

Then she slipped the tablet back into her Hermès bag, burying it alongside Livia's drive and the ledger beneath her silk scarf. The screen went dark. As far as she was concerned, their job was done.

She went into the small, attached private restroom—a ridiculously luxurious space of marble and gold. She carefully peeled the latex prosthetic from her right hand. The heating strips were cool now, inert. She flushed the ghostly skin and its embedded technology down the toilet in three separate pieces. Her own hand, pale and scarred, was a relief to see.

She pressed the call button.

***

Herr Ziegler returned a moment later, his face a mask of polite, professional calm. "Everything in order, Frau Baros?"

"Perfectly," Sloane said, her own voice a perfect, cool Helena. She stood up, her handbag heavy on her shoulder. "Thank you for your assistance."

"It is our pleasure," he said with a small bow.

He escorted her back through the labyrinth of security, through the titanium door, through the steel-grilled gate, back into the world of wood-paneled corridors. The journey out felt even more tense than the journey in. She had the weapon now. She was a smuggler, a thief, walking out of the dragon's lair with its heart in her handbag.

They reached his office. He held out his hand. "Until next time, Frau Baros."

"Until next time, Herr Ziegler," she said, shaking his hand, her own hand now bare.

She walked out of his office, down the silent corridor, through the unmarked door, and back into the vast, marble hall of the main bank.

The light from the tall, arched windows was blinding after the dim, quiet intimacy of the vault. She walked toward the main entrance, her heels clicking a steady, confident rhythm on the floor. *Don't run. Don't rush. You are Helena Baros. You have just concluded a piece of tedious but satisfactory business.*

She was ten feet from the heavy, bronze doors, ten feet from the sunlight, from Nico, from the first, real taste of victory.

And then she saw him.

He was standing just inside the entrance, pretending to read a newspaper. A man built like a concrete pillar, poured into a perfectly tailored gray suit that couldn't quite conceal his brutality.

Kovac Sokolov.

The ghost from the gala. Roman's enforcer.

How?

Her mind reeled. This bank. This day. This exact time.

Katarina? She had mapped the last-minute escape route. *Or Nico—*

No. Not Nico. But then—

Kovac lowered the newspaper, and his eyes—small, dark, and utterly devoid of light—met hers. He smiled. A slow, calm, and utterly terrifying smile.

He had not waited outside. He had been here all along. Watching. Waiting.

The trap had not been at Argentis. The trap had not been the vault.

The trap was here.

***

Nico's voice was a sharp, urgent hiss in her ear. "Sloane. He's inside. I see him. Abort. Abort now. There's a service exit to your left. Go. Now."

But it was too late. Kovac took a step forward, blocking her path to the door. Two other men, big, square-shouldered men in dark suits, materialized from the crowd, flanking him.

"Miss Devereaux," Kovac said, his voice a silken, conversational murmur. "What a remarkable coincidence to see you here."

Sloane's mind went white with a pure, animal panic. It was over. After all of it—the escape, the chase, the perfect, impossible heist—it was all for nothing. He had just been waiting for her to do the hard work for him.

She clutched her handbag, Livia's key a heavy, sacred weight inside.

Kovac's gaze dropped to the bag, his smile widening. "It seems you have something that belongs to me," he said.

He took another step toward her. His men moved with him.

And then, the world exploded.

The great, bronze doors of the bank burst open. Nico. He was not a ghost anymore. He was a storm. He moved with a brutal, violent grace, a blur of motion.

He took out the first of Kovac's men with a single, precise shot to the chest, the sound of the silenced gunshot a soft, ugly cough in the vast, echoing hall.

Chaos erupted. People screamed, ducking for cover. Alarms began to blare, a high, piercing shriek.

Kovac's face, for the first time, showed a flicker of surprise, of annoyance. This was not part of his perfect, elegant plan.

His second man drew a weapon, a sleek black pistol, and fired wildly in Nico's direction. Nico was already moving, using a marble pillar for cover, but the shot was lucky. Sloane saw him flinch, a sharp, almost imperceptible intake of breath, as the bullet tore a furrow across his left shoulder.

He didn't slow down. He returned fire, two quick, controlled shots, and the second man went down, a look of shocked surprise on his face.

"Sloane! Run!" Nico yelled, his voice a raw, commanding bark, betraying none of the pain she knew he had to be feeling.

Sloane was already running. She sprinted for the doors, for the sunlight, for the chaos of the street.

Kovac did not chase her. He simply stood there, a still point in the chaos, his eyes locked on Nico, memorizing, analyzing. Then he turned, melting back into the screaming crowd, a ghost disappearing back into the machine.

Sloane burst out onto the Bahnhofstrasse, into a world that had suddenly gone mad. People were screaming, running. The sound of the bank alarm was a frantic, terrifying heartbeat.

A black car, a powerful Audi, screeched to a halt at the curb in front of her, its door flying open. Nico. He had taken out Kovac's men and gotten to the car in less than ten seconds, a dark stain already spreading on the shoulder of his gray sweater.

She dove into the passenger seat, not even waiting for the door to close. "Go!" she screamed.

Nico slammed the accelerator. The tires shrieked as the Audi shot out into the traffic, a gray bullet fleeing a war zone.

In the rearview mirror, Sloane saw Kovac walk out of the bank, flanked by two new men who had appeared from nowhere. He stood on the steps, watching them go, a still, calm point in a world of chaos. He didn't run. He didn't scream for a car. He simply raised his phone, his thumb tapping the screen with clinical calm. He wasn't calling for backup. He was recording their exit—specifically, the rear of the Audi.

"He got the plate," Sloane gasped, clutching the tablet to her chest.

Nico didn't flinch, even as he wrenched the wheel to avoid a passing tram, his jaw tight with the effort of ignoring the fire in his shoulder. "One crisis at a time. How did it go with the Dark Ledger?"

Sloane pulled the tablet from her bag. The screen was glowing.

"It worked," she breathed.

"Status?" Nico asked, his eyes darting from the rearview to the narrow street ahead.

"Decrypted," she said. "The Seed unlocked Manny's file. It's all readable. We have the gun and the bullets."

They had the weapon. But they had also just declared open war in the heart of Zurich. Nico was bleeding. And the hunter was now in plain sight.

Chapter 77: The World Will Know

The Audi screamed through the orderly, terrified streets of Zurich, a gray shark in a school of startled fish. Nico drove with a focused, feral intensity, his hands a blur on the wheel, his eyes constantly moving, scanning, analyzing. He was no longer the silent, watchful sentinel. He was a combat operator, his training a visceral, instinctive thing that had taken over his body.

Sloane was a ball of pure, raw adrenaline. She was crouched low in the passenger seat, her heart a wild, frantic drum against her ribs. The handbag containing Livia's vengeance was clutched in her lap like a shield.

"Are they following us?" she gasped, daring a glance out the back window. The streets were a chaos of screeching trams and scattering pedestrians.

"Not yet," Nico said, his voice a low, hard growl, his face pale under a sheen of sweat. "But they will be. He won't let this go. He can't." He took a sharp, squealing turn into a narrow side street. "We have to get off the grid. Now."

He drove for another ten minutes, a dizzying, labyrinthine journey through the city's ancient, winding alleys, a route he had clearly memorized from the maps in the bunker. He finally pulled the car into a small, dark, underground parking garage and killed the engine. The sudden silence was a deafening, ringing thing after the chaos of the chase.

They were safe. For a moment.

Nico didn't check his wound first. He stumbled out of the driver's side, his face pale under a sheen of cold sweat. He leaned heavily against the Audi's rear quarter panel, then reached down toward the license plate.

With a sharp, plastic *snap*, he peeled back a thin, magnetized vinyl strip.

Sloane let out a sharp, jagged gasp, her eyes widening as the Zurich registration she'd memorized during the chase simply... vanished. It was like watching a face being peeled away.

"Nico?" she whispered, her voice a mix of shock and dawning awe. "How many masks did you give this car?"

He didn't look up, his fingers already dropping the fake strip onto the greasy concrete. He kicked it deep under a dumpster with a grunt of effort. "Only two," he rasped, his voice tight with the fire in his shoulder. "The one Roman saw, and the one that's going to keep us invisible."

He turned to her, his breath hitching as the adrenaline began to ebb. "How did it go with the Dark Ledger?"

Sloane retrieved the silver USB drive from her pocket, the metal cool and heavy in her trembling hand. "We have it," she breathed, showing it to him. "All decrypted, and ready to upload."

"Good," Nico said, his voice a raw, exhausted thing. "Now we have to make sure the world sees them without getting us killed first." He looked at her. "Are you okay?"

"I think so," she said. Then she saw it. The dark stain on the shoulder of his gray sweater. "Nico," she whispered. "You're hit."

"It's nothing," he lied. "We need to get to the second floor. The apartment is clear."

***

The safe house was a small, nondescript apartment in a working-class neighborhood on the outskirts of the city, another of Livia's contingencies. It was clean, spartan, and utterly forgettable.

The first thing they did was tend to Nico's wound.

"It's a graze," he lied, his voice tight with pain as Sloane helped him out of his jacket.

"Stop talking," she ordered, her voice a firm, steady thing she didn't recognize as her own. She pointed to a kitchen chair. "Sit."

He sat. The graze was not a graze. It was a deep, ugly furrow, ploughed through the muscle of his shoulder where one of Kovac's men's bullets had torn through. The blood was welling up, dark and thick.

Sloane opened the military-grade first-aid kit, her hands surprisingly steady. The actress who had learned field medicine for a role was now a medic in a real war. She cleaned the wound with antiseptic wipes. He hissed in pain, a sharp, involuntary intake of breath, but he did not make another sound, his eyes locked on her face.

As she worked in the quiet, dim apartment, her fingers brushing against his skin, the air between them became thick with a new, different kind of tension. This was not the adrenaline of the chase. It was the quiet, profound intimacy of two people who had survived a battle together, who had seen the raw, vulnerable truth of each other. She could feel the hard, coiled muscle of his shoulder under her fingers. She could smell the scent of his skin, a mixture of sweat, iron, and something else, something uniquely, elementally him.

When she finished applying the sterile dressing, her fingers lingered for a moment on his uninjured shoulder.

"Thank you," he said, his voice a low, rough murmur.

"We take care of each other," she replied, the words a quiet, simple vow.

He nodded, a slow, painful movement.

"Now," he said, his voice a grim, determined thing, "we finish it. Get the laptop. We force the upload through the hardline."

But before they could breathe, the encrypted satellite phone Katarina had given them buzzed harshly on the table. A single, encrypted text.

Nico snatched it up. Sloane watched as his face went rigid, all the color draining from it. The look in his eyes was one of raw, catastrophic defeat.

"What is it?" Sloane asked, her own heart seizing. "Did they track us?"

He handed her the phone without a word. The message was from Katarina, a timestamp from two minutes ago.

The signing is done. Moved up to early this morning. Go live in a week. Damian has outlived his usefulness. Roman is en route to seize the Core personally. Prepare for the worst. I'm sorry.

The words hit Sloane like a physical blow.

After everything—the escape, the firefight, the heist, the successful decryption—they were too late. Roman had won. He had seen their move coming and simply executed the deal before the news cycle could catch him.

Sloane sank onto a rickety kitchen chair, the triumph of the morning curdling into a black, sickening horror. "So it's over," she whispered. "He won. The governments have the tech. Even if the scandal breaks tomorrow, they already own the machine. They'll just bury the story and keep the weapon."

Nico stared out the window, his wounded shoulder a dark stain, his posture that of a soldier surveying a battle he has already lost. "Worse than over. The deal is done. Panopticon is sold. We're not just fugitives from Lazar anymore. We're fugitives from twelve of the world's most powerful intelligence agencies. And they now own the most powerful surveillance system ever built."

It was hopeless. They had the evidence, but the crime had already been committed and sanctioned at the highest levels.

It was in that moment of absolute despair that Sloane Devereaux, the counterfeit, the ghost, the survivor, found the last, hard, diamond-like core of her rage. She stood up, her movement so abrupt it startled Nico.

"No," she said. The word was quiet, but it was filled with a cold, terrifying certainty. "The papers are signed. But the system isn't deployed yet."

Nico turned, a flicker of disbelief in his eyes. "Sloane, the deal is done. The Twelve own it now. Even if we—"

"But the system isn't live yet," she pressed.

"No," he admitted. "The official integration schedule is one week. But I know Roman. He won't wait. He'll want to demonstrate full, operational control to his new partners as soon as possible to solidify his position. He'll have the primary systems handed over and the network locked down within forty-eight hours. We don't have a week. We have two days. At most."

"Two days... then we go to Argentis," she interrupted, her eyes blazing with a new, wild, and utterly insane fire. "Right now. We can't undo the sale. But we can destroy what they just bought. We burn Panopticon to the ground before they can deploy it. Make their five-trillion-dollar asset worthless. Contracts signed for a system that no longer exists."

Nico stared at her, the sheer, audacious brilliance of the gambit dawning on his face. They couldn't stop the deal. But they could make the five-trillion-dollar asset they were signing for cease to exist, in real time.

He looked at the laptop where they were about to send the evidence, then back at her. "The data upload..."

"...exposes Roman as a criminal while the world leaders are in a room with him," Sloane finished. "And the attack on the Core destroys the product they're buying. It's a two-front war. We make the deal collapse from the inside out and the outside in, all at the same time."

The despair in Nico's eyes was replaced by a dangerous, feral light. He looked at the clock. 11:15 AM.

"We have maybe two hours," he said, his voice a low growl.

"Then we'd better hurry," Sloane replied.

Chapter 78: Livia's Gift

He sat at the rickety kitchen table, the matte-black, hardened laptop from the bunker open in front of him. "Give me the drive," Nico said.

Sloane pulled the silver USB drive from her pocket—the backup Nico had given her at the hotel. She plugged it into the laptop.

"Mounting the drive," Nico muttered, his fingers flying across the keyboard. "Files are clean. Launching Livia's distribution script. It's pre-configured to route through the dark web relays she set up."

The laptop screen flashed a stark, command-line interface:

> MOUNTING: /VOL/EXTERNAL_01> STATUS: READ/WRITE> EXECUTING: HYDRA_BROADCAST.EXE> TARGET LIST: GLOBAL_MEDIA_TIER_1 [LOADED]> AWAITING CONFIRMATION... [PRESS ENTER]

Nico hit the enter key on the laptop. A new window opened. BROADCASTING TO GLOBAL MEDIA...

0%...

The screen flickered. Lists of recipients scrolled by at blinding speed. BBC. The New York Times. Der Spiegel. Al Jazeera. Interpol. The Hague.

"It's going," Nico said softly.

15%...

The satellite phone buzzed, a harsh, jarring sound in the quiet room. An unknown number.

Sloane looked at Nico. He nodded. She answered.

"Hello, Sloane."

The voice was calm. Amused. Roman Lazar.

Ice formed in Sloane's stomach. Katarina had sworn this phone was secure. Military-grade. Untraceable. There was only one way he could have this number.

Katarina.

Was the "escape" just another level of the maze? Was the "ally" just another warden holding the door open only to slam it shut?

"Congratulations on your escape," he said. "It was... impressive. A well-executed, if brutishly loud, operation."

"It's over, Roman," Sloane said, her voice cold. "The files are broadcasting."

"Oh, Sloane," he sighed. "You still think you're playing a game of chess. This has never been about the board. It's always been about the players."

"What do you want?"

"I have a proposal. A final offer. I have Mr. Goldman's exoneration ready to file. All it takes is one phone call to my lawyer, and your friend is a free man."

The offer was a punch to the gut. Manny's freedom.

"The deal is simple. You destroy the drive. You walk away with the hundred million dollars. Everyone lives."

"And you?" Sloane asked. "You just... keep going?"

"The machine lives. The world needs a shepherd, Sloane. Even if it doesn't know it."

His voice dropped, becoming intimate. "Join me, and you will have a seat at the table. Defy me, and you will be just another piece of chaos—another problem requiring cleanup."

It was the ultimate temptation. Money. Freedom. And Manny's life.

She looked at Nico. He was watching her, his face a mask of pain. The choice was hers.

She looked at the screen. 18%. It was moving too slowly.

And then, the realization hit her with blinding clarity.

Roman wasn't calling to trace a signal. He was calling to break her will. He needed her to surrender, to validate his worldview, to admit that his order was inevitable. It was a mind game.

Two can play that game, Sloane thought.

There was no deal. There never was. If she destroyed the drive, Manny would suffer anyway. They all would. The only way out was through.

"You're right about one thing, Roman," she said, her voice low. "It is about the players. And you've misunderstood your opponent."

"Have I?" he asked. "Enlighten me."

"You think you're a god, building a new world order," she said, her voice dropping to a whisper of pure, distilled ice. "But I've seen the files, Roman. All of them. I know exactly what you are."

She paused, letting the silence stretch.

"Vienna. 1976. The fire. The accelerants in the master bedroom. You told the shrink you heard them arguing about leaving you. You didn't survive that fire, Roman. You started it."

The silence on the other end was absolute. Glacial.

"And the empire?" she pressed. "The 'genius investor'? You built it on corpses. The fifty million dollars in stolen art your father looted from the Kremlin. You didn't build a business, Roman. You fenced a crime scene."

"Careful, Sloane," Roman whispered. The amusement was gone.

"And Katya," she said, the name landing like a slap. "You think building a machine that sees everything will absolve you? You think if you watch the whole world, you won't have to watch her fall again?"

"That is enough." His voice was shaking with rage.

"No, I'm not done," Sloane said. "Because I know about the music box. The Serpent's Heart. The one that plays Brahms. That's not a keepsake, Roman. It's a trophy. You took it from your mother's room before you lit the match."

She delivered the final verdict.

"You aren't a visionary. You're just a scared little boy who burned down his house because mommy and daddy didn't want him anymore."

For a second, there was silence.

Then, a raw, guttural noise came through the phone. It was the sound of a caged animal, a god stripped of his divinity.

"Goodbye, Ms. Devereaux."

The line went dead.

"He hung up," Sloane said, her hand shaking.

Nico looked at the screen. "22%... Come on..."

Suddenly, the screen flashed red.

CONNECTION TERMINATED.

"He found us," Nico yelled. "He's jamming the signal."

Then, the laptop screen turned a violent, washing-out white. Text scrolled frantically across the command line.

> INTRUSION DETECTED.> EXTERNAL VOLUME TARGETED.> EXECUTING REMOTE WIPE...

"No!" Nico lunged for the USB drive, yanking it from the port.

He stared at the silver stick in his hand. Then he plugged it back in. The screen flashed:

> VOLUME CORRUPT. NO DATA FOUND.

"He fried it," Nico whispered, the horror dawning on him. "He sent a logic bomb back down the line. The drive is blank. It's gone. All of it."

She stared at Katarina's satellite phone. "He called us. How did he even have this number?"

"I don't know," Nico said, his voice raw. "But that's not how he found us. Tracking an encrypted satellite phone is impossible—even for him."

He pointed at the laptop. "The upload was the flare. We thought the hardline was a dark node, but Roman has the Consortium now. They monitored every high-bandwidth encrypted stream in Zurich and traced this one straight to our building."

"So the phone call—"

"Was him gloating. He already knew where we were from the upload. He was just rubbing it in."

The realization was absolute. He slammed the laptop shut and yanked the battery.

"We have to move," Nico said. "They'll be here any moment. We'll call for the jet from a public phone. Donaueschingen is an hour-plus north. If we make the border, we disappear."

"No," Sloane said. "Running is not a victory. We have no evidence left. We can't expose him."

She looked at Nico, her eyes hard.

"The digital bomb failed. So we become a physical one."

"Argentis," Nico breathed. "South."

"We don't just expose him," she said. "We end him. Since the world won't do it for us."

Nico stared at her. The soldier in him was screaming that it was a suicide mission. But the man, the father, the ghost who had been hunting this monster for a year, knew she was right.

He grabbed the laptop. He hesitated over the manila envelope—Livia's final gift—then shoved it deep into his jacket. "Then we drive."

They were heading south. Back to the mountain. Back to the fire.

Chapter 79: The Siege

The drive from Zurich was a blur of gray highway and silent tension. They made one stop—at the ravine east of Küssnacht—to retrieve the waterproof bag Nico had buried in the loose rocks.

Armed, they drove the Audi up the winding mountain road.

They didn't take the main approach. Roman's perimeter security would be active, but his eyes were turned inward, focused on the Core and the cleanup. He expected his enemies to be halfway to the border, not driving back into the fire.

They stopped five minutes short of the main gate, driving the car deep into a dense patch of pines to hide it.

Nico killed the engine. He reached into the back seat and grabbed the heavy-duty waterproof bag.

He cracked the seal. Inside lay the two Glock 19s, dry and cold.

He handed the first one to Sloane, butt-first. Then he took the second for himself, racking the slide with a sharp, metallic clack.

"Load and make ready," he whispered.

Sloane didn't hesitate. She seated the magazine with a solid click and racked the slide. The motion was fluid, practiced—muscle memory taking over where fear tried to freeze her. The weight was familiar now. A heavy, solid presence in her hand.

"On foot from here," Nico said.

They moved through the woods, shadows slipping through the tree line, untangling the back roads until they reached the rusted corrugated fence of the upper service intake.

The tunnel was exactly where Nico knew it would be—a forgotten artery in the mountain's stone heart, hidden behind a curtain of ivy. It was a dark, narrow hole that smelled of damp earth and deep, ancient silence.

Nico went first, a ghost melting into the darkness. Sloane followed, the cold, rough stone scraping against her back.

They moved in a tense, claustrophobic crouch for what felt like a mile, the only sound the soft scuff of their boots and their own ragged, controlled breaths.

The tunnel ended at a heavy, steel maintenance hatch. Nico produced a small, specialized tool, and with a series of soft, precise clicks, the lock disengaged. He pushed the hatch open a crack, his eye pressed to the opening, scanning.

"We're in," he whispered. "Sublevel three. Utility corridor. West wing. Clear for now."

He slipped through the opening, and Sloane followed, emerging into a narrow, brightly lit corridor of polished concrete and exposed conduit. The air was cold, sterile, and hummed with the faint, almost subliminal vibration of immense power. They were inside the machine.

"The Core is this way," Nico murmured, his voice a low, urgent command. He was no longer the quiet sentinel. He was a combat operator in his element, his movements fluid, certain, and deadly. "The schematics show a primary access route and a secondary ventilation shaft. The main route will be guarded. We take the shaft."

They moved like shadows through the labyrinthine service corridors of Argentis's underbelly, a world of humming servers, hissing pipes, and stark, fluorescent light that was a universe away from the curated, sunlit luxury of the floors above.

They reached the ventilation access point, a grilled hatch set high on a wall. Nico gave Sloane a boost, and she climbed up, her fingers finding purchase on the cold metal. He followed, pulling himself up with a silent, economic grace.

The shaft was a tight, dark, metal box, a claustrophobic's nightmare. They crawled on their hands and knees, the sound of their movements echoing in the enclosed space. Below them, through the metal grilles, they could see into the main corridors of the sublevel.

They saw them almost immediately. Lazar's men. Three of them, dressed in black tactical gear, armed with short-barreled rifles, moving in a tight, professional formation. An occupying force.

They were heading for the Sanctum.

***

Damian Crestwell sat in his study, a glass of Macallan 1926 in his trembling hand. He was a king in a fallen kingdom.

But the enemy wasn't at the gates. The enemy was in the room.

On the desk before him lay the black Moleskine notebook. Sloane had left it. A final, silent explanation for why she had run.

He had read it. All of it. But he kept staring at the entry dated December 20th. A week before they left for Naples.

"Damian presented it to me as a plea... He has no idea he's the one leading me into the trap."

The words blurred through the tears he couldn't stop. He remembered that night. He remembered begging her to come on the yacht. He remembered feeling so proud that he had fixed their marriage.

He hadn't fixed anything. He had walked her into the slaughterhouse.

He looked at the empty chair across the room where Roman used to sit. The kind eyes. The mentorship. It was all a long con. Roman hadn't just killed Livia; he had used Damian's love to do it.

He set the glass down. The grief was gone, replaced by a cold, mathematical clarity.

The equation was flawed. And it was time to wipe the board.

He heard a sound. The soft, electronic chime of his study door opening. He looked up, expecting Katarina.

It was Roman Lazar.

He stood in the doorway, a dark, calm figure, flanked by two of his silent, black-clad soldiers. He was not smiling. His face was a mask of cold, serene fury.

"Damian," Lazar said, his voice a quiet, dangerous thing. "You have been a profound disappointment."

"It's over, Roman," Damian whispered, his voice a dry, broken rasp.

"Over?" Lazar gave a small, incredulous laugh. "My dear, naive boy. Nothing is ever over. It simply... changes management."

He walked into the room, his movements the slow, deliberate glide of a predator.

"Your muse has fled, Damian. You are spiraling. The Consortium deal is signed, the funds are in escrow, and I cannot risk a grieving widower damaging a five-trillion-dollar asset in a fit of melancholy."

He stopped in front of Damian's desk.

"I am taking the Core. Not in partnership. In totality. We are going down there to transfer the root administrative privileges to my biometric signature. Then I will lock you out of your own creation. For its own protection."

Damian looked at him. He didn't argue. He didn't fight. He let the exhaustion wash over him, hiding the sharp, cold clarity beneath.

"You want the machine," Damian said softly, standing up. He didn't look at Roman; he looked at the empty space where a life used to be. "I lost her twice, Roman. Both times for the machine. Take it. It's yours."

Lazar smiled, the sound of deep, paternal satisfaction. He had expected a tantrum; he got surrender. "A wise choice. Do not worry. The machine will be in safe hands."

He gestured to his men. "Escort him."

***

From the ventilation shaft above the main corridor, Sloane and Nico watched as Lazar's men escorted Damian toward the elevator that led down to the Core. Damian was not fighting. He was a ghost, a hollowed-out man being led to the final sacrifice.

"Roman's seizing the core," Nico whispered, his voice a low, hard thing. "He's forcing an admin transfer to lock Damian out."

"We can't let him take it," Sloane said, her hand tightening on the grip of her Glock.

"We won't," he replied. "They'll have two men on Lazar, and one in the control room. We have the element of surprise." He looked at her, his eyes dark and serious in the dim light of the shaft. "You ready for this?"

She thought of Manny. Of Livia. Of the gun in her hand. "Yes," she said.

They moved quickly, silently, crawling through the shaft until they were directly over the entrance to the Core. They could hear the voices below them.

"Initiate the Root Transfer protocol," Lazar's voice commanded. "Sign it over, Damian."

They had seconds.

Nico kicked out the grille beneath them. It fell with a loud, metallic clang. He dropped to the floor below, landing in a perfect, silent crouch, his weapon already up. Sloane followed, her own landing a clumsy, adrenaline-fueled thud.

The scene in front of them was a tableau of controlled chaos. Damian was at the keyboard; Lazar stood over him. One of Lazar's men was monitoring the console. The other stood guard, his rifle now swinging toward them.

Nico fired twice, two quick, controlled shots. The guard at the door went down, a look of shocked surprise on his face.

The man at the console spun around, drawing a sidearm. Sloane raised the Glock, just as Nico had taught her. Her finger found the trigger. She had the high center mass. She had the breath control. Everything was ready.

But she couldn't pull it.

The man was young—her own age, maybe less. His tactical vest—thick with ceramic plates—and practiced stance marked him as one of Roman's handpicked elite, a soldier who cost six figures a year. But Sloane didn't see the operative; she saw the man beneath the ceramic plates. She saw the frantic, desperate pulse in his neck. She saw the way his hand shook—a micro-tremor of raw mortality that no amount of conditioning could kill. He wasn't a target. He was a person. A human being with a life, a family, and a name she'd never know.

The hesitation cost her a second. A heartbeat of humanity in a room built for monsters.

It was almost enough to kill them both.

Nico's shot cracked past her shoulder, the heat of the muzzle blast stinging her cheek. The round took the man dead-center in the forehead, a surgical strike that bypassed the ceramic plates entirely. His head snapped back, the light in his eyes vanishing instantly.

He didn't stagger. He simply disconnected. He hit the server rack with the heavy, hollow thud of a machine being unplugged and slid to the floor, leaving a dark, final smear on the metal.

Nico grabbed her arm, his grip iron, hauling her back from the abyss of her own conscience. "Sloane. Move. Now."

She stared at the body on the ground—the man Nico had killed because she couldn't. The smoke from Nico's gun felt like a physical weight on her chest.

"I couldn't—" she started, her voice a broken whisper.

"Later," Nico said, his voice hard but not unkind. "We process later. Right now, we survive."

He didn't wait for her to answer. He lunged for the stairs leading up to the command platform, and Sloane followed on wooden legs, her boots ringing hollow against the metal grating. They crested the top of the stairs, weapons raised, the air here smelling of ozone and the heavy, electric scent of a god's funeral.

Nico fanned left, cutting off the exit. Sloane took the center.

***

It was down to the four of them. Sloane and Nico, their guns up, a fragile, desperate alliance. And on the platform, Damian, the broken king, and Roman Lazar, the cornered god.

Lazar did not look surprised. He did not look scared. He looked... disappointed.

"So predictable," he sighed, shaking his head. "Violence. The last, desperate argument of the unimaginative." He looked at Sloane, and his eyes were full of a strange, sad pity. "I had hoped for more from you. I thought you, of all people, would understand. I didn't pick you just for the resemblance, Sloane. I picked you for the damage. I needed someone broken enough to make Damian believe he was being healed. You were the only one capable of selling the lie because you wanted it to be true just as badly as he did."

"You're a monster," Sloane said, her voice shaking but clear, the gun steady in her hands. "And your reign is over."

"My reign?" Lazar laughed, a soft, genuine, and utterly chilling sound. "Ms. Devereaux, my reign is not a thing that can be overthrown. It is an idea. An algorithm. You think you have won because you leaked a few files? You think you can stop the future with a bullet? I am the future." He gestured to the humming, silent servers around them. "This... this is just a body. A vessel. The idea will survive long after this hardware is melted slag."

"Then we'll burn that one down, too," Nico growled, his gun trained on Lazar's chest.

"Perhaps you will," Lazar conceded with a small, gracious nod. "But the need for order, for control... it is fundamental. In the end, the world will beg for a man like me. You have not saved them. You have merely... delayed the inevitable."

He looked at Damian, who was standing beside him, his face a pale, catatonic mask of terror.

"Transfer the admin rights, Damian," Lazar said, his voice a soft, reasonable command. "I promised myself I would never be blind again. I built this to see the chaos before it strikes. Now give me the eyes."

Damian did not move. He was a statue, frozen in the crossfire of his own failed morality.

"Damian," Sloane said, her voice a low, urgent plea. "Don't do it. It's not over. You can still make a choice. The right choice. For her. For Livia."

The name was a key. It unlocked something in the frozen, terrified man. He looked at Sloane, at the woman who wore his wife's face, who was now fighting his wife's war. He looked at Lazar, the man who had been his mentor, his patron, his devil. He looked at the dead men on the floor. At the blood. At the ruin of his beautiful, perfect machine.

And for the first time in two decades, he saw the truth with a clarity that was both liberating and utterly devastating.

"She tried to tell me," he said quietly, his voice no longer shaking, but filled with a profound, hollow calm. "Livia. She showed me the truth, and I called her paranoid. Because I needed to believe in the beautiful lie."

He looked at Roman, at the kind eyes that had been his anchor for twenty years. "I loved a vision, not the truth. And everyone who tried to save me paid the price for my blindness."

"Damian," Roman warned, tightening his grip. "Don't be dramatic. Transfer the admin rights. *Now.*"

"I worshipped you, Roman," Damian whispered, the fight draining out of him. Tears spilled over, unchecked. "For twelve years, I gave you everything. My mind. My life. I built this... thing... because I believed you when you said we were saving the world."

He looked up at Roman, his eyes full of a child's shattered trust.

"And my reward was a lie," he said softly. "You killed the only woman I ever loved. And you made me thank you for a counterfeit."

Damian turned to the console, his fingers moving across the keyboard in a blur of motion, muscle memory overriding fear. He wasn't accessing the transfer protocol. He was accessing something else. Something deeper.

Lazar moved closer, leaning over Damian's shoulder. His eyes scanned the terminal.

And then he saw it.

At the top of the screen:

CHAOS PROTOCOL - INITIALIZING

The code was a strobe of frantic logic across the monitor. Recursive loops were already devouring the kernel. The system's foundations were hemorrhaging into pure entropy.

Not a transfer.

A detonation.

"Damian, stop!" Lazar's voice was ice and rage. "What are you—"

Red warnings flashed across the screens.

"I've thought about nothing else," Damian said quietly, his fingers never slowing. A sad, broken smile crossed his face. "Iago had Othello. You had me. Same play. Different stage."

Roman lunged for the keyboard.

Damian was faster.

He entered the second sequence. His voice rose to a shout, shattering his calm facade. "You kept me in a trance for twelve years! Playing the benevolent mentor. The friend. You controlled every decision. And you conned me into thinking I was the one choosing!"

He glared at the man he had worshipped, his eyes burning with absolute, final rage. "No more!"

He pressed enter.

Roman's hand closed on empty air.

For a single, crystalline second, nothing happened.

Then the world exploded into chaos.

Alarms shrieked—a high, piercing wail that echoed off the concrete walls. The gunmetal gray servers, which had hummed with quiet, godlike power just moments before, began to scream, their cooling fans whining in futile, high-pitched protest against the rising heat. Red warning lights strobed across the room, painting everything in a hellish, pulsating glow.

On every screen, the same message appeared in blood-red text:

CHAOS PROTOCOL INITIATEDTHERMAL SAFEGUARDS: DISABLEDCOOLING SYSTEMS: OFFLINEVOLTAGE REGULATORS: MAX

Damian hadn't just turned it off. He had commanded the quantum core to consume itself. He had bypassed the limiters, flooding the delicate circuits with a lethal surge of raw, unregulated current. And with zero cooling to check the rising heat, he was forcing the machine to commit suicide.

Sloane stared at the screens, Livia's journal entry flashing in her mind: *"Chaos is the one thing the patron cannot stand."*

Damian hadn't just built a bomb. He had built poetic justice.

The machine was dying.

And Roman Lazar, god-king of the Panopticon, finally understood that he'd lost.

His face twisted into something inhuman—pure, unrestrained fury stripped of all pretense of civility. He moved. Not toward the console to save his legacy.

Toward Damian.

Revenge. Even now. Even at the end of the world.

Nico's shot cracked through the chaos, but Lazar was already moving.

"No!" Sloane screamed.

And the siege became a war.

Chapter 80: The Kill Switch

The Core was dying, and it was taking the world with it.

Sloane stood on the elevated platform overlooking the vast underground chamber, her Glock heavy in her hand, her heart a frantic drum against her ribs. Below her, the monolithic black server racks—Panopticon's digital heart—shrieked and wailed like dying gods. Damian had done it. He'd triggered the kill switch, initiated a cascade failure that would corrupt every backup, every redundancy, every tentacle of the surveillance machine his genius had built. But Roman Lazar, architect of nightmares, was not a man who accepted defeat gracefully.

And now Damian was going to pay for his defiance.

***

The Core was a symphony of destruction. Alarms shrieked, a high, piercing wail that echoed off the concrete walls and burrowed into Sloane's skull. The monolithic black servers, which had hummed with a quiet, godlike power just moments before, were now screaming, their cooling fans whining in a futile, high-pitched protest against the rising heat. Red warning lights strobed across the room, painting everything in a hellish, pulsating glow. The air was thick with the smell of burning electronics and ozone, an acrid chemical tang that coated the back of her throat.

The machine was dying.

But not fast enough.

Sloane's eyes tracked the scene below. Nico stood near the main entrance, twenty feet to her left, his weapon raised. Damian was at the central console, his fingers still on the keyboard.

And then Lazar bridged the distance.

He moved with the speed of a striking serpent. Not toward safety. Not toward escape. Toward vengeance. He was reclaiming the hostage.

His hand shot out, clamping onto the front of Damian's shirt, yanking the taller, thinner man into his personal space. The move was so fluid, so practiced, that it bypassed the reaction time of the two professionals in the room.

Nico's shot rang out, aimed with surgical precision for Lazar's center mass. But the target had already vanished behind the human shield of his own architect. The round went wide, striking one of the server racks with a deafening, metallic clang. Sparks erupted in a shower of orange and white, adding to the chaos.

"No!" Sloane screamed, her own gun wavering, her finger frozen on the trigger. She couldn't shoot. Not with Damian in the way.

Roman's free hand swept to the small of his back, producing a sleek, stainless Sig Sauer that had been hidden beneath his jacket. Lazar had Damian in a choke-hold now, his arm locked across the younger man's throat. The gun—gleaming silver, Swiss-made, and terrifyingly elegant—was pressed to Damian's temple. Damian's face was pale, his eyes wide with shock and the terrible clarity of a man who'd just made a choice he couldn't take back.

"Predictable, Mr. Sorrento," Lazar hissed, his face a mask of cold, controlled fury. His kind eyes, those warm, grandfatherly eyes that had smiled at her across a hundred dinners, were now flat and dead as a shark's. "So brutally, predictably violent."

He began to back away, dragging Damian with him, toward a small, unmarked service door at the back of the platform. His steps were careful, measured, even now maintaining the control that had made him a god in this digital kingdom.

"It's over, Lazar," Nico growled, his weapon steady now, tracking the small sliver of Lazar's head that was visible behind Damian's. His voice was ice and steel. "There's no way out."

"There is always a way out," Lazar replied, his voice a low, confident murmur, even in the face of absolute defeat. He was a king, even in the ruins of his kingdom. "This particular vessel may be sinking. But I am a very strong swimmer." His eyes flicked past them, toward the distant exit, toward a future only he could see. "The idea will find a new home. Another Damian. Another machine. The world needs what I built. They just don't know it yet."

The arrogance was breathtaking. The machine was dying around him, his empire crumbling, his secrets about to spill into the world, and still he believed he would escape. Still he believed he was inevitable.

He reached the service door and fumbled with the keypad, his arm still locked around Damian's throat. His fingers moved quickly, muscle memory overriding panic. The keypad beeped. A light turned green.

Sloane felt her heart stop. He was going to get away. He was going to drag Damian through that door, use him as a bargaining chip, escape into the network of tunnels that honeycombed the mountain, and vanish. And they would never find him. Men like Roman Lazar didn't go to prison. They went to ground. They resurfaced years later with new names, new fortunes, new machines.

Unless someone stopped him.

Damian, who had been a limp, catatonic doll in Lazar's grip, suddenly came to life.

He looked at Sloane across the strobing, smoke-filled chamber. His eyes found hers, and in that moment, she saw everything.

"Livia..." he whispered, his voice a raw, broken thing. He looked at her as if he were finally seeing the woman instead of the mask. "She would have hated you."

Sloane flinched, the words a knife to the chest.

"Too angry," Damian continued, a faint, sad smile touching his lips even with the gun pressed to his head. "Too loud. Too... alive. She was a masterpiece of control, Sloane. A Stradivarius that only played the notes on the page. But you—" His voice caught. "You were never afraid to be human. To be messy. To feel things."

The alarm wailed. The servers screamed. The world was ending around them in fire and chaos.

"She would have hated you because you are the version of her she was too afraid to be," Damian said, his eyes shining with tears and a terrifying, final clarity. "But she would have been proud of you for having the courage to burn down the cage she only knew how to decorate. And I..."

He held her gaze across the impossible distance, and in that final, shared look, she saw the full, tragic weight of his impossible love.

"I think I love you more."

"Damian, no—" Sloane's voice broke. She knew what he was going to do. She could see it in his eyes, in the set of his jaw, in the way his body tensed.

"Enough!" Lazar snarled, tightening his grip, the gun digging harder into Damian's temple. "We're leaving. Now."

But Damian wasn't listening. He was looking at Sloane, memorizing her face, saying goodbye with his eyes.

Then he did the last thing any of them expected.

He acted.

With a sudden, convulsive movement, he slammed his head backward, into Lazar's face. There was a sickening crunch of bone and cartilage. Lazar roared in pain and fury, his nose exploding in a spray of blood, his grip loosening for a fraction of a second.

It was the opening Damian needed. The only opening he was going to get.

He shoved himself away from Lazar with all his strength, not toward Sloane and Nico, not toward safety, but sideways. Toward the primary power distribution unit—a massive cabinet of high-voltage conductors feeding the server farm. The cascade failure had torn it open, exposing a nest of thick cables arcing and sparking with lethal current.

Damian didn't hesitate.

He grabbed the exposed wiring with both hands.

Chapter 81: The Judgment

The sound was a horrific, wet sizzle—the sound of flesh meeting current, of a human body taking the full force of the high-voltage discharge. A massive arc of blue-white electrical energy erupted from the torn power distribution unit, engulfing Damian. His body convulsed, a terrible, silent dance of death, his arms thrown wide like a man embracing the sky. The smell of burning flesh and ozone hit Sloane like a physical blow, choking and acrid.

For a single, horrifying second, he was a man made of pure, white light. Beautiful and terrible, like a star going supernova.

The cabinet exploded in a cascade of sparks and flame, the overload traveling back through the failing grid. More servers erupted, adding their death screams to the chaos. The main lights flickered and died. Emergency power kicked in, bathing everything in dim, red emergency lighting.

And then Damian was gone.

Collapsed. A charred, unrecognizable shape against the blackened metal, smoke rising from what had been a man, a genius, a lover, a hero.

"DAMIAN!" Sloane's scream was lost in the chaos.

She fell to her knees on the platform, her legs giving out beneath her. The Glock clattered from her hand. A sound came from her throat—half-sob, half-scream—that she didn't recognize as her own voice.

Below, on the main floor, a new sound cut through the wail of the alarms. The sharp crack of a gunshot, then another—muffled, distant, coming from the corridor beyond the main entrance. Katarina, Sloane realized dimly, fighting her way through the last of Roman's security. Clearing the path.

***

Time fractured.

Sloane didn't know if she knelt there for seconds or minutes. Her mind was a screaming void, unable to process what she'd just witnessed. The man who'd kissed her, who'd held her, who'd told her she made him feel human—reduced to ash and silence. He'd sacrificed himself. The final, absolute, and heroic act of a man who'd chosen to destroy the weapon, even if it meant destroying himself.

"Sloane!"

Nico's voice cut through the fog. Urgent. Warning.

She looked up, her vision blurred with tears and smoke.

Lazar stood by the service door, his nose a bloody ruin, his face a mask of pure, unrestrained fury stripped of all pretense of civility. His shield was gone. His machine was dead. His escape route blocked by flame and wreckage.

He was exposed.

And he was aiming his pistol directly at her.

His hand was steady. His eyes were cold. He had nothing left to lose, and that made him the most dangerous thing in the room.

"You took everything," Lazar said, his voice a low rasp through the blood and pain. "My machine. My architect. My future. You were supposed to be a tool. A prop. A useful ghost. But you became a weapon."

His finger tightened on the trigger.

Two shots cracked through the screaming chaos of the dying Core, so close together they were almost a single sound.

One from Nico, sharp and professional, fired from his position near the entrance.

One from a new, unexpected direction—the main doorway, where Katarina Zimina had appeared, her Makarov PM held steady in a two-handed grip, wisps of smoke still curling from the barrel. Blood spattered her tactical vest—not hers. The guards who'd tried to stop her hadn't succeeded.

Lazar staggered back, not from the force of the bullets, but from the shock of the new player on the board. A red bloom spread across his shoulder, dark and spreading. Another blossomed on his thigh, shattering his leg. He collapsed to his knees, his pistol clattering to the floor, skittering across the blood-slicked concrete. He was wounded, broken, but not dead.

Not yet.

Katarina walked slowly into the room, her weapon held steady**, the barrel still pointed at Roman's center mass**. Her silver hair caught the emergency lighting, making her look like an avenging angel. Or a reaper. Her face was a mask of cold, serene, and absolute satisfaction—the expression of a woman who'd been waiting years for this moment.

She reached into the breast pocket of her jacket and pulled out a small, silver compass. Old. Worn. The kind a sailor might carry on long, dangerous voyages. She opened it with a soft click. Pressed beneath the glass was a lock of dark blonde hair.

Livia's.

She held it up so Lazar could see, crossing to stand over him like a victor over the vanquished.

"Checkmate, mon cœur," she whispered, her voice soft and intimate and final. My heart.

Lazar's eyes widened, blood bubbling at his lips. He looked from the compass to Katarina, recognition and understanding dawning in his eyes. Then his gaze shifted to Sloane, still kneeling on the platform, and finally back to Katarina.

He understood now. He had not been playing a game against one woman. He had been playing against three. Against Livia's ghost, against the actress who'd worn her face, against the woman who'd loved her. A triangle of vengeance, closing around him like a trap he'd never seen coming.

And they had won.

Katarina closed the compass with a soft, final click. She slipped it back into her jacket, over her heart, and stepped aside. Her eyes met Sloane's across the smoking ruins.

This kill belonged to someone else.

***

The screaming of the servers began to die down, replaced by the low, ominous hum of emergency power. The strobing red lights painted everything in hellish, pulsating waves—red, then shadow, then red again. In that flickering darkness, Sloane stood. She walked to the edge of the platform and descended the metal stairs, her footsteps ringing hollow in the vast space. Her legs were unsteady, but her hands were not. She bent and picked up her Glock from where it had fallen on the platform grating.

She walked forward, her steps sure on the blood-slicked floor, past the burning servers, past the emergency lights, past the point of no return.

She stopped ten feet from the kneeling, bleeding monster.

The gun was heavier than it looked in movies. But she was used to the weight now.

Roman Lazar looked up at her, and despite the blood streaming down his face, despite the ruin of his body, despite the smoking wreckage of his kingdom around him, he smiled. A strange, horrifying, almost tender smile. And in that smile was something she had not expected: relief.

"You know what the difference is between you and me, Sloane?" His voice was soft, labored, each word purchased with pain. Blood flecked his lips. "I was willing to lose everything to win."

He tilted his head, that same gesture of academic curiosity she'd seen at a hundred dinners in Argentis, over wine and imported delicacies, when he'd played the kindly mentor. He was waiting for her answer. Even now, dying on his knees in the ruins of his empire, he wanted to understand. He wanted to know if she'd learned his lesson.

"Were you?"

The question hung in the smoke.

Sloane looked down at him. She thought of the eviction notice and the dusty Oscar gathering cobwebs on top of her fridge. She thought of a sixteen-year-old girl on a Greyhound bus from Oklahoma who had promised herself she would never be invisible again.

She thought of Manny, who had mortgaged his soul for her. Of Livia, who had gambled her legacy on a successor. Of Damian, who had given his last breath to destroy a god.

Yes, she thought, the answer crystallizing with absolute clarity. I was willing to burn it all down.

But the difference between us, Roman?

You were fighting to own. I was fighting to exist. You became a god to take lives. I became a ghost to save them.

And gods die, too.

She didn't say it aloud. Her answer was simpler.

She adjusted her stance, shifting her weight to her back foot. She dropped her shoulders, unclenched her jaw, and tilted her chin—catching the strobing red emergency light perfectly in her eyes. It was a masterpiece of focus.

She found her mark.

"Scene," she whispered.

She pulled the trigger.

Chapter 82: Ashes and Silence

The sound of the shot was the last loud thing. A single, clean crack that cut through the chaos of the dying Core. After it, there was only the low hum of emergency power and the smell of cordite.

Roman Lazar jerked back, the strange, relieved smile freezing on his face. It was replaced by something that might have been surprise, or final understanding, or simply the blank emptiness of a man whose calculations had finally run out.

His body slumped forward, hitting the floor with a heavy, final thud. No last words. No final revelation. Just silence and stillness and the smell of cordite and death.

The false god fell.

Sloane stood there, the Glock still raised, smoke curling from its barrel like a ghost taking flight. The recoil had split the webbing between her thumb and forefinger, a hot, clean pain she barely felt. She stared at the man who'd paid her a hundred million dollars to play a dead woman.

Instead, she'd made him a ghost.

Katarina walked to Lazar's body and knelt, her movements precise and professional. She pressed two fingers to his neck, checking for a pulse with the clinical efficiency of someone who'd done this many times before. After a long moment, she looked up at Sloane and gave a single, slow nod.

Confirmation. Closure. Victory.

The screaming of the servers finally stopped. The last of the alarms cut off mid-wail, leaving only the low hum of emergency power. The strobing red lights went out, replaced by the dim, blue glow of the backup systems. Emergency power. End-of-the-world lighting for the end of a world.

Silence.

It was over.

***

Nico was at her side, his hand gentle on her shoulder, his presence a solid anchor in the chaos. "Sloane," he said, his voice a low, careful thing. "It's over. Are you okay?"

She looked down at the Glock in her hand, still warm from firing. She'd killed a man. She'd walked into his kingdom, worn a dead woman's face, played his game, survived his traps, and won. She'd become exactly what she'd needed to become to survive.

The realization should have devastated her. Should have broken something essential inside her. Should have made her feel like a monster.

Instead, she felt only a strange, cold, absolute clarity.

She looked at Nico, at his dark, steady eyes that had seen too much death and still chose to protect, to fight, to love. Then at Katarina, who stood like a sentinel over Lazar's body, finally at peace after years of grief and rage. Then at the charred servers where Damian had made his final, heroic choice, where his body lay in the wreckage of the machine he'd destroyed.

"I'm okay," she said. Another performance. The easiest one yet.

She wasn't okay. She was a void.

She had been willing to lose everything to win.

And she had.

***

Katarina holstered her weapon and stood, brushing invisible dust from her tactical pants. She looked at them both, her pale gray eyes unreadable in the dim emergency lighting.

She studied Sloane with a clinical, almost unnerving intensity—taking in the soot-stained face, the split skin on her thumb, and the raw, hollowed-out look of a woman who had just completed the final stage of an impossible mission that she hadn't even contracted for.

"You believe you failed in Zurich, don't you?" Katarina asked, and there was something almost like amusement flickering in her ice-cold eyes. "You believe Lazar forced you to abort the upload—that he won that round of the game."

"He did," Nico said, his voice a low growl, raw with the frustration of a soldier who hated losing. "He cut the hardline at the safe house. We barely got out alive. The drive was fried."

"No," Katarina said, and her smile was thin, sharp, cold. The smile of a chess master revealing a checkmate. "Roman didn't just jam the Flare. He attacked it. Livia programmed the laptop to upload the heavy freight first—the video archives, the large audio files, high-resolution images. Megabytes before kilobytes. It was huge, loud, and impossible to miss. Roman focused all his resources on crushing that stream. He sent a kill command down the line to wipe that USB drive. He thought he was destroying the evidence at the source."

She took a step closer, her voice dropping to a whisper in the humming, dying room.

"But the tablet was the dagger. You thought its job ended with the decryption, but that was just the handshake. Livia designed the script to run in the background, the tablet's integrated modem hunting for a signal while Roman was distracted by the laptop. She reversed the upload priorities for the tablet. It triggered the upload of the Dark Ledger the moment you cleared the bank vault and continued silently."

Sloane stared at her, the sheer, magnificent magnitude of it settling in. "The dead man's switch," she whispered. "It was running the whole time?"

"Yes," Katarina confirmed. "Livia's Hydra protocol. It prioritized the text files—the needles. Since they were tiny, they flew fast. Images, audio, and video followed in that order. The upload finished while you were still on the road. By the time you arrived, the story was all over the global media, just as Livia had intended."

She paused, letting the weight of it settle. "Roman thought he was hunting a girl. He didn't know he was fighting a legacy. By the time his men breached the safe house in Zurich, key parts of the story were already being read in newsrooms from London to Tokyo. The machine was already dead. It just took a few more hours for the body to hit the floor."

"You see," Katarina added, her gaze shifting to the ruined servers, "Roman was arrogant. He needed to teach Damian's machine how to predict corruption, but he couldn't do it without a textbook. He had to feed it real data. His data. He ordered Livia to build a Black Box to hide his crimes from Damian. He thought because he ordered the encryption, he controlled the secrets. He didn't realize she'd rigged the door to open for the one person brave enough to turn the handle."

The silence that followed was profound, broken only by the distant drip of water and the hum of emergency power. Sloane felt something unlock in her chest—a weight she'd been carrying since the safe house. They hadn't just survived; they had already won. Livia hadn't just haunted this house. She had reached out from the dark and guided Sloane's hand to the trigger.

Katarina's comms unit chirped—a sharp, digital bird-call that shattered the moment. She pressed the earpiece into her canal, listened for three seconds, then turned to them, her face snapping back into the clinical mask of the professional.

"The local authorities have been... delayed," she said, her voice now tight with operational urgency. "Conflicting reports have sent the initial response to the lower pass, but they are correcting course. You have approximately thirty minutes before they breach the perimeter. The path to the service exit is clear; Lazar's men have no interest in fighting for a ghost whose accounts are being frozen as we speak."

She looked at Nico, then at Sloane, her gaze hard. "But that window is closing. You have what you came for. You have the victory. Now, leave. You've been through enough tonight. You'll answer their questions later. But not here, not while the bodies are still warm. I'll ensure the scene tells the right story."

"We need to go," Nico said quietly, his hand on Sloane's arm. "Before those thirty minutes run out."

Sloane nodded, but she couldn't move yet. She looked one last time at the Core—at the dying servers, at Roman Lazar's body, at the charred remains of Damian against the blackened equipment.

"What about him?" she whispered, her voice breaking. "We can't just leave him here."

Katarina's expression softened, just for a moment. "I will make sure Damian Crestwell is remembered as a hero," she said quietly. "The man who destroyed

Panopticon. The whistleblower who gave his life to stop the Chairman's machine."

She let the title hang in the air, cold and final. It stripped Roman of any personal connection, reducing him to his official role: the man in charge of the corrupt enterprise.

"That is the story the world will hear," she finished. "That is the truth."

It wasn't justice. It wouldn't restart his heart. But it was something.

"Thank you," Sloane whispered.

Katarina nodded once, then turned toward the exit. "Go," she said over her shoulder. "I will handle the rest. I am very good at handling the rest."

Nico pulled Sloane gently toward the door, and this time, she let him. They left the Core behind—left the death and the fire and the ruins of an empire built on surveillance and control. Left Roman Lazar to his final, silent judgment. Left Damian Crestwell to become a legend.

They climbed the stairs in silence, Nico leading the way with his weapon drawn, clearing each corner with professional efficiency. The house above was empty, silent, the staff and guards gone or dead or fled. They emerged into the cold Swiss night, the stars impossibly bright above the mountains, the air clean and sharp after the smoke and death below.

Sloane breathed in deep, filling her lungs with freedom.

She had walked into a fortress as a ghost.

She was walking out as herself.

And Roman Lazar, the man who'd tried to own the world, was nothing but a body cooling in the dark.

Chapter 83: Aftermath

The cold hit her first.

Sloane burst through the service exit into the Swiss night, and the air was a knife against her smoke-choked lungs. She gasped, stumbled, nearly fell. Nico caught her, his arm around her waist, holding her upright as they ran across the snow-dusted grass toward the tree line. Behind them, Argentis loomed like a glass cathedral, beautiful and cold and full of death.

Sirens wailed in the distance. Multiple sirens. Police, fire, ambulance—the whole machinery of Swiss emergency response converging on the estate. Katarina's thirty-minute window was closing.

"Keep moving," Nico urged, his voice low and urgent. "Almost there."

Sloane's legs were lead. Her hands were shaking so violently she could barely hold onto the Glock Nico had shoved back into her grip. The smell of burning flesh clung to her clothes, her hair, her skin. Every time she blinked, she saw it: Damian, engulfed in blue-white light. Damian, becoming ash and smoke. Damian, gone.

I think I love you more.

His last words. His final gift. And she hadn't said it back. She hadn't told him—

"Sloane." Nico's voice cut through the spiral. "I need you here. Stay with me."

She nodded. Forced her legs to keep moving. One foot in front of the other. Survival first. Grief later.

They reached the tree line and plunged into darkness. The forest swallowed them, thick pine branches shutting out the moonlight. Nico moved like a ghost, sure-footed even in the dark, his hand never leaving hers. He led her down a narrow trail she hadn't known existed, deeper into the woods, away from the sirens and the lights and the glass fortress where she'd been a prisoner.

After what felt like hours but was probably only minutes, they reached the dense patch of pines where they'd left the car. The Audi sat exactly where they'd stashed it—a dark, cold silhouette buried beneath the low-hanging boughs.

Nico chirped the locks, the sound sharp and metallic in the quiet forest. He shoved Sloane into the passenger seat, his movements a blur of practiced urgency.

"Get in," Nico said, slamming her door and vaulting over the hood to the driver's side. "We have maybe five minutes before the roadblocks go up."

Sloane climbed in, her movements mechanical. Nico slid into the driver's seat, threw the vehicle into gear, and they were moving, bouncing down a narrow forest road barely wider than the SUV itself. No headlights. Just moonlight and Nico's perfect spatial memory.

She looked back once. Through the trees, she could see Argentis—a constellation of lights, beautiful and deadly. Emergency vehicles were arriving now, red and blue strobes painting the glass walls. She watched it recede into the distance, that glass cage where she'd been Livia, where she'd fallen in love, where she'd killed a god.

Where Damian had died to save her. And the world. By destroying his own creation.

She turned away and didn't look back again.

***

They drove in silence for twenty minutes, taking back roads and forest tracks that didn't appear on any map, until they finally emerged onto a proper highway. Nico flipped on the headlights and merged into sparse late-night traffic. Just another car. Just another couple driving through the Swiss night.

"Where are we going?" Sloane asked. Her voice sounded strange to her own ears—flat, distant, like it belonged to someone else.

"Safe house," Nico said. "Not one of Katarina's. One of mine."

She nodded. Didn't ask any more questions. Her mind felt like static, like a radio stuck between stations, picking up fragments of signal but unable to form coherent thought.

She looked down at her hands. They were covered in soot. Blood on her knuckles. The webbing between her thumb and forefinger was split from the recoil, a thin line of red against pale skin. She'd killed a man. She'd watched another man die. She'd walked out of hell.

And she felt nothing.

No. That wasn't true. She felt everything. Too much. A tidal wave of emotion pressing against a dam that was starting to crack, and she knew—*knew*—that when it broke, it would destroy her.

Not yet. Hold it together. Just a little longer.

Nico's hand found hers in the darkness. Warm. Solid. Real.

"You did it," he said quietly. "You survived."

She didn't feel like a survivor. She felt like a ghost.

***

The safe house was a small, unremarkable apartment in a suburb of Lucerne, the kind of place where no one asked questions and everyone minded their own business. Third floor, back entrance, two exits. Nico had been planning this, she realized. Even before tonight. Even before they'd gone into the Core. He'd been preparing for the escape, for the aftermath, for the moment when the war ended and they had to become human again.

He unlocked the door and ushered her inside. The apartment was sparse but clean: a small living room, a kitchenette, a bedroom barely big enough for a double bed. A temporary sanctuary. A place to breathe.

Sloane stood in the middle of the living room, still holding the Glock, not sure what to do with it, not sure what to do with herself. The adrenaline was draining out of her body, leaving her hollow and shaking.

"Bathroom's through there," Nico said gently, taking the gun from her hand and setting it on the counter. "There's a shower. Clean clothes. Take your time."

She nodded. Moved toward the bathroom like a sleepwalker.

The face in the mirror was a stranger's. Soot-streaked. Hollow-eyed. Hair wild and tangled. She looked like she'd been to war.

She had.

She turned on the shower, made it as hot as she could stand, and stepped under the spray fully clothed. Watched the water turn gray, then brown, then pink as it washed away the smoke and the blood and the ash. Watched pieces of the night swirl down the drain—evidence, memory, trauma.

She stood there until the water ran clear. Until her clothes were soaked and heavy. Until the heat made her dizzy.

Then she peeled off the wet fabric—Livia's clothes, she realized with a jolt, the last costume she'd ever wear—and let them fall in a heap on the tile. She stood under the spray, naked and raw, and let the water pound against her skull until she couldn't think anymore.

When she finally emerged, wrapped in a towel, her skin was red and her fingers were pruned and she still felt dirty. Like the smoke and death had soaked all the way down to her bones.

Nico had set out clean clothes on the bed: soft gray sweats, a black t-shirt. Not hers. Probably his. She put them on, rolled up the sleeves and pant legs. They smelled like detergent and safety.

She found him in the kitchen, making tea. A strangely domestic gesture after a night of violence and death. He looked up when she entered, his dark eyes scanning her face with professional efficiency, cataloging damage.

"You should eat something," he said.

"I can't."

"You should try."

"Nico." Her voice cracked. "I can't."

He nodded. Set down the kettle. Crossed to her in two strides and pulled her into his arms.

That's when the dam broke.

The sob came from somewhere deep inside her, somewhere primal and animal. It tore out of her throat, violent and ugly, and once it started, she couldn't stop. She collapsed against him, her legs giving out, and he caught her, lowered them both to the floor, held her while she shattered.

She cried for Damian. For the man he'd been, the man he'd almost become. For the impossible love she'd felt and never spoken. For his final words, his final sacrifice, his final, terrible courage.

She cried for herself. For the girl from Oklahoma who'd thought Hollywood was the hardest war she'd ever fight. For the actress who'd been so desperate for a role she'd sold her face and her name. For the woman who'd had to become a killer to survive.

She cried for Livia, who she'd never met but who'd saved her life from beyond the grave. For Manny, who'd gone to war for her. For Nico, who'd been a prisoner as long as she had.

She cried until there was nothing left, until her throat was raw and her eyes were swollen and her chest ached from the force of it.

And through it all, Nico held her. Didn't speak. Didn't try to fix it. Just held her while she broke, his hand moving in slow circles on her back, his presence the only solid thing in a world that had just exploded.

When the storm finally passed, she pulled back, wiping her face with shaking hands. "I'm sorry," she whispered.

"Don't," he said firmly. "Don't apologize for being human."

"I killed him, Nico. I looked Roman Lazar in the eyes and pulled the trigger."

"I know."

"And Damian—" Her voice broke again. "He died thinking I—I never told him—"

"He knew," Nico said quietly. "I saw the way he looked at you. He knew."

The words were a gift she didn't deserve. She buried her face in her hands, trying to breathe, trying to think, trying to figure out how to exist in a world where she'd done what she'd done.

But beneath the grief, a sharp, jagged piece of business remained. She couldn't save Damian. But there was someone she could still save.

She lifted her head. Her eyes were red, but the steel was back in her voice.

"Manny," she said.

She looked at Nico. "Roman told me he had an exoneration file ready. Proof of the frame-up. He said all it took was one call to his lawyer."

She held out her hand. "Give me the phone."

Nico handed it to her. She dialed the number she had memorized from the business card Fairweather had given her in the glass tower a lifetime ago.

It rang once.

"Fairweather." A crisp, tense voice.

"Mr. Fairweather," Sloane said. "It's Sloane Devereaux."

A pause. "Ms. Devereaux. I am seeing... disturbing reports regarding Argentis." He sounded like a man watching his firm's stock price plummet.

"The contract is concluded," she said. "Roman is... unavailable."

A long silence followed. Fairweather was a survivor; she could hear him recalculating in real time. The King was dead. The pawn had reached the last rank and been promoted. Long live the Queen.

"I understand," he said carefully.

"Roman had you prepare an exoneration package for Emanuel Goldman," Sloane said. "Proof of the frame-up."

"I can neither confirm nor deny the existence of such a file," Fairweather replied, his voice smooth as glass but tightening. "And even if it did exist, it would be a work product prepared for a specific client. Without an instruction from that client, my hands are tied."

"The client is gone, Mr. Fairweather," she cut him off, her voice dropping to a dangerous, icy floor. "And since Roman's estate is about to be incinerated by global asset forfeitures, he is no longer in a position to have 'interests.' Roman's money is gone. Mine isn't. That makes me the only account you should care about. I am retaining you—effective immediately—to perform a 'corrective filing' to rectify a fraud on the court."

She let the offer land.

"You aren't breaking privilege; you're mitigating your firm's liability for Roman's subornation of perjury. File the package. Personally. Send it to the FBI, and release it to the press right after."

"Ms. Devereaux," he paused, the sound of a man weighing the probability of a disbarment hearing against the certainty of a nine-figure retainer. "Executing such a filing... as a matter of 'professional ethics' to rectify this fraud... would entail significant costs."

"Spare no expense." She let the words hang there, heavy with implication. "You know I'm good for it."

She paused, letting the weight of the new power dynamic settle. She wasn't the desperate actress in the chair anymore. She was the woman controlling the account.

"Very well," Fairweather said, realizing he was talking to a hundred-million-dollar client. His tone wasn't servile; it was efficient. He had swapped horses mid-stream without getting his boots wet. "I will process the filing as an expedited submission. The Bureau will have it within the hour."

"Good," Sloane said, letting the word fall like a verdict. "The future of our association depends on how quickly Manny walks out of that cell. Goodbye, Mr. Fairweather."

She hung up and handed the phone back to Nico. Her hands had stopped shaking.

"He'll do it," she said, a ghost of a confident smile touching her lips.

Then the adrenaline finally ran out.

They sat in the small, tidy living room as the morning light shifted across the floor. Nico finally got her to drink the tea. They didn't talk. There were no words left. There was only the waiting—the heavy, suffocating silence after lighting a fuse, before the explosion.

Two hours later, the phone buzzed in Nico's hand.

Harsh. Intrusive.

He glanced at the screen, and his expression shifted—alert, focused.

"It's Katarina," he said.

Sloane's head snapped up. "What does it say?"

He opened the message, read silently, then turned the phone so she could see.

It was a news link. BBC World Service. Posted twelve minutes ago.

BREAKING: Panopticon Data Leak Exposes Global Surveillance Network

Below it, a second link. New York Times. Posted eight minutes ago.

Panopticon Whistleblower Damian Crestwell Killed in Armed Incursion at His Estate; Attacker Roman Lazar Also Dies

And a third. The Guardian.

'Panopticon Papers' Reveal Massive Corporate and Government Surveillance Operation

Beneath the links, a single line of text from Katarina:

The ghost protocol is active. The world is watching. You won.

Sloane stared at the screen, her mind struggling to process the words. Won. She'd won. Livia's plan had worked. The Zurich upload—the real one, the silent one that had been spreading like a virus through the world's media networks for days—had finally reached critical mass.

"What about Manny?" Sloane asked, her voice tight. "The file... did it work?"

Nico tapped the screen, searching. He stopped. Let out a long, sharp breath.

"Look," he said.

He turned the phone toward her. A breaking news alert from the LA Times.

BREAKING: FBI Drops Charges Against Manny Goldman: New Evidence Reveals "Digital Plant" by Unknown Perpetrator

"He's out," Nico said. "Or he will be within the hour. You didn't just clear his name, Sloane. You made him Roman's first victim to be vindicated."

Sloane stared at the headline. The knot in her chest, the one that had been tightening since his arrest, finally let go.

"We should watch," Nico said, gesturing to the small TV mounted on the wall. "See what the world is learning."

Sloane nodded. He turned it on, flipped to BBC World Service.

The anchor's face was grave, professional, but there was an edge of barely contained shock in her voice:

"—unprecedented leak of confidential documents has revealed the existence of a massive global surveillance operation code-named Panopticon..."

The screen cut to a panel of experts, talking over each other. Phrases jumped out: *Biggest intelligence leak since Snowden... Governments complicit... Pre-crime surveillance...*

Sloane watched it all in numb silence. The enormity of what they'd stopped—what Livia had stopped—was too big to fully comprehend. Millions of people. Billions, maybe. All of them living under Panopticon's invisible eye, their every move tracked, predicted, controlled.

And now they were free.

Because a dead woman had built a weapon. Because an actress had been desperate enough to wear her face. Because a broken genius had sacrificed himself to destroy his own creation.

"Turn it off," she whispered.

Nico clicked the remote. The silence was sudden and profound.

They sat there on the floor of the anonymous safe house, their backs against the couch, the weight of what they'd done settling over them like snow.

"What happens now?" Sloane asked.

"Now?" Nico looked at her, his dark eyes steady. "Now we disappear. At least for a while. Let the authorities sort through the mess. Let the world process what they've learned. And when the dust settles—" He paused. "Then you decide who you want to be."

"I don't know who that is anymore."

"You will," he said. "Give it time."

Time. She had that now. For the first time in months—maybe years—she had time. No one was hunting her. No one was watching her. Roman Lazar was dead. Panopticon was destroyed. The contract was fulfilled.

She was free.

So why did she feel so empty?

Nico stood, held out his hand. "Come on. You need to sleep."

"I can't sleep."

"You need to try."

She let him pull her to her feet, lead her to the small bedroom. The bed looked impossibly soft, impossibly safe. She crawled under the covers, still wearing his clothes, and he lay down beside her, on top of the blankets, his presence a guard against the nightmares that were coming.

"Nico?" she whispered in the darkness.

"Yeah?"

"Thank you. For everything. For getting me out. For—" Her voice broke. "For keeping me alive."

"You kept yourself alive, Sloane. I just drove the getaway car."

The cadence of Manny. She almost smiled.

Almost.

She closed her eyes and tried to sleep. Tried not to see Damian's face. Tried not to hear his final words. Tried not to feel the weight of the Glock in her hand, the recoil splitting her skin, the moment when Roman Lazar's eyes had gone empty and still.

But even with Nico beside her, even in the safety of the anonymous apartment, even knowing she'd won—

The ghosts followed her into sleep.

And she wondered if they'd ever leave.

Chapter 84: The Weight of Ghosts

The nightmares started in the safe house.

They had made it to Lucerne, to the small, anonymous apartment Nico had prepared, a ghost's haven in a city of strangers. But sleep was not a sanctuary. It was an ambush.

Sloane would wake gasping, Roman's smiling, bloody face burned into her retinas like a camera flash. In the dreams, he thanked her. Over and over.

She had killed a man. She had looked him in the eyes, heard the hollow logic of his ruin, and pulled the trigger anyway. And in the end, he seemed relieved.

"You're not sleeping," Nico said. It was three in the morning. He was sitting in the single armchair in the small living room, cleaning his weapon, the soft, rhythmic click of metal on metal the only sound.

Sloane sat by the window, staring out at the dark, silent street, a cup of cold tea in her hands. "I'm fine."

"No, you're not," he said, not looking up from his work. "You haven't slept more than an hour at a time since we left Argentis. Talk to me."

"What do you want me to say?" Sloane asked, her voice flat. "That I'm having nightmares? That I wake up feeling his blood on my hands? That I killed a man who looked relieved to finally stop, and that somehow makes it worse?"

"Yes," Nico said simply, finally looking up, his dark eyes steady in the dim light. "Say all of that. Because it's true. And it's normal."

"Normal?" Sloane laughed, the sound harsh and broken. "What's normal about any of this?"

"You did what you had to do," he said carefully. "Roman Lazar was going to sell Panopticon to governments that would use it to disappear dissidents, crush protests, eliminate anyone who dared to speak the truth. You stopped that. You saved lives. Millions, maybe."

"He was willing to lose everything to win," Sloane whispered, finally saying it out loud. The thing that had been eating at her since that moment in the Core. "So who won? Him or me?"

Nico was quiet for a long time, choosing his words. "The difference is choice," he said finally. "He chose to die. You're choosing to live. Every morning you wake up from those nightmares and you're still here, you're still fighting... that's a choice. That's a victory."

"It doesn't feel like enough."

"It never does," Nico said, and there was something ancient and weary in his voice. "I remember every single face. The ones who deserved it. The ones who didn't. And the day I stop remembering, the day it stops hurting, that's the day I stop being human."

He stood and walked over to her, kneeling in front of her chair so they were eye-level. "You're asking yourself if you're a monster now. And the answer is yes. It changed you. You can't take a life and stay the same person. But the fact that you're asking the question? The fact that you're having nightmares? That means you're still human, Sloane."

"How long until I stop seeing his face?" she asked, her voice small.

"I don't know," he answered honestly. "Maybe never. But you learn to carry it." His hand came up, gently taking the cold teacup from her trembling fingers and setting it aside. His hand found hers. "And you don't have to carry it alone."

The simple, quiet statement was an anchor in the storm of her guilt. She looked at him, at this man who understood the weight of ghosts, and for the first time since the Core, she felt a flicker of something other than horror.

"I don't want to do this work," she said. "I don't want to be an assassin. I don't want to be a spy. I just want to... I don't even know what I want anymore."

"Then you're exactly where you should be," Nico said softly. "Because the ones who enjoy it? The ones who don't question it? They're the real monsters."

She leaned into him, and for the first time in days, she slept without nightmares.

Chapter 85: Reckoning

The interrogation room in the Zurich Federal Police headquarters was nothing like the ones Sloane had seen in movies. No flickering fluorescent lights, no two-way mirror, no good cop-bad cop routine. Just a quiet, well-lit conference room with tasteful modern furniture, a pitcher of water, and two extremely polite Swiss investigators who asked their questions in flawless English and took meticulous notes.

They'd been at it for three hours.

"And you're certain," Inspector Keller said, her voice calm and professional, "that Roman Lazar threatened your life directly?"

"Yes," Sloane said. Again. For the third time. "He aimed a gun at me. He was going to kill me. Nico and Katarina Zimina shot him to stop him."

"And you fired the final shot."

"Yes."

"In self-defense."

"Yes."

Inspector Keller made a note. Her partner, Inspector Weber, leaned forward slightly. He was older, gray-haired, with the weary eyes of someone who'd seen too much and believed too little.

"Ms. Devereaux," he said quietly, "you understand that Switzerland takes firearms offenses with extreme gravity. You discharged a weapon on Swiss soil. A man is dead by your hand."

Sloane's throat tightened, but she didn't look away. "An intruder is dead. A man who brought a private army into my home to commit a series of executions."

Weber conceded the point with a slow, heavy nod. "Our forensics teams have spent forty-eight hours processing the site. Under Article 15 of our Criminal Code, the right to ward off an unlawful attack is fundamental. But more importantly, under Swiss law, the *Hausrecht*—the authority of the home—is sacred. Roman Lazar didn't just threaten you; he launched a paramilitary breach of a private, lawful residence. He wasn't a visitor. He was a combatant."

"The security footage confirms the arrival of his tactical team," Keller added, her voice clinical. "They bypassed the perimeter, jammed the domestic alerts, and entered with suppressed weapons. They weren't there to talk, Ms. Devereaux. They were there to liquidate the occupants of Argentis."

"However," Weber continued, and something in his voice shifted—not quite warmth, but a grim pragmatism. "The evidence supports your account. The surveillance footage, Ms. Zimina's testimony, Mr. Sorrento's statement—all of it corroborates a claim of justifiable defense of self and domicile. And given the nature of what Mr. Lazar was involved in—" He gestured to the thick folder of Panopticon files. "Well. Let us simply say the Federal Department of Justice and Police has no appetite to prosecute the people who stopped a global blackmail engine from being activated on our soil. The optics of a trial would be... catastrophic for our international standing."

Sloane blinked. "What are you saying?"

Inspector Keller closed her notebook. "We're saying that no charges will be filed against you, Ms. Zimina, or Mr. Sorrento. Roman Lazar's death will be ruled justifiable defense of occupied domicile against armed intrusion. Damian Crestwell's death will be recorded as an act of heroic intervention to disable the unauthorized Core. The public record will show he died stopping the monster he realized he'd helped create." She met Sloane's eyes. "You are free to go, Ms. Devereaux. Though we would appreciate if you remained in Switzerland for the next few weeks. In case we have follow-up questions."

"Of course," Sloane whispered.

"There is, however, one more thing." Weber pulled a different folder from his briefcase. This one was thinner, marked with official-looking seals. "The matter of your contract with Mr. Lazar's estate. One hundred million dollars, paid through a Zurich escrow account, for your... services."

Sloane's stomach dropped. They knew. Of course they knew. The whole ugly, desperate transaction was probably documented in excruciating detail.

"The escrow agent," Weber continued, his voice neutral but his eyes tracking Sloane's reaction, "has confirmed that the terms of your contract were fulfilled. A formal completion notice was filed this morning by Ms. Zimina, acting as interim estate administrator. She was... remarkably efficient... in her attestation of your performance."

Katarina. Still directing from the wings, making sure her lead actress got paid before the theater burned to the ground.

She nodded, her throat too tight to form words.

"The Swiss banking authorities have reviewed the contract. It is, technically, legal. Eccentric, certainly. Morally complicated, absolutely. But legal." He slid the folder across the table. "These are the transfer documents. You'll need to sign them and provide banking information. The funds will be released within seventy-two hours."

Sloane stared at the folder like it was a snake. Blood money. Money paid for wearing a dead woman's face, for playing a role in a sick man's delusion, for being the bait in Livia's trap.

But also: freedom. Security. The ability to help Manny, to honor her mother's memory, to build something good from the wreckage.

She picked up the pen and signed.

***

Nico was waiting for her in the lobby, his face carefully neutral, but his body language radiating tension. He relaxed fractionally when he saw her.

"How bad?" he asked.

"Not bad. No charges. Justified defense of the home."

"Good." He studied her face. "You okay?"

"I don't know," she said honestly. "Ask me in a year."

They walked out into the gray Zurich morning. Five days. That's all it had been since the Core. Since Damian died. Since she'd killed Roman Lazar. It felt like five years.

Her phone buzzed in her pocket. She pulled it out, saw Manny's name on the screen, and her eyes immediately filled with tears. She'd been texting him—brief, cryptic messages to let him know she was alive—but they hadn't actually spoken.

She answered. "Manny."

"Jesus Christ, kid." His voice was rough, choked. "Jesus fucking Christ."

"I'm okay. I'm—"

"Don't you dare tell me you're okay. I've been watching the news. I know what happened. I know what you—" He broke off, and she heard him fighting for control. "I'm at the airport. I'm on the next flight to Zurich. I don't care what you say, I don't care if it's safe, I'm coming."

"Manny, you don't have to—"

"Like hell I don't. You're my family, Sloane. You're my—" His voice cracked. "I'm coming. Text me where you are. I'll be there tomorrow."

He hung up before she could argue.

Sloane stood on the steps of the police headquarters, the phone still pressed to her ear, and felt something crack open in her chest. Manny. Her constant. Her north star. The man who'd gone to war for her when she had nothing, who'd never stopped believing even when she'd been toxic and broken and impossible to save.

He was coming.

"He's on his way, isn't he?" Nico said, a small smile touching his lips.

"Yeah."

"Good. You need him."

She did. God, she did.

***

Manny Goldman burst into the safe house apartment like a hurricane late next morning, dropped his carry-on bag, and pulled Sloane into a crushing hug that smelled like airport coffee and expensive cologne and home.

"You crazy, brilliant, terrifying kid," he muttered into her hair. "You beautiful goddamn disaster. I thought I lost you. I thought—"

"I'm here," she whispered. "I'm okay."

"You're not okay. You're not even close to okay." He pulled back, holding her at arm's length, his eyes scanning her face with the intensity of someone looking for damage. And finding it. "But you're alive. And that's—" His voice broke. "That's all that matters."

He looked past her to where Nico stood by the kitchen, giving them space. "You must be Nico."

"I am."

"You kept her alive."

"She kept herself alive. I just helped."

"Bullshit," Manny said, but there was no heat in it. "Thank you. For whatever you did. For being there when I couldn't."

Nico nodded once, a gesture of acknowledgment between two men who understood the weight of that responsibility.

Manny turned back to Sloane, his hands on her shoulders. "Okay. Talk to me. What the hell is happening? I've got reporters camping outside my office. The FBI came to my house—my house, Sloane—asking questions about Panopticon. And the internet—Jesus, the internet is losing its goddamn mind. They're calling Damian Crestwell a hero. They're calling Roman Lazar a monster. And you—" He paused. "They don't know about you yet. They don't know Livia's face was you."

"Katarina is controlling the narrative," Sloane said. "She issued a press statement this morning via the Crestwell Foundation."

She recited the lie that had bought her freedom.

"'Livia Crestwell, physically recovered but devastated by the tragic loss of her husband, has retreated into absolute, indefinite seclusion.' The world thinks the grieving widow has locked the doors to mourn. They aren't looking for an actress. They're respecting a tragedy."

"Can she do that?" Manny asked, skepticism warring with hope. "Can she actually keep the lid on this?"

"She kept herself a ghost for twenty-five years," Nico said. "She knows how to make people disappear in plain sight. As long as Sloane stays quiet and out of sight for a while, the world will forget to look."

Manny absorbed this, his agent-brain clearly spinning through the implications. "So you're a ghost. Again."

"Yeah," Sloane said. "Again."

He pulled her to the couch, sat her down, and settled in beside her like he was preparing for a long conversation. Which, she realized, he was.

"Alright," he said. "Start from the beginning. The real beginning. And don't leave anything out."

So she told him. Everything.

By the time she finished, tears were streaming down her face, and Manny's jaw was clenched so tight she thought he might crack a tooth.

"That son of a bitch," he said quietly. "That evil, manipulative son of a bitch. If you hadn't already killed him, I'd fly to Switzerland just to kill the bastard and piss on his grave."

Despite everything, Sloane laughed. It came out half-sob, but it was a laugh.

"And Damian," Manny said, his voice gentler now. "You loved him."

It wasn't a question.

"Yes," she whispered. "I did. I do. Even though I shouldn't. Even though he was—"

"Human," Manny finished. "He was human. Flawed and broken and trying to do better. That's all any of us are, kid."

Chapter 86: The Price of Peace

She leaned against him, and he wrapped an arm around her shoulders, and for a few minutes they just sat there in the quiet of the safe house while the world outside spun and burned and tried to make sense of the Panopticon revelations.

"There's something else," Sloane said finally. "The money. The contract. It's real. It's legal. Ninety-nine million dollars. They're going to transfer it to me."

Manny went very still. "Jesus Christ."

"I'm going to set up a five-million-dollar trust for Mona's children—Sofia and Marco," she said, her voice steady. "It doesn't bring her back, and it isn't justice. But it secures their future. And I'm going to set up a foundation. In my mother's name. For women and kids trying to escape bad situations."

Manny looked at her for a long moment, then nodded slowly. "Caroline would have liked that."

"And I want to give you twenty million."

"Sloane—"

"Non-negotiable, Manny. You taught me how to negotiate. Don't try to out-stubborn the student."

He stared at her, his eyes shining. "You're serious."

"Dead serious. You saved my life. Multiple times. Let me say thank you."

"That's a very big thank you."

"It's not big enough," she said, her voice catching.

He pulled her into another hug, and this time she felt him shaking. "You're going to make an old man cry," he muttered.

"Good. You've earned it."

***

The memorial service for Damian Crestwell was held two weeks later in a small, private chapel in Zurich. It was a quiet affair—no press, no cameras, just a handful of people who'd known him before Roman Lazar had transformed him into a weapon. His parents, both tenured professors at prestigious institutions, had been notified by the executor's office. They had sent their regrets—a brief, formal email citing academic obligations that could not be postponed.

Sloane attended in the back row, wearing dark sunglasses and a black dress that wasn't from Livia's wardrobe. Nico sat beside her, solid and present. Manny was on her other side, his hand occasionally squeezing hers when the grief threatened to overwhelm her.

A former MIT professor spoke about the young Damian he'd taught twenty years ago: curious, idealistic, obsessed with using quantum computing to solve climate models, to predict famines, to save lives.

"He wanted to save the world," the old man said, his voice breaking. "He just forgot to ask if the world wanted to be saved that way. But in the end—in the very end—he made the right choice. He destroyed the machine. He saved millions of people from a surveillance state that would have made Orwell weep. He died a hero, even if the world will never fully understand what he prevented."

Sloane bit her lip. Damian. A hero. It was true. It was all true. But it didn't bring him back.

After the service, she visited his grave—a simple stone in a private cemetery overlooking Lake Zurich. A quiet corner he'd purchased years ago. Next to Livia's empty marker.

She knelt in the grass, not caring that it was damp and cold, and spoke to him as if he could hear.

"You saved us," she whispered. "You saved all of us. And I'm so angry at you for it. I wanted more time. I wanted to know who you could have been, after all of this. I wanted—"

Her voice broke. She pressed her palm flat against the cold stone, feeling its solidity, its finality.

"I loved you," she said, the confession ripped from somewhere deep inside her. "I know that makes me a fool. I know it was complicated and messy and probably not even real, but I did. And I'm sorry I never told you. I'm sorry I let you die thinking I was just performing."

The stone said nothing.

But the wind off the lake was gentle, and somewhere overhead, a bird sang, and for just a moment, Sloane let herself believe he'd heard her.

When she finally stood, her knees were stiff and her eyes were swollen, but something inside her had shifted. Not healed—not even close. But... settled. Like a bone set after a break, painful but aligned.

***

Before she left Zurich, Sloane found herself wandering back into the quiet halls of Argentis—the part untouched by fire, untouched by investigators, untouched by everything except silence. Damian's study looked exactly as she remembered: the neat desk, the whiskey bottle still half full, the chess board frozen mid-play. A life paused, not ended.

Something on the edge of the desk caught her eye. A paperback. Worn. Softened at the corners from use.

Alan Turing: The Enigma.

She lifted it, and the weight of it felt heavier than the pages should allow. Damian had underlined passages in his precise, elegant handwriting. Small marginalia. Quiet notes. The private thoughts of a man who had never truly spoken for himself.

One line was starred three times, the ink nearly gouged into the page: "We can only see a short distance ahead, but we can see plenty there that needs to be done."

Below it, scrawled in the margin, was a single word in Damian's hand: *Sloane.*

Not Livia. Sloane. He'd seen the woman behind the counterfeit—and he'd believed she was the only one who could finish what Livia had started.

Her breath shuddered.

Damian had seen himself in these pages—a brilliant, gentle man crushed by the system he helped build, punished for the very mind that made him extraordinary. A man whose genius had metastasized into a burden he could not set down.

Next to the Turing book, partially hidden beneath a stack of papers, sat Livia's journal.

Sloane's hand trembled as she reached for it. The leather was worn, the pages soft from repeated readings. He'd found it. In her room, where she'd accidentally left it. And he'd read it. Every word.

She opened to a page marked with a folded corner. Livia's handwriting, urgent and precise:

I will not let Damian become another beautiful mind broken by ugly men.

Sloane's eyes burned. She'd tried. God, she'd tried.

And so had he. In the end.

She placed the book and journal back exactly where she found them, side by side. The two texts that had shaped his final choice. The warning from his wife. The parallel from history. Together, they'd given him the courage to act.

"Goodbye, Damian," she whispered. This time, it didn't feel like a confession. It felt like a benediction.

***

Nico was waiting by the car, giving her space but not leaving her alone. Manny was already inside, probably making phone calls, probably already planning her next move even though she hadn't decided what that was yet.

"You okay?" Nico asked as she approached.

"No," she said honestly. "But I will be. Someday."

He nodded. Didn't try to fix it. Just opened the car door for her.

"Where to?" he asked.

Sloane looked back at the cemetery one last time. At the simple stone marking the grave of a brilliant, broken man who'd died trying to be better.

"Somewhere far away," she said. "Somewhere quiet. Somewhere I can figure out who I am when I'm not running."

Nico's lips quirked. "Katarina tells me that she might know a place."

***

Before they could leave Zurich, Sloane had one last meeting. Katarina had summoned her with a single, encrypted text: The Dolder Grand. Terrace bar. One hour.

Sloane found her sitting at a secluded table, a glass of vodka in her hand, looking out over the city.

"The files are out there now," Sloane said, sitting down. "It's working. Panopticon is destroyed. We won."

"Did we?" Katarina asked. She took a sip of her vodka. "Half the world won't believe the files are real. They'll call them deepfakes, disinformation. Roman's clients will spin it. Governments will deny everything."

Sloane felt something cold settle in her stomach. "So we failed?"

"No." Katarina turned to look at her. "We made it impossible for them to win cleanly. The truth is out there now. Messy, complicated, contested—but out there. Some journalists will chase it. Some governments will fall. Some victims will get justice." She paused. "Not all of them. Maybe not even most of them. But some. And that is more than they had last week."

"It's not enough," Sloane whispered.

"It never is," Katarina said. "But it's what we get."

Sloane looked out at the clean, orderly city, and she finally understood. Real victory was messy. Incomplete.

It wasn't the ending she'd wanted. But it was the ending she'd earned.

Katarina finished her vodka and placed a keycard and a leather portfolio on the table. "These are the final documents. The escrow transfer is complete. The foundation paperwork is filed. And this," she tapped the keycard, "is for the villa in Lake Como. Private. Secure. Yours."

Sloane stared at the card. The breath hitched in her throat.

On Lake Como. Somewhere quiet... I'll ask Katarina to finalize the paperwork. I want it ready for us.

Damian's voice rang in her mind, hopeful and shy in the morning light.

"He bought it," Sloane whispered, her eyes stinging. "He actually bought it."

"He wanted a sanctuary," Katarina said softly. "He wanted a life with you. Not Livia. You. He just didn't know how to say it."

Sloane looked up at the older woman. The walls were down. No more spy games.

"I loved him, Katarina. In the end... I really loved him."

"I know," Katarina said. And for the first time, her eyes weren't cold. They were just sad. "That is why I am giving you the house. Go there. Be a ghost for a while. Heal."

"Thank you," Sloane said. "For everything."

"We are even," Katarina said. "Livia saved my life once. You avenged her death. The debt is paid." She stood to leave. "The media is still digging. Disappear. Let the storm pass."

"I'm not Livia Crestwell," Sloane said.

Katarina's smile was small and sad. "No. You're not. You're Sloane Devereaux. Don't forget that."

And then she was gone, dissolving into the city like smoke.

Chapter 87: Homecoming

Spring arrived in Lake Como like a slow awakening, painting the hillsides in soft greens and the delicate white of fruit tree blossoms. The winter cold retreated up into the mountains, leaving the small lakeside towns to emerge from hibernation—the morning bells of the church ringing longer, the fishermen returning to the water, the smell of bread baking in stone ovens that had been warm for three hundred years.

For the first time in her life, Sloane Devereaux was learning what it meant to simply be.

She woke up with the sun. She made coffee. She wrote.

She had bought a simple Moleskine notebook. Just like Livia's. And she began to fill its empty pages with her story. Not Livia's story. Not the sensational story the tabloids had tried to tell. Her own. She wrote about the butterfly jar. About the Greyhound bus. About the cold, hard desperation of a girl who had refused to be invisible. She wrote about the blinding lights of Hollywood and the suffocating darkness of Argentis.

She wrote about Manny, who'd refused the money at first, then cried when she'd insisted. About the foundation named after her mother.

She wrote about Damian, too.

About a brilliant man who'd built a machine to see the future and paid for it with his life. About falling in love at the worst possible time, and losing him before she could tell him what he'd meant to her. His letter sat in a wooden box beside her bed—she couldn't bring herself to read it more than once, but she couldn't throw it away either. Some grief was too big to look at directly. You had to visit it in small doses, like staring at the sun.

She'd loved two men in that glass fortress. She'd lost one to fire and saved one from ice. And both had changed her in ways she was only beginning to understand.

She was not writing a memoir. She was performing an exorcism, pulling the ghosts out of her head and trapping them in ink on a page. And with every word she wrote, she felt a little more real.

But the Moleskine journal was just the first step. It was the raw material. The therapy.

When the story was finally clear in her own head, she put the journal away. She placed her hands on the keyboard.

She remembered the stack of dog-eared, half-finished scripts on her coffee table in North Hollywood—stories that went nowhere because no one was reading. She smiled. This was different. She was finally writing the one story that mattered—the one she'd lived. This was not a story she was writing for them. This was a story she was writing for herself.

She was no longer the actress performing a role. She was the author. And this time, she would control the ending.

The loneliness was still there, a quiet, constant ache. But it was no longer a prison. It was a room of her own—quiet, vast, and finally hers to furnish.

***

A large box had arrived from Los Angeles last week, arranged by Manny. Inside were the last relics of her old life.

She unpacked the Celine blazer first. The perfect black fabric felt familiar in her hands. She tried it on. It still fit. She looked at her reflection, expecting to see a ghost. Instead, she just saw a woman in a beautiful, slightly outdated blazer. A costume from a role she no longer played. She folded it carefully and placed it in the back of her closet. A memory, not a lifeline.

The Oscar was last. She held it in her hands, feeling its familiar, surprising weight. The golden man who had once been her tombstone.

She didn't put it on a mantelpiece. She didn't hide it away. She placed it on the corner of her desk where she wrote each morning. It wasn't a trophy anymore. It was just a beautiful object. A reminder not of what she had lost, but of the talent she still possessed, a talent she would now use on her own terms.

***

The phone buzzed on the small wrought-iron table on her balcony. A text from Manny.

Signed three new clients today, kid. A brilliant young writer from NYU, a kid from Juilliard who's going to be the next Pacino, and an actress from Oklahoma with fire in her eyes who reminds me of someone I used to know. I'M BACK, BABY! Also, when are you coming home? Gable's misses you. I miss you. Get your ass back to LA. - Manny

Sloane smiled, a real, genuine smile that reached her eyes. Manny was more than back. He was a legend. Vindicated. A Hollywood lion back in his prime, more powerful and respected than ever before. His agency was now the hottest boutique in town. Manny had even brought on his old friend Jerry Bostrom as his Business Manager. A six-figure salary, full benefits, and the one role Manny had always needed to fill: someone he actually trusted with the numbers.

The first in a bombshell series of articles had run on the front page of the LA Times last week, a deep-dive into the human cost of Panopticon, written by Sarah Jensen.

It began with the girl in the New Mexico facility—Oliver Harrow's daughter—and ended with the woman who brought the system down.

While every outlet in the world had the Ledger files, only Sarah had an exclusive source—someone who'd been there when it all came down. Manny had kept his promise, connecting Sarah to Sloane for deep background, on the condition that Sloane's name and role remained off the record.

It had already been nominated for a Pulitzer. And in New Mexico, the young woman whose tragedy had opened Sarah's investigation—Oliver Harrow's daughter—had spoken her first words in a decade. The truth had set more than one person free. Sarah Jensen was back. Not just as a journalist, but as the most respected investigative reporter in the country.

Home. The word was a strange, foreign country she was no longer sure she had a passport for.

She texted back: *Soon. Promise. Love you, old man.*

A moment later, his reply came. *Love you too, superstar. Now go be happy. That's an order.*

She was trying. She truly was.

***

Three weeks earlier, Nico had stood on a cobblestone street in Buenos Aires, watching the entrance to an arts academy. The door opened, and a young woman emerged—dark curly hair, his eyes, her mother's smile. She was laughing with a friend, a portfolio case slung over her shoulder.

Elena.

She didn't see him. He was a shadow on the other side of the street. But he saw her. Alive. Safe. Free.

"You kept her safe," a voice said beside him.

Katarina Zimina stood there, holding a coffee. "Livia asked me to protect her," she said, her gaze on Elena. "Roman's surveillance was real. He needed his leverage visible to keep you compliant."

She took a sip of her coffee.

"But the moment you broke protocol at Klausjagen, the game changed. Roman ordered a team to kidnap her. I sent a faster team. I extracted Elena and Tía Sofia an hour before Roman's men breached the apartment. By the time you stormed the Core in Argentis, Elena was already in a safe house."

Nico felt something break in his chest. His daughter. Safe. Because a dead woman had planned it, and the woman standing beside him had kept the promise.

"Why didn't you tell me?" he asked.

"Because you needed the fear," Katarina said simply. "Fear makes us sharp. Fear keeps us alive."

Across the street, Elena laughed, the sound a bright, joyful bell.

"Thank you," Nico whispered.

Katarina finished her coffee. "You are welcome. Now go. Live your life. She earned it for you."

"Where will you go?" Nico asked.

A faint smile touched her lips. "Wherever the next war is," she said.

And then she was gone.

***

He found her on the balcony in Bellagio three months after Argentis.

Three months of nightmares. Three months of jumping at shadows. Three months of learning to live in the daylight again.

She'd been watching the sunset, drinking cheap wine, wondering if the hollow feeling in her chest was permanent.

"I was in the neighborhood."

The voice was a low, gravelly rumble, so close behind her that she flinched, wine sloshing in her glass.

Her heart stopped. She knew that voice. She turned, slowly.

He was standing in the doorway, a dark silhouette against the warm, golden light of her apartment. He was holding a bottle of cheap American cabernet. He looked thinner, the shadows under his eyes deeper. He looked like a man who'd been carrying his own ghosts.

Nico.

"Buenos Aires is a long way from Lake Como," she managed, her voice breathless.

"Like I said," he replied, and the corner of his mouth quirked into that rare, devastating smile. "The neighborhood."

She didn't move. Couldn't. She just stared at him, drinking in the impossible reality of him. Here. Real. Alive.

He walked onto the balcony, placing the bottle of wine on the small table. "How's Elena?" she asked.

"Good," he said, and his voice was full of a deep, quiet joy. "Really good. She can't wait to finish this semester and go to the pre-college summer intensive at UCLA."

"She has her father's courage," Sloane said softly.

"She has her mother's talent," he corrected. "I just taught her how to run."

They stood there in the warm Italian twilight, the comfortable silence settling between them.

"Do you ever think about going back?" he asked. "To acting?"

"Sometimes," she said. "But on my terms. When I'm ready. When I remember who Sloane Devereaux is."

"I know who she is," Nico said quietly. He turned to look at her, his eyes dark and serious. "She's a survivor. A fighter. The bravest woman I've ever met."

The air between them crackled.

"Nico," she whispered, the name a prayer.

He reached out, his hand coming up to cup her face, his thumb gently tracing the line of her cheekbone. His eyes searched hers. "When we were in that bunker," he said, his voice low and rough, "I made you a promise. I said we'd wait. Until we were free. Until we were real."

He held her gaze. "Are we real now, Sloane?"

Her heart was suddenly, blessedly still. She leaned into his touch. "We are," she whispered.

"I'm in love with you, Nico," she said, the words simple, quiet, and the truest thing she had ever said.

She saw the surprise, the hope, and the fear warring in his eyes. "Sloane, my life... it's complicated. It's looking over my shoulder. It's never being able to stay in one place for too long."

"I know," she said, her hand coming up to cup his face. "I'm not asking for a white picket fence. I'm asking for you. All of it. The scars, the ghosts, the running. As long as we're running together."

The last of his walls crumbled. "I love you, too," he said, his voice rough. "God help me, I do."

He kissed her. It was not the desperate, frantic kiss of two soldiers on the eve of battle. It was slow. Tender. Sure. A question and an answer. A promise made and a promise kept. It was a kiss that tasted of cheap wine, and Italian air, and the impossible, beautiful, hard-won taste of a new beginning.

It was the taste of home.

***

Later, they made dinner together. Pasta. The cheap cabernet. Laughter.

It was mundane. Domestic. Ordinary.

It was the most extraordinary night of her life.

"What are you thinking?" Nico asked.

"That I'm happy," she said.

"Good," he said, kissing her forehead. "You deserve to be."

And for the first time in her life, Sloane Devereaux believed him.

Her phone buzzed. A text from Manny—a photo of him standing in front of his new production company office, grinning like a fool, holding a bottle of champagne.

Grand opening next week. You better be there, kid. Black tie. I mean it. - Manny

She smiled and texted back a promise she intended to keep.

Nico poured them both more wine, and they took their glasses to the small balcony overlooking the lake. The sun had set, leaving the sky bruised purple and gold.

"Do you think it's really over?" she asked quietly.

Nico was silent for a moment, then: "Roman is dead. Panopticon is destroyed. The files are out. The world knows." He looked at her. "But will you ever stop looking over your shoulder? Probably not. Neither will I. That's the price we pay."

"So we just... live with it?"

"We just live," he corrected. "That's the gift. That's what we fought for."

She leaned against him, feeling his warmth, his solidity. Real. Here. Hers.

They finished their wine, then went inside, back to the warmth and the beautiful, messy reality of building a life together.

***

Later that night, as she lay in bed beside Nico, listening to his breathing slow into sleep, she felt herself drifting.

She dreamed.

In the dream, she was underwater again. But this time, the water wasn't cold. It wasn't dark. It was warm, crystalline, shot through with shafts of golden sunlight. She wasn't drowning. She was floating, suspended in that quiet space between surface and depth, and for the first time in her life, she wasn't afraid.

She could see the surface above her, shimmering and close. She could reach it anytime she wanted.

But she didn't need to. Not yet.

She opened her eyes.

Outside, the lake was black glass under a moonless sky. And somewhere in that darkness, far across the water, a single light flickered on in a villa that had stood empty for months.

A figure stood on a balcony across the water, silhouetted against the glow. It looked exactly like Roman on the night of the gala—standing at the railing, back turned to the world, believing himself immortal.

Her breath caught. The same tightness in her chest as the nightmares. The same sense of being watched.

Probably just new owners. Or fishermen. Or her imagination playing tricks in the dark. Or a ghost she was summoning because she didn't know how to live without an enemy.

Or something else. Something patient. Something that could wait.

For a moment, the script in her head demanded a twist. A final scare. A monster that refused to die.

But she wasn't just the actress anymore. She was the author. And she got to decide when the scene ended.

She closed her eyes.

"Cut," she whispered.

And she chose not to look again. Because some ghosts, she'd learned, only had power if you kept watching.

Author's Note

Dear Reader,

Thank you for spending your time in the world of *The Counterfeit Wife*.

The question that sparked this novel was a simple one: *What would you be willing to become for a second chance?* For Sloane Devereaux, a woman forged in the fires of both poverty and fame, that question arrives in the form of an impossible offer—a deal with a devil who lives in a glass fortress in the Swiss Alps.

I've always been fascinated by the masks we wear, the roles we play to survive, and the terrifying, exhilarating moment when we are forced to discover who we are when the performance ends. Sloane's journey from a ghost in Hollywood to a warrior in a secret war is, at its heart, a story about the fight for authenticity in a world that rewards illusion.

Writing this book was a journey into a world of breathtaking glamour and chilling paranoia. I found myself lost in the hushed corridors of Zurich's private banks, the chaotic, fiery streets of the Klausjagen festival, and the silent, beautiful, and deeply dangerous landscape of the Swiss Alps. My hope is that, for a little while, you were lost there too.

Ultimately, this is a story about the kind of quiet, tenacious courage it takes to fight a monster who can see your every move. It is a story about the ghosts we inherit and the ones we choose to become.

Thank you for taking the journey with Sloane. The greatest privilege a writer has is a reader's time, and I am deeply grateful for yours.

Yours,

– *Nathan Case*

www.ingramcontent.com/pod-product-compliance
Lightning Source LLC
LaVergne TN
LVHW050913080826
845145LV00001B/67

* 9 7 8 1 9 6 9 3 4 2 1 5 8 *